Charlotte Perkins Gilman (1860–1935), a major American feminist and prolific writer, published a dozen books of social analysis, almost 200 poems and close to 200 short stories and novels. Born in Hartford, Connecticut, a grandniece of Harriet Beecher Stowe, she attended the Rhode Island School of Design before marrying her first husband, Charles Walter Stetson. Her mental breakdown after the birth of her daughter led to the writing of her now classic short story, "The Yellow Wallpaper." She left her husband in 1888, supporting herself by lecturing, editing, writing, and teaching. After she obtained a divorce, she created a public scandal by allowing her daughter to live with her ex-husband and his new wife. In 1900 she married George Houghton Gilman. Her writings include *Women and Economics* (1898), hailed as "the Bible" of the women's movement, *Concerning Children* (1900), *Human Work* (1904), *Man-Made World* (1911), *Herland* (1915), and *The Living of Charlotte Perkins Gilman: An Autobiography* (1935). After being diagnosed as having breast cancer, she committed suicide in 1935 in Pasadena, California.

HERLAND

and

Selected Stories by
Charlotte Perkins Gilman

EDITED AND WITH AN INTRODUCTION BY
BARBARA H. SOLOMON

C

A SIGNET CLASSIC

SIGNET CLASSIC
Published by the Penguin Group
Penguin Books USA Inc., 375 Hudson Street,
New York, New York 10014, U.S.A.
Penguin Books Ltd, 27 Wrights Lane,
London W8 5TZ, England
Penguin Books Australia Ltd, Ringwood,
Victoria, Australia
Penguin Books Canada Ltd, 10 Alcorn Avenue,
Toronto, Ontario, Canada M4V 3B2
Penguin Books (N.Z.) Ltd, 182-190 Wairau Road,
Auckland 10, New Zealand

Penguin Books Ltd, Registered Offices:
Harmondsworth, Middlesex, England

Published by Signet Classic, an imprint of New American Library, a
division of Penguin Books USA Inc.

First Signet Classic Printing, July, 1992
10 9 8 7 6 5 4 3 2 1

Ⓒ   REGISTERED TRADEMARK—MARCA REGISTRADA
Library of Congress Catalog Card Number: 92-080441

Printed in the United States of America

This book is lovingly dedicated to my mother
Rose Hochster.

CONTENTS

ACKNOWLEDGMENTS

I would like to acknowledge the role of the Iona students studying "Images of Women in Modern American Literature" during the fall of 1991. Their enthusiastic reception of *Herland* helped to make my work on this text very rewarding. To Kenneth Hedman and Charlotte Snyder of the United States Military Academy Library at West Point, I am indebted for considerable help in locating Gilman materials. A great deal of assistance was offered by Mary A. Bruno and the staff of Iona's Secretarial Services Center: Teresa Alifante, Patti Besen, Nancy Girardi, and Teresa Martin, as well as by Adrienne Franco and Anthony Todman of Ryan Library. At the Department of English, I was cheerfully aided by two student assistants: Susan Pavliscak and Shigeko Yamaguchi.

INTRODUCTION

In the spring of 1887, a depressed and desperate young woman from Providence, Rhode Island, traveled to Philadelphia to consult Dr. Silas Weir Mitchell, the famous physician and specialist in nervous disorders. She had been ill for about three years, experiencing symptoms which today might well lead to a medical diagnosis of clinical depression. Moreover, her situation and misery were perfect examples of the condition which would be described so accurately three-quarters of a century later by Betty Friedan in *The Feminine Mystique* as "The Problem That Has No Name."

After a month of treatment at S. Weir Mitchell's sanitarium, the young woman was discharged with the following prescription: "Live as domestic a life as possible. . . . Have but two hours' intellectual life a day. And never touch pen, brush, or pencil as long as you live."

Fortunately for posterity, the patient, who was Charlotte Perkins Gilman (though at the time she was Charlotte Perkins Stetson), found it impossible to live according to the doctor's instructions. She later wrote in her autobiography that those directions caused her to come very close to losing her mind.

Thus, in the fall of 1888, still in poor health and with little money, Charlotte Perkins Stetson did the unthinkable. She left Walter Stetson, her husband of four years, and traveled with her three-year-old daughter, Katharine, to Pasadena, California. There she began a life characterized by the independence, determination, and hard work which were to be her salvation.

Charlotte Perkins Gilman did not become America's lead-

ing feminist writer and lecturer at the turn of the century
through a casual or purely intellectual inclination. She had
attempted to live her life according to the collective wisdom
of her era about women, and she had found the precepts
handed down to women by respected authorities to be not
merely misguided or wrong, but deadly, leading to unlived
lives, to stultification, depression, and desperation. Gilman
turned to writing both fiction and nonfiction as she explored
her own personal experience as girl and woman, as wife
and mother, and as she studied the economic and social
facts of the communal experience of American women. Like
the majority of women of her generation, Charlotte was
reared in a world which considered her being female as the
foremost fact about her. Thus, she was raised to take her
place in the domestic sphere in which it was assumed all
normal women would find happiness and fulfillment. As she
attempted to live in the sphere assigned to women, with the
goals which were described in her era as "the cult of true
womanhood," she learned first-hand that no matter how fervently the religious, political, and social leaders expounded
upon the responsibilities and duties of women to their parents, husbands, and children, a life lived vicariously was not
a real life at all.

Charlotte Perkins Gilman's experience of the destructive-
ness of America's cult of feminine domesticity began in infancy with the relationship of her parents. Soon after
Charlotte's birth, her mother, Mary Perkins, was abandoned
by her husband, Frederick Beecher Perkins. He may well
have left after being told by a physician that his wife must
never again become pregnant. A member of the illustrious
Beecher family, which included the preacher Lyman Beecher, the famous authors Harriet Beecher Stowe and Catherine Beecher, as well as the abolitionist minister and writer
Henry Ward Beecher, Frederick, in contrast, was an unsuc-
cessful and debt-ridden man who seemed eager to avoid all
family responsibilities. Mary was forced to raise her two
young children alone, often living in the households and on
the charity of relatives. She, Charlotte, and Thomas, who
was a year older than his sister, were forced to move some
nineteen times during Charlotte's youth.

Mary Perkins appears to have been a woman with few
inner resources and little wisdom. Suffering pathetically
from the lack of her husband's love, she thought that if she

denied all signs of affection to Charlotte, her daughter would never need nor long for them. Mary only revealed her love or tenderness for Charlotte was when she believed that the child was asleep. Having discovered this pattern, the affection-starved girl tried to remain awake until her mother came to her bed, "even using pins to prevent dropping off. . . . Then," writes Gilman in her autobiography, "how carefully I pretended to be sound asleep and how rapturously I enjoyed being gathered into her arms, held close and kissed."

By the time she was a young woman, Charlotte had formed unusual and strong resolutions against marrying. In a journal entry written when she was twenty-one, she recorded a number of reasons for remaining single which included her desire for "freedom," for having her own "unaided will" in all matters, and her preference for providing for herself rather than trusting another to provide for her. She added a description of one of her goals: "I love to be *able* and *free* to help any and every one, as I never could be if my time and thoughts were taken by that extended self—a family."

Ironically, only a few days after writing this diary entry, Charlotte met Charles Walter Stetson, an attractive artist. He assiduously courted her, overcame her misgivings and objections, and two years later, they were married. As we have seen from the disastrous effects and psychological distress Charlotte suffered during the years they lived as husband and wife, their marriage brought together two people whose characters, ambitions, values, and needs made them totally unsuited for one another.

One aspect of Walter's character which would prove destructive to Charlotte was his romanticized ideal of male dominance. Even during their courtship, Walter had noted his desire to have Charlotte "look up to me as if I were superior . . . that my love of her has conquered." He resented her independent nature and recorded his pleasure in his belief that her "spirit is broken."

Often well meaning, and certainly not malicious, Walter was simply a rather conventional specimen of a turn-of-the-century American male, one who resented the idea of his wife's having ambitions and desiring accomplishments other than those associated with the roles of wife and mother. Vulnerable as a painter who was struggling to win recognition of his own work, he undoubtedly thought of Charlotte's desire for literary achievements as unnatural and as reflecting unfavorably upon him.

Their inevitable problems were exacerbated by the birth of Katharine less than a year after the marriage and the straitened circumstances of the household. Unable to function as a wife or mother, unable to cope with her deteriorating mental and physical state, and unable to find helpful medical advice, Charlotte left Providence, never to return to Walter.

She settled in Pasadena, choosing to live near the Channing family. Charlotte had become very close to them, particularly to Grace Ellery Channing, during the years when they had lived in Providence. William F. Channing, his wife, and two daughters were an affectionate, lively, and well-educated family. In their congenial household, Charlotte had enjoyed stimulating discussions and literary activities in a cheerful and relaxed atmosphere. They were sympathetic to Charlotte and willing to help her as much as they could, even locating the small wooden house in Pasadena which Charlotte rented for Katharine and herself.

Charlotte and Grace were especial girlhood friends who had a great deal in common. Grace, too, wrote fiction and poetry, and the two women had amused themselves by writing a comic play together during a vacation trip. Interestingly, their friendship was not destroyed by Grace's subsequent marriage to Walter not long after he and Charlotte had finalized their divorce. On the contrary, because Charlotte knew Grace to be a gentle, affectionate, and dependable woman, and because during that period Charlotte was traveling extensively and preoccupied with earning a living, she arranged for Katharine, then nine years old, to live with Grace and Walter when they married in 1894.

When Charlotte first arrived in Pasadena, she struggled to support herself and her child, but the move to California proved to be curative and revitalizing. Within a surprisingly short time, she began to earn money through writing and lecturing. Her poem "Similar Cases" (published in 1890 in the *Nationalist*) brought her work to the attention of William Dean Howells, the influential author and the editor of the *Atlantic Monthly*. She began to establish first a local and later a national reputation as an inspiring speaker on women's issues and on socialism. The topics of her lectures anticipated those which would be discussed in American women's consciousness-raising groups of the late 1960s and 1970s. She recognized that women's economic dependence, relegation to drudgery in the home, exclusion from work in the professions, industry, and commerce, and submission to male authority were preventing women from leading fully human and productive lives. Most important, she understood that women's problems were not individual or isolated instances, and that only reform on a national, system-wide basis could ameliorate their conditions. Gilman crisscrossed America for more than three decades preaching the need for economic, political, and social reform in the ways that people live together as families and work at their occupations.

Her successful career as a lecturer was inextricably linked to her career as a writer. The themes of her first and best-known work of nonfiction, *Women and Economics: A Study of the Economic Relation Between Men and Women as a Factor in Social Evolution* (1898), were those she had been presenting in her provocative lectures.

During the time Charlotte was writing this book, in which she focused in a public way on the most important issues of her life, she was also writing about herself in a private way in an extraordinary series of letters to her cousin, George Houghton Gilman. Charlotte and Houghton had been fond acquaintances as children. An unusually scholarly and cultured individual, he had become a New York attorney. Although he was obviously competent and professional in his work, he was not particularly ambitious or career-oriented. After a brief meeting in 1897, he and Charlotte began to correspond. Her letters became increasingly lengthy and introspective as she found herself describing her fears, self-doubts, needs, hopes, and beliefs to this gentle and understanding relative.

During this courtship by correspondence—for this is, indeed, what it turned out to be—Charlotte revealed all of the character traits and aspirations which she must have imagined had made her unlovable. To her great delight, she found that these self-revelations did not dismay Houghton at all. Instead, he repaid her confidences with an approval and affirmation of her innermost self that made true intimacy possible. In 1900 they were married.

As Charlotte recalled her thirty-four-year marriage to Houghton in her autobiography, *The Living of Charlotte Perkins Gilman*, she judged that they had "lived happily ever after." Always thinking as a writer, she added, "If this were a novel, now, here's that happy ending."

Secure as a beloved wife and increasingly self-confident as a famous author of national stature, Gilman followed *Women and Economics* with four additional and closely related volumes: *Concerning Children* (1900), *The Home: Its Work and Influence* (1903), *Human Work* (1904), and *The Man-Made World; or, Our Androcentric Culture* (1911).

Although she had written and published poetry and short stories for more than two decades, with the founding of her own monthly magazine, the *Forerunner*, in 1909, Charlotte Perkins Gilman entered an astounding creative period of eight years. The magazine, which was entirely written by Gilman, typically contained one fully developed short story, one very brief and didactic story, a chapter of a novel (generally serialized over the twelve issues of a single year), as well as several poems, articles, and book reviews. During Gilman's lifetime, three of the novels serialized in the *Forerunner* were subsequently published as separate books: *What Diantha Did* (1910), *The Crux* (1911), and *Moving the Mountain* (1911). The other novels preserved in the issues of the *Forerunner* are *Mag-Marjorie* (1912), *Won Over* (1913), *Benigna Machiavelli* (1914), *Herland* (1915) and *With Her in Ourland* (1916).

A prolific writer and tireless activist for women's rights, Charlotte Perkins Gilman believed that far-reaching change could be brought about through education and experience. If human beings could abandon their caves, their huts, their tenements to embrace the well-built and technologically sophisticated homes of the best modern architects, they could also abandon their ideas about women's and men's lives which were just as primitive and useless as a cave home would be to a twentieth-century family.

Gilman believed in her work of bringing this message to women everywhere much in the same way that her Beecher ancestors had preached about sin and salvation to their throngs of listeners. In spite of a painful and terminal illness, cancer, she struggled to write and lecture during her last months of life. Knowing that the end must come soon, Gilman returned to Pasadena, the sanctuary to which she had fled so many years earlier and now the home of her married daughter, Katharine. During Charlotte's final weeks, Grace Channing Stetson—now, like Charlotte, a widow—also returned to help care for her old and dear friend. With Charlotte's days of work behind her and only the agony of an incurable disease ahead, Charlotte Perkins Gilman ended her life, by chloroform, in the summer of 1935.

During subsequent decades, it appeared that Gilman had been greatly mistaken about the significance of her work, especially her writing. Descriptions of her life and contributions simply disappeared. For example, the 1962 edition of *The Reader's Encyclopedia of American Literature* profiles three Gilmans, Arthur Gilman, Daniel Gilman, and Lawrence Gilman. No Charlotte. Similarly, the 1965 edition of *The Oxford Companion to American Literature* includes sketches of Caroline Howard Gilman and Daniel Gilman. No Charlotte. But at about this time, a burgeoning interest in feminist issues led historians, social critics, teachers, and students to search for the best sources about the conditions of women. And their search inevitably led to Charlotte Perkins Gilman. Thus, 1966 marked the republication of *Women and Economics*, the first of her numerous works to be reissued during the following years. Although the readers' interest appeared to be concentrated on Gilman's nonfiction, the publication of *The Yellow Wallpaper* by the Feminist Press in 1973 led to a rediscovery and appreciation of Gilman as a powerful American literary force.

* * *

Ironically, Gilman's best-known and most artistically successful story "The Yellow Wallpaper" is not typical of her fiction in three important aspects: the point of view, the use of symbolic imagery, and the unhappy ending. The story, originally published in 1892, records the anguish and decline of a young wife and mother who is being treated for mental illness by her physician husband. The wife, the first-person narrator, explains that although she has "nervous troubles [that] are dreadfully depressing," her husband, John, believes that she must use her "will and self-control" and that "there is really nothing the matter with one but temporary nervous depression—a slight hysterical tendency. . . ." John's treatment, including a tonic, specific foods, isolation, and a great deal of rest with "a schedule prescription for each hour in the day," is obviously exacerbating his wife's psychological problems, although he is oblivious to all of the signs that this is so. The woman believes "that congenial work, with excitement and change" would be good for her, but of course the views of the sufferer are not to be taken seriously. The wife is subject to her husband's authority in her two central roles: as a dutiful, subservient turn-of-the-century wife and as a fanciful, emotional female patient.

The powerful imagery of the story revolves around the pattern of the wallpaper in the couple's bedroom—the room which John has chosen—in the country house he has rented for a three-month stay. Early in the story, the wife examines her reactions to the wallpaper:

> It is dull enough to confuse the eye in following, pronounced enough to constantly irritate and provoke study, and when you follow the lame uncertain curves for a little distance they suddenly commit suicide—plunge off at outrageous angles, destroy themselves in unheard of contradictions.
>
> The color is repellent, almost revolting; a smoldering unclean yellow, strangely faded by the slow-turning sunlight.
>
> It is a dull yet lurid orange in some places, a sickly sulphur tint in others.

As the story progresses and the wife becomes more severely ill, her perceptions of the wallpaper become increasingly dramatic and are clearly linked to her own condition. At night, the pattern is revealed to her as a series of bars behind which a woman is imprisoned. The narrator describes her discovery:

> The front pattern *does* move—and no wonder! The woman behind shakes it!
>
> Sometimes I think there are a great many women behind, and sometimes only one, and she crawls around fast, and her crawling shakes it all over.
>
> Then in the very bright spots she keeps still, and in the very shady spots she just takes hold of the bars and shakes them hard.
>
> And she is all the time trying to climb through. But nobody could climb through that pattern—it strangles so: I think that is why it has so many heads.

The behavior of the woman trapped in the wallpaper is a symbolic parallel for the situation of the wife who is trapped by her severe mental illness and by a husband and household in which control of her life has been taken from her. Increasingly, the narrator behaves like a hostage, hiding her writing and her thoughts from her husband/captor. The story concludes with the ultimate breakdown of the narrator, in an unusual—but fitting—ending.

With the exception of one or two very early stories, most of Gilman's fiction ends very differently from "The Yellow Wallpaper." An analysis of "Three Thanksgivings" (1909), which was among the first stories Gilman published in the *Forerunner,* reveals a number of the conflicts, heroines, and important themes which are characteristic of her fiction.

Delia Morrison, a widow with two married children, would prefer to live in her own spacious house, but needs to generate an annual income as well as to raise $2,000 to pay off the mortgage. Her financial problems would be resolved if she were to accept the marriage proposal of Peter Butts, a man she does not love.

Andrew and Jean, Mrs. Morrison's children, have suggested that their mother sell her house and live with one of them. She visits each on two successive Thanksgiving holidays and discovers the kind of life she would experience in their households.

Andrew, a minister, and his wife, Annie, live in a house that Delia finds overheated and small. The "home" they offer is, in fact, a room which measures twelve by fifteen feet. Annie, who has no children, is a precise and efficient housekeeper who needs no help from her mother-in-law. Delia is invited out with the couple:

> Waited upon and watched over and set down among the old ladies and gentlemen—she had never realized so keenly that she was no longer young. Here nothing recalled her youth, every careful provision anticipated age.

During the second Thanksgiving, Mrs. Morrison stays with Jean and her husband, Joseph, for a week. They have four small children including a new baby. The room they provide is about the same size as the one in Andrew's house, but it has a sloped ceiling and is an additional flight up.

There was no going visiting here. Jeannie could not leave the babies. And few visitors; all the little suburb being full of similarly overburdened mothers. Such as called found Mrs. Morrison charming. What she found them, she did not say.

A final similarity of the offers of both children concerns the funds which would be realized by the sale of Delia's large house when she moves. Andrew believes he can profitably invest the money on his mother's behalf and Joseph, her son-in-law, wants to put the money into his own store and pay interest for its use. Both children assume that she will be financially dependent upon them and send Mrs. Morrison the fare for her Thanksgiving visits.

When Delia returns home after the first visit, she evaluates her situation. Her house is quite large and comfortable, but she has accommodated boarders in the past and thoroughly disliked running a boarding house. She lives with an energetic black servant, Sally, who has carefully preserved many of the assets of the house: napkins, tablecloths, towels, and china. Mrs. Morrison briefly considers the possibility of opening either a hotel or a girls' school, but rejects these ideas as unattractive and impractical. Her solution to the problem, founding and running the Haddleton Rest and Improvement Club, is one which enables Delia to continue to live independently, to use her management skills, to enjoy her pleasant home, and to serve other women.

Delia Morrison typifies the women Charlotte Perkins Gilman depicted in stories written during more than three decades. Sensible and intelligent, she is at an economic disadvantage as a woman in a society with low expectations for women. She is one of a number of older heroines, about fifty years of age, such as Mary Crosley of "Old Mrs. Crosley," Mrs. Gordins of "Making a Change" and Grace Elder of "Mrs. Elder's Idea," who are dismayed to find that although they feel competent, are energetic, and want to perform satisfying work, they have been written off by family members as old ladies who should confine themselves to porch rocking chairs.

Since the most crucial events of Charlotte Perkins Gilman's life were leaving her husband and reconstructing her life around her work, it is not surprising that one of Gilman's major lifelong themes was the need of women to do useful and meaningful work. Clearly, the benefits of a congenial occupation go far beyond simply earning a salary. Gilman was one of America's first writers to understand the ways in which paid labor outside the home helped women to achieve a strong identity and a healthy sense of self-respect.

"Three Thanksgivings," which is representative of much of Gilman's fiction, also dramatizes the social good which is accomplished by Delia Morrison in her newly established business. Her organization responds to the pressing needs of the farm wife. When she travels to town for the day, she often feels isolated and weary. She lacks the companionship and support of other women who lead similar lives. The streets of the town are filled with shops where she is welcome as long as she is a customer who is spending money. The usual cafés or restaurants of the town are places she would find too expensive, but also they are places where she would be expected to eat a meal without lingering.

Like Delia Morrison, numerous Gilman heroines find that in addressing their own desire to do meaningful work, they can aid other women, bringing about significant and much-needed social change. The changes or improvements are generally in areas in which American politicians have shown little interest or initiative.

For example, Mrs. Joyce, in "Martha's Mother," longs to live in the city and to be surrounded by people, as well as to use her talent and energy in working. The enterprise that provides a solution to her problems also improves the lives of urban working girls. Similarly, the resolution of the crisis of Julia Gordins and her mother-in-law leads to the establishment of a childcare facility which would be the envy of any contemporary community.

In much of Gilman's fiction, the satisfying work undertaken by women leads to both reasonable profits and community enrichment. Among the realistic details Gilman's heroines very willingly supply in several stories are an accounting of their costs for supplies, labor, and rent, as well as the resulting income. In "Three Thanksgivings," for example, we learn that

> on Saturday Mrs. Morrison hired two helpers for half a day, for half a dollar each. She stocked the library with

many magazines for fifty dollars a year. She covered fuel, light and small miscellanies with another hundred. And she fed her multitude with the plain viands agreed upon, at about four cents apiece.

Even when a woman's work does not particularly benefit others, the wealth she earns can enrich her own life in admirable ways. In "Her Beauty," for example, the clothes which Amaryllis Delong designs and sells are well made and flattering, but not inexpensive. There is, however, nothing frivolous in the way Amaryllis uses her profits from the clothing business:

> She was able to travel, to study to her heart's content, to meet people, to hear lectures, to read books, to see pictures, to attend plays, to feed her soul with knowledge and to enjoy, as far as it exists in the modern world, the beauty she desired.

As dramatized by Gilman, independence is usually the essential goal of a woman's occupational success. The heroine who performs work efficiently, has original ideas, is well organized, and has a successful career is a woman who can make choices based on her preferences. She will not be coerced by economic circumstances. Furthermore, marriage is not the only option for such a woman, not her only way of attaining respect, social status, and financial support.

Delia's proposal from Peter, in "Three Thanksgivings," introduces another of Gilman's recurring motifs, the evaluation of possible or existing marriages from the perspective of whether they are desirable for the woman. Peter Butts is an unpleasant suitor in several respects. In the first place, Delia has known him since girlhood and has never found him attractive. In the second, as a self-made, affluent man, he is pompous and tactless. Finally, he has no qualms about trying to manipulate Delia through his economic power over her and envisions possessing her as his experienced wife-housekeeper. Obviously, if Delia is to triumph, she must reject Butt's unwanted proposal.

In an era in which so much popular fiction concluded with a proposal signaling a happy ending for the heroine, Gilman often portrayed marriage as an impediment to a woman's

continued growth and happiness, depicting inappropriate
suitors who were not admirable or marriageable males. Instead, the wise Gilman heroine knows that a single life in
which she finds fulfilling work is a better choice than a marriage based on such elements as the need for economic se-
curity or on the flattering attentions of an admiring male.
For example, in one of her earliest stories, ''My Poor Aunt''
(1891), Gilman briefly surveys the marriages of three sisters, Ellen, Lucy, and Kate. The youngest, Kate, had divorced her husband many years before the opening of the
story because ''she found the shame and injury heaped upon
her by the scoundrel she had so trustfully married too much
for a woman to bear in honor.'' The two conventional sisters who remained married—one wealthy, one impover-
ished—have led difficult and equally unrewarding lives,
filled with ''uninterrupted trials and disappointments.''
Surprisingly, their experiences as wives have not made them
very perceptive or critical of the institution of marriage.
Gilman clearly concludes that the divorced sister, who has
pursued a career as an editor and publisher, is the happily
unmarried heroine of the story.

In one of her last stories, ''Mrs. Beazley's Deeds'' (1916),
Gilman effectively dramatizes her belief that a marriage to
a cruel and destructive husband is not a sacred or irrevo-
cable bond. The woman in this situation, Maria Beazley,
must be helped so that she does not sacrifice her life and
the lives of her young children to an unworthy man.

On the other hand, in a number of stories by Gilman,
intelligent and sympathetic suitors do appear. The happy
marriages she dramatizes, however, are never based on superficial romantic attraction. A wise Gilman heroine wants
the man who courts her to understand who she is and what
she needs in order to be happy. The young widow, Mrs.
Leland, of ''Her Housekeeper'' (1910) is completely forth-
right in explaining the reasons she does not want to marry
again. She is now a successful actress and would not give
up her work for any man. Moreover, she knows herself and
is not self-conscious about describing the freedom and comfort which are all-important to her sense of well-being.

In Gilman's fiction, there are good marriages that are satisfying, nurturing, and pleasant for both wives and husbands. But these marriages occur between articulate and
thoughtful individuals who have considerable self-

knowledge and insight into one another, and who both engage in interesting work outside of the home.

The happy conclusion of a typical Gilman short story, like that of "Three Thanksgivings," is generally neither a forced nor a tacked-on ending. It develops from the characters' traits and the events and has an emotional as well as a logical rightness. Readers might have found tragic endings marked by continued sacrifice or suffering or even death more dramatic and moving, but Gilman clearly intended to create fiction in which women were not to be pitied or mourned, but emulated and celebrated.

* * *

Given the lifetime preoccupations and optimism of Charlotte Perkins Gilman, we are not surprised that *Herland,* a feminist utopian novel, was her quintessential work of fiction. By 1915, the year of its publication, she had written more than one hundred short stories, six novels, and five volumes of nonfiction on topics related to women's lives. Central to her thought was the need for reform. America, she knew, needed to change its view of women. Men had to relinquish their stereotypical ideas about the differences between males and females and the kinds of lives that, as a result of these supposed differences, were suitable for each. The many women who shared or accepted such stereotypical views of themselves had to rethink their assumptions and reeducate themselves to discover the truth about their potential and about the kind of individuals they could become in a world where they were not limited by society's narrow expectations.

Utopian fiction was the ideal genre for Gilman's fervently held beliefs and designs for reform. Utopias are landscapes of the imagination where the inhabitants lead the best possible—or even perfect—lives. In one, a writer can dramatize how a society ought to be organized according to rational principles and for the good of all. Gilman's objectives were to instruct, to question, to stimulate reevaluation—perhaps by shocking—and to entertain. And she succeeded.

Herland is a country in which there are no males and have not been any for two thousand years. With no experience of courtship and no expectation of romantic love, the women of this nation have become different from other women around the world, but these differences are positive and far-reaching. Without the need to dress or behave in ways that are pleasing to men, these women are free to fulfill their own expectations, to depend on themselves and on other women for a civilized life.

In the central action of *Herland,* three young American men, Vandyke Jennings, Terry O. Nicholson, and Jeff Margrave, explore this land without males. The three are characterized almost exclusively in terms of one quality: their views of women. Terry, at one extreme, is a womanizer, seeing all females as sex objects who—no matter how much they protest—want to be mastered by a man. Jeff, at the other extreme, is the chivalric romantic who idealizes women and would like them to remain on their pedestals where they can be beautiful, charming, useless, and protected by men. Vandyke, the novel's first-person narrator, is the character who is most moderate in his views about women and most open to the new ideas and experiences he encounters.

As the visitors learn about the way the women of Herland live, the novel's readers make two kinds of discovery. First, we learn about the three explorers' beliefs and expectations of women—one source of the novel's gentle comedy. In this regard, many of the most successful scenes of the novel depict the ways in which the women of Herland innocently challenge the "truths" about women which Van, Terry, and Jeff have always accepted and—more important—acted upon when relating to women. Without ever being aware that they are doing so, the inhabitants of Herland demonstrate that many well-known "truths" or "facts" about women are really unfounded stereotypes.

The second type of discovery results from the contrast between the comments, actions, and goals of the admirable women of Herland and some of the typical practices and ideals of conventional American women. Many of Gilman's female contemporaries had never seriously or critically examined the traditional attitudes about themselves which they had absorbed and always accepted. The author's method for urging reform was to depict the inspiring women of Herland so as to enable American women to observe their own world from a new vantage point and with an enriched consciousness.

For example, the women of Herland are dressed very differently from the way women in America, and in Europe as well, would dress. In his first encounter with several young girls, Van notes: "We saw short hair, hatless, loose, and shining; a suit of some light firm stuff, the closest of tunics and kneebreeches, met by trim gaiters." Shortly afterwards, Van records the men's behavior with a group of older Herland women and Terry's foolish attempt to impress them with gifts for ornamenting themselves:

He stepped forward, with his brilliant ingratiating smile, and made low obeisance to the women before him. Then he produced another tribute, a broad soft scarf of filmy texture, rich in color and pattern, a lovely thing, even to my eye, and offered it with a deep bow to the tall unsmiling woman who seemed to head the ranks before him. She took it with a gracious nod of acknowledgment, and passed it on to those behind her.

He tried again, this time bringing out a circlet of rhinestones, a glittering crown that should have pleased any woman on earth. He made a brief address, including Jeff and me as partners in his enterprise, and with another bow presented this. Again his gift was accepted and, as before, passed out of sight.

Gilman did not consider matters of women's clothing and accessories trivial issues. In fact, throughout 1915, she had serialized the twelve chapters of an extensive, nonfiction work titled *The Dress of Women* in the same issues of the *Forerunner* in which *Herland* appeared.

The conventional and elaborate clothing worn by women in Gilman's era had, she understood, significant consequences. It reflected society's insistence that women wear "the mask of beauty," and the intense quest of many women for finery to help make them appear more beautiful helped, instead, to make them vain, petty, and inappropriately competitive. Judged and valued on the basis of their appearance, many women exerted their energy in the pursuit of beauty instead of the pursuit of education, strength of character, and meaningful work.

There were compelling reasons beyond those effects of "the mask of beauty" for Gilman's attack on the fashion of her day. Women's tightly-laced corsets, ill-fitting shoes, and layers of petticoats under long skirts, prevented them from engaging in normal physical activities and gave support to those stereotypes of literature, painting, and advertising, which portrayed them as delicate creatures, unsuited to strenuous life outside the home.

Moreover, women's clothing sometimes caused serious illness and even death. We now know that the pressure exerted by steel and whalebone corsets could injure and displace a woman's internal organs and could prevent the normal circulation of blood. The small and pointed shoes into which women were encouraged to cram their feet could damage their arches and calf muscles, as well as causing bunions and clawed toes. The trailing skirts made them vulnerable to accidents such as falls and fires. Even women's large and extravagant hats, though not physically dangerous, had the damaging effect of making it difficult for the world to take their wearers seriously.

Thus in one of *Herland*'s typical scenes of discovery, the men describe their ideas of ladies' hats to these unadorned women, possibly to inspire emulation. Terry illustrates the kind of hats he knows and approves, "with plumes and quills and those various tickling things that stick out so far. . . ."

As for them, they said they only wore hats for shade when working in the sun; and those were big light straw hats, something like those used in China and Japan. In cold weather they wore caps or hoods.

"But for decorative purposes—don't you think they would be becoming?" pursued Terry, making as pretty a picture as he could of a lady with a plumed hat.

They by no means agreed to that, asking quite simply if the men wore the same kind. We hastened to assure her that they did not—drew for them our kind of headgear.

"And do no men wear feathers in their hats?"

"Only Indians," Jeff explained. "Savages, you know." And he sketched a war bonnet to show them.

"And soldiers," I added, drawing a military hat with plumes.

They never expressed horror or disapproval, nor indeed much surprise—just a keen interest. And the notes they made!—miles of them!

In this exchange and, indeed, throughout the novel, Gilman explores America's double standard for males and females. Similarly, almost all of the ideals and practices in Herland become topics of discovery, often leading to explicit comparisons with life in America as articulated by the surprised male characters.

The function of our homes is one of the most significant of these. As Van, Jeff, and Terry attempt to set up conventional households as couples with their Herland wives, the women and men describe their expectations of a home. For Ellador, Celis, and Alima, home is a place for rest and relaxation after they have finished their strenuous outside work. They assume that the usual housekeeping services will be performed, as they are throughout Herland, by well-paid, well-trained professionals who have an aptitude for this work. For Van, Jeff, and Terry, home is the place where their wives are supposed to serve them, to cook, to clean, to launder clothes. A home, for a husband, is a place where he rests from his labor and is nurtured; a home, for a wife, is often a place where she performs work, usually of the most unrewarding menial type. The issue for Gilman can be simply phrased: why can't homes nurture women as well as men and children?

Among Gilman's most serious concerns in the novel is the nurturing of children. The common bond which holds the society of Herland together and provides the impetus for the women's noblest activities is the rearing of the young. Gilman had long despaired of the practice in middle-class American families of shunting the care of infants and children off to the least-trained female laborers, whose work skills and education were so minimal that they did not qualify for any other type of employment.

Repeatedly, Van, the narrator of *Herland*, is awed by the way babies and children are treated in the many scenes in which he observes and discusses them. Concluding that the women have created a "perfect system of child rearing," he explains that because of their desire to raise their young "in an environment calculated to allow the richest, freest growth, they had deliberately remodeled and improved the whole state." Throughout it, all inhabitants focus their intelligence and talents on the real future of their world, the next generation. Here, each child's well-being, development, and happiness are of the greatest concern not only of the woman to whom the child was born but to the entire community. The birth mothers are joined by all of Herland's women in sharing a sacred obligation to the young. An inescapable comparison occurs to Van:

> The big difference was that whereas our children grow up in private homes and families, with every effort made to protect and seclude them from a dangerous world, here they grew up in a wide friendly world, and knew it for theirs, from the first.

Gilman recognized that in America the rearing of children was a burdensome and isolating responsibility only of women. While the joys of motherhood were extolled and many expressed concern about the needs of children, the reality was that few resources were forthcoming and the sacrifices expected from mothers had no parallels in sacrifices of fathers.

Throughout the pages of *Herland*, Gilman dramatizes attractive alternatives. The women in her imagined country emphasize goals which are different from ours. Their daily mode of living and structuring of family life and society demonstrate alternatives for raising our children, running our households, performing our work, and relating to one another in humane and fulfilling terms. Gilman's *Herland*, as well as her other fiction, is the vehicle through which she attempted, first, to ameliorate the condition of women, but also to better the lives of men as well. She believed that while one half of the human race lacked the same opportunities, respect, and comfort afforded the other half, neither could find satisfaction or pleasure in their relationships. As a believer in progress, she used her considerable skill to transport her readers to a distant place, where like Gulliver among the Brobdingnagians, they could look at human behavior from a radically different perspective. As we struggle today to improve the quality of our lives in a world that seems increasingly materialistic, violent, stressful, and indifferent to individuals, Charlotte Perkins Gilman's vision of a humane utopia becomes more poignant with each passing year.

—Barbara H. Solomon

Selected Biographical and Critical Sources

Allen, Polly Wynn. *Building Domestic Liberty: Charlotte Perkins Gilman's Architectural Feminism*. Amherst: University of Massachusetts Press, 1988.

Bader, Julia. "The Dissolving Vision: Realism in Jewett, Freeman and Gilman." In *American Realism: New Essays*, ed. Eric J. Sundquist, pp. 176–98. Baltimore: Johns Hopkins University Press, 1982.

Bartkowski, Frances. *Feminist Utopias*. Lincoln: University of Nebraska Press, 1989.

Degler, Carl N. "Charlotte Perkins Gilman on the Theory and Practice of Feminism," *American Quarterly*, 8 (Spring 1956). 21–39; reprinted in Meyering.

Gilman, Charlotte Perkins. *The Living of Charlotte Perkins Gilman: An Autobiography*. New York: D. Appleton-Century Co., 1935; reprinted by Arno Press, 1972 and Harper & Row, 1975.

Golden, Catherine, ed. *The Captive Imagination: A Casebook on "The Yellow Wallpaper."* New York: Feminist Press, 1991.

Hill, Mary A. *Charlotte Perkins Gilman: The Making of a Radical Feminist 1860–1896*. Philadelphia: Temple University Press, 1980.

Hill, Mary A., ed. *Endure: The Diaries of Charles Walter Stetson*. Philadelphia: Temple University Press, 1985.

Howe, Harriet. "Charlotte Perkins Gilman—As I Knew Her." *Equal Rights: Independent Feminist Weekly*, II, no. 27 (Sept. 5, 1936), 211–16.

Karpinski, Joanne B. "When the Marriage of True Minds Admits Impediments: Charlotte Perkins Gilman and William Dean Howells." In *Patrons and Protegees: Gender, Friendship, and Writing in Nineteenth-Century America*, ed. Shirley Marchalonis, pp. 212–34. New Brunswick, NJ: Rutgers University Press, 1988.

Lane, Ann J. *To "Herland" and Beyond: The Life and Work of Charlotte Perkins Gilman*. New York: Pantheon 1990; reprinted by Meridian, 1991.

Meyering, Sheryl L., ed. *Charlotte Perkins Gilman: The*

Woman and Her Work. Ann Arbor: UMI Research Press, 1989.

Nies, Judith. ''Charlotte Perkins Gilman.'' In *Seven Women: Portraits from the American Radical Tradition*. New York: Viking, 1977.

Scharnhost, Gary. *Charlotte Perkins Gilman*. Boston: Twayne, 1985.

———. *Charlotte Perkins Gilman: A Bibliography*. Metuchen, NJ: Scarecrow, 1985.

Wilson, Christopher P. ''Charlotte Perkins Gilman's Steady Burghers: The Terrain of *Herland*,'' *Women's Studies* 12 (1986), 271–92; reprinted in Meyering.

HERLAND

1. A Not Unnatural Enterprise

This is written from memory, unfortunately. If I could have brought with me the material I so carefully prepared, this would be a very different story. Whole books full of notes, carefully copied records, firsthand descriptions, and the pictures—that's the worst loss. We had some bird's-eyes of the cities and parks; a lot of lovely views of streets, of buildings, outside and in, and some of those gorgeous gardens, and, most important of all, of the women themselves.

Nobody will ever believe how they looked. Descriptions aren't any good when it comes to women, and I never was good at descriptions anyhow. But it's got to be done somehow; the rest of the world needs to know about that country.

I haven't said where it was for fear some self-appointed missionaries, or traders, or land-greedy expansionists, will take it upon themselves to push in. They will not be wanted, I can tell them that, and will fare worse than we did if they do find it.

It began this way. There were three of us, classmates and friends—Terry O. Nicholson (we used to call him the Old Nick, with good reason), Jeff Margrave, and I, Vandyck Jennings.

We had known each other years and years, and in spite of our differences we had a good deal in common. All of us were interested in science.

Terry was rich enough to do as he pleased. His great aim was exploration. He used to make all kinds of a row because there was nothing left to explore now, only patchwork and filling in, he said. He filled in well enough—he had a lot of talents—great on mechanics and electricity. Had all kinds of boats and motorcars, and was one of the best of our airmen.

We never could have done the thing at all without Terry.

Jeff Margrave was born to be a poet, a botanist—or both—but his folks persuaded him to be a doctor instead. He was a good one, for his age, but his real interest was in what he loved to call "the wonders of science."

As for me, sociology's my major. You have to back that up with a lot of other sciences, of course. I'm interested in them all.

Terry was strong on facts—geography and meteorology and those; Jeff could beat him any time on biology, and I didn't care what it was they talked about, so long as it connected with human life, somehow. There are few things that don't.

We three had a chance to join a big scientific expedition. They needed a doctor, and that gave Jeff an excuse for dropping his just opening practice; they needed Terry's experience, his machine, and his money; and as for me, I got in through Terry's influence.

The expedition was up among the thousand tributaries and enormous hinterland of a great river, up where the maps had to be made, savage dialects studied, and all manner of strange flora and fauna expected.

But this story is not about that expedition. That was only the merest starter for ours.

My interest was first roused by talk among our guides. I'm quick at languages, know a good many, and pick them up readily. What with that and a really good interpreter we took with us, I made out quite a few legends and folk myths of these scattered tribes.

And as we got farther and farther upstream, in a dark tangle of rivers, lakes, morasses, and dense forests, with here and there an unexpected long spur running out from the big mountains beyond, I noticed that more and more of these savages had a story about a strange and terrible Woman Land in the high distance.

"Up yonder," "Over there," "Way up"—was all the direction they could offer, but their legends all agreed on the main point—that there was this strange country where no men lived—only women and girl children.

None of them had ever seen it. It was dangerous, deadly,

they said, for any man to go there. But there were tales of long ago, when some brave investigator had seen it—a Big Country, Big Houses, Plenty People—All Women.

Had no one else gone? Yes—a good many—but they never came back. It was no place for me—of that they seemed sure.

I told the boys about these stories, and they laughed at them. Naturally I did myself. I knew the stuff that savage dreams are made of.

But when we had reached our farthest point, just the day before we all had to turn around and start for home again, as the best of expeditions must in time, we three made a discovery.

The main encampment was on a spit of land running out into the main stream, or what we thought was the main stream. It had the same muddy color we had been seeing for weeks past, the same taste.

I happened to speak of that river to our last guide, a rather superior fellow with quick, bright eyes.

He told me that there was another river—"over there, short river, sweet water, red and blue."

I was interested in this and anxious to see if I had understood, so I showed him a red and blue pencil I carried, and asked again.

Yes, he pointed to the river, and then to the southwestward. "River—good water—red and blue."

Terry was close by and interested in the fellow's pointing. "What does he say, Van?"

I told him.

Terry blazed up at once.

"Ask him how far it is."

The man indicated a short journey; I judged about two hours, maybe three.

"Let's go," urged Terry. "Just us three. Maybe we can really find something. May be cinnabar in it."

"May be indigo," Jeff suggested, with his lazy smile.

It was early yet; we had just breakfasted; and leaving word that we'd be back before night, we got away quietly, not wishing to be thought too gullible if we failed, and secretly hoping to have some nice little discovery all to ourselves.

It was a long two hours, nearer three. I fancy the savage could have done it alone much quicker. There was a desperate tangle of wood and water and a swampy patch we never should have found our way across alone. But there was one, and I could see Terry, with compass and notebook, marking directions and trying to place landmarks.

We came after a while to a sort of marshy lake, very big, so that the circling forest looked quite low and dim across it. Our guide told us that boats could go from there to our camp—but "long way—all day."

This water was somewhat clearer than that we had left, but we could not judge well from the margin. We skirted it for another half hour or so, the ground growing firmer as we advanced, and presently we turned the corner of a wooded promontory and saw a quite different country—a sudden view of mountains, steep and bare.

"One of those long easterly spurs," Terry said appraisingly. "May be hundreds of miles from the range. They crop out like that."

Suddenly we left the lake and struck directly toward the cliffs. We heard running water before we reached it, and the guide pointed proudly to his river.

It was short. We could see where it poured down a narrow vertical cataract from an opening in the face of the cliff. It was sweet water. The guide drank eagerly and so did we.

"That's snow water," Terry announced. "Must come from way back in the hills."

But as to being red and blue—it was greenish in tint. The guide seemed not at all surprised. He hunted about a little and showed us a quiet marginal pool where there were smears of red along the border; yes, and of blue.

Terry got out his magnifying glass and squatted down to investigate.

"Chemicals of some sort—I can't tell on the spot. Look to me like dyestuffs. Let's get nearer," he urged, "up there by the fall."

We scrambled along the steep banks and got close to the pool that foamed and boiled beneath the falling water. Here we searched the border and found traces of color beyond dispute. More—Jeff suddenly held up an unlooked-for trophy.

It was only a rag, a long, raveled fragment of cloth. But it was a well-woven fabric, with a pattern, and of a clear scarlet that the water had not faded. No savage tribe that we had heard of made such fabrics.

The guide stood serenely on the bank, well pleased with our excitement.

"One day blue—one day red—one day green," he told us, and pulled from his pouch another strip of bright-hued cloth.

"Come down," he said, pointing to the cataract. "Woman Country—up there."

Then we were interested. We had our rest and lunch right there and pumped the man for further information. He could tell us only what the others had—a land of women—no men—babies, but all girls. No place for men—dangerous. Some had gone to see—none had come back.

I could see Terry's jaw set at that. No place for men? Dangerous? He looked as if he might shin up the waterfall on the spot. But the guide would not hear of going up, even if there had been any possible method of scaling that sheer cliff, and we had to get back to our party before night.

"They might stay if we told them," I suggested.

But Terry stopped in his tracks. "Look here, fellows," he said. "This is our find. Let's not tell those cocky old professors. Let's go on home with 'em, and then come back—just us—have a little expedition of our own."

We looked at him, much impressed. There was something attractive to a bunch of unattached young men in finding an undiscovered country of strictly Amazonian nature.

Of course we didn't believe the story—but yet!

"There is no such cloth made by any of these local tribes," I announced, examining those rags with great care. "Somewhere up yonder they spin and weave and dye as well as we do."

"That would mean a considerable civilization, Van. There couldn't be such a place—and not known about."

"Oh, well, I don't know. What's that old republic up in the Pyrenees somewhere—Andorra? Precious few people know anything about that, and it's been minding its own business for a thousand years. Then there's Montenegro—splendid little state—you could lose a dozen Montenegroes up and down these great ranges."

We discussed it hotly all the way back to camp. We discussed it with care and privacy on the voyage home. We discussed it after that, still only among ourselves, while Terry was making his arrangements.

He was hot about it. Lucky he had so much money—we

might have had to beg and advertise for years to start the thing, and then it would have been a matter of public amusement—just sport for the papers.

But T. O. Nicholson could fix up his big steam yacht, load his specially-made big motorboat aboard, and tuck in a "dissembled" biplane without any more notice than a snip in the society column.

We had provisions and preventives and all manner of supplies. His previous experience stood him in good stead there. It was a very complete little outfit.

We were to leave the yacht at the nearest safe port and go up that endless river in our motorboat, just the three of us and a pilot; then drop the pilot when we got to that last stopping place of the previous party, and hunt up that clear water stream ourselves.

The motorboat we were going to leave at anchor in that wide shallow lake. It had a special covering of fitted armor, thin but strong, shut up like a clamshell.

"Those natives can't get into it, or hurt it, or move it," Terry explained proudly. "We'll start our flier from the lake and leave the boat as a base to come back to."

"If we come back," I suggested cheerfully.

" 'Fraid the ladies will eat you?" he scoffed.

"We're not so sure about those ladies, you know," drawled Jeff. "There may be a contingent of gentlemen with poisoned arrows or something."

"You don't need to go if you don't want to," Terry remarked drily.

"Go? You'll have to get an injunction to stop me!" Both Jeff and I were sure about that.

But we did have differences of opinion, all the long way.

An ocean voyage is an excellent time for discussion. Now we had no eavesdroppers, we could loll and loaf in our deck chairs and talk and talk—there was nothing else to do. Our absolute lack of facts only made the field of discussion wider.

"We'll leave papers with our consul where the yacht stays," Terry planned. "If we don't come back in—say a month—they can send a relief party after us."

"A punitive expedition," I urged. "If the ladies do eat us we must make reprisals."

"They can locate that last stopping place easy enough,

and I've made a sort of chart of that lake and cliff and waterfall.''

"Yes, but how will they get up?" asked Jeff.

"Same way we do, of course. If three valuable American citizens are lost up there, they will follow somehow—to say nothing of the glittering attractions of that fair land—let's call it 'Feminisia,' '' he broke off.

"You're right, Terry. Once the story gets out, the river will crawl with expeditions and the airships rise like a swarm of mosquitoes." I laughed as I thought of it. "We've made a great mistake not to let Mr. Yellow Press in on this. Save us! What headlines!"

"Not much!" said Terry grimly. "This is our party. We're going to find that place alone."

"What are you going to do with it when you do find it—if you do?" Jeff asked mildly.

Jeff was a tender soul. I think he thought that country—if there was one—was just blossoming with roses and babies and canaries and tidies, and all that sort of thing.

And Terry, in his secret heart, had visions of a sort of sublimated summer resort—just Girls and Girls and Girls—and that he was going to be—well, Terry was popular among women even when there were other men around, and it's not to be wondered at that he had pleasant dreams of what might happen. I could see it in his eyes as he lay there, looking at the long blue rollers slipping by, and fingering that impressive mustache of his.

But I thought—then—that I could form a far clearer idea of what was before us than either of them.

"You're all off, boys," I insisted. "If there is such a place—and there does seem some foundation for believing it—you'll find it's built on a sort of matriarchal principle, that's all. The men have a separate cult of their own, less socially developed than the women, and make them an annual visit—a sort of wedding call. This is a condition known to have existed—here's just a survival. They've got some peculiarly isolated valley or tableland up there, and their primeval customs have survived. That's all there is to it."

"How about the boys?" Jeff asked.

"Oh, the men take them away as soon as they are five or six, you see."

"And how about this danger theory all our guides were so sure of?"

"Danger enough, Terry, and we'll have to be mighty careful. Women of that stage of culture are quite able to defend themselves and have no welcome for unseasonable visitors."

We talked and talked.

And with all my airs of sociological superiority I was no nearer than any of them.

It was funny though, in the light of what we did find, those extremely clear ideas of ours as to what a country of women would be like. It was no use to tell ourselves and one another that all this was idle speculation. We were idle and we did speculate, on the ocean voyage and the river voyage, too.

"Admitting the improbability," we'd begin solemnly, and then launch out again.

"They would fight among themselves," Terry insisted. "Women always do. We mustn't look to find any sort of order and organization."

"You're dead wrong," Jeff told him. "It will be like a nunnery under an abbess—a peaceful, harmonious sisterhood."

I snorted derision at this idea.

"Nuns, indeed! Your peaceful sisterhoods were all celibate, Jeff, and under vows of obedience. These are just women, and mothers, and where there's motherhood you don't find sisterhood—not much."

"No, sir—they'll scrap," agreed Terry. "Also we mustn't look for inventions and progress; it'll be awfully primitive."

"How about that cloth mill?" Jeff suggested.

"Oh, cloth! Women have always been spinsters. But there they stop—you'll see."

We joked Terry about his modest impression that he would be warmly received, but he held his ground.

"You'll see," he insisted. "I'll get solid with them all—and play one bunch against another. I'll get myself elected king in no time—whew! Solomon will have to take a back seat!"

"Where do we come in on that deal?" I demanded. "Aren't we Viziers or anything?"

"Couldn't risk it," he asserted solemnly. "You might start a revolution—probably would. No, you'll have to be beheaded, or bowstrung—or whatever the popular method of execution is.''

''You'd have to do it yourself, remember,'' grinned Jeff. ''No husky black slaves and mamelukes! And there'd be two of us and only one of you—eh, Van?''

Jeff's ideas and Terry's were so far apart that sometimes it was all I could do to keep the peace between them. Jeff idealized women in the best Southern style. He was full of chivalry and sentiment, and all that. And he was a good boy; he lived up to his ideals.

You might say Terry did, too, if you can call his views about women anything so polite as ideals. I always liked Terry. He was a man's man, very much so, generous and brave and clever; but I don't think any of us in college days was quite pleased to have him with our sisters. We weren't very stringent, heavens no! But Terry was ''the limit.'' Later on—why, of course a man's life is his own, we held, and asked no questions.

But barring a possible exception in favor of a not impossible wife, or of his mother, or, of course, the fair relatives of his friends, Terry's idea seemed to be that pretty women were just so much game and homely ones not worth considering.

It was really unpleasant sometimes to see the notions he had.

But I got out of patience with Jeff, too. He had such rose-colored halos on his womenfolks. I held a middle ground, highly scientific, of course, and used to argue learnedly about the physiological limitations of the sex.

We were not in the least ''advanced'' on the woman question, any of us, then.

So we joked and disputed and speculated, and after an interminable journey, we got to our old camping place at last.

It was not hard to find the river, just poking along that side till we came to it, and it was navigable as far as the lake.

When we reached that and slid out on its broad glistening bosom, with that high gray promontory running out toward us, and the straight white fall clearly visible, it began to be really exciting.

There was some talk, even then, of skirting the rock wall

and seeking a possible footway up, but the marshy jungle made that method look not only difficult but dangerous.

Terry dismissed the plan sharply.

"Nonsense, fellows! We've decided that. It might take months—we haven't the provisions. No, sir—we've got to take our chances. If we get back safe—all right. If we don't, why, we're not the first explorers to get lost in the shuffle. There are plenty to come after us."

So we got the big biplane together and loaded it with our scientifically compressed baggage: the camera, of course; the glasses; a supply of concentrated food. Our pockets were magazines of small necessities, and we had our guns, of course—there was no knowing what might happen.

Up and up and up we sailed, way up at first, to get "the lay of the land" and make note of it.

Out of that dark green sea of crowding forest this high-standing spur rose steeply. It ran back on either side, apparently to the far-off white-crowned peaks in the distance, themselves probably inaccessible.

"Let's make the first trip geographical," I suggested. "Spy out the land, and drop back here for more gasoline. With your tremendous speed we can reach that range and back all right. Then we can leave a sort of map on board—for that relief expedition."

"There's sense in that," Terry agreed. "I'll put off being king of Ladyland for one more day."

So we made a long skirting voyage, turned the point of the cape which was close by, ran up one side of the triangle at our best speed, crossed over the base where it left the higher mountains, and so back to our lake by moonlight.

"That's not a bad little kingdom," we agreed when it was roughly drawn and measured. We could tell the size fairly by our speed. And from what we could see of the sides—and that icy ridge at the back end—"It's a pretty enterprising savage who would manage to get into it," Jeff said.

Of course we had looked at the land itself—eagerly, but we were too high and going too fast to see much. It appeared to be well forested about the edges, but in the interior there were wide plains, and everywhere parklike meadows and open places.

There were cities, too; that I insisted. It looked—well, it looked like any other country—a civilized one, I mean.

We had to sleep after that long sweep through the air, but we turned out early enough next day, and again we rose softly up the height till we could top the crowning trees and see the broad fair land at our pleasure.

"Semitropical. Looks like a first-rate climate. It's wonderful what a little height will do for temperature." Terry was studying the forest growth.

"Little height! Is that what you call little?" I asked. Our instruments measured it clearly. We had not realized the long gentle rise from the coast perhaps.

"Mighty lucky piece of land, I call it," Terry pursued. "Now for the folks—I've had enough scenery."

So we sailed low, crossing back and forth, quartering the country as we went, and studying it. We saw—I can't remember now how much of this we noted then and how much was supplemented by our later knowledge, but we could not help seeing this much, even on that excited day—a land in a state of perfect cultivation, where even the forests looked as if they were cared for; a land that looked like an enormous park, only it was even more evidently an enormous garden.

"I don't see any cattle," I suggested, but Terry was silent. We were approaching a village.

I confess that we paid small attention to the clean, well-built roads, to the attractive architecture, to the ordered beauty of the little town. We had our glasses out; even Terry, setting his machine for a spiral glide, clapped the binoculars to his eyes.

They heard our whirring screw. They ran out of the houses—they gathered in from the fields, swift-running light figures, crowds of them. We stared and stared until it was almost too late to catch the levers, sweep off and rise again; and then we held our peace for a long run upward.

"Gosh!" said Terry, after a while.

"Only women there—and children," Jeff urged excitedly.

"But they look—why, this is a *civilized* country!" I protested. "There must be men."

"Of course there are men," said Terry. "Come on, let's find 'em."

He refused to listen to Jeff's suggestion that we examine the country further before we risked leaving our machine.

"There's a fine landing place right there where we came over," he insisted, and it was an excellent one—a wide, flat-topped rock, overlooking the lake, and quite out of sight from the interior.

"They won't find this in a hurry," he asserted, as we scrambled with the utmost difficulty down to safer footing. "Come on, boys—there were some good lookers in that bunch."

Of course it was unwise of us.

It was quite easy to see afterward that our best plan was to have studied the country more fully before we left our swooping airship and trusted ourselves to mere foot service. But we were three young men. We had been talking about this country for over a year, hardly believing that there was such a place, and now—we were in it.

It looked safe and civilized enough, and among those upturned, crowding faces, though some were terrified enough, there was great beauty—on that we all agreed.

"Come on!" cried Terry, pushing forward. "Oh, come on! Here goes for Herland!"

2. Rash Advances

Not more than ten or fifteen miles we judged it from our landing rock to that last village. For all our eagerness we thought it wise to keep to the woods and go carefully.

Even Terry's ardor was held in check by his firm conviction that there were men to be met, and we saw to it that each of us had a good stock of cartridges.

"They may be scarce, and they may be hidden away somewhere—some kind of a matriarchate, as Jeff tells us; for that matter, they may live up in the mountains yonder and keep the women in this part of the country—sort of a national harem! But there are men somewhere—didn't you see the babies?"

We had all seen babies, children big and little, everywhere that we had come near enough to distinguish the people. And though by dress we could not be sure of all the grown persons, still there had not been one man that we were certain of.

"I always liked that Arab saying, 'First tie your camel and then trust in the Lord,' " Jeff murmured; so we all had our weapons in hand, and stole cautiously through the forest. Terry studied it as we progressed.

"Talk of civilization," he cried softly in restrained enthusiasm. "I never saw a forest so petted, even in Germany. Look, there's not a dead bough—the vines are trained—actually! And see here"—he stopped and looked about him, calling Jeff's attention to the kinds of trees.

They left me for a landmark and made a limited excursion on either side.

"Food-bearing, practically all of them," they announced

returning. "The rest, splendid hardwood. Call this a forest? It's a truck farm!"

"Good thing to have a botanist on hand," I agreed. "Sure there are no medicinal ones? Or any for pure ornament?"

As a matter of fact they were quite right. These towering trees were under as careful cultivation as so many cabbages. In other conditions we should have found those woods full of fair foresters and fruit gatherers; but an airship is a conspicuous object, and by no means quiet—and women are cautious.

All we found moving in those woods, as we started through them, were birds, some gorgeous, some musical, all so tame that it seemed almost to contradict our theory of cultivation—at least until we came upon occasional little glades, where carved stone seats and tables stood in the shade beside clear fountains, with shallow bird baths always added.

"They don't kill birds, and apparently they do kill cats," Terry declared. *"Must* be men here. Hark!"

We had heard something: something not in the least like a birdsong, and very much like a suppressed whisper of laughter—a little happy sound, instantly smothered. We stood like so many pointers, and then used our glasses, swiftly, carefully.

"It couldn't have been far off," said Terry excitedly. "How about this big tree?"

There was a very large and beautiful tree in the glade we had just entered, with thick wide-spreading branches that sloped out in lapping fans like a beech or pine. It was trimmed underneath some twenty feet up, and stood there like a huge umbrella, with circling seats beneath.

"Look," he pursued. "There are short stumps of branches left to climb on. There's someone up that tree, I believe."

We stole near, cautiously.

"Look out for a poisoned arrow in your eye," I suggested, but Terry pressed forward, sprang up on the seatback, and grasped the trunk. "In my heart, more likely," he answered. "Gee! Look, boys!"

We rushed close in and looked up. There among the boughs overhead was something—more than one something—that clung motionless, close to the great trunk at first, and then, as one and all we started up the tree, separated into three swift-moving figures and fled upward. As we climbed we could catch glimpses of them scattering above us. By the time we had reached about as far as three men together dared push, they had left the main trunk and moved outward, each one balanced on a long branch that dipped and swayed beneath the weight.

We paused uncertain. If we pursued further, the boughs would break under the double burden. We might shake them off, perhaps, but none of us was so inclined. In the soft dappled light of these high regions, breathless with our rapid climb, we rested awhile, eagerly studying our objects of pursuit; while they in turn, with no more terror than a set of frolicsome children in a game of tag, sat as lightly as so many big bright birds on their precarious perches and frankly, curiously, stared at us.

"Girls!" whispered Jeff, under his breath, as if they might fly if he spoke aloud.

"Peaches!" added Terry, scarcely louder. "Peacherinos—apricot-nectarines! Whew!"

They were girls, of course, no boys could ever have shown that sparkling beauty, and yet none of us was certain at first.

We saw short hair, hatless, loose, and shining; a suit of some light firm stuff, the closest of tunics and knee-breeches, met by trim gaiters. As bright and smooth as parrots and as unaware of danger, they swung there before us, wholly at ease, staring as we stared, till first one, and then all of them burst into peals of delighted laughter.

Then there was a torrent of soft talk tossed back and forth; no savage sing-song, but clear musical fluent speech.

We met their laughter cordially, and doffed our hats to them, at which they laughed again, delightedly.

Then Terry, wholly in his element, made a polite speech, with explanatory gestures, and proceeded to introduce us, with pointing finger. "Mr. Jeff Margrave," he said clearly; Jeff bowed as gracefully as a man could in the fork of a great limb. "Mr. Vandyck Jennings"—I also tried to make an effective salute and nearly lost my balance.

Then Terry laid his hand upon his chest—a fine chest he had, too, and introduced himself; he was braced carefully for the occasion and achieved an excellent obeisance.

Again they laughed delightedly, and the one nearest me followed his tactics.

"Celis," she said distinctly, pointing to the one in blue;

"Alima"—the one in rose; then, with a vivid imitation of Terry's impressive manner, she laid a firm delicate hand on her gold-green jerkin—"Ellador." This was pleasant, but we got no nearer.

"We can't sit here and learn the language," Terry protested. He beckoned to them to come nearer, most winningly—but they gaily shook their heads. He suggested, by signs, that we all go down together; but again they shook their heads, still merrily. Then Ellador clearly indicated that we should go down, pointing to each and all of us, with unmistakable firmness; and further seeming to imply by the sweep of a lithe arm that we not only go downward, but go away altogether—at which we shook our heads in turn.

"Have to use bait," grinned Terry. "I don't know about you fellows, but I came prepared." He produced from an inner pocket a little box of purple velvet, that opened with a snap—and out of it he drew a long sparkling thing, a necklace of big varicolored stones that would have been worth a million if real ones. He held it up, swung it, glittering in the sun, offered it first to one, then to another, holding it out as far as he could reach toward the girl nearest him. He stood braced in the fork, held firmly by one hand—the other, swinging his bright temptation, reached far out along the bough, but not quite to his full stretch.

She was visibly moved, I noted, hesitated, spoke to her companions. They chattered softly together, one evidently warning her, the other encouraging. Then, softly and slowly, she drew nearer. This was Alima, a tall long-limbed lass, well-knit and evidently both strong and agile. Her eyes were splendid, wide, fearless, as free from suspicion as a child's who has never been rebuked. Her interest was more that of an intent boy playing a fascinating game than of a girl lured by an ornament.

The others moved a bit farther out, holding firmly, watching. Terry's smile was irreproachable, but I did not like the look in his eyes—it was like a creature about to spring. I could already see it happen—the dropped necklace, the sudden clutching hand, the girl's sharp cry as he seized her and drew her in. But it didn't happen. She made a timid reach with her right hand for the gay swinging thing—he held it a little nearer—then, swift as light, she seized it from him with her left, and dropped on the instant to the bough below.

He made his snatch, quite vainly, almost losing his position as his hand clutched only air; and then, with inconceivable rapidity, the three bright creatures were gone. They dropped from the ends of the big boughs to those below, fairly pouring themselves off the tree, while we climbed downward as swiftly as we could. We heard their vanishing gay laughter, we saw them fleeting away in the wide open reaches of the forest, and gave chase, but we might as well have chased wild antelopes; so we stopped at length somewhat breathless.

"No use," gasped Terry. "They got away with it. My word! The men of this country must be good sprinters!"

"Inhabitants evidently arboreal," I grimly suggested. "Civilized and still arboreal—peculiar people."

"You shouldn't have tried that way," Jeff protested. "They were perfectly friendly; now we've scared them."

But it was no use grumbling, and Terry refused to admit any mistake. "Nonsense," he said. "They expected it. Women like to be run after. Come on, let's get to that town; maybe we'll find them there. Let's see, it was in this direction and not far from the woods, as I remember."

When we reached the edge of the open country we reconnoitered with our field glasses. There it was, about four miles off, the same town, we concluded, unless, as Jeff ventured, they all had pink houses. The broad green fields and closely cultivated gardens sloped away at our feet, a long easy slant, with good roads winding pleasantly here and there, and narrower paths besides.

"Look at that!" cried Jeff suddenly. "There they go!"

Sure enough, close to the town, across a wide meadow, three bright-hued figures were running swiftly.

"How could they have got that far in this time? It can't be the same ones," I urged. But through the glasses we could identify our pretty tree-climbers quite plainly, at least by costume.

Terry watched them, we all did for that matter, till they disappeared among the houses. Then he put down his glass and turned to us, drawing a long breath. "Mother of Mike, boys—what Gorgeous Girls! To climb like that! to run like that! and afraid of nothing. This country suits me all right. Let's get ahead."

"Nothing venture, nothing have," I suggested, but Terry preferred "Faint heart ne'er won fair lady."

We set forth in the open, walking briskly. "If there are any men, we'd better keep an eye out," I suggested, but Jeff seemed lost in heavenly dreams, and Terry in highly practical plans.

"What a perfect road! What a heavenly country! See the flowers, will you?"

This was Jeff, always an enthusiast; but we could agree with him fully.

The road was some sort of hard manufactured stuff, sloped slightly to shed rain, with every curve and grade and gutter as perfect as if it were Europe's best. "No men, eh?" sneered Terry. On either side a double row of trees shaded the footpaths; between the tree bushes or vines, all fruit-bearing, now and then seats and little wayside fountains; everywhere flowers.

"We'd better import some of these ladies and set 'em to parking the United States," I suggested. "Mighty nice place they've got here." We rested a few moments by one of the fountains, tested the fruit that looked ripe, and went on, impressed, for all our gay bravado by the sense of quiet potency which lay about us.

Here was evidently a people highly skilled, efficient, caring for their country as a florist cares for his costliest orchids. Under the soft brilliant blue of that clear sky, in the pleasant shade of those endless rows of trees, we walked unharmed, the placid silence broken only by the birds.

Presently there lay before us at the foot of a long hill the town or village we were aiming for. We stopped and studied it.

Jeff drew a long breath. "I wouldn't have believed a collection of houses could look so lovely," he said.

"They've got architects and landscape gardeners in plenty, that's sure," agreed Terry.

I was astonished myself. You see, I come from California, and there's no country lovelier, but when it comes to towns—! I have often groaned at home to see the offensive mess man made in the face of nature, even though I'm no art sharp, like Jeff. But this place! It was built mostly of a sort of dull rose-colored stone, with here and there some clear white houses; and it lay abroad among the green groves and gardens like a broken rosary of pink coral.

"Those big white ones are public buildings evidently,"

Terry declared. "This is no savage country, my friend. But no men? Boys, it behooves us to go forward most politely."

The place had an odd look, more impressive as we approached. "It's like an exposition." "It's too pretty to be true." "Plenty of palaces, but where are the homes?" "Oh there are little ones enough—but—." It certainly was different from any towns we had ever seen.

"There's no dirt," said Jeff suddenly. "There's no smoke," he added after a little.

"There's no noise," I offered; but Terry snubbed me—"That's because they are laying low for us; we'd better be careful how we go in there."

Nothing could induce him to stay out, however, so we walked on.

Everything was beauty, order, perfect cleanness, and the pleasantest sense of home over it all. As we neared the center of the town the houses stood thicker, ran together as it were, grew into rambling palaces grouped among parks and open squares, something as college buildings stand in their quiet greens.

And then, turning a corner, we came into a broad paved space and saw before us a band of women standing close together in even order, evidently waiting for us.

We stopped a moment and looked back. The street behind was closed by another band, marching steadily, shoulder to shoulder. We went on—there seemed no other way to go—and presently found ourselves quite surrounded by this close-massed multitude, women, all of them, but—

They were not young. They were not old. They were not, in the girl sense, beautiful. They were not in the least ferocious. And yet, as I looked from face to face, calm, grave, wise, wholly unafraid, evidently assured and determined, I had the funniest feeling—a very early feeling—a feeling that I traced back and back in memory until I caught up with it at last. It was that sense of being hopelessly in the wrong that I had so often felt in early youth when my short legs' utmost effort failed to overcome the fact that I was late to school.

Jeff felt it too; I could see he did. We felt like small boys, very small boys, caught doing mischief in some gracious lady's house. But Terry showed no such consciousness. I saw his quick eyes darting here and there, estimating numbers, measuring distances, judging chances of escape. He examined the close ranks about us, reaching back far on every side, and murmured softly to me, "Every one of 'em over forty as I'm a sinner."

Yet they were not old women. Each was in the full bloom of rosy health, erect, serene, standing sure-footed and light as any pugilist. They had no weapons, and we had, but we had no wish to shoot.

"I'd as soon shoot my aunts," muttered Terry again. "What do they want with us anyhow? They seem to mean business." But in spite of that businesslike aspect, he determined to try his favorite tactics. Terry had come armed with a theory.

He stepped forward, with his brilliant ingratiating smile, and made low obeisance to the women before him. Then he produced another tribute, a broad soft scarf of filmy texture, rich in color and pattern, a lovely thing, even to my eye, and offered it with a deep bow to the tall unsmiling woman who seemed to head the ranks before him. She took it with a gracious nod of acknowledgment, and passed it on to those behind her.

He tried again, this time bringing out a circlet of rhinestones, a glittering crown that should have pleased any woman on earth. He made a brief address, including Jeff and me as partners in his enterprise, and with another bow presented this. Again his gift was accepted and, as before, passed out of sight.

"If they were only younger," he muttered between his teeth. "What on earth is a fellow to say to a regiment of old Colonels like this?"

In all our discussions and speculations we had always unconsciously assumed that the women, whatever else they might be, would be young. Most men do think that way, I fancy.

"Woman" in the abstract is young, and, we assume, charming. As they get older they pass off the stage, somehow, into private ownership mostly, or out of it altogether. But these good ladies were very much on the stage, and yet any one of them might have been a grandmother.

We looked for nervousness—there was none.

For terror, perhaps—there was none.

For uneasiness, for curiosity, for excitement—and all we saw was what might have been a vigilance committee of women doctors, as cool as cucumbers, and evidently meaning to take us to task for being there.

Six of them stepped forward now, one on either side of each of us, and indicated that we were to go with them. We thought it best to accede, at first anyway, and marched along, one of these close at each elbow, and the others in close masses before, behind, on both sides.

A large building opened before us, a very heavy thick-walled impressive place, big, and old-looking; of gray stone, not like the rest of the town.

"This won't do!" said Terry to us, quickly. "We mustn't let them get us in this, boys. All together, now—"

We stopped in our tracks. We began to explain, to make signs pointing away toward the big forest—indicating that we would go back to it—at once.

It makes me laugh, knowing all I do now, to think of us three boys—nothing else; three audacious impertinent boys—butting into an unknown country without any sort of a guard or defense. We seemed to think that if there were men we could fight them, and if there were only women— why, they would be no obstacles at all.

Jeff, with his gentle romantic old-fashioned notions of women as clinging vines. Terry, with his clear decided practical theories that there were two kinds of women—those he wanted and those he didn't; Desirable and Undesirable was his demarcation. The latter as a large class, but negligible— he had never thought about them at all.

And now here they were, in great numbers, evidently indifferent to what he might think, evidently determined on some purpose of their own regarding him, and apparently well able to enforce their purpose.

We all thought hard just then. It had not seemed wise to object to going with them, even if we could have; our one chance was friendliness—a civilized attitude on both sides.

But once inside that building, there was no knowing what these determined ladies might do to us. Even a peaceful detention was not to our minds, and when we named it imprisonment it looked even worse.

So we made a stand, trying to make clear that we preferred the open country. One of them came forward with a sketch of our flier, asking by signs if we were the aerial visitors they had seen.

This we admitted.

They pointed to it again, and to the outlying country, in different directions—but we pretended we did not know where it was, and in truth we were not quite sure and gave a rather wild indication of its whereabouts.

Again they motioned us to advance, standing so packed about the door that there remained but the one straight path open. All around us and behind they were massed solidly—there was simply nothing to do but go forward—or fight.

We held a consultation.

"I never fought with women in my life," said Terry, greatly perturbed, "but I'm not going in there. I'm not going to be—herded in—as if we were in a cattle chute."

"We can't fight them, of course," Jeff urged. "They're all women, in spite of their nondescript clothes; nice women, too; good strong sensible faces. I guess we'll have to go in."

"We may never get out, if we do," I told them. "Strong and sensible, yes; but I'm not so sure about the good. Look at those faces!"

They had stood at ease, waiting while we conferred together, but never relaxing their close attention.

Their attitude was not the rigid discipline of soldiers; there was no sense of compulsion about them. Terry's term of a "vigilance committee" was highly descriptive. They had just the aspect of sturdy burghers, gathered hastily to meet some common need or peril, all moved by precisely the same feelings, to the same end.

Never, anywhere before, had I seen women of precisely this quality. Fishwives and market women might show similar strength, but it was coarse and heavy. These were merely athletic—light and powerful. College professors, teachers, writers—many women showed similar intelligence but often wore a strained nervous look, while these were as calm as cows, for all their evident intellect.

We observed pretty closely just then, for all of us felt that it was a crucial moment.

The leader gave some word of command and beckoned us on, and the surrounding mass moved a step nearer.

"We've got to decide quick," said Terry.

"I vote to go in," Jeff urged. But we were two to one against him and he loyally stood by us. We made one more effort to be let go, urgent, but not imploring. In vain.

"Now for a rush, boys!" Terry said. "And if we can't break 'em, I'll shoot in the air."

Then we found ourselves much in the position of the suffragette trying to get to the Parliament buildings through a triple cordon of London police.

The solidity of those women was something amazing. Terry soon found that it was useless, tore himself loose for a moment, pulled his revolver, and fired upward. As they caught at it, he fired again—we heard a cry—.

Instantly each of us was seized by five women, each holding arm or leg or head; we were lifted like children, straddling helpless children, and borne onward, wriggling indeed, but most ineffectually.

We were borne inside, struggling manfully, but held secure most womanfully, in spite of our best endeavors.

So carried and so held, we came into a high inner hall, gray and bare, and were brought before a majestic gray-haired woman who seemed to hold a judicial position.

There was some talk, not much, among them, and then suddenly there fell upon each of us at once a firm hand holding a wetted cloth before mouth and nose—an odor of swimming sweetness—anesthesia.

3. A Peculiar Imprisonment

From a slumber as deep as death, as refreshing as that of a healthy child, I slowly awakened.

It was like rising up, up, up through a deep warm ocean, nearer and nearer to full light and stirring air. Or like the return to consciousness after concussion of the brain. I was once thrown from a horse while on a visit to a wild mountainous country quite new to me, and I can clearly remember the mental experience of coming back to life, through lifting veils of dream. When I first dimly heard the voices of those about me, and saw the shining snowpeaks of that mighty range, I assumed that this too would pass, and I should presently find myself in my own home.

That was precisely the experience of this awakening: receding waves of half-caught swirling vision, memories of home, the steamer, the boat, the airship, the forest—at last all sinking away one after another, till my eyes were wide open, my brain clear, and I realized what had happened.

The most prominent sensation was of absolute physical comfort. I was lying in a perfect bed: long, broad, smooth; firmly soft and level; with the finest linen, some warm light quilt of blanket, and a counterpane that was a joy to the eye. The sheet turned down some fifteen inches, yet I could stretch my feet at the foot of the bed free but warmly covered.

I felt as light and clean as a white feather. It took me some time to consciously locate my arms and legs, to feel the vivid sense of life radiate from the wakening center to the extremities.

A big room, high and wide, with many lofty windows whose closed blinds let through soft green-lit air; a beautiful room, in proportion, in color, in smooth simplicity; a scent of blossoming gardens outside.

I lay perfectly still, quite happy, quite conscious, and yet not actively realizing what had happened till I heard Terry.

"Gosh!" was what he said.

I turned my head. There were three beds in this chamber, and plenty of room for them.

Terry was sitting up, looking about him, alert as ever. His remark, though not loud, roused Jeff also. We all sat up.

Terry swung his legs out of bed, stood up, stretched himself mightily. He was in a long nightrobe, a sort of seamless garment, undoubtedly comfortable—we all found ourselves so covered. Shoes were beside each bed, also quite comfortable and good-looking though by no means like our own.

We looked for our clothes—they were not there, nor anything of all the varied contents of our pockets.

A door stood somewhat ajar; it opened into a most attractive bathroom, copiously provided with towels, soap, mirrors, and all such convenient comforts, with indeed our toothbrushes and combs, our notebooks, and thank goodness, our watches—but no clothes.

Then we made a search of the big room again and found a large airy closet, holding plenty of clothing, but not ours.

"A council of war!" demanded Terry. "Come on back to bed—the bed's all right anyhow. Now then, my scientific friend, let us consider our case dispassionately."

He meant me, but Jeff seemed most impressed.

"They haven't hurt us in the least!" he said. "They could have killed us—or—or anything—and I never felt better in my life."

"That argues that they are all women," I suggested, "and highly civilized. You know you hit one in the last scrimmage—I heard her sing out—and we kicked awfully."

Terry was grinning at us. "So you realize what these ladies have done to us?" he pleasantly inquired. "They have taken away all our possessions, all our clothes—every stitch. We have been stripped and washed and put to bed like so many yearling babies—by these highly civilized women."

Jeff actually blushed. He had a poetic imagination. Terry had imagination enough, of a different kind. So had I, also different. I always flattered myself I had the scientific imagination, which, incidentally, I considered the highest sort.

One has a right to a certain amount of egotism if founded on fact—and kept to one's self—I think.

"No use kicking, boys," I said. "They've got us, and apparently they're perfectly harmless. It remains for us to cook up some plan of escape like any other bottled heroes. Meanwhile we've got to put on these clothes—Hobson's choice."

The garments were simple in the extreme, and absolutely comfortably, physically, though of course we all felt like supes in the theater. There was a one-piece cotton undergarment, thin and soft, that reached over the knees and shoulders, something like the one-piece pajamas some fellows wear, and a kind of half-hose, that came up to just under the knee and stayed there—had elastic tops of their own, and covered the edges of the first.

Then there was a thicker variety of union suit, a lot of them in the closet, of varying weights and somewhat sturdier material—evidently they would do at a pinch with nothing further. Then there were tunics, knee-length, and some long robes. Needless to say, we took tunics.

We bathed and dressed quite cheerfully.

"Not half bad," said Terry, surveying himself in a long mirror. His hair was somewhat longer than when we left the last barber, and the hats provided were much like those seen on the prince in the fairy tale, lacking the plume.

The costume was similar to that which we had seen on all the women, though some of them, those working in the fields, glimpsed by our glasses when we first flew over, wore only the first two.

I settled my shoulders and stretched my arms, remarking: "They have worked out a mighty sensible dress, I'll say that for them." With which we all agreed.

"Now then," Terry proclaimed, "we've had a fine long sleep—we've had a good bath—we're clothed and in our right minds, though feeling like a lot of neuters. Do you think these highly civilized ladies are going to give us any breakfast?"

"Of course they will," Jeff asserted confidently. "If they had meant to kill us, they would have done it before. I believe we are going to be treated as guests."

"Hailed as deliverers, I think," said Terry.

"Studied as curiosities," I told them. "But anyhow, we want food. So now for a sortie!"

A sortie was not so easy.

The bathroom only opened into our chamber, and that had but one outlet, a big heavy door, which was fastened.

We listened.

"There's someone outside," Jeff suggested. "Let's knock."

So we knocked, whereupon the door opened.

Outside was another large room, furnished with a great table at one end, long benches or couches against the wall, some smaller tables and chairs. All these were solid, strong, simple in structure, and comfortable in use—also, incidentally, beautiful.

This room was occupied by a number of women, eighteen to be exact, some of whom we distinctly recalled.

Terry heaved a disappointed sigh. "The Colonels!" I heard him whisper to Jeff.

Jeff, however, advanced and bowed in his best manner; so did we all, and we were saluted civilly by the tall-standing women.

We had no need to make pathetic pantomime of hunger; the smaller tables were already laid with food, and we were gravely invited to be seated. The tables were set for two; each of us found ourselves placed vis-à-vis with one of our hosts, and each table had five other stalwarts nearby, unobtrusively watching. We had plenty of time to get tired of those women!

The breakfast was not profuse, but sufficient in amount and excellent in quality. We were all too good travelers to object to novelty, and this repast with its new but delicious fruit, its dish of large rich-flavored nuts, and its highly satisfactory little cakes was most agreeable. There was water to drink, and a hot beverage of a most pleasing quality, some preparation like cocoa.

And then and there, willy-nilly, before we had satisfied our appetites, our education began.

By each of our plates lay a little book, a real printed book, though different from ours both in paper and binding, as well, of course, as in type. We examined them curiously.

"Shades of Sauveur!" muttered Terry. "We're to learn the language!"

We were indeed to learn the language, and not only that, but to teach our own. There were blank books with parallel columns, neatly ruled, evidently prepared for the occasion, and in these, as fast as we learned and wrote down the name of anything, we were urged to write our own name for it by its side.

The book we had to study was evidently a schoolbook, one in which children learned to read, and we judged from this, and from their frequent consultation as to methods, that they had had no previous experience in the art of teaching foreigners their language, or of learning any other.

On the other hand, what they lacked in experience, they made up for in genius. Such subtle understanding, such instant recognition of our difficulties, and readiness to meet them, were a constant surprise to us.

Of course, we were willing to meet them halfway. It was wholly to our advantage to be able to understand and speak with them, and as to refusing to teach them—why should we? Later on we did try open rebellion, but only once.

That first meal was pleasant enough, each of us quietly studying his companion, Jeff with sincere admiration, Terry with that highly technical look of his, as of a past master— like a lion tamer, a serpent charmer, or some such professional. I myself was intensely interested.

It was evident that those sets of five were there to check any outbreak on our part. We had no weapons, and if we did try to do any damage, with a chair, say, why five to one was too many for us, even if they were women; that we had found out to our sorrow. It was not pleasant, having them always around, but we soon got used to it.

"It's better than being physically restrained ourselves," Jeff philosophically suggested when we were alone. "They've given us a room—with no great possibility of escape—and personal liberty—heavily chaperoned. It's better than we'd have been likely to get in a man-country."

"Man-Country! Do you really believe there are no men here, you innocent? Don't you know there must be?" demanded Terry.

"Ye—es," Jeff agreed. "Of course—and yet—"

"And yet—what! Come, you obdurate sentimentalist— what are you thinking about?"

"They may have some peculiar division of labor we've never heard of," I suggested. "The men may live in separate towns, or they may have subdued them—somehow— and keep them shut up. But there must be some."

"That last suggestion of yours is a nice one, Van," Terry

protested. "Same as they've got us subdued and shut up! You make me shiver."

"Well, figure it out for yourself, anyway you please. We saw plenty of kids, the first day, and we've seen those girls—"

"Real girls!" Terry agreed, in immense relief. "Glad you mentioned 'em. I declare, if I thought there was nothing in the country but those grenadiers I'd jump out the window."

"Speaking of windows," I suggested, "let's examine ours."

We looked out of all the windows. The blinds opened easily enough, and there were no bars, but the prospect was not reassuring.

This was not the pink-walled town we had so rashly entered the day before. Our chamber was high up, in a projecting wing of a sort of castle, built out on a steep spur of rock. Immediately below us were gardens, fruitful and fragrant, but their high walls followed the edge of the cliff which dropped sheer down, we could not see how far. The distant sound of water suggested a river at the foot.

We could look out east, west, and south. To the southeastward stretched the open country, lying bright and fair in the morning light, but on either side, and evidently behind, rose great mountains.

"This thing is a regular fortress—and no women built it, I can tell you that," said Terry. We nodded agreeingly. "It's right up among the hills—they must have brought us a long way."

"We saw some kind of swift-moving vehicles the first day," Jeff reminded us. "If they've got motors, they *are* civilized."

"Civilized or not, we've got our work cut out for us to get away from here. I don't propose to make a rope of bedclothes and try those walls till I'm sure there is no better way."

We all concurred on this point, and returned to our discussion as to the women.

Jeff continued thoughtful. "All the same, there's something funny about it," he urged. "It isn't just that we don't see any men—but we don't see any signs of them. The—the—reaction of those women is different from any that I've ever met."

"There is something in what you say, Jeff," I agreed. "There is a different—atmosphere."

"They don't seem to notice our being men," he went on. "They treat us—well—just as they do one another. It's as if our being men was a minor incident."

I nodded. I'd noticed it myself. But Terry broke in rudely.

"Fiddlesticks!" he said. "It's because of their advanced age. They're all grandmas, I tell you—or ought to be. Great aunts, anyhow. Those girls were girls all right, weren't they?"

"Yes—" Jeff agreed, still slowly. "But they weren't afraid—they flew up that tree and hid, like schoolboys caught out of bounds—not like shy girls."

"And they ran like marathon winners—you'll admit that, Terry," he added.

Terry was moody as the days passed. He seemed to mind our confinement more than Jeff or I did; and he harped on Alima, and how near he'd come to catching her. "If I had—" he would say, rather savagely, "we'd have had a hostage and could have made terms."

But Jeff was getting on excellent terms with his tutor, and even his guards, and so was I. It interested me profoundly to note and study the subtle difference between these women and other women, and try to account for them. In the matter of personal appearance, there was a great difference. They all wore short hair, some few inches at most; some curly, some not; all light and clean and fresh-looking.

"If their hair was only long," Jeff would complain, "they would look so much more feminine."

I rather liked it myself, after I got used to it. Why we should so admire "a woman's crown of hair" and not admire a Chinaman's queue is hard to explain, except that we are so convinced that the long hair "belongs" to a woman. Whereas the "mane" in horses is on both, and in lions, buffalos, and such creatures only on the male. But I did miss it—at first.

Our time was quite pleasantly filled. We were free of the garden below our windows, quite long in its irregular rambling shape, bordering the cliff. The walls were perfectly smooth and high, ending in the masonry of the building; and as I studied the great stones I became convinced that the whole structure was extremely old. It was built like the pre-Incan architecture in Peru, of enormous monoliths, fitted as closely as mosaics.

"These folks have a history, that's sure," I told the others. "And *some* time they were fighters—else why a fortress?"

I said we were free of the garden, but not wholly alone in it. There was always a string of those uncomfortably strong women sitting about, always one of them watching us even if the others were reading, playing games, or busy at some kind of handiwork.

"When I see them knit," Terry said, "I can almost call them feminine."

"That doesn't prove anything," Jeff promptly replied. "Scotch shepherds knit—always knitting."

"When we get out—" Terry stretched himself and looked at the far peaks, "when we get out of this and get to where the real women are—the mothers, and the girls—"

"Well, what'll we do then?" I asked, rather gloomily. "How do you know we'll ever get out?"

This was an unpleasant idea, which we unanimously considered, returning with earnestness to our studies.

"If we are good boys and learn our lessons well," I suggested. "If we are quiet and respectful and polite and they are not afraid of us—then perhaps they will let us out. And anyway—when we do escape, it is of immense importance that we know the language."

Personally, I was tremendously interested in that language, and seeing they had books, was eager to get at them, to dig into their history, if they had one.

It was not hard to speak, smooth and pleasant to the ear, and so easy to read and write that I marveled at it. They had an absolutely phonetic system, the whole thing was as scientific as Esperanto yet bore all the marks of an old and rich civilization.

We were free to study as much as we wished, and were not left merely to wander in the garden for recreation but introduced to a great gymnasium, partly on the roof and partly in the story below. Here we learned real respect for our tall guards. No change of costume was needed for this work, save to lay off outer clothing. The first one was as perfect a garment for exercise as need be devised, absolutely free to move in, and, I had to admit, much betterlooking than our usual one.

"Forty—over forty—some of 'em fifty, I bet—and look at 'em!" grumbled Terry in reluctant admiration.

There were no spectacular acrobatics, such as only the young can perform, but for all-around development they had a most excellent system. A good deal of music went with it, with posture dancing and, sometimes, gravely beautiful processional performances.

Jeff was much impressed by it. We did not know then how small a part of their physical culture methods this really was, but found it agreeable to watch, and to take part in.

Oh yes, we took part all right! It wasn't absolutely compulsory, but we thought it better to please.

Terry was the strongest of us, though I was wiry and had good staying power, and Jeff was a great sprinter and hurdler, but I can tell you those old ladies gave us cards and spades. They ran like deer, by which I mean that they ran not as if it was a performance, but as if it was their natural gait. We remembered those fleeting girls of our first bright adventure, and concluded that it was.

They leaped like deer, too, with a quick folding motion of the legs, drawn up and turned to one side with a sidelong twist of the body. I remembered the sprawling spread-eagle way in which some of the fellows used to come over the line—and tried to learn the trick. We did not easily catch up with these experts, however.

"Never thought I'd live to be bossed by a lot of elderly lady acrobats," Terry protested.

They had games, too, a good many of them, but we found them rather uninteresting at first. It was like two people playing solitaire to see who would get it first; more like a race or a—a competitive examination, than a real game with some fight in it.

I philosophized a bit over this and told Terry it argued against their having any men about. "There isn't a man-size game in the lot," I said.

"But they are interesting—I like them," Jeff objected, "and I'm sure they are educational."

"I'm sick and tired of being educated," Terry protested. "Fancy going to a dame school—at our age. I want to Get Out!"

But we could not get out, and we were being educated swiftly. Our special tutors rose rapidly in our esteem. They seemed of rather finer quality than the guards, though all were on terms of easy friendliness. Mine was named Somel, Jeff's Zava, and Terry's Moadine. We tried to generalize from the names, those of the guards, and of our three girls, but got nowhere.

"They sound well enough, and they're mostly short, but there's no similarity of termination—and no two alike. However, our acquaintance is limited as yet."

There were many things we meant to ask—as soon as we could talk well enough. Better teaching I never saw. From morning to night there was Somel, always on call except between two and four; always pleasant with a steady friendly kindness that I grew to enjoy very much. Jeff said Miss Zava—he would put on a title, though they apparently had none—was a darling, that she reminded him of his Aunt Esther at home; but Terry refused to be won, and rather jeered at his own companion, when we were alone.

"I'm sick of it!" he protested. "Sick of the whole thing. Here we are cooped up as helpless as a bunch of three-year-old orphans, and being taught what they think is necessary—whether we like it or not. Confound their old-maid impudence!"

Nevertheless we were taught. They brought in a raised map of their country, beautifully made, and increased our knowledge of geographical terms; but when we inquired for information as to the country outside, they smilingly shook their heads.

They brought pictures, not only the engravings in the books but colored studies of plants and trees and flowers and birds. They brought tools and various small objects— we had plenty of "material" in our school.

If it had not been for Terry we would have been much more contented, but as the weeks ran into months he grew more and more irritable.

"Don't act like a bear with a sore head," I begged him. "We're getting on finely. Every day we can understand them better, and pretty soon we can make a reasonable plea to be let out—"

"*Let* out!" he stormed. "*Let* out—like children kept after school. I want to Get Out, and I'm going to. I want to find the men of this place and fight!—or the girls—"

"Guess it's the girls you're most interested in," Jeff commented. "What are you going to fight *with*—your fists?"

"Yes—or sticks and stones—I'd just like to!" And Terry

squared off and tapped Jeff softly on the jaw. "Just for instance," he said.

"Anyhow," he went on, "we could get back to our machine and clear out."

"If it's there," I cautiously suggested.

"Oh, don't croak, Van! If it isn't there, we'll find our way down somehow—the boat's there, I guess."

It was hard on Terry, so hard that he finally persuaded us to consider a plan of escape. It was difficult, it was highly dangerous, but he declared that he'd go alone if we wouldn't go with him, and of course we couldn't think of that.

It appeared he had made a pretty careful study of the environment. From our end window that faced the point of the promontory we could get a fair idea of the stretch of wall, and the drop below. Also from the roof we could make out more, and even, in one place, glimpse a sort of path below the wall.

"It's a question of three things," he said. "Ropes, agility, and not being seen."

"That's the hardest part," I urged, still hoping to dissuade him. "One or another pair of eyes is on us every minute except at night."

"Therefore we must do it at night," he answered. "That's easy."

"We've got to think that if they catch us we may not be so well treated afterward," said Jeff.

"That's the business risk we must take. I'm going—if I break my neck." There was no changing him.

The rope problem was not easy. Something strong enough to hold a man and long enough to let us down into the garden, and then down over the wall. There were plenty of strong ropes in the gymnasium—they seemed to love to swing and climb on them—but we were never there by ourselves.

We should have to piece it out from our bedding, rugs, and garments, and moreover, we should have to do it after we were shut in for the night, for every day the place was cleaned to perfection by two of our guardians.

We had no shears, no knives, but Terry was resourceful. "These Jennies have glass and china, you see. We'll break a glass from the bathroom and use that. 'Love will find out a way,' " he hummed. "When we're all out of the window, we'll stand three-man high and cut the rope as far up as we can reach, so as to have more for the wall. I know just where I saw that bit of path below, and there's a big tree there, too, or a vine or something—I saw the leaves."

It seemed a crazy risk to take, but this was, in a way, Terry's expedition, and we were all tired of our imprisonment.

So we waited for full moon, retired early, and spent an anxious hour or two in the unskilled manufacture of man-strong ropes.

To retire into the depths of the closet, muffle a glass in thick cloth, and break it without noise was not difficult, and broken glass will cut, though not as deftly as a pair of scissors.

The broad moonlight streamed in through four of our windows—we had not dared leave our lights on too long—and we worked hard and fast at our task of destruction.

Hangings, rugs, robes, towels, as well as bed-furniture—even the mattress covers—we left not one stitch upon another, as Jeff put it.

Then at an end window, as less liable to observation, we fastened one end of our cable, strongly, to the firm-set hinge of the inner blind, and dropped our coiled bundle of rope softly over.

"This part's easy enough—I'll come last, so as to cut the rope," said Terry.

So I slipped down first, and stood, well braced against the wall; then Jeff on my shoulders, then Terry, who shook us a little as he sawed through the cord above his head. Then I slowly dropped to the ground, Jeff following, and at last we all three stood safe in the garden, with most of our rope with us.

"Good-bye, Grandma!" whispered Terry, under his breath, and we crept softly toward the wall, taking advantage of the shadow of every bush and tree. He had been foresighted enough to mark the very spot, only a scratch of stone on stone, but we could see to read in that light. For anchorage there was a tough, fair-sized shrub close to the wall.

"Now I'll climb up on you two again and go over first," said Terry. "That'll hold the rope firm till you both get up on top. Then I'll go down to the end. If I can get off safely, you can see me and follow—or, say, I'll twitch it three times. If I find there's absolutely no footing—why I'll climb up again, that's all. I don't think they'll kill us.''

From the top he reconnoitered carefully, waved his hand, and whispered, ''OK,'' then slipped over. Jeff climbed up and I followed, and we rather shivered to see how far down that swaying, wavering figure dropped, hand under hand, till it disappeared in a mass of foliage far below.

Then there were three quick pulls, and Jeff and I, not without a joyous sense of recovered freedom, successfully followed our leader.

4. Our Venture

We were standing on a narrow, irregular, all too slanting little ledge, and should doubtless have ignominiously slipped off and broken our rash necks but for the vine. This was a thick-leaved, wide-spreading thing, a little like Amphelopsis.

"It's not *quite* vertical here, you see," said Terry, full of pride and enthusiasm. "This thing never would hold our direct weight, but I think if we sort of slide down on it, one at a time, sticking in with hands and feet, we'll reach that next ledge alive."

"As we do not wish to get up our rope again—and can't comfortably stay here—I approve," said Jeff solemnly.

Terry slid down first—said he'd show us how a Christian meets his death. Luck was with us. We had put on the thickest of those intermediate suits, leaving our tunics behind, and made this scramble quite successfully, though I got a pretty heavy fall just at the end, and was only kept on the second ledge by main force. The next stage was down a sort of "chimney"—a long irregular fissure; and so with scratches many and painful and bruises not a few, we finally reached the stream.

It was darker there, but we felt it highly necessary to put as much distance as possible behind us; so we waded, jumped, and clambered down that rocky riverbed, in the flickering black and white moonlight and leaf shadow, till growing daylight forced a halt.

We found a friendly nut-tree, those large, satisfying, soft-shelled nuts we already knew so well, and filled our pockets.

I see that I have not remarked that these women had pockets in surprising number and variety. They were in all their garments, and the middle one in particular was shingled with them. So we stocked up with nuts till we bulged like Prussian privates in marching order, drank all we could hold, and retired for the day.

It was not a very comfortable place, not at all easy to get at, just a sort of crevice high up along the steep bank, but it was well veiled with foliage and dry. After our exhausting three- or four-hour scramble and the good breakfast food, we all lay down along that crack—heads and tails, as it were—and slept till the afternoon sun almost toasted our faces.

Terry poked a tentative foot against my head.

"How are you, Van? Alive yet?"

"Very much so," I told him. And Jeff was equally cheerful.

We had room to stretch, if not to turn around; but we could very carefully roll over, one at a time, behind the sheltering foliage.

It was no use to leave there by daylight. We could not see much of the country, but enough to know that we were now at the beginning of the cultivated area, and no doubt there would be an alarm sent out far and wide.

Terry chuckled softly to himself, lying there on that hot narrow little rim of rock. He dilated on the discomfiture of our guards and tutors, making many discourteous remarks.

I reminded him that we had still a long way to go before getting to the place where we'd left our machine, and no probability of finding it there; but he only kicked me, mildly, for a croaker.

"If you can't boost, don't knock," he protested. "I never said 'twould be a picnic. But I'd run away in the Antarctic ice fields rather than be a prisoner."

We soon dozed off again.

The long rest and penetrating dry heat were good for us, and that night we covered a considerable distance, keeping always in the rough forested belt of land which we knew bordered the whole country. Sometimes we were near the outer edge, and caught sudden glimpses of the tremendous depths beyond.

"This piece of geography stands up like a basalt column," Jeff said. "Nice time we'll have getting down if they have confiscated our machine!'' For which suggestion he received summary chastisement.

What we could see inland was peaceable enough, but only moonlit glimpses; by daylight we lay very close. As Terry said, we did not wish to kill the old ladies—even if we could; and short of that they were perfectly competent to pick us up bodily and carry us back, if discovered. There was nothing for it but to lie low, and sneak out unseen if we could do it.

There wasn't much talking done. At night we had our marathon-obstacle race; we ''stayed not for brake and we stopped not for stone,'' and swam whatever water was too deep to wade and could not be got around; but that was only necessary twice. By day, sleep, sound and sweet. Mighty lucky it was that we could live off the country as we did. Even that margin of forest seemed rich in foodstuffs.

But Jeff thoughtfully suggested that that very thing showed how careful we should have to be, as we might run into some stalwart group of gardeners or foresters or nut-gatherers at any minute. Careful we were, feeling pretty sure that if we did not make good this time we were not likely to have another opportunity; and at last we reached a point from which we could see, far below, the broad stretch of that still lake from which we had made our ascent.

''That looks pretty good to me!'' said Terry, gazing down at it. ''Now, if we can't find the 'plane, we know where to aim if we have to drop over this wall some other way.''

The wall at that point was singularly uninviting. It rose so straight that we had to put our heads over to see the base, and the country below seemed to be a far-off marshy tangle of rank vegetation. We did not have to risk our necks to that extent, however, for at last, stealing along among the rocks and trees like so many creeping savages, we came to that flat space where we had landed; and there, in unbelievable good fortune, we found our machine.

''Covered, too, by jingo! Would you think they had that much sense?'' cried Terry.

''If they had that much, they're likely to have more,'' I warned him, softly. ''Bet you the thing's watched.''

We reconnoitered as widely as we could in the failing moonlight—moons are of a painfully unreliable nature; but the growing dawn showed us the familiar shape, shrouded in some heavy cloth like canvas, and no slightest sign of any watchman near. We decided to make a quick dash as soon as the light was strong enough for accurate work.

"I don't care if the old thing'll go or not," Terry declared. "We can run her to the edge, get aboard, and just plane down—plop!—beside our boat there. Look there—see the boat!"

Sure enough—there was our motor, lying like a gray cocoon on the flat pale sheet of water.

Quietly but swiftly we rushed forward and began to tug at the fastenings of that cover.

"Confound the thing!" Terry cried in desperate impatience. "They've got it sewed up in a bag! And we've not a knife among us!"

Then, as we tugged and pulled at that tough cloth we heard a sound that made Terry lift his head like a war horse—the sound of an unmistakable giggle, yes—three giggles.

There they were—Celis, Alima, Ellador—looking just as they had when we first saw them, standing a little way off from us, as interested, as mischievous as three schoolboys.

"Hold on, Terry—hold on!" I warned. "That's too easy. Look out for a trap."

"Let us appeal to their kind hearts," Jeff urged. "I think they will help us. Perhaps they've got knives."

"It's no use rushing them, anyhow." I was absolutely holding on to Terry. "We know they can out-run and out-climb us."

He reluctantly admitted this; and after a brief parley among ourselves, we all advanced slowly toward them, holding out our hands in token of friendliness.

They stood their ground till we had come fairly near, and then indicated that we should stop. To make sure, we advanced a step or two and they promptly and swiftly withdrew. So we stopped at the distance specified. Then we used their language, as far as we were able, to explain our plight, telling how we were imprisoned, how we had escaped—a good deal of pantomime here and vivid interest on their part—how we had traveled by night and hidden by day, living on nuts—and here Terry pretended great hunger.

I know he could not have been hungry; we had found plenty to eat and had not been sparing in helping ourselves. But they seemed somewhat impressed; and after a murmured consultation they produced from their pockets cer-

little packages, and with the utmost ease and accuracy tossed them into our hands.

Jeff was most appreciative of this; and Terry made extravagant gestures of admiration, which seemed to set them off, boy-fashion, to show their skill. While we ate the excellent biscuits they had thrown us, and while Ellador kept a watchful eye on our movements, Celis ran off to some distance, and set up a sort of "duck-on-a-rock" arrangement, a big yellow nut on top of three balanced sticks; Alima, meanwhile, gathering stones.

They urged us to throw at it, and we did, but the thing was a long way off, and it was only after a number of failures, at which those elvish damsels laughed delightedly, that Jeff succeeded in bringing the whole structure to the ground. It took me still longer, and Terry, to his intense annoyance, came third.

Then Celis set up the little tripod again, and looked back at us, knocking it down, pointing at it, and shaking her short curls severely. "No," she said. "Bad—wrong!" We were quite able to follow her.

Then she set it up once more, put the fat nut on top, and returned to the others; and there those aggravating girls sat and took turns throwing little stones at that thing, while one stayed by as a setter-up; and they just popped that nut off, two times out of three, without upsetting the sticks. Pleased as Punch they were, too, and we pretended to be, but weren't.

We got very friendly over this game, but I told Terry we'd be sorry if we didn't get off while we could, and then we begged for knives. It was easy to show what we wanted to do, and they each proudly produced a sort of strong clasp-knife from their pockets.

"Yes," we said eagerly, "that's it! Please—" We had learned quite a bit of their language, you see. And we just begged for those knives, but they would not give them to us. If we came a step too near they backed off, standing light and eager for flight.

"It's no sort of use," I said. "Come on—let's get a sharp stone or something—we must get this thing off."

So we hunted about and found what edged fragments we could, and hacked away, but it was like trying to cut sailcloth with a clamshell.

Terry hacked and dug, but said to us under his breath,

"Boys, we're in pretty good condition—let's make a life and death dash and get hold of those girls—we've got to."

They had drawn rather nearer to watch our efforts, and we did take them rather by surprise; also, as Terry said, our recent training had strengthened us in wind and limb, and for a few desperate moments those girls were scared and we almost triumphant.

But just as we stretched out our hands, the distance between us widened; they had got their pace apparently, and then, though we ran at our utmost speed, and much farther than I thought wise, they kept just out of reach all the time.

We stopped breathless, at last, at my repeated admonitions.

"This is stark foolishness," I urged. "They are doing it on purpose—come back or you'll be sorry."

We went back, much slower than we came, and in truth we were sorry.

As we reached our swaddled machine, and sought again to tear loose its covering, there rose up from all around the sturdy forms, the quiet determined faces we knew so well.

"Oh Lord!" groaned Terry. "The Colonels! It's all up—they're forty to one."

It was no use to fight. These women evidently relied on numbers, not so much as a drilled force but as a multitude actuated by a common impulse. They showed no sign of fear, and since we had no weapons whatever and there were at least a hundred of them, standing ten deep about us, we gave in as gracefully as we might.

Of course we looked for punishment—a closer imprisonment, solitary confinement maybe—but nothing of the kind happened. They treated us as truants only, and as if they quite understood our truancy.

Back we went, not under an anesthetic this time but skimming along in electric motors enough like ours to be quite recognizable, each of us in a separate vehicle with one ablebodied lady on either side and three facing him.

They were all pleasant enough, and talked to us as much as was possible with our limited powers. And though Terry was keenly mortified, and at first we all rather dreaded harsh treatment, I for one soon began to feel a sort of pleasant confidence and to enjoy the trip.

Here were my five familiar companions, all good-natured as could be, seeming to have no worse feeling than a mild triumph as of winning some simple game; and even that they politely suppressed.

This was a good opportunity to see the country, too, and the more I saw of it, the better I liked it. We went too swiftly for close observation, but I could appreciate perfect roads, as dustless as a swept floor; the shade of endless lines of trees; the ribbon of flowers that unrolled beneath them; and the rich comfortable country that stretched off and away, full of varied charm.

We rolled through many villages and towns, and I soon saw that the parklike beauty of our first-seen city was no exception. Our swift high-sweeping view from the plane had been most attractive, but lacked detail; and in that first day of struggle and capture, we noticed little. But now we were swept along at an easy rate of some thirty miles an hour and covered quite a good deal of ground.

We stopped for lunch in quite a sizable town, and here, rolling slowly through the streets, we saw more of the population. They had come out to look at us everywhere we had passed, but here were more; and when we went in to eat, in a big garden place with little shaded tables among the trees and flowers, many eyes were upon us. And everywhere, open country, village, or city—only women. Old women and young women and a great majority who seemed neither young nor old, but just women; young girls, also, though these, and the children, seeming to be in groups by themselves generally, were less in evidence. We caught many glimpses of girls and children in what seemed to be schools or in playgrounds, and so far as we could judge there were no boys. We all looked, carefully. Everyone gazed at us politely, kindly, and with eager interest. No one was impertinent. We could catch quite a bit of the talk now, and all they said seemed pleasant enough.

Well—before nightfall we were all safely back in our big room. The damage we had done was quite ignored; the beds as smooth and comfortable as before, new clothing and towels supplied. The only thing those women did was to illuminate the gardens at night, and to set an extra watch. But they called us to account next day. Our three tutors, who had not joined in the recapturing expedition, had been quite busy in preparing for us, and now made explanation.

They knew well we would make for our machine, and also that there was no other way of getting down—alive. So our flight had troubled no one; all they did was to call the inhabitants to keep an eye on our movements all along the edge of the forest between the two points. It appeared that many of those nights we had been seen, by careful ladies sitting snugly in big trees by the riverbed, or up among the rocks.

Terry looked immensely disgusted, but it struck me as extremely funny. Here we had been risking our lives, hiding and prowling like outlaws, living on nuts and fruit, getting wet and cold at night, and dry and hot by day, and all the while these estimable women had just been waiting for us to come out.

Now they began to explain, carefully using such words as we could understand. It appeared that we were considered as guests of the country—sort of public wards. Our first violence had made it necessary to keep us safeguarded for a while, but as soon as we learned the language—and would agree to do no harm—they would show us all about the land.

Jeff was eager to reassure them. Of course he did not tell on Terry, but he made it clear that he was ashamed of himself, and that he would now conform. As to the language— we all fell upon it with redoubled energy. They brought us books, in greater numbers, and I began to study them seriously.

"Pretty punk literature," Terry burst forth one day, when we were in the privacy of our own room. "Of course one expects to begin on child-stories, but I would like something more interesting now."

"Can't expect stirring romance and wild adventure without men, can you?" I asked. Nothing irritated Terry more than to have us assume that there were no men; but there were no signs of them in the books they gave us, or the pictures.

"Shut up!" he growled. "What infernal nonsense you talk! I'm going to ask 'em outright—we know enough now."

In truth we had been using our best efforts to master the language, and were able to read fluently and to discuss what we read with considerable ease.

That afternoon we were all sitting together on the roof— we three and the tutors gathered about a table, no guards about. We had been made to understand some time earlier that if we would agree to do no violence they would withdraw their constant attendance, and we promised most willingly.

So there we sat, at ease; all in similar dress; our hair, by now, as long as theirs, only our beards to distinguish us. We did not want those beards, but had so far been unable to induce them to give us any cutting instruments.

"Ladies," Terry began, out of a clear sky, as it were, " are there no men in this country?"

"Men?" Somel answered. "Like you?"

"Yes, men," Terry indicated his beard, and threw back his broad shoulders. "Men, real men."

"No," she answered quietly. "There are no men in this country. There has not been a man among us for two thousand years."

Her look was clear and truthful and she did not advance this astonishing statement as if it was astonishing, but quite as a matter of fact.

"But—the people—the children," he protested, not believing her in the least, but not wishing to say so.

"Oh yes," she smiled. "I do not wonder you are puzzled. We are mothers—all of us—but there are no fathers. We thought you would ask about that long ago—why have you not?" Her look was as frankly kind as always, her tone quite simple.

Terry explained that we had not felt sufficiently used to the language, making rather a mess of it, I thought, but Jeff was franker.

"Will you excuse us all," he said, "if we admit that we find it hard to believe? There is no such—possibility—in the rest of the world."

"Have you no kind of life where it is possible?" asked Zava.

"Why, yes—some low forms, of course."

"How low—or how high, rather?"

"Well—there are some rather high forms of insect life in which it occurs. Parthenogenesis, we call it—that means virgin birth."

She could not follow him.

"*Birth,* we know, of course; but what is *virgin?*"

Terry looked uncomfortable, but Jeff met the question quite calmly. "Among mating animals, the term *virgin* is applied to the female who has not mated," he answered.

"Oh, I see. And does it apply to the male also? Or is there a different term for him?"

He passed this over rather hurriedly, saying that the same term would apply, but was seldom used.

"No?" she said. "But one cannot mate without the other surely. Is not each then—virgin—before mating? And, tell me, have you any forms of life in which there is birth from a father only?"

"I know of none," he answered, and I inquired seriously.

"You ask us to believe that for two thousand years there have been only women here, and only girl babies born?"

"Exactly," answered Somel, nodding gravely. "Of course we know that among other animals it is not so, that there are fathers as well as mothers; and we see that you are fathers, that you come from a people who are of both kinds. We have been waiting, you see, for you to be able to speak freely with us, and teach us about your country and the rest of the world. You know so much, you see, and we know only our own land."

In the course of our previous studies we had been at some pains to tell them about the big world outside, to draw sketches, maps, to make a globe, even, out of a spherical fruit, and show the size and relation of the countries, and to tell of the numbers of their people. All this had been scant and in outline, but they quite understood.

I find I succeed very poorly in conveying the impression I would like to of these women. So far from being ignorant, they were deeply wise—that we realized more and more; and for clear reasoning, for real brain scope and power they were A No. 1, but there were a lot of things they did not know.

They had the evenest tempers, the most perfect patience and good nature—one of the things most impressive about them all was the absence of irritability. So far as we had only this group to study, but afterward I found it a common trait.

We had gradually come to feel that we were in the hands of friends, and very capable ones at that—but we couldn't form any opinion yet of the general level of these women.

"We want you to teach us all you can," Somel went on, her firm shapely hands clasped on the table before her, her clear quiet eyes meeting ours frankly. "And we want to teach you what we have that is novel and useful. You can well imagine that it is a wonderful event to us, to have men among us—after two thousand years. And we want to know about your women.''

What she said about our importance gave instant pleasure to Terry. I could see by the way he lifted his head that it pleased him. But when she spoke of our women—someway I had a queer little indescribable feeling, not like any feeling I ever had before when ''women'' were mentioned.

''Will you tell us how it came about?'' Jeff pursued. ''You said 'for two thousand years'—did you have men here before that?''

''Yes,'' answered Zava.

They were all quiet for a little.

''You should have our full history to read—do not be alarmed—it has been made clear and short. It took us a long time to learn how to write history. Oh, how I should love to read yours!''

She turned with flashing eager eyes, looking from one to the other of us.

''It would be so wonderful—would it not? To compare the history of two thousand years, to see what the differences are—between us, who are only mothers, and you, who are mothers and fathers, too. Of course we see, with our birds, that the father is as useful as the mother, almost. But among insects we find him of less importance, sometimes very little. Is it not so with you?''

''Oh, yes, birds and bugs,'' Terry said, ''but not among animals—have you *no* animals?''

''We have cats,'' she said. ''The father is not very useful.''

''Have you no cattle—sheep—horses?'' I drew some rough outlines of these beasts and showed them to her.

''We had, in the very old days, these,'' said Somel, and sketched with swift sure touches a sort of sheep or llama, ''and these''—dogs, of two or three kinds, ''and that''— pointing to my absurd but recognizable horse.

''What became of them?'' asked Jeff.

''We do not want them anymore. They took up too much room—we need all our land to feed our people. It is such a little country, you know.''

''Whatever do you do without milk?'' Terry demanded incredulously.

''Milk? We have milk in abundance—our own.''

"But—but—I mean for cooking—for grown people," Terry blundered, while they looked amazed and a shade displeased.

Jeff came to the rescue. "We keep cattle for their milk, as well as for their meat," he explained. "Cow's milk is a staple article of diet. There is a great milk industry—to collect and distribute it."

Still they looked puzzled. I pointed to my outline of a cow. "The farmer milks the cow," I said, and sketched a milk pail, the stool, and in pantomime showed the man milking. "Then it is carried to the city and distributed by milkmen—everybody has it at the door in the morning."

"Has the cow no child?" asked Somel earnestly.

"Oh, yes, of course, a calf, that is."

"Is there milk for the calf and you, too?"

It took some time to make clear to those three sweet-faced women the process which robs the cow of her calf, and the calf of its true food; and the talk led us into a further discussion of the meat business. They heard it out, looking very white, and presently begged to be excused.

5. A Unique History

It is no use for me to try to piece out this account with adventures. If the people who read it are not interested in these amazing women and their history, they will not be interested at all.

As for us—three young men to a whole landful of women—what could we do? We did get away, as described, and were peacefully brought back again without, as Terry complained, even the satisfaction of hitting anybody.

There were no adventures because there was nothing to fight. There were no wild beasts in the country and very few tame ones. Of these I might as well stop to describe the one common pet of the country. Cats, of course. But such cats!

What do you suppose these lady Burbanks had done with their cats? By the most prolonged and careful selection and exclusion they had developed a race of cats that did not sing! That's a fact. The most those poor dumb brutes could do was to make a kind of squeak when they were hungry or wanted the door open, and, of course, to purr, and make the various mother-noises to their kittens.

Moreover, they had ceased to kill birds. They were rigorously bred to destroy mice and moles and all such enemies of the food supply; but the birds were numerous and safe.

While we were discussing birds, Terry asked them if they used feathers for their hats, and they seemed amused at the idea. He made a few sketches of our women's hats, with plumes and quills and those various tickling things that stick out so far; and they were eagerly interested, as at everything about our women.

As for them, they said they only wore hats for shade when working in the sun; and those were big light straw hats, something like those used in China and Japan. In cold weather they wore caps or hoods.

"But for decorative purposes—don't you think they would be becoming?" pursued Terry, making as pretty a picture as he could of a lady with a plumed hat.

They by no means agreed to that, asking quite simply if the men wore the same kind. We hastened to assure her that they did not—drew for them our kind of headgear.

"And do no men wear feathers in their hats?"

"Only Indians," Jeff explained. "Savages, you know." And he sketched a war bonnet to show them.

"And soldiers," I added, drawing a military hat with plumes.

They never expressed horror or disapproval, nor indeed much surprise—just a keen interest. And the notes they made!—miles of them!

But to return to our pussycats. We were a good deal impressed by this achievement in breeding, and when they questioned us—I can tell you we were well pumped for information—we told of what had been done for dogs and horses and cattle, but that there was no effort applied to cats, except for show purposes.

I wish I could represent the kind, quiet, steady, ingenious way they questioned us. It was not just curiosity—they weren't a bit more curious about us than we were about them, if as much. But they were bent on understanding our kind of civilization, and their lines of interrogation would gradually surround us and drive us in till we found ourselves up against some admissions we did not want to make.

"Are all these breeds of dogs you have made useful?" they asked.

"Oh—useful! Why, the hunting dogs and watchdogs and sheepdogs are useful—and sleddogs of course!—and ratters, I suppose, but we don't keep dogs for their *usefulness*. The dog is 'the friend of man,' we say—we love them."

That they understood. "We love our cats that way. They surely are our friends, and helpers, too. You can see how intelligent and affectionate they are."

It was a fact. I'd never seen such cats, except in a few rare instances. Big, handsome silky things, friendly with everyone and devotedly attached to their special owners.

"You must have a heartbreaking time drowning kittens," we suggested. But they said, "Oh, no! You see we care for them as you do for your valuable cattle. The fathers are few compared to the mothers, just a few very fine ones in each town; they live quite happily in walled gardens and the houses of their friends. But they only have a mating season once a year."

"Rather hard on Thomas, isn't it?" suggested Terry.

"Oh, no—truly! You see, it is many centuries that we have been breeding the kind of cats we wanted. They are healthy and happy and friendly, as you see. How do you manage with your dogs? Do you keep them in pairs, or segregate the fathers, or what?"

Then we explained that—well, that it wasn't a question of fathers exactly; that nobody wanted a—a mother dog; that, well, that practically all our dogs were males—there was only a very small percentage of females allowed to live.

Then Zava, observing Terry with her grave sweet smile, quoted back at him: "Rather hard on Thomas, isn't it? Do they enjoy it—living without mates? Are your dogs as uniformly healthy and sweet-tempered as our cats?"

Jeff laughed, eyeing Terry mischievously. As a matter of fact we began to feel Jeff something of a traitor—he so often flopped over and took their side of things; also his medical knowledge gave him a different point of view somehow.

"I'm sorry to admit," he told them, "that the dog, with us, is the most diseased of any animal—next to man. And as to temper—there are always some dogs who bite people—especially children."

That was pure malice. You see, children were the—the *raison d'être* in this country. All our interlocutors sat up straight at once. They were still gentle, still restrained, but there was a note of deep amazement in their voices.

"Do we understand that you keep an animal—an unmated male animal—that bites children? About how many are there of them, please?"

"Thousands—in a large city," said Jeff, "and nearly every family has one in the country."

Terry broke in at this. "You must not imagine they are all dangerous—it's not one in a hundred that ever bites anybody. Why, they are the best friends of the children—a boy doesn't have half a chance that hasn't a dog to play with!"

"And the girls?" asked Somel.

"Oh—girls—why they like them too," he said, but his voice flatted a little. They always noticed little things like that, we found later.

Little by little they wrung from us the fact that the friend of man, in the city, was a prisoner; was taken out for his meager exercise on a leash; was liable not only to many diseases but to the one destroying horror of rabies; and, in many cases, for the safety of the citizens, had to go muzzled. Jeff maliciously added vivid instances he had known or read of injury and death from mad dogs.

They did not scold or fuss about it. Calm as judges, those women were. But they made notes; Moadine read them to us.

"Please tell me if I have the facts correct," she said. "In your country—and in others too?"

"Yes," we admitted, "in most civilized countries."

"In most civilized countries a kind of animal is kept which is no longer useful—"

"They are a protection," Terry insisted. "They bark if burglars try to get in."

Then she made notes of "burglars" and went on: "because of the love which people bear to this animal."

Zava interrupted here. "Is it the men or the women who love this animal so much?"

"Both!" insisted Terry.

"Equally?" she inquired.

And Jeff said, "Nonsense, Terry—you know men like dogs better than women do—as a whole."

"Because they love it so much—especially men. This animal is kept shut up, or chained."

"Why?" suddenly asked Somel. "We keep our father cats shut up because we do not want too much fathering; but they are not chained—they have large grounds to run in."

"A valuable dog would be stolen if he was let loose," I said. "We put collars on them, with the owner's name, in case they do stray. Besides, they get into fights—a valuable dog might easily be killed by a bigger one."

"I see," she said. "They fight when they meet—is that common?" We admitted that it was.

"They are kept shut up, or chained." She paused again, and asked, "Is not a dog fond of running? Are they not built for speed?'' That we admitted, too, and Jeff, still malicious, enlightened them further.

"I've always thought it was a pathetic sight, both ways—to see a man or a woman taking a dog to walk—at the end of a string.''

"Have you bred them to be as neat in their habits as cats are?'' was the next question. And when Jeff told them of the effect of dogs on sidewalk merchandise and the streets generally, they found it hard to believe.

You see, their country was as neat as a Dutch kitchen, and as to sanitation—but I might as well start in now with as much as I can remember of the history of this amazing country before further description.

And I'll summarize here a bit as to our opportunities for learning it. I will not try to repeat the careful, detailed account I lost; I'll just say that we were kept in that fortress a good six months all told, and after that, three in a pleasant enough city where—to Terry's infinite disgust—there were only "Colonels" and little children—no young women whatever. Then we were under surveillance for three more—always with a tutor or a guard or both. But those months were pleasant because we were really getting acquainted with the girls. That was a chapter!—or will be—I will try to do justice to it.

We learned their language pretty thoroughly—had to; and they learned ours much more quickly and used it to hasten our own studies.

Jeff, who was never without reading matter of some sort, had two little books with him, a novel and a little anthology of verse; and I had one of those pocket encyclopedias—a fat little thing, bursting with facts. These were used in our education—and theirs. Then as soon as we were up to it, they furnished us with plenty of their own books, and I went in for the history part—I wanted to understand the genesis of this miracle of theirs.

And this is what happened, according to their records:

As to geography—at about the time of the Christian era this land had a free passage to the sea. I'm not saying where, for good reasons. But there was a fairly easy pass through that wall of mountains behind us, and there is no doubt in my mind that these people were of Aryan stock, and were once in contact with the best civilization of the old world.

They were "white," but somewhat darker than our northern races because of their constant exposure to sun and air.

The country was far larger then, including much land beyond the pass, and a strip of coast. They had ships, commerce, an army, a king—for at that time they were what they so calmly called us—a bi-sexual race.

What happened to them first was merely a succession of historic misfortunes such as have befallen other nations often enough. They were decimated by war, driven up from their coastline till finally the reduced population, with many of the men killed in battle, occupied this hinterland, and defended it for years, in the mountain passes. Where it was open to any possible attack from below they strengthened the natural defenses so that it became unscalably secure, as we found it.

They were a polygamous people, and a slave-holding people, like all of their time; and during the generation or two of this struggle to defend their mountain home they built the fortresses, such as the one we were held in, and other of their oldest buildings, some still in use. Nothing but earthquakes could destroy such architecture—huge solid blocks, holding by their own weight. They must have had efficient workmen and enough of them in those days.

They made a brave fight for their existence, but no nation can stand up against what the steamship companies call "an act of God." While the whole fighting force was doing its best to defend their mountain pathway, there occurred a volcanic outburst, with some local tremors, and the result was the complete filling up of the pass—their only outlet. Instead of a passage, a new ridge, sheer and high, stood between them and the sea; they were walled in, and beneath that wall lay their whole little army. Very few men were left alive, save the slaves; and these now seized their opportunity, rose in revolt, killed their remaining masters even to the youngest boy, killed the old women too, and the mothers, intending to take possession of the country with the remaining young women and girls.

But this succession of misfortunes was too much for those infuriated virgins. There were many of them, and but few of these would-be masters, so the young women, instead of submitting, rose in sheer desperation and slew their brutal conquerors.

This sounds like Titus Andronicus, I know, but that is

their account. I suppose they were about crazy—can you blame them?

There was literally no one left on this beautiful high garden land but a bunch of hysterical girls and some older slave women.

That was about two thousand years ago.

At first there was a period of sheer despair. The mountains towered between them and their old enemies, but also between them and escape. There was no way up or down or out—they simply had to stay there. Some were for suicide, but not the majority. They must have been a plucky lot, as a whole, and they decided to live—as long as they did live. Of course they had hope, as youth must, that something would happen to change their fate.

So they set to work, to bury the dead, to plow and sow, to care for one another.

Speaking of burying the dead, I will set down while I think of it, that they had adopted cremation in about the thirteenth century, for the same reason that they had left off raising cattle—they could not spare the room. They were much surprised to learn that we were still burying—asked our reasons for it, and were much dissatisfied with what we gave. We told them of the belief in the resurrection of the body, and they asked if our God was not as well able to resurrect from ashes as from long corruption. We told them of how people thought it repugnant to have their loved ones burn, and they asked if it was less repugnant to have them decay. They were inconveniently reasonable, those women.

Well—that original bunch of girls set to work to clean up the place and make their living as best they could. Some of the remaining slave women rendered invaluable service, teaching such trades as they knew. They had such records as were then kept, all the tools and implements of the time, and a most fertile land to work in.

There were a handful of the younger matrons who had escaped slaughter, and a few babies were born after the cataclysm—but only two boys, and they both died.

For five or ten years they worked together, growing stronger and wiser and more and more mutually attached, and then the miracle happened—one of these young women bore a child. Of course they all thought there must be a man somewhere, but none was found. Then they decided it must be a direct gift from the gods, and placed the proud mother in the Temple of Maaia—their Goddess of Motherhood—under strict watch. And there, as years passed, this wonder-woman bore child after child, five of them—all girls.

I did my best, keenly interested as I have always been in sociology and social psychology, to reconstruct in my mind the real position of these ancient women. There were some five or six hundred of them, and they were harem-bred; yet for the few preceding generations they had been reared in the atmosphere of such heroic struggle that the stock must have been toughened somewhat. Left alone in that terrific orphanhood, they had clung together, supporting one another and their little sisters, and developing unknown powers in the stress of new necessity. To this pain-hardened and work-strengthened group, who had lost not only the love and care of parents, but the hope of ever having children of their own, there now dawned the new hope.

Here at last was Motherhood, and though it was not for all of them personally, it might—if the power was inherited—found here a new race.

It may be imagined how those five Daughters of Maaia, Children of the Temple, Mothers of the Future—they had all the titles that love and hope and reverence could give—were reared. The whole little nation of women surrounded them with loving service, and waited, between a boundless hope and an equally boundless despair, to see if they, too, would be mothers.

And they were! As fast as they reached the age of twenty-five they began bearing. Each of them, like her mother, bore five daughters. Presently there were twenty-five New Women, Mothers in their own right, and the whole spirit of the country changed from mourning and mere courageous resignation to proud joy. The older women, those who remembered men, died off; the youngest of all the first lot of course died too, after a while, and by that time there were left one hundred and fifty-five parthenogenetic women, founding a new race.

They inherited all that the devoted care of that declining band of original ones could leave them. Their little country was quite safe. Their farms and gardens were all in full production. Such industries as they had were in careful order. The records of their past were all preserved, and for years the older women had spent their time in the best teaching they were capable of, that they might leave to the little group of sisters and mothers all they possessed of skill and knowledge.

There you have the start of Herland! One family, all descended from one mother! She lived to a hundred years old; lived to see her hundred and twenty-five great-granddaughters born; lived as Queen-Priestess-Mother of them all; and died with a nobler pride and a fuller joy than perhaps any human soul has ever known—she alone had founded a new race!

The first five daughters had grown up in an atmosphere of holy calm, of awed watchful waiting, of breathless prayer. To them the longed-for motherhood was not only a personal joy, but a nation's hope. Their twenty-five daughters in turn, with a stronger hope, a richer, wider outlook, with the devoted love and care of all the surviving population, grew up as a holy sisterhood, their whole ardent youth looking forward to their great office. And at last they were left alone; the white-haired First Mother was gone, and this one family, five sisters, twenty-five first cousins, and a hundred and twenty-five second cousins, began a new race.

Here you have human beings, unquestionably, but what we were slow in understanding was how these ultra-women, inheriting only from women, had eliminated not only certain masculine characteristics, which of course we did not look for, but so much of what we had always thought essentially feminine.

The tradition of men as guardians and protectors had quite died out. These stalwart virgins had no men to fear and therefor no need of protection. As to wild beasts—there were none in their sheltered land.

The power of mother-love, that maternal instinct we so highly laud, was theirs of course, raised to its highest power; and a sister-love which, even while recognizing the actual relationship, we found it hard to credit.

Terry, incredulous, even contemptuous, when we were alone, refused to believe the story. "A lot of traditions as old as Herodotus—and about as trustworthy!" he said. "It's unlikely women—just a pack of women—would have hung together like that! We all know women can't organize—that they scrap like anything—are frightfully jealous."

"But these New ladies didn't have anyone to be jealous of, remember," drawled Jeff.

"That's a likely story," Terry sneered.

"Why don't you invent a likelier one?" I asked him. "Here *are* the women—nothing but women, and you yourself admit there's no trace of a man in the country." This was after we had been about a good deal.

"I'll admit that," he growled. "And it's a big miss, too. There's not only no fun without 'em—no real sport—no competition; but these women aren't *womanly*. You know they aren't."

That kind of talk always set Jeff going; and I gradually grew to side with him. "Then you don't call a breed of women whose one concern is motherhood—womanly?" he asked.

"Indeed I don't," snapped Terry. "What does a man care for motherhood—when he hasn't a ghost of a chance at fatherhood? And besides—what's the good of talking sentiment when we are just men together? What a man wants of women is a good deal more than all this 'motherhood'!"

We were as patient as possible with Terry. He had lived about nine months among the "Coloncls" when he made that outburst; and with no chance at any more strenuous excitement than our gymnastics gave us—save for our escape fiasco. I don't suppose Terry had ever lived so long with neither Love, Combat, nor Danger to employ his superabundant energies, and he was irritable. Neither Jeff nor I found it so wearing. I was so much interested intellectually that our confinement did not wear on me; and as for Jeff, bless his heart!—he enjoyed the society of that tutor of his almost as much as if she had been a girl—I don't know but more.

As to Terry's criticism, it was true. These women, whose essential distinction of motherhood was the dominant note of their whole culture, were strikingly deficient in what we call "femininity." This led me very promptly to the conviction that those "feminine charms" we are so fond of are not feminine at all, but mere reflected masculinity—developed to please us because they had to please us, and in no way essential to the real fulfillment of their great process. But Terry came to no such conclusion.

"Just you wait till I get out!" he muttered.

Then we both cautioned him. "Look here, Terry, my boy! You be careful! They've been mighty good to us—but do you remember the anesthesia? If you do any mischief in this virgin land, beware of the vengeance of the Maiden Aunts! Come, be a man! It won't be forever.''

To return to the history.

They began at once to plan and build for their children, all the strength and intelligence of the whole of them devoted to that one thing. Each girl, of course, was reared in full knowledge of her Crowning Office, and they had, even then, very high ideas of the molding powers of the mother, as well as those of education.

Such high ideals as they had! Beauty, Health, Strength, Intellect, Goodness—for these they prayed and worked.

They had no enemies; they themselves were all sisters and friends. The land was fair before them, and a great future began to form itself in their minds.

The religion they had to begin with was much like that of old Greece—a number of gods and goddesses; but they lost all interest in deities of war and plunder, and gradually centered on their Mother Goddess altogether. Then, as they grew more intelligent, this had turned into a sort of Maternal Pantheism.

Here was Mother Earth, bearing fruit. All that they ate was fruit of motherhood, from seed or egg or their product. By motherhood they were born and by motherhood they lived—life was, to them, just the long cycle of motherhood.

But very early they recognized the need of improvement as well as of mere repetition, and devoted their combined intelligence to that problem—how to make the best kind of people. First this was merely the hope of bearing better ones, and then they recognized that however the children differed at birth, the real growth lay later—through education.

Then things began to hum.

As I learned more and more to appreciate what these women had accomplished, the less proud I was of what we, with all our manhood, had done.

You see, they had had no wars. They had had no kings, and no priests, and no aristocracies. They were sisters, and as they grew, they grew together—not by competition, but by united action.

We tried to put in a good word for competition, and they were keenly interested. Indeed, we soon found from their earnest questions of us that they were prepared to believe our world must be better than theirs. They were not sure;

they wanted to know; but there was no such arrogance about them as might have been expected.

We rather spread ourselves, telling of the advantages of competition: how it developed fine qualities; that without it there would be "no stimulus to industry." Terry was very strong on that point.

"No stimulus to industry," they repeated, with that puzzled look we had learned to know so well. *"Stimulus? To Industry?* But don't you *like* to work?"

"No man would work unless he had to," Terry declared.

"Oh, no *man!* You mean that is one of your sex distinctions?"

"No, indeed!" he said hastily. "No one, I mean, man or woman, would work without incentive. Competition is the—the motor power, you see."

"It is not with us," they explained gently, "so it is hard for us to understand. Do you mean, for instance, that with you no mother would work for her children without the stimulus of competition?"

No, he admitted that he did not mean that. Mothers, he supposed, would of course work for their children in the home; but the world's work was different—that had to be done by men, and required the competitive element.

All our teachers were eagerly interested.

"We want so much to know—you have the whole world to tell us of, and we have only our little land! And there are two of you—the two sexes—to love and help one another. It must be a rich and wonderful world. Tell us—what is the work of the world, that men do—which we have not here?"

"Oh, everything," Terry said grandly. "The men do everything, with us." He squared his broad shoulders and lifted his chest. "We do not allow our women to work. Women are loved—idolized—honored—kept in the home to care for the children."

"What is 'the home'?" asked Somel a little wistfully.

But Zava begged: "Tell me first, do *no* women work, really?"

"Why, yes," Terry admitted. "Some have to, of the poorer sort."

"About how many—in your country?"

"About seven or eight million," said Jeff, as mischievous as ever.

6. Comparisons
Are Odious

I had always been proud of my country, of course. Everyone is. Compared with the other lands and other races I knew, the United States of America had always seemed to me, speaking modestly, as good as the best of them.

But just as a clear-eyed, intelligent, perfectly honest, and well-meaning child will frequently jar one's self-esteem by innocent questions, so did these women, without the slightest appearance of malice or satire, continually bring up points of discussion which we spent our best efforts in evading.

Now that we were fairly proficient in their language, had read a lot about their history, and had given them the general outlines of ours, they were able to press the questions closer.

So when Jeff admitted the number of "women wage earners" we had, they instantly asked for the total population, for the proportion of adult women, and found that there were but twenty million or so at the outside.

"Then at least a third of your women are—what is it you call them—wage earners? And they are all *poor*. What is *poor*, exactly?"

"Ours is the best country in the world as to poverty," Terry told them. "We do not have the wretched paupers and beggars of the older countries, I assure you. Why, European visitors tell us we don't know what poverty is."

"Neither do we," answered Zava. "Won't you tell us?"

Terry put it up to me, saying I was the sociologist, and I explained that the laws of nature require a struggle for existence, and that in the struggle the fittest survive, and the unfit perish. In our economic struggle, I continued, there was always plenty of opportunity for the fittest to reach the top, which they did, in great numbers, particularly in our country; that where there was severe economic pressure the lowest classes of course felt it the worst, and that among the poorest of all the women were driven into the labor market by necessity.

They listened closely, with the usual note-taking.

"About one-third, then, belong to the poorest class," observed Moadine gravely. "And two-thirds are the ones who are—how was it you so beautifully put it?—'loved, honored, kept in the home to care for the children.' This inferior one-third have no children, I suppose?"

Jeff—he was getting as bad as they were—solemnly replied that, on the contrary, the poorer they were, the more children they had. That too, he explained, was a law of nature: "Reproduction is in inverse proportion to individuation."

"These 'laws of nature,' " Zava gently asked, "are they all the laws you have?"

"I should say not!" protested Terry. "We have systems of law that go back thousands and thousands of years—just as you do, no doubt," he finished politely.

"Oh no," Moadine told him. "We have no laws over a hundred years old, and most of them are under twenty. In a few weeks more," she continued, "we are going to have the pleasure of showing you over our little land and explaining everything you care to know about. We want you to see our people."

"And I assure you," Somel added, "that our people want to see you."

Terry brightened up immensely at this news, and reconciled himself to the renewed demands upon our capacity as teachers. It was lucky that we knew so little, really, and had no books to refer to, else, I fancy we might all be there yet, teaching those eager-minded women about the rest of the world.

As to geography, they had the tradition of the Great Sea, beyond the mountains; and they could see for themselves the endless thick-forested plains below them—that was all. But from the few records of their ancient condition—not "before the flood" with them, but before that mighty quake which had cut them off so completely—they were aware that there were other peoples and other countries.

In geology they were quite ignorant.

As to anthropology, they had those same remnants of information about other peoples, and the knowledge of the savagery of the occupants of those dim forests below. Nevertheless, they had inferred (marvelously keen on inference and deduction their minds were!) the existence and development of civilization in other places, much as we infer it on other planets.

When our biplane came whirring over their heads in that first scouting flight of ours, they had instantly accepted it as proof of the high development of Some Where Else, and had prepared to receive us as cautiously and eagerly as we might prepare to welcome visitors who came "by meteor" from Mars.

Of history—outside their own—they knew nothing, of course, save for their ancient traditions.

Of astronomy they had a fair working knowledge—that is a very old science; and with it, a surprising range and facility in mathematics.

Physiology they were quite familiar with. Indeed, when it came to the simpler and more concrete sciences, wherein the subject matter was at hand and they had but to exercise their minds upon it, the results were surprising. They had worked out a chemistry, a botany, a physics, with all the blends where a science touches an art, or merges into an industry, to such fullness of knowledge as made us feel like schoolchildren.

Also we found this out—as soon as we were free of the country, and by further study and question—that what one knew, all knew, to a very considerable extent.

I talked later with little mountain girls from the fir-dark valleys away up at their highest part, and with sunburned plainswomen and agile foresters, all over the country, as well as those in the towns, and everywhere there was the same high level of intelligence. Some knew far more than others about one thing—they were specialized, of course; but all of them knew more about everything—that is, about everything the country was acquainted with—than is the case with us.

We boast a good deal of our "high level of general intelligence" and our "compulsory public education," but in proportion to their opportunities they were far better educated than our people.

With what we told them, from what sketches and models we were able to prepare, they constructed a sort of working outline to fill in as they learned more.

A big globe was made, and our uncertain maps, helped out by those in that precious yearbook thing I had, were tentatively indicated upon it.

They sat in eager groups, masses of them who came for the purpose, and listened while Jeff roughly ran over the geologic history of the earth, and showed them their own land in relation to the others. Out of that same pocket reference book of mine came facts and figures which were seized upon and placed in right relation with unerring acumen.

Even Terry grew interested in this work. "If we can keep this up, they'll be having us lecture to all the girls' schools and colleges—how about that?" he suggested to us. "Don't know as I'd object to being an Authority to such audiences."

They did, in fact, urge us to give public lectures later, but not to the hearers or with the purpose we expected.

What they were doing with us was like—like—well, say like Napolean extracting military information from a few illiterate peasants. They knew just what to ask, and just what use to make of it; they had mechanical appliances for disseminating information almost equal to ours at home; and by the time we were led forth to lecture, our audiences had thoroughly mastered a well-arranged digest of all we had previously given to our teachers, and were prepared with such notes and questions as might have intimidated a university professor.

They were not audiences of girls, either. It was some time before we were allowed to meet the young women.

"Do you mind telling what you intend to do with us?" Terry burst forth one day, facing the calm and friendly Moadine with that funny half-blustering air of his. At first he used to storm and flourish quite a good deal, but nothing seemed to amuse them more; they would gather around and watch him as if it was an exhibition, politely, but with evident interest. So he learned to check himself, and was almost reasonable in his bearing—but not quite.

She announced smoothly and evenly: "Not in the least. I thought it was quite plain. We are trying to learn of you all we can, and to teach you what you are willing to learn of our country."

"Is that all?" he insisted.

She smiled a quiet enigmatic smile. "That depends."

"Depends on what?"

"Mainly on yourselves," she replied.

"Why do you keep us shut up so closely?"

"Because we do not feel quite safe in allowing you at large where there are so many young women."

Terry was really pleased at that. He had thought as much, inwardly; but he pushed the question. "Why should you be afraid? We are gentlemen."

She smiled that little smile again, and asked: "Are 'gentlemen' always safe?"

"You surely do not think that any of us," he said it with a good deal of emphasis on the "us," "would hurt your young girls?"

"Oh no," she said quickly, in real surprise. "The danger is quite the other way. They might hurt you. If, by any accident, you did harm any one of us, you would have to face a million mothers."

He looked so amazed and outraged that Jeff and I laughed outright, but she went on gently.

"I do not think you quite understand yet. You are but men, three men, in a country where the whole population are mothers—or are going to be. Motherhood means to us something which I cannot yet discover in any of the countries of which you tell us. You have spoken"—she turned to Jeff, "of Human Brotherhood as a great idea among you, but even that I judge is far from a practical expression?"

Jeff nodded rather sadly. "Very far—" he said.

"Here we have Human Motherhood—in full working use," she went on. "Nothing else except the literal sisterhood of our origin, and the far higher and deeper union of our social growth.

"The children in this country are the one center and focus of all our thoughts. Every step of our advance is always considered in its effect on them—on the race. You see, we are *Mothers*," she repeated, as if in that she had said it all.

"I don't see how that fact—which is shared by all women—constitutes any risk to us," Terry persisted. "You mean they would defend their children from attack. Of course. Any mothers would. But we are not savages, my dear lady; we are not going to hurt any mother's child.''

They looked at one another and shook their heads a little, but Zava turned to Jeff and urged him to make us see—said he seemed to understand more fully than we did. And he tried.

I can see it now, or at least much more of it, but it has taken me a long time, and a good deal of honest intellectual effort.

What they call Motherhood was like this:

They began with a really high degree of social development, something like that of Ancient Egypt or Greece. Then they suffered the loss of everything masculine, and supposed at first that all human power and safety had gone too. Then they developed this virgin birth capacity. Then, since the prosperity of their children depended on it, the fullest and subtlest coordination began to be practiced.

I remember how long Terry balked at the evident unanimity of these women—the most conspicuous feature of their whole culture. "It's impossible!" he would insist. "Women cannot cooperate—it's against nature."

When we urged the obvious facts he would say: "Fiddle-sticks!" or "Hang your facts—I tell you it can't be done!" And we never succeeded in shutting him up till Jeff dragged in the hymenoptera.

" 'Go to the ant, thou sluggard'—and learn something,'' he said triumphantly. "Don't they cooperate pretty well? You can't beat it. This place is just like an enormous ant-hill—you know an anthill is nothing but a nursery. And how about bees? Don't they manage to cooperate and love one another?

> *As the birds do love the Spring*
> *Or the bees their careful king,*

as that precious Constable had it. Just show me a combination of male creatures, bird, bug, or beast, that works as well, will you? Or one of our masculine countries where the people work together as well as they do here! I tell you, women are the natural cooperators, not men!''

Terry had to learn a good many things he did not want to.

To go back to my little analysis of what happened:

They developed all this close inter-service in the interests of their children. To do the best work they had to specialize, of course; the children needed spinners and weavers, farmers and gardeners, carpenters and masons, as well as mothers.

Then came the filling up of the place. When a population multiplies by five every thirty years it soon reaches the limits of a country, especially a small one like this. They very soon eliminated all the grazing cattle—sheep were the last to go, I believe. Also, they worked out a system of intensive agriculture surpassing anything I ever heard of, with the very forests all reset with fruit- or nut-bearing trees.

Do what they would, however, there soon came a time when they were confronted with the problem of "the pressure of population" in an acute form. There was really crowding, and with it, unavoidably, a decline in standards.

And how did those women meet it?

Not by a "struggle for existence" which would result in an everlasting writhing mass of underbred people trying to get ahead of one another—some few on top, temporarily, many constantly crushed out underneath, a hopeless substratum of paupers and degenerates, and no serenity or peace for anyone, no possibility for really noble qualities among the people at large.

Neither did they start off on predatory excursions to get more land from somebody else, or to get more food from somebody else, to maintain their struggling mass.

Not at all. They sat down in council together and thought it out. Very clear, strong thinkers they were. They said: "With our best endeavors this country will support about so many people, with the standard of peace, comfort, health, beauty, and progress we demand. Very well. That is all the people we will make."

There you have it. You see, they were Mothers, not in our sense of helpless involuntary fecundity, forced to fill and overfill the land, every land, and then see their children suffer, sin, and die, fighting horribly with one another; but in the sense of Conscious Makers of People. Mother-love with them was not a brute passion, a mere "instinct," a wholly personal feeling; it was—a religion.

It included that limitless feeling of sisterhood, that wide

unity in service which was so difficult for us to grasp. And it was National, Racial, Human—oh, I don't know how to say it.

We are used to seeing what we call "a mother" completely wrapped up in her own pink bundle of fascinating babyhood, and taking but the faintest theoretic interest in anybody else's bundle, to say nothing of the common needs of *all* the bundles. But these women were working all together at the grandest of tasks—they were Making People—and they made them well.

There followed a period of "negative eugenics" which must have been an appalling sacrifice. We are commonly willing to "lay down our lives" for our country, but they had to forgo motherhood for their country—and it was precisely the hardest thing for them to do.

When I got this far in my reading I went to Somel for more light. We were as friendly by that time as I had ever been in my life with any woman. A mighty comfortable soul she was, giving one the nice smooth mother-feeling a man likes in a woman, and yet giving also the clear intelligence and dependableness I used to assume to be masculine qualities. We had talked volumes already.

"See here," said I. "Here was this dreadful period when they got far too thick, and decided to limit the population. We have a lot of talk about that among us, but your position is so different that I'd like to know a little more about it.

"I understand that you make Motherhood the highest social service—a sacrament, really; that it is only undertaken once, by the majority of the population; that those held unfit are not allowed even that; and that to be encouraged to bear more than one child is the very highest reward and honor in the power of the state."

(She interpolated here that the nearest approach to an aristocracy they had was to come of a line of "Over Mothers"—those who had been so honored.)

"But what I do not understand, naturally, is how you prevent it. I gathered that each woman had five. You have no tyrannical husbands to hold in check—and you surely do not destroy the unborn—"

The look of ghastly horror she gave me I shall never forget. She started from her chair, pale, her eyes blazing.

"Destroy the unborn—!" she said in a hard whisper. "Do men do that in your country?"

"Men!" I began to answer, rather hotly, and then saw the gulf before me. None of us wanted these women to think that *our* women, of whom we boasted so proudly, were in any way inferior to them. I am ashamed to say that I equivocated. I told her of certain criminal types of women—perverts, or crazy, who had been known to commit infanticide. I told her, truly enough, that there was much in our land which was open to criticism, but that I hated to dwell on our defects until they understood us and our conditions better.

And, making a wide detour, I scrambled back to my question of how they limited the population.

As for Somel, she seemed sorry, a little ashamed even, of her too clearly expressed amazement. As I look back now, knowing them better, I am more and more and more amazed as I appreciate the exquisite courtesy with which they had received over and over again statements and admissions on our part which must have revolted them to the soul.

She explained to me, with sweet seriousness, that as I had supposed, at first each woman bore five children; and that, in their eager desire to build up a nation, they had gone on in that way for a few centuries, till they were confronted with the absolute need of a limit. This fact was equally plain to all—all were equally interested.

They were now as anxious to check their wonderful power as they had been to develop it; and for some generations gave the matter their most earnest thought and study.

"We were living on rations before we worked it out," she said. "But we did work it out. You see, before a child comes to one of us there is a period of utter exaltation—the whole being is uplifted and filled with a concentrated desire for that child. We learned to look forward to that period with the greatest caution. Often our young women, those to whom motherhood had not yet come, would voluntarily defer it. When the deep inner demand for a child began to be felt she would deliberately engage in the most active work, physical and mental; and even more important, would solace her longing by the direct care and service of the babies we already had."

She paused. Her wise sweet face grew deeply, reverently tender.

"We soon grew to see that mother-love has more than

one channel of expression. I think the reason our children are so—so fully loved, by all of us, is that we never—any of us—have enough of our own.''

This seemed to me infinitely pathetic, and I said so. "We have much that is bitter and hard in our life at home," I told her, "but this seems to me piteous beyond words—a whole nation of starving mothers!"

But she smiled her deep contented smile, and said I quite misunderstood.

"We each go without a certain range of personal joy," she said, "but remember—we each have a million children to love and serve—*our* children."

It was beyond me. To hear a lot of women talk about "our children"! But I suppose that is the way the ants and bees would talk—do talk, maybe.

That was what they did, anyhow.

When a woman chose to be a mother, she allowed the child-longing to grow within her till it worked its natural miracle. When she did not so choose she put the whole thing out of her mind, and fed her heart with the other babies.

Let me see—with us, children—minors, that is—constitute about three-fifths of the population; with them only about one-third, or less. And precious—! No sole heir to an empire's throne, no solitary millionaire baby, no only child of middle-aged parents, could compare as an idol with these Herland children.

But before I start on that subject I must finish up that little analysis I was trying to make.

They did effectually and permanently limit the population in numbers, so that the country furnished plenty for the fullest, richest life for all of them: plenty of everything, including room, air, solitude even.

And then they set to work to improve that population in quality—since they were restricted in quantity. This they had been at work on, uninterruptedly, for some fifteen hundred years. Do you wonder they were nice people?

Physiology, hygiene, sanitation, physical culture—all that line of work had been perfected long since. Sickness was almost wholly unknown among them, so much so that a previously high development in what we call the "science of medicine" had become practically a lost art. They were a clean-bred, vigorous lot, having the best of care, the most perfect living conditions always.

When it came to psychology—there was no one thing which left us so dumbfounded, so really awed, as the everyday working knowledge—and practice—they had in this line. As we learned more and more of it, we learned to appreciate the exquisite mastery with which we ourselves, strangers of alien race, of unknown opposite sex, had been understood and provided for from the first.

With this wide, deep, thorough knowledge, they had met and solved the problems of education in ways some of which I hope to make clear later. Those nation-loved children of theirs compared with the average in our country as the most perfectly cultivated, richly developed roses compare with— tumbleweeds. Yet they did not *seem* "cultivated" at all—it had all become a natural condition.

And this people, steadily developing in mental capacity, in will power, in social devotion, had been playing with the arts and sciences—as far as they knew them—for a good many centuries now with inevitable success.

Into this quiet lovely land, among these wise, sweet, strong women, we, in our easy assumption of superiority, had suddenly arrived; and now, tamed and trained to a degree they considered safe, we were at last brought out to see the country, to know the people.

7. Our Growing Modesty

Being at last considered sufficiently tamed and trained to be trusted with scissors, we barbered ourselves as best we could. A close-trimmed beard is certainly more comfortable than a full one. Razors, naturally, they could not supply.

"With so many old women you'd think there'd be some razors," sneered Terry. Whereat Jeff pointed out that he never before had seen such complete absence of facial hair on women.

"Looks to me as if the absence of men made them more feminine in that regard, anyhow," he suggested.

"Well, it's the only one then," Terry reluctantly agreed. "A less feminine lot I never saw. A child apiece doesn't seem to be enough to develop what I call motherliness."

Terry's idea of motherliness was the usual one, involving a baby in arms, or "a little flock about her knees," and the complete absorption of the mother in said baby or flock. A motherliness which dominated society, which influenced every art and industry, which absolutely protected all childhood, and gave to it the most perfect care and training, did not seem motherly—to Terry.

We had become well used to the clothes. They were quite as comfortable as our own—in some ways more so—and undeniably better looking. As to pockets, they left nothing to be desired. That second garment was fairly quilted with pockets. They were most ingeniously arranged, so as to be convenient to the hand and not inconvenient to the body, and were so placed as at once to strengthen the garment and add decorative lines of stitching.

In this, as in so many other points we had now to observe, there was shown the action of a practical intelligence, coupled with fine artistic feeling, and, apparently, untrammeled by any injurious influences.

Our first step of comparative freedom was a personally conducted tour of the country. No pentagonal bodyguard now! Only our special tutors, and we got on famously with them. Jeff said he loved Zava like an aunt—"only jollier than any aunt I ever saw''; Somel and I were as chummy as could be—the best of friends; but it was funny to watch Terry and Moadine. She was patient with him, and courteous, but it was like the patience and courtesy of some great man, say a skilled, experienced diplomat, with a schoolgirl. Her grave acquiescence with his most preposterous expression of feeling; her genial laughter, not only with, but, I often felt, at him—though impeccably polite; her innocent questions, which almost invariably led him to say more than he intended—Jeff and I found it all amusing to watch.

He never seemed to recognize that quiet background of superiority. When she dropped an argument he always thought he had silenced her; when she laughed he thought it tribute to his wit.

I hated to admit to myself how much Terry had sunk in my esteem. Jeff felt it too, I am sure; but neither of us admitted it to the other. At home we had measured him with other men, and, though we knew his failings, he was by no means an unusual type. We knew his virtues too, and they had always seemed more prominent than the faults. Measured among women—our women at home, I mean—he had always stood high. He was visibly popular. Even where his habits were known, there was no discrimination against him; in some cases his reputation for what was felicitously termed "gaiety" seemed a special charm.

But here, against the calm wisdom and quiet restrained humor of these women, with only that blessed Jeff and my inconspicuous self to compare with, Terry did stand out rather strong.

As "a man among men," he didn't; as a man among—I shall have to say, "females," he didn't; his intense masculinity seemed only fit complement to their intense femininity. But here he was all out of drawing.

Moadine was a big woman, with a balanced strength that seldom showed. Her eye was as quietly watchful as a fencer's. She maintained a pleasant relation with her charge, but I doubt if many, even in that country, could have done as well.

He called her "Maud," amongst ourselves, and said she was "a good old soul, but a little slow"; wherein he was quite wrong. Needless to say, he called Jeff's teacher "Java," and sometimes "Mocha," or plain "Coffee"; when specially mischievous, "Chicory," and even "Postum." But Somel rather escaped this form of humor, save for a rather forced "Some 'ell."

"Don't you people have but one name?" he asked one day, after we had been introduced to a whole group of them, all with pleasant, few-syllabled strange names, like the ones we knew.

"Oh yes," Moadine told him. "A good many of us have another, as we get on in life—a descriptive one. That is the name we earn. Sometimes even that is changed, or added to, in an unusually rich life. Such as our present Land Mother—what you call president or king, I believe. She was called Mera, even as a child; that means 'thinker.' Later there was added Du—Du-mera—the wise thinker, and now we all know her as O-du-mera—great and wise thinker. You shall meet her."

"No surnames at all then?" pursued Terry, with his somewhat patronizing air. "No family name?"

"Why no," she said. "Why should we? We are all descended from a common source—all one 'family' in reality. You see, our comparatively brief and limited history gives us that advantage at least."

"But does not each mother want her own child to bear her name?" I asked.

"No—why should she? The child has its own."

"Why for—for identification—so people will know whose child she is."

"We keep the most careful records," said Somel. "Each one of us has our exact line of descent all the way back to our dear First Mother. There are many reasons for doing that. But as to everyone knowing which child belongs to which mother—why should she?"

Here, as in so many other instances, we were led to feel the difference between the purely maternal and the paternal attitude of mind. The element of personal pride seemed strangely lacking.

"How about your other works?" asked Jeff. "Don't you sign your name to them—books and statues and so on?"

"Yes, surely, we are all glad and proud to. Not only books and statues, but all kinds of work. You will find names on the houses, on the furniture, on the dishes sometimes. Because otherwise one is likely to forget, and we want to know to whom to be grateful."

"You speak as if it were done for the convenience of the consumer—not the pride of the producer," I suggested.

"It's both," said Somel. "We have pride enough in our work."

"Then why not in your children?" urged Jeff.

"But we have! We're magnificently proud of them," she insisted.

"Then why not sign 'em?" said Terry triumphantly.

Moadine turned to him with her slightly quizzical smile. "Because the finished product is not a private one. When they are babies, we do speak of them, at times, as 'Essa's Lato,' or 'Novine's Amel'; but that is merely descriptive and conversational. In the records, of course, the child stands in her own line of mothers; but in dealing with it personally it is Lato, or Amel, without dragging in its ancestors."

"But have you names enough to give a new one to each child?"

"Assuredly we have, for each living generation."

Then they asked about our methods, and found first that "we" did so and so, and then that other nations did differently. Upon which they wanted to know which method has been proved best—and we had to admit that so far as we knew there had been no attempt at comparison, each people pursuing its own custom in the fond conviction of superiority, and either despising or quite ignoring the others.

With these women the most salient quality in all their institutions was reasonableness. When I dug into the records follow out any line of development, that was the most astonishing thing—the conscious effort to make it better.

They had early observed the value of certain improvements, had easily inferred that there was room for more, and took the greatest pains to develop two kinds of minds—the critic and inventor. Those who showed an early tendency to observe, to discriminate, to suggest, were given special training for that function; and some of their highest officials spent their time in the most careful study of one or another branch of work, with a view to its further improvement.

In each generation there was sure to arrive some new mind to detect faults and show need of alterations; and the whole corps of inventors was at hand to apply their special faculty at the point criticized, and offer suggestions.

We had learned by this time not to open a discussion on any of their characteristics without first priming ourselves to answer questions about our own methods; so I kept rather quiet on this matter of conscious improvement. We were not prepared to show our way was better.

There was growing in our minds, at least in Jeff's and mine, a keen appreciation of the advantages of this strange country and its management. Terry remained critical. We laid most of it to his nerves. He certainly was irritable.

The most conspicuous feature of the whole land was the perfection of its food supply. We had begun to notice from that very first walk in the forest, the first partial view from our 'plane. Now we were taken to see this mighty garden, and shown its methods of culture.

The country was about the size of Holland, some ten or twelve thousand square miles. One could lose a good many Hollands along the forest-smothered flanks of those mighty mountains. They had a population of about three million—not a large one, but quality is something. Three million is quite enough to allow for considerable variation, and these people varied more widely than we could at first account for.

Terry had insisted that if they were parthenogenetic they'd be as alike as so many ants or aphids; he urged their visible differences as proof that there must be men—somewhere.

But when we asked them, in our later, more intimate conversations, how they accounted for so much divergence without cross-fertilization, they attributed it partly to the careful education, which followed each slight tendency to differ, and partly to the law of mutation. This they had found in their work with plants, and fully proven in their own case.

Physically they were more alike than we, as they lacked all morbid or excessive types. They were tall, strong, healthy, and beautiful as a race, but differed individually in a wide range of feature, coloring, and expression.

"But surely the most important growth is in mind—and

in the things we make," urged Somel. "Do you find your physical variation accompanied by a proportionate variation in ideas, feelings, and products? Or, among people who look more alike, do you find their internal life and their work as similar?"

We were rather doubtful on this point, and inclined to hold that there was more chance of improvement in greater physical variation.

"It certainly should be," Zava admitted. "We have always thought it a grave initial misfortune to have lost half our little world. Perhaps that is one reason why we have so striven for conscious improvement."

"But acquired traits are not transmissible," Terry declared. "Weissman has proved that."

They never disputed our absolute statements, only made notes of them.

"If that is so, then our improvement must be due either to mutation, or solely to education," she gravely pursued. "We certainly have improved. It may be that all these higher qualities were latent in the original mother, that careful education is bringing them out, and that our personal differences depend on slight variations in prenatal condition."

"I think it is more in your accumulated culture," Jeff suggested. "And in the amazing psychic growth you have made. We know very little about methods of real soul culture—and you seem to know a great deal."

Be that as it might, they certainly presented a higher level of active intelligence, and of behavior, than we had so far really grasped. Having known in our lives several people who showed the same delicate courtesy and were equally pleasant to live with, at least when they wore their "company manners," we had assumed that our companions were a carefully chosen few. Later we were more and more impressed that all this gentle breeding was breeding; that they were born to it, reared in it, that it was as natural and universal with them as the gentleness of doves or the alleged wisdom of serpents.

As for the intelligence, I confess that this was the most impressive and, to me, most mortifying, of any single feature of Herland. We soon ceased to comment on this or other matters which to them were such obvious commonplaces as to call forth embarrassing questions about our own conditions.

This was nowhere better shown than in that matter of food supply, which I will now attempt to describe.

Having improved their agriculture to the highest point, and carefully estimated the number of persons who could comfortably live on their square miles; having then limited their population to that number, one would think that was all there was to be done. But they had not thought so. To them the country was a unit—it was theirs. They themselves were a unit, a conscious group; they thought in terms of the community. As such, their time-sense was not limited to the hopes and ambitions of an individual life. Therefore, they habitually considered and carried out plans for improvement which might cover centuries.

I had never seen, had scarcely imagined, human beings undertaking such a work as the deliberate replanting of an entire forest area with different kinds of trees. Yet this seemed to them the simplest common sense, like a man's plowing up an inferior lawn and reseeding it. Now every tree bore fruit—edible fruit, that is. In the case of one tree, in which they took especial pride, it had originally no fruit at all—that is, none humanly edible—yet was so beautiful that they wished to keep it. For nine hundred years they had experimented, and now showed us this particularly lovely graceful tree, with a profuse crop of nutritious seeds.

They had early decided that trees were the best food plants, requiring far less labor in tilling the soil, and bearing a larger amount of food for the same ground space; also doing much to preserve and enrich the soil.

Due regard had been paid to seasonable crops, and their fruit and nuts, grains and berries, kept on almost the year through.

On the higher part of the country, near the backing wall of mountains, they had a real winter with snow. Toward the southeastern point, where there was a large valley with a lake whose outlet was subterranean, the climate was like that of California, and citrus fruits, figs, and olives grew abundantly.

What impressed me particularly was their scheme of fertilization. Here was this little shut-in piece of land where one would have thought an ordinary people would have been starved out long ago or reduced to an annual struggle for life. These careful culturists had worked out a perfect scheme of refeeding the soil with all that came out of it. All the scraps and leavings of their food, plant waste from lumber work or textile industry, all the solid matter from the sewage, properly treated and combined—everything which came from the earth went back to it.

The practical result was like that in any healthy forest; an increasingly valuable soil was being built, instead of the progressive impoverishment so often seen in the rest of the world.

When this first burst upon us we made such approving comments that they were surprised that such obvious common sense should be praised; asked what our methods were; and we had some difficulty in—well, in diverting them, by referring to the extent of our own land, and the—admitted—carelessness with which we had skimmed the cream of it.

At least we thought we had diverted them. Later I found that besides keeping a careful and accurate account of all we told them, they had a sort of skeleton chart, on which the things we said and the things we palpably avoided saying were all set down and studied. It really was child's play for those profound educators to work out a painfully accurate estimate of our conditions—in some lines. When a given line of observation seemed to lead to some very dreadful inference they always gave us the benefit of the doubt, leaving it open to further knowledge. Some of the things we had grown to accept as perfectly natural, or as belonging to our human limitations, they literally could not have believed; and, as I have said, we had all of us joined in a tacit endeavor to conceal much of the social status at home.

"Confound their grandmotherly minds!" Terry said. "Of course they can't understand a Man's World! They aren't human—they're just a pack of Fe-Fe-Females!" This was after he had to admit their parthenogenesis.

"I wish our grandfatherly minds had managed as well," said Jeff. "Do you really think it's to our credit that we have muddled along with all our poverty and disease and the like? They have peace and plenty, wealth and beauty, goodness and intellect. Pretty good people, I think!"

"You'll find they have their faults too," Terry insisted; and partly in self-defense, we all three began to look for those faults of theirs. We had been very strong on this subject before we got there—in those baseless speculations of ours.

"Suppose there is a country of women only," Jeff had put in, over and over. "What'll they be like?"

And we had been cocksure as to the inevitable limitations, the faults and vices, of a lot of women. We had expected them to be given over to what we called "feminine vanity"—"frills and furbelows," and we found they had evolved a costume more perfect than the Chinese dress, richly beautiful when so desired, always useful, of unfailing dignity and good taste.

We had expected a dull submissive monotony, and found a daring social inventiveness far beyond our own, and a mechanical and scientific development fully equal to ours.

We had expected pettiness, and found a social consciousness besides which our nations looked like quarreling children—feebleminded ones at that.

We had expected jealousy, and found a broad sisterly affection, a fair-minded intelligence, to which we could produce no parallel.

We had expected hysteria, and found a standard of health and vigor, a calmness of temper, to which the habit of profanity, for instance, was impossible to explain—we tried it.

All these things even Terry had to admit, but he still insisted that we should find out the other side pretty soon.

"It stands to reason, doesn't it?" he argued. "The whole thing's deuced unnatural—I'd say impossible if we weren't in it. And an unnatural condition's sure to have unnatural results. You'll find some awful characteristics—see if you don't! For instance—we don't know yet what they do with their criminals—their defectives—their aged. You notice we haven't seen any! There's got to be something!"

I was inclined to believe that there had to be something, so I took the bull by the horns—the cow, I should say!—and asked Somel.

"I want to find some flaw in all this perfection," I told her flatly. "It simply isn't possible that three million people have no faults. We are trying our best to understand and learn—would you mind helping us by saying what, to your minds, are the worst qualities of this unique civilization of yours?"

We were sitting together in a shaded arbor, in one of those eating-gardens of theirs. The delicious food had been eaten, a plate of fruit still before us. We could look out on one side over a stretch of open country, quietly rich and lovely; on the other, the garden, with tables here and there, far apart enough for privacy. Let me say right here that with all their careful "balance of population" there was no crowding in this country. There was room, space, a sunny breezy freedom everywhere.

Somel set her chin upon her hand, her elbow on the low wall beside her, and looked off over the fair land.

"Of course we have faults—all of us," she said. "In one way you might say that we have more than we used to—that is, our standard of perfection seems to get farther and farther away. But we are not discouraged, because our records do show gain—considerable gain.

"When we began—even with the start of one particularly noble mother—we inherited the characteristics of a long race-record behind her. And they cropped out from time to time—alarmingly. But it is—yes, quite six hundred years since we have had what you call a 'criminal.'

"We have, of course, made it our first business to train out, to breed out, when possible, the lowest types."

"Breed out?" I asked. "How could you—with parthenogenesis?"

"If the girl showing the bad qualities had still the power to appreciate social duty, we appealed to her, by that, to renounce motherhood. Some of the few worst types were, fortunately, unable to reproduce. But if the fault was in a disproportionate egotism—then the girl was sure she had the right to have children, even that hers would be better than others."

"I can see that," I said. "And then she would be likely to rear them in the same spirit."

"That we never allowed," answered Somel quietly.

"Allowed?" I queried. "Allowed a mother to rear her own children?"

"Certainly not," said Somel, "unless she was fit for that supreme task."

This was rather a blow to my previous convictions.

"But I thought motherhood was for each of you—"

"Motherhood—yes, that is, maternity, to bear a child. But education is our highest art, only allowed to our highest artists."

"Education?" I was puzzled again. "I don't mean education. I mean by motherhood not only child-bearing, but the care of babies."

"The care of babies involves education, and is entrusted only to the most fit," she repeated.

"Then you separate mother and child!" I cried in cold horror, something of Terry's feeling creeping over me, that there must be something wrong among these many virtues.

"Not usually," she patiently explained. "You see, almost every woman values her maternity above everything else. Each girl holds it close and dear, an exquisite joy, a crowning honor, the most intimate, most personal, most precious thing. That is, the child-rearing has come to be with us a culture so profoundly studied, practiced with such subtlety and skill, that the more we love our children the less we are willing to trust that process to unskilled hands—even our own."

"But a mother's love—" I ventured.

She studied my face, trying to work out a means of clear explanation.

"You told us about your dentists," she said, at length, "those quaintly specialized persons who spend their lives filling little holes in other persons' teeth—even in children's teeth sometimes."

"Yes?" I said, not getting her drift.

"Does mother-love urge mothers—with you—to fill their own children's teeth? Or to wish to?"

"Why no—of course not," I protested. "But that is a highly specialized craft. Surely the care of babies is open to any woman—any mother!"

"We do not think so," she gently replied. "Those of us who are the most highly competent fulfill that office; and a majority of our girls eagerly try for it—I assure you we have the very best."

"But the poor mother—bereaved of her baby—"

"Oh no!" she earnestly assured me. "Not in the least bereaved. It is her baby still—it is with her—she has not lost it. But she is not the only one to care for it. There are others whom she knows to be wiser. She knows it because she has studied as they did, practiced as they did, and honors their real superiority. For the child's sake, she is glad to have for it this highest care."

I was unconvinced. Besides, this was only hearsay; I had yet to see the motherhood of Herland.

8. The Girls of Herland

At last Terry's ambition was realized. We were invited, always courteously and with free choice on our part, to address general audiences and classes of girls.

I remember the first time—and how careful we were about our clothes, and our amateur barbering. Terry, in particular, was fussy to a degree about the cut of his beard, and so critical of our combined efforts, that we handed him the shears and told him to please himself. We began to rather prize those beards of ours; they were almost our sole distinction among those tall and sturdy women, with their cropped hair and sexless costume. Being offered a wide selection of garments, we had chosen according to our personal taste, and were surprised to find, on meeting large audiences, that we were the most highly decorated, especially Terry.

He was a very impressive figure, his strong features softened by the somewhat longer hair—though he made me trim it as closely as I knew how; and he wore his richly embroidered tunic with its broad, loose girdle with quite a Henry V air. Jeff looked more like—well, like a Huguenot Lover; and I don't know what I looked like, only that I felt very comfortable. When I got back to our own padded armor and its starched borders I realized with acute regret how comfortable were those Herland clothes.

We scanned that audience, looking for the three bright faces we knew; but they were not to be seen. Just a multitude of girls: quiet, eager, watchfull, all eyes and ears to listen and learn.

We had been urged to give, as fully as we cared to, a sort

of synopsis of world history, in brief, and to answer questions.

"We are so utterly ignorant, you see," Moadine had explained to us. "We know nothing but such science as we have worked out for ourselves, just the brain work of one small half-country; and you, we gather, have helped one another all over the globe, sharing your discoveries, pooling your progress. How wonderful, how supremely beautiful your civilization must be!"

Somel gave a further suggestion.

"You do not have to begin all over again, as you did with us. We have made a sort of digest of what we have learned from you, and it has been eagerly absorbed, all over the country. Perhaps you would like to see our outline?"

We were eager to see it, and deeply impressed. To us, at first, these women, unavoidably ignorant of what to us was the basic commonplace of knowledge, had seemed on the plane of children, or of savages. What we had been forced to admit, with growing acquaintance, was that they were ignorant as Plato and Aristotle were, but with a highly developed mentality quite comparable to that of Ancient Greece.

Far be it from me to lumber these pages with an account of what we so imperfectly strove to teach them. The memorable fact is what they taught us, or some faint glimpse of it. And at present, our major interest was not at all in the subject matter of our talk, but in the audience.

Girls—hundreds of them—eager, bright-eyed, attentive young faces; crowding questions, and, I regret to say, an increasing inability on our part to answer them effectively.

Our special guides, who were on the platform with us, and sometimes aided in clarifying a question or, oftener, an answer, noticed this effect, and closed the formal lecture part of the evening rather shortly.

"Our young women will be glad to meet you," Somel suggested, "to talk with you more personally, if you are willing?"

Willing! We were impatient and said as much, at which I saw a flickering little smile cross Moadine's face. Even then, with all those eager young things waiting to talk to us, a sudden question crossed my mind: "What was their point of view? What did they think of us?" We learned that later.

Terry plunged in among those young creatures with a sort

of rapture, somewhat as a glad swimmer takes to the sea. Jeff, with a rapt look on his high-bred face, approached as to a sacrament. But I was a little chilled by that last thought of mine, and kept my eyes open. I found time to watch Jeff, even while I was surrounded by an eager group of questioners—as we all were—and saw how his worshipping eyes, his grave courtesy, pleased and drew some of them; while others, rather stronger spirits they looked to be, drew away from his group to Terry's or mine.

I watched Terry with special interest, knowing how he had longed for this time, and how irresistible he had always been at home. And I could see, just in snatches, of course, how his suave and masterful approach seemed to irritate them; his too-intimate glances were vaguely resented, his compliments puzzled and annoyed. Sometimes a girl would flush, not with drooped eyelids and inviting timidity, but with anger and a quick lift of the head. Girl after girl turned on her heel and left him, till he had but a small ring of questioners, and they, visibly, were the least "girlish" of the lot.

I saw him looking pleased at first, as if he thought he was making a strong impression; but finally, casting a look at Jeff, or me, he seemed less pleased—and less.

As for me, I was most agreeably surprised. At home I never was "popular." I had my girl friends, good ones, but they were friends—nothing else. Also they were of somewhat the same clan, not popular in the sense of swarming admirers. But here, to my astonishment, I found my crowd was the largest.

I have to generalize, of course, rather telescoping many impressions; but the first evening was a good sample of the impression we made. Jeff had a following, if I may call it that, of the more sentimental—though that's not the word I want. The less practical, perhaps; the girls who were artists of some sort, ethicists, teachers—that kind.

Terry was reduced to a rather combative group: keen, logical, inquiring minds, not overly sensitive, the very kind he liked least, while, as for me—I became quite cocky over my general popularity.

Terry was furious about it. We could hardly blame him.

"Girls!" he burst forth, when that evening was over and we were by ourselves once more. "Call those *girls!*"

"Most delightful girls, I call them," said Jeff, his blue eyes dreamily contented.

"What do *you* call them?" I mildly inquired.

"Boys! Nothing but boys, most of 'em. A standoffish, disagreeable lot at that. Critical, impertinent youngsters. No girls at all."

He was angry and severe, not a little jealous, too, I think. Afterward, when he found out just what it was they did not like, he changed his manner somewhat and got on better. He had to. For, in spite of his criticism, they were girls, and, furthermore, all the girls there were! Always excepting our three!—with whom we presently renewed our acquaintance.

When it came to courtship, which it soon did, I can of course best describe my own—and am least inclined to. But of Jeff I heard somewhat; he was inclined to dwell reverently and admiringly, at some length, on the exalted sentiment and measureless perfection of his Celis; and Terry—Terry made so many false starts and met so many rebuffs, that by the time he really settled down to win Alima, he was considerably wiser. At that, it was not smooth sailing. They broke and quarreled, over and over; he would rush off to console himself with some other fair one—the other fair one would have none of him—and he would drift back to Alima, becoming more and more devoted each time.

She never gave an inch. A big, handsome creature, rather exceptionally strong even in that race of strong women, with a proud head and sweeping level brows that lined across above her dark eager eyes like the wide wings of a soaring hawk.

I was good friends with all three of them but best of all with Ellador, long before that feeling changed, for both of us.

From her, and from Somel, who talked very freely with me, I learned at last something of the viewpoint of Herland toward its visitors.

Here they were, isolated, happy, contented, when the booming buzz of our biplane tore the air above them.

Everybody heard it—saw it—for miles and miles, word flashed all over the country, and a council was held in every town and village.

And this was their rapid determination:

"From another country. Probably men. Evidently highly

civilized. Doubtless possessed of much valuable knowledge. May be dangerous. Catch them if possible; tame and train them if necessary. This may be a chance to re-establish a bi-sexual state for our people.''

They were not afraid of us—three million highly intelligent women—or two million, counting only grown-ups—were not likely to be afraid of three young men. We thought of them as "Women," and therefore timid; but it was two thousand years since they had had anything to be afraid of, and certainly more than one thousand since they had outgrown the feeling.

We thought—at least Terry did—that we could have our pick of them. They thought—very cautiously and farsightedly—of picking us, if it seemed wise.

All that time we were in training they studied us, analyzed us, prepared reports about us, and this information was widely disseminated all about the land.

Not a girl in that country had not been learning for months as much as could be gathered about our country, our culture, our personal characters. No wonder their questions were hard to answer. But I am sorry to say, when we were at last brought out and—exhibited (I hate to call it that, but that's what it was), there was no rush of takers. Here was poor old Terry fondly imagining that at last he was free to stray in "a rosebud garden of girls"—and behold! the rosebuds were all with keen appraising eye, studying us.

They were interested, profoundly interested, but it was not the kind of interest we were looking for.

To get an idea of their attitude you have to hold in mind their extremely high sense of solidarity. They were not each choosing a lover; they hadn't the faintest idea of love—sex-love, that is. These girls—to each of whom motherhood was a lodestar, and that motherhood exalted above a mere personal function, looked forward to as the highest social service, as the sacrament of a lifetime—were now confronted with an opportunity to make the great step of changing their whole status, of reverting to their earlier bi-sexual order of nature.

Beside this underlying consideration there was the limitless interest and curiosity in our civilization, purely impersonal, and held by an order of mind beside which we were like—schoolboys.

It was small wonder that our lectures were not a success;

and none at all that our, or at least Terry's, advances were
so ill received. The reason for my own comparative success
was at first far from pleasing to my pride.

"We like you the best," Somel told me, "because you
seem more like us."

"More like a lot of women!" I thought to myself dis-
gustedly, and then remembered how little like "women,"
in our derogatory sense, they were. She was smiling at me,
reading my thought.

"We can quite see that we do not seem like—women—to
you. Of course, in a bi-sexual race the distinctive feature of
each sex must be intensified. But surely there are characteristics enough which belong to People, aren't there? That's
what I mean about you being more like us—more like People. We feel at ease with you."

Jeff's difficulty was his exalted gallantry. He idealized
women, and was always looking for a chance to "protect"
or to "serve" them. These needed neither protection nor
service. They were living in peace and power and plenty;
we were their guests, their prisoners, absolutely dependent.

Of course we could promise whatsoever we might of advantages, if they would come to our country; but the more
we knew of theirs, the less we boasted.

Terry's jewels and trinkets they prized as curios; handed
them about, asking questions as to workmanship, not in the
least as to value; and discussed not ownership, but which
museum to put them in.

When a man has nothing to give a woman, is dependent
wholly on his personal attraction, his courtship is under limitations.

They were considering these two things: the advisability
of making the Great Change; and the degree of personal
adaptability which would best serve that end.

Here we had the advantage of our small personal experience with those three fleet forest girls; and that served to
draw us together.

As for Ellador: Suppose you come to a strange land and
find it pleasant enough—just a little more than ordinarily
pleasant—and then you find rich farmland, and then gardens, gorgeous gardens, and then palaces full of rare and
curious treasures—incalculable, inexhaustible, and then—
mountains—like the Himalayas, and then the sea.

I liked her that day she balanced on the branch before me

and named the trio. I thought of her most. Afterward I turned to her like a friend when we met for the third time, and continued the acquaintance. While Jeff's ultra-devotion rather puzzled Celis, really put off their day of happiness, while Terry and Alima quarreled and parted, re-met and re-parted, Ellador and I grew to be close friends.

We talked and talked. We took long walks together. She showed me things, explained them, interpreted much that I had not understood. Through her sympathetic intelligence I became more and more comprehending of the spirit of the people of Herland, more and more appreciative of its marvelous inner growth as well as outer perfection.

I ceased to feel a stranger, a prisoner. There was a sense of understanding, of identity, of purpose. We discussed—everything. And, as I traveled farther and farther, exploring the rich, sweet soul of her, my sense of pleasant friendship became but a broad foundation for such height, such breadth, such interlocked combination of feeling as left me fairly blinded with the wonder of it.

As I've said, I had never cared very much for women, nor they for me—not Terry-fashion. But this one—

At first I never even thought of her ''in that way,'' as the girls have it. I had not come to the country with any Turkish-harem intentions, and I was no woman-worshipper like Jeff. I just liked that girl ''as a friend,'' as we say. That friendship grew like a tree. She was *such* a good sport! We did all kinds of things together. She taught me games and I taught her games, and we raced and rowed and had all manner of fun, as well as higher comradeship.

Then, as I got on farther, the palace and treasures and snowy mountain ranges opened up. I had never known there could be such a human being. So—great. I don't mean talented. She was a forester—one of the best—but it was not that gift I mean. When I say *great,* I mean great—big, all through. If I had known more of those women, as intimately, I should not have found her so unique; but even among them she was noble. Her mother was an Over Mother—and her grandmother, too, I heard later.

So she told me more and more of her beautiful land; and I told her as much, yes, more than I wanted to, about mine; and we became inseparable. Then this deeper recognition came and grew. I felt my own soul rise and lift its wings, as it were. Life got bigger. It seemed as if I understood—

as I never had before—as if I could Do things—as if I too could grow—if she would help me. And then It came—to both of us, all at once.

A still day—on the edge of the world, their world. The two of us, gazing out over the far dim forestland below, talking of heaven and earth and human life, and of my land and other lands and what they needed and what I hoped to do for them—

"If you will help me," I said.

She turned to me, with that high, sweet look of hers, and then, as her eyes rested in mine and her hands too—then suddenly there blazed out between us a farther glory, instant, overwhelming—quite beyond any words of mine to tell.

Celis was a blue-and-gold-and-rose person; Alima, black-and-white-and-red, a blazing beauty. Ellador was brown: hair dark and soft, like a seal coat; clear brown skin with a healthy red in it; brown eyes—all the way from topaz to black velvet they seemed to range—splendid girls, all of them.

They had seen us first of all, far down in the lake below, and flashed the tidings across the land even before our first exploring flight. They had watched our landing, flitted through the forest with us, hidden in that tree and—I shrewdly suspect—giggled on purpose.

They had kept watch over our hooded machine, taking turns at it; and when our escape was announced, had followed alongside for a day or two, and been there at the last, as described. They felt a special claim on us—called us "their men"—and when we were at liberty to study the land and people, and be studied by them, their claim was recognized by the wise leaders.

But I felt, we all did, that we should have chosen them among millions, unerringly.

And yet, "the path of true love never did run smooth"; this period of courtship was full of the most unsuspected pitfalls.

Writing this as late as I do, after manifold experiences both in Herland and, later, in my own land, I can now understand and philosophize about what was then a continual astonishment and often a temporary tragedy.

The "long suit" in most courtships is sex attraction, of course. Then gradually develops such comradeship as the two temperaments allow. Then, after marriage, there is either the establishment of a slow-growing, widely based friendship, the deepest, tenderest, sweetest of relations, all lit and warmed by the recurrent flame of love; or else that process is reversed, love cools and fades, no friendship grows, the whole relation turns from beauty to ashes.

Here everything was different. There was no sex-feeling to appeal to, or practically none. Two thousand years' disuse had left very little of the instinct; also we must remember that those who had at times manifested it as atavistic exceptions were often, by that very fact, denied motherhood.

Yet while the mother process remains, the inherent ground for sex-distinction remains also; and who shall say what long forgotten feeling, vague and nameless, was stirred in some of these mother hearts by our arrival?

What left us even more at sea in our approach was the lack of any sex-tradition. There was no accepted standard of what was "manly" and what was "womanly."

When Jeff said, taking the fruit basket from his adored one, "A woman should not carry anything," Celis said, "Why?" with the frankest amazement. He could not look that fleet-footed, deep-chested young forester in the face and say, "Because she is weaker." She wasn't. One does not call a race horse weak because it is visibly not a cart horse.

He said, rather lamely, that women were not built for heavy work.

She looked out across the fields to where some women were working, building a new bit of wall out of large stones; looked back at the nearest town with its woman-built houses; down at the smooth, hard road we were walking on; and then at the little basket he had taken from her.

"I don't understand," she said quite sweetly. "Are the women in your country so weak that they could not carry such a thing as that?"

"It is a convention," he said. "We assume that motherhood is a sufficient burden—that men should carry all the others."

"What a beautiful feeling!" she said, her blue eyes shining.

"Does it work?" asked Alima, in her keen, swift way.

"Do all men in all countries carry everything? Or is it only in yours?"

"Don't be so literal," Terry begged lazily. "Why aren't you willing to be worshipped and waited on? We like to do it."

"You don't like to have us do it to you," she answered.

"That's different," he said, annoyed; and when she said, "Why is it?" he quite sulked, referring her to me, saying, "Van's the philosopher."

Ellador and I talked it all out together, so that we had an easier experience of it when the real miracle time came. Also, between us, we made things clearer to Jeff and Celis. But Terry would not listen to reason.

He was madly in love with Alima. He wanted to take her by storm, and nearly lost her forever.

You see, if a man loves a girl who is in the first place young and inexperienced; who in the second place is educated with a background of caveman tradition, a middleground of poetry and romance, and a foreground of unspoken hope and interest all centering upon the one Event; and who has, furthermore, absolutely no other hope or interest worthy of the name—why, it is a comparatively easy matter to sweep her off her feet with a dashing attack. Terry was a past master in this process. He tried it here, and Alima was so affronted, so repelled, that it was weeks before he got near enough to try again.

The more coldly she denied him, the hotter his determination; he was not used to real refusal. The approach of flattery she dismissed with laughter, gifts and such "attentions" we could not bring to bear, pathos and complaint of cruelty stirred only a reasoning inquiry. It took Terry a long time.

I doubt if she ever accepted her strange lover as fully as did Celis and Ellador theirs. He had hurt and offended her too often; there were reservations.

But I think Alima retained some faint vestige of long-descended feeling which made Terry more possible to her than to others; and that she had made up her mind to the experiment and hated to renounce it.

However it came about, we all three at length achieved full understanding, and solemnly faced what was to them a step of measureless importance, a grave question as well as a great happiness; to us a strange, new joy.

Of marriage as a ceremony they knew nothing. Jeff was for bringing them to our country for the religious and the civil ceremony, but neither Celis nor the others would consent.

"We can't expect them to want to go with us—yet," said Terry sagely. "Wait a bit, boys. We've got to take 'em on their own terms—if at all." This, in rueful reminiscence of his repeated failures.

"But our time's coming," he added cheerfully. "These women have never been mastered, you see—" This, as one who had made a discovery.

"You'd better not try to do any mastering if you value your chances," I told him seriously; but he only laughed, and said, "Every man to his trade!"

We couldn't do anything with him. He had to take his own medicine.

If the lack of tradition of courtship left us much at sea in our wooing, we found ourselves still more bewildered by lack of tradition of matrimony.

And here again, I have to draw on later experience, and as deep an acquaintance with their culture as I could achieve, to explain the gulfs of difference between us.

Two thousand years of one continuous culture with no men. Back of that, only traditions of the harem. They had no exact analogue for our word *home,* any more than they had for our Roman-based *family.*

They loved one another with a practically universal affection, rising to exquisite and unbroken friendships, and broadening to a devotion to their country and people for which our word *patriotism* is no definition at all.

Patriotism, red hot, is compatible with the existence of a neglect of national interests, a dishonesty, a cold indifference to the suffering of millions. Patriotism is largely pride, and very largely combativeness. Patriotism generally has a chip on its shoulder.

This country had no other country to measure itself by— save the few poor savages far below, with whom they had no contact.

They loved their country because it was their nursery, playground, and workshop—theirs and their children's. They were proud of it as a workshop, proud of their record of ever-increasing efficiency; they had made a pleasant garden of it, a very practical little heaven; but most of all they valued it—and here it is hard for us to understand them—as a cultural environment for their children.

That, of course, is the keynote of the whole distinction—their children.

From those first breathlessly guarded, half-adored race mothers, all up the ascending line, they had this dominant thought of building up a great race through the children.

All the surrendering devotion our women have put into their private families, these women put into their country and race. All the loyalty and service men expect of wives, they gave, not singly to men, but collectively to one another.

And the mother instinct, with us so painfully intense, so thwarted by conditions, so concentrated in personal devotion to a few, so bitterly hurt by death, disease, or barrenness, and even by the mere growth of the children, leaving the mother alone in her empty nest—all this feeling with them flowed out in a strong, wide current, unbroken through the generations, deepening and widening through the years, including every child in all the land.

With their united power and wisdom, they had studied and overcome the ''diseases of childhood''—their children had none.

They had faced the problems of education and so solved them that their children grew up as naturally as young trees; learning through every sense; taught continuously but unconsciously—never knowing they were being educated.

In fact, they did not use the word as we do. Their idea of education was the special training they took, when half grown up, under experts. Then the eager young minds fairly flung themselves on their chosen subjects, and acquired with an ease, a breadth, a grasp, at which I never ceased to wonder.

But the babies and little children never felt the pressure of that ''forcible feeding'' of the mind that we call ''education.'' Of this, more later.

9. Our Relations
and Theirs

What I'm trying to show here is that with these women the whole relationship of life counted in a glad, eager growing-up to join the ranks of workers in the line best loved; a deep, tender reverence for one's own mother—too deep for them to speak of freely—and beyond that, the whole, free, wide range of sisterhood, the splendid service of the country, and friendships.

To these women we came, filled with the ideas, convictions, traditions, of our culture, and undertook to rouse in them the emotions which—to us—seemed proper.

However much, or little, of true sex-feeling there was between us, it phrased itself in their minds in terms of friendship, the one purely personal love they knew, and of ultimate parentage. Visibly we were not mothers, nor children, nor compatriots; so, if they loved us, we must be friends.

That we should pair off together in our courting days was natural to them; that we three should remain much together, as they did themselves, was also natural. We had as yet no work, so we hung about them in their forest tasks; that was natural, too.

But when we began to talk about each couple having "homes" of our own, they could not understand it.

"Our work takes us all around the country," explained Celis. "We cannot live in one place all the time."

"We are together now," urged Alima, looking proudly at Terry's stalwart nearness. (This was one of the times when they were "on," though presently "off" again.)

"It's not the same thing at all," he insisted. "A man wants a home of his own, with his wife and family in it."

"Staying in it? All the time?" asked Ellador. "Not imprisoned, surely!"

"Of course not! Living there—naturally," he answered.

"What does she do there—all the time?" Alima demanded. "What is her work?"

Then Terry patiently explained again that our women did not work—with reservations.

"But what do they do—if they have no work?" she persisted.

"They take care of the home—and the children."

"At the same time?" asked Ellador.

"Why yes. The children play about, and the mother has charge of it all. There are servants, of course."

It seemed so obvious, so natural to Terry, that he always grew impatient; but the girls were honestly anxious to understand.

"How many children do your women have?" Alima had her notebook out now, and a rather firm set of lip. Terry began to dodge.

"There is no set number, my dear," he explained. "Some have more, some have less."

"Some have none at all," I put in mischievously.

They pounced on this admission and soon wrung from us the general fact that those women who had the most children had the least servants, and those who had the most servants had the least children.

"There!" triumphed Alima. "One or two or no children, and three or four servants. Now what do those women *do?*"

We explained as best we might. We talked of "social duties," disingenuously banking on their not interpreting the words as we did; we talked of hospitality, entertainment, and various "interests." All the time we knew that to these large-minded women whose whole mental outlook was so collective, the limitations of a wholly personal life were inconceivable.

"We cannot really understand it," Ellador concluded. "We are only half a people. We have our woman-ways and they have their man-ways and their both-ways. We have worked out a system of living which is, of course, limited. They must have a broader, richer, better one. I should like to see it."

"You shall, dearest," I whispered.

* * *

"There's nothing to smoke," complained Terry. He was in the midst of a prolonged quarrel with Alima, and needed a sedative. "There's nothing to drink. These blessed women have no pleasant vices. I wish we could get out of here!"

This wish was vain. We were always under a certain degree of watchfulness. When Terry burst forth to tramp the streets at night he always found a "Colonel" here or there; and when, on an occasion of fierce though temporary despair, he had plunged to the cliff edge with some vague view to escape, he found several of them close by. We were free—but there was a string to it.

"They've no unpleasant ones, either," Jeff reminded him.

"Wish they had!" Terry persisted. "They've neither the vices of men, nor the virtues of women—they're neuters!"

"You know better than that. Don't talk nonsense," said I, severely.

I was thinking of Ellador's eyes when they gave me a certain look, a look she did not at all realize.

Jeff was equally incensed. "I don't know what 'virtues of women' you miss. Seems to me they have all of them."

"They've no modesty," snapped Terry. "No patience, no submissiveness, none of that natural yielding which is woman's greatest charm."

I shook my head pityingly. "Go and apologize and make friends again, Terry. You've got a grouch, that's all. These women have the virtue of humanity, with less of its faults than any folks I ever saw. As for patience—they'd have pitched us over the cliffs the first day we lit among 'em, if they hadn't that."

"There are no—distractions," he grumbled. "Nowhere a man can go and cut loose a bit. It's an everlasting parlor and nursery."

"And workshop," I added. "And school, and office, and laboratory, and studio, and theater, and—home."

"Home!" he sneered. "There isn't a home in the whole pitiful place."

"There isn't anything else, and you know it," Jeff retorted hotly. "I never saw, I never dreamed of, such universal peace and good will and mutual affection."

"Oh, well, of course, if you like a perpetual Sunday school, it's all very well. But I like Something Doing. Here it's all done."

There was something to this criticism. The years of pioneering lay far behind them. Theirs was a civilization in which the initial difficulties had long since been overcome. The untroubled peace, the unmeasured plenty, the steady health, the large good will and smooth management which ordered everything, left nothing to overcome. It was like a pleasant family in an old established, perfectly run country place.

I liked it because of my eager and continued interest in the sociological achievements involved. Jeff liked it as he would have liked such a family and such a place anywhere.

Terry did not like it because he found nothing to oppose, to struggle with, to conquer.

"Life is a struggle, has to be," he insisted. "If there is no struggle, there is no life—that's all."

"You're talking nonsense—masculine nonsense," the peaceful Jeff replied. He was certainly a warm defender of Herland. "Ants don't raise their myriads by a struggle, do they? Or the bees?"

"Oh, if you go back to insects—and want to live in an anthill—! I tell you the higher grades of life are reached only through struggle—combat. There's no Drama here. Look at their plays! They make me sick!"

He rather had us there. The drama of the country was—to our taste—rather flat. You see, they lacked the sex motive and, with it, jealousy. They had no interplay of warring nations, no aristocracy and its ambitions, no wealth and poverty opposition.

I see I have said little about the economics of the place; it should have come before, but I'll go on about the drama now.

They had their own kind. There was a most impressive array of pageantry, of processions, a sort of grand ritual, with their arts and their religion broadly blended. The very babies joined in it. To see one of their great annual festivals, with the massed and marching stateliness of those great mothers; the young women brave and noble, beautiful and strong; and then the children, taking part as naturally as ours would frolic round a Christmas tree—it was overpowering in the impression of joyous, triumphant life.

They had begun at a period when the drama, the dance, music, religion, and education were all very close together; and instead of developing them in detached lines, they had kept the connection. Let me try again to give, if I can, a faint sense of the difference in the life view—the background and basis on which their culture rested.

Ellador told me a lot about it. She took me to see the children, the growing girls, the special teachers. She picked out books for me to read. She always seemed to understand just what I wanted to know, and how to give it to me.

While Terry and Alima struck sparks and parted—he always madly drawn to her and she to him—she must have been, or she'd never have stood the way he behaved—Ellador and I had already a deep, restful feeling, as if we'd always had one another. Jeff and Celis were happy; there was no question of that; but it didn't seem to me as if they had the good times we did.

Well, here is the Herland child facing life—as Ellador tried to show it to me. From the first memory, they knew Peace, Beauty, Order, Safety, Love, Wisdom, Justice, Patience, and Plenty. By "plenty" I mean that the babies grew up in an environment which met their needs, just as young fawns might grow up in dewy forest glades and brook-fed meadows. And they enjoyed it as frankly and utterly as the fawns would.

They found themselves in a big bright lovely world, full of the most interesting and enchanting things to learn about and to do. The people everywhere were friendly and polite. No Herland child ever met the overbearing rudeness we so commonly show to children. They were People, too, from the first; the most precious part of the nation.

In each step of the rich experience of living, they found the instance they were studying widen out into contact with an endless range of common interests. The things they learned were *related,* from the first; related to one another, and to the national prosperity.

"It was a butterfly that made me a forester," said Ellador. "I was about eleven years old, and I found a big purple-and-green butterfly on a low flower. I caught it, very carefully, by the closed wings, as I had been told to do, and carried it to the nearest insect teacher"—I made a note there to ask her what on earth an insect teacher was—"to ask her its name. She took it from me with a little cry of delight. 'Oh, you blessed child,' she said. 'Do you like obernuts?' Of course I liked obernuts, and said so. It is our best food-nut, you know. 'This is a female of the obernut moth,' she told me. 'They are almost gone. We have been trying to exterminate them for centuries. If you had not caught this one, it might have laid eggs enough to raise worms enough to destroy thousands of our nut trees—thousands of bushels of nuts—and make years and years of trouble for us.'

"Everybody congratulated me. The children all over the country were told to watch for that moth, if there were any more. I was shown the history of the creature, and an account of the damage it used to do and of how long and hard our foremothers had worked to save that tree for us. I grew a foot, it seemed to me, and determined then and there to be a forester."

This is but an instance; she showed me many. The big difference was that whereas our children grow up in private homes and families, with every effort made to protect and seclude them from a dangerous world, here they grew up in a wide, friendly world, and knew it for theirs, from the first.

Their child-literature was a wonderful thing. I could have spent years following delicate subtleties, the smooth simplicities with which they had bent that great art to the service of the child mind.

We have two life cycles: the man's and the woman's. To the man there is growth, struggle, conquest, the establishment of his family, and as much further sucess in gain or ambition as he can achieve.

To the woman, growth, the securing of a husband, the subordinate activities of family life, and afterward such "social" or charitable interests as her position allows.

Here was but one cycle, and that a large one.

The child entered upon a broad open field of life, in which motherhood was the one great personal contribution to the national life, and all the rest the individual share in their common activities. Every girl I talked to, at any age above babyhood, had her cheerful determination as to what she was going to be when she grew up.

What Terry meant by saying they had no "modesty" was that this great life-view had no shady places; they had a high sense of personal decorum, but no shame—no knowledge of anything to be ashamed of.

Even their shortcomings and misdeeds in childhood never were presented to them as sins; merely as errors and misplays—as in a game. Some of them, who were palpably less agreeable than others or who had a real weakness of fault, were treated with cheerful allowance, as a friendly group at whist would treat a poor player.

Their religion, you see, was maternal; and their ethics, based on the full perception of evolution, showed the principle of growth and the beauty of wise culture. They had no theory of the essential opposition of good and evil; life to them was growth; their pleasure was in growing, and their duty also.

With this background, with their sublimated mother-love, expressed in terms of widest social activity, every phase of their work was modified by its effect on the national growth. The language itself they had deliberately clarified, simplified, made easy and beautiful, for the sake of the children.

This seemed to us a wholly incredible thing: first, that any nation should have the foresight, the strength, and the persistence to plan and fulfill such a task; and second, that women should have had so much initiative. We have assumed, as a matter of course, that women had none; that only the man, with his natural energy and impatience of restriction, would ever invent anything.

Here we found that the pressure of life upon the environment develops in the human mind its inventive reactions, regardless of sex; and further, that a fully awakened motherhood plans and works without limit, for the good of the child.

That the children might be most nobly born, and reared in an environment calculated to allow the richest, freest growth, they had deliberately remodeled and improved the whole state.

I do not mean in the least that they stopped at that, any more than a child stops at childhood. The most impressive part of their whole culture beyond this perfect system of child-rearing was the range of interests and associations open to them all, for life. But in the field of literature I was most struck, at first, by the child-motive.

They had the same gradation of simple repetitive verse and story that we are familiar with, and the most exquisite, imaginative tales; but where, with us, these are the dribbled remnants of ancient folk myths and primitive lullabies, theirs were the exquisite work of great artists; not only simple and unfailing in appeal to the child-mind, but *true,* true to the living world about them.

To sit in one of their nurseries for a day was to change

one's views forever as to babyhood. The youngest ones, rosy fatlings in their mothers' arms, or sleeping lightly in the flower-sweet air, seemed natural enough, save that they never cried. I never heard a child cry in Herland, save once or twice at a bad fall; and then people ran to help, as we would at a scream of agony from a grown person.

Each mother had her year of glory; the time to love and learn, living closely with her child, nursing it proudly, often for two years or more. This perhaps was one reason for their wonderful vigor.

But after the baby-year the mother was not so constantly in attendance, unless, indeed, her work was among the little ones. She was never far off, however, and her attitude toward the co-mothers, whose proud child-service was direct and continuous, was lovely to see.

As for the babies—a group of those naked darlings playing on short velvet grass, clean-swept; or rugs as soft; or in shallow pools of bright water; tumbling over with bubbling joyous baby laughter—it was a view of infant happiness such as I had never dreamed.

The babies were reared in the warmer part of the country, and gradually acclimated to the cooler height as they grew older.

Sturdy children of ten and twelve played in the snow as joyfully as ours do; there were continuous excursions of them, from one part of the land to another, so that to each child the whole country might be home.

It was all theirs, waiting for them to learn, to love, to use, to serve; as our own little boys plan to be "a big soldier," or "a cowboy," or whatever pleases their fancy; and our little girls plan for the kind of home they mean to have, or how many children; these planned, freely and gaily with much happy chattering, of what they would do for the country when they were grown.

It was the eager happiness of the children and young people which first made me see the folly of that common notion of ours—that if life was smooth and happy, people would not enjoy it. As I studied these youngsters, vigorous, joyous, eager little creatures, and their voracious appetite for life, it shook my previous ideas so thoroughly that they have never been re-established. The steady level of good health gave them all that natural stimulus we used to call "animal spirits"—an odd contradiction in terms. They found themselves in an immediate environment which was agreeable and interesting, and before them stretched the years of learning and discovery, the fascinating, endless process of education.

As I looked into these methods and compared them with our own, my strange uncomfortable sense of race-humility grew apace.

Ellador could not understand my astonishment. She explained things kindly and sweetly, but with some amazement that they needed explaining, and with sudden questions as to how we did it that left me meeker than ever.

I betook myself to Somel one day, carefully not taking Ellador. I did not mind seeming foolish to Somel—she was used to it.

"I want a chapter of explanation," I told her. "You know my stupidities by heart, and I do not want to show them to Ellador—she things me so wise!"

She smiled delightedly. "It is beautiful to see," she told me, "this new wonderful love between you. The whole country is interested, you know—how can we help it!"

I had not thought of that. We say: "All the world loves a lover," but to have a couple of million people watching one's courtship—and that a difficult one—was rather embarrassing.

"Tell me about your theory of education," I said. "Make it short and easy. And, to show you what puzzles me, I'll tell you that in our theory great stress is laid on the forced exertion of the child's mind; we think it is good for him to overcome obstacles."

"Of course it is," she unexpectedly agreed. "All our children do that—they love to."

That puzzled me again. If they loved to do it, how could it be educational?

"Our theory is this," she went on carefully. "Here is a young human being. The mind is as natural a thing as the body, a thing that grows, a thing to use and to enjoy. We seek to nourish, to stimulate, to exercise the mind of a child as we do the body. There are the two main divisions in education—you have those of course?—the things it is necessary to know, and the things it is necessary to do."

"To do? Mental exercises, you mean?"

"Yes. Our general plan is this: In the matter of feeding the mind, of furnishing information, we use our best powers to meet the natural appetite of a healthy young brain; not to overfeed it, to provide such amount and variety of impressions as seem most welcome to each child. That is the easiest part. The other division is in arranging a properly graduated series of exercises which will best develop each mind; the common faculties we all have, and most carefully, the especial faculties some of us have. You do this also, do you not?''

''In a way,'' I said rather lamely. ''We have not so subtle and highly developed a system as you, not approaching it; but tell me more. As to the information—how do you manage? It appears that all of you know pretty much everything—is that right?''

This she laughingly disclaimed. ''By no means. We are, as you soon found out, extremely limited in knowledge. I wish you could realize what a ferment the country is in over the new things you have told us; the passionate eagerness among thousands of us to go to your country and learn—learn—learn! But what we do know is readily divisible into common knowledge and special knowledge. The common knowledge we have long since learned to feed into the minds of our little ones with no waste of time or strength; the special knowledge is open to all, as they desire it. Some of us specialize in one line only. But most take up several—some for their regular work, some to grow with.''

''To grow with?''

''Yes. When one settles too close in one kind of work there is a tendency to atrophy in the disused portions of the brain. We like to keep on learning, always.''

''What do you study?''

''As much as we know of the different sciences. We have, within our limits, a good deal of knowledge of anatomy, physiology, nutrition—all that pertains to a full and beautiful personal life. We have our botany and chemistry, and so on—very rudimentary, but interesting; our own history, with its accumulating psychology.''

''You put psychology with history—not with personal life?''

''Of course. It is ours; it is among and between us, and it changes with the succeeding and improving generations. We are at work, slowly and carefully, developing our whole people along these lines. It is glorious work—splendid! To see the thousands of babies improving, showing stronger clearer minds, sweeter dispositions, higher capacities—don't you find it so in your country?''

This I evaded flatly. I remembered the cheerless claim that the human mind was no better than in its earliest period of savagery, only better informed—a statement I had never believed.

"We try most earnestly for two powers," Somel continued. "The two that seem to us basically necessary for all noble life: a clear, far-reaching judgment, and a strong well-used will. We spend our best efforts, all through childhood and youth, in developing these faculties, individual judgment and will."

"As part of your system of education, you mean?"

"Exactly. As the most valuable part. With the babies, as you may have noticed, we first provide an environment which feeds the mind without tiring it; all manner of simple and interesting things to do, as soon as they are old enough to do them; physical properties, of course, come first. But as early as possible, going very carefully, not to tax the mind, we provide choices, simple choices, with very obvious causes and consequences. You've noticed the games?"

I had. The children seemed always playing something; or else, sometimes, engaged in peaceful researches of their own. I had wondered at first when they went to school, but soon found that they never did—to their knowledge. It was all education but no schooling.

"We have been working for some sixteen hundred years, devising better and better games for children," continued Somel.

I sat aghast. "Devising games?" I protested. "Making up new ones, you mean?"

"Exactly," she answered. "Don't you?"

Then I remembered the kindergarten, and the "material" devised by Signora Montessori, and guardedly replied: "To some extent." But most of our games, I told her, were very old—came down from child to child, along the ages, from the remote past.

"And what is their effect?" she asked. "Do they develop the faculties you wish to encourage?"

Again I remembered the claims made by the advocates of "sports," and again replied guardedly that that was, in part, the theory.

"But do the children *like* it?" I asked. "Having things

made up and set before them that way? Don't they want the old games?''

''You can see the children,'' she answered. ''Are yours more contented—more interested—happier?''

Then I thought, as in truth I never had thought before, of the dull, bored children I had seen, whining: ''What can I do now?''; of the little groups and gangs hanging about; of the value of some one strong spirit who possessed initiative and would ''start something''; of the children's parties and the onerous duties of the older people set to ''amuse the children''; also of that troubled ocean of misdirected activity we call ''mischief,'' the foolish, destructive, sometimes evil things done by unoccupied children.

''No,'' said I grimly. ''I don't think they are.''

The Herland child was born not only into a world carefully prepared, full of the most fascinating materials and opportunities to learn, but into the society of plentiful numbers of teachers, teachers born and trained, whose business it was to accompany the children along that, to us, impossible thing—the royal road to learning.

There was no mystery in their methods. Being adapted to children it was at least comprehensible to adults. I spent many days with the little ones, sometimes with Ellador, sometimes without, and began to feel a crushing pity for my own childhood, and for all others that I had known.

The houses and gardens planned for babies had in them nothing to hurt—no stairs, no corners, no small loose objects to swallow, no fire—just a babies' paradise. They were taught, as rapidly as feasible, to use and control their own bodies, and never did I see such sure-footed, steady-handed, clear-headed little things. It was a joy to watch a row of toddlers learning to walk, not only on a level floor, but, a little later, on a sort of rubber rail raised an inch or two above the soft turf or heavy rugs, and falling off with shrieks of infant joy, to rush back to the end of the line and try again. Surely we have noticed how children love to get up on something and walk along it! But we have never thought to provide that simple and inexhaustible form of amusement and physical education for the young.

Water they had, of course, and could swim even before they walked. If I feared at first the effects of a too intensive system of culture, that fear was dissipated by seeing the long sunny days of pure physical merriment and natural sleep in which these heavenly babies passed their first years. They never knew they were being educated. They did not dream that in this association of hilarious experiment and achievement they were laying the foundation for that close beautiful group feeling into which they grew so firmly with the years. This was education for citizenship.

10. Their Religions and Our Marriages

It took me a long time, as a man, a foreigner, and a species of Christian—I was that as much as anything—to get any clear understanding of the religion of Herland.

Its deification of motherhood was obvious enough; but there was far more to it than that; or, at least, than my first interpretation of that.

I think it was only as I grew to love Ellador more than I believed anyone could love anybody, as I grew faintly to appreciate her inner attitude and state of mind, that I began to get some glimpses of this faith of theirs.

When I asked her about it, she tried at first to tell me, and then, seeing me founder, asked for more information about ours. She soon found that we had many, that they varied widely, but had some points in common. A clear methodical luminous mind had my Ellador, not only reasonable, but swiftly perceptive.

She made a sort of chart, superimposing the different religions as I described them, with a pin run through them all, as it were; their common basis being a Dominant Power or Powers, and some Special Behavior, mostly taboos, to please or placate. There were some common features in certain groups of religions, but the one always present was this Power, and the things which must be done or not done because of it. It was not hard to trace our human imagery of the Divine Force up through successive stages of blood-thirsty, sensual, proud, and cruel gods of early times to the conception of a Common Father with its corollary of a Common Brotherhood.

This pleased her very much, and when I expatiated on the Omniscience, Omnipotence, Omnipresence, and so on, of our God, and of the loving kindness taught by his Son, she was much impressed.

The story of the Virgin birth naturally did not astonish her, but she was greatly puzzled by the Sacrifice, and still more by the Devil, and the theory of Damnation.

When in an inadvertent moment I said that certain sects had believed in infant damnation—and explained it—she sat very still indeed.

"They believed that God was Love—and Wisdom—and Power?"

"Yes—all of that."

Her eyes grew large, her face ghastly pale.

"And yet that such a God could put little new babies to burn—for eternity?" She fell into a sudden shuddering and left me, running swiftly to the nearest temple.

Every smallest village had its temple, and in those gracious retreats sat wise and noble women, quietly busy at some work of their own until they were wanted, always ready to give comfort, light, or help, to any applicant.

Ellador told me afterward how easily this grief of hers was assuaged, and seemed ashamed of not having helped herself out of it.

"You see, we are not accustomed to horrible ideas," she said, coming back to me rather apologetically. "We haven't any. And when we get a thing like that into our minds it's like—oh, like red pepper in your eyes. So I just ran to her, blinded and almost screaming, and she took it out so quickly—so easily!"

"How?" I asked, very curious.

"'Why, you blessed child,' she said, 'you've got the wrong idea altogether. You do not have to think that there ever was such a God—for there wasn't. Or such a happening—for there wasn't. Nor even that this hideous false idea was believed by anybody. But only this—that people who are utterly ignorant will believe anything—which you certainly knew before.'

"Anyhow," pursued Ellador, "she turned pale for a minute when I first said it."

This was a lesson to me. No wonder this whole nation of women was peaceful and sweet in expression—they had no horrible ideas.

"Surely you had some when you began," I suggested.

"Oh, yes, no doubt. But as soon as our religion grew to any height at all we left them out, of course."

From this, as from many other things, I grew to see what I finally put in words.

"Have you no respect for the past? For what was thought and believed by your foremothers?"

"Why, no," she said. "Why should we? They are all gone. They knew less than we do. If we are not beyond them, we are unworthy of them—and unworthy of the children who must go beyond us."

This set me thinking in good earnest. I had always imagined—simply from hearing it said, I suppose—that women were by nature conservative. Yet these women, quite unassisted by any masculine spirit of enterprise, had ignored their past and built daringly for the future.

Ellador watched me think. She seemed to know pretty much what was going on in my mind.

"It's because we began in a new way, I suppose. All our folks were swept away at once, and then, after that time of despair, came those wonder children—the first. And then the whole breathless hope of us was for *their* children—if they should have them. And they did! Then there was the period of pride and triumph till we grew too numerous; and after that, when it all came down to one child apiece, we began to really work—to make better ones."

"But how does this account for such a radical difference in your religion?" I persisted.

She said she couldn't talk about the difference very intelligently, not being familiar with other religions, but that theirs seemed simple enough. Their great Mother Spirit was to them what their own motherhood was—only magnified beyond human limits. That meant that they felt beneath and behind them an upholding, unfailing, serviceable love—perhaps it was really the accumulated mother-love of the race they felt—but it was a Power.

"Just what is your theory of worship?" I asked her.

"Worship? What is that?"

I found it singularly difficult to explain. This Divine Love which they felt so strongly did not seem to ask anything of them—"any more than our mothers do," she said.

"But surely your mothers expect honor, reverence, obedience, from you. You have to do things for your mothers, surely?"

"Oh, no," she insisted, smiling, shaking her soft brown hair. "We do things *from* our mothers—not *for* them. We don't have to do things *for* them—they don't need it, you know. But we have to live on—splendidly—because of them; and that's the way we feel about God."

I meditated again. I thought of that God of Battles of ours, that Jealous God, that Vengeance-is-mine God. I thought of our world-nightmare—Hell.

"You have no theory of eternal punishment then, I take it?"

Ellador laughed. Her eyes were as bright as stars, and there were tears in them, too. She was so sorry for me.

"How could we?" she asked, fairly enough. "We have no punishments in life, you see, so we don't imagine them after death."

"Have you *no* punishments? Neither for children nor criminals—such mild criminals as you have?" I urged.

"Do you punish a person for a broken leg or a fever? We have preventive measures, and cures; sometimes we have to 'send the patient to bed,' as it were; but that's not a punishment—it's only part of the treatment," she explained.

Then studying my point of view more closely, she added: "You see, we recognize, in our human motherhood, a great tender limitless uplifting force—patience and wisdom and all subtlety of delicate method. We credit God—our idea of God—with all that and more. Our mothers are not angry with us—why should God be?"

"Does God mean a person to you?"

This she thought over a little. "Why—in trying to get close to it in our minds we personify the idea, naturally; but we certainly do not assume a Big Woman somewhere, who is God. What we call God is a Pervading Power, you know, an Indwelling Spirit, something inside of us that we want more of. Is your God a Big Man?" she asked innocently.

"Why—yes, to most of us, I think. Of course we call it an Indwelling Spirit just as you do, but we insist that it is Him, a Person, and a Man—with whiskers."

"Whiskers? Oh yes—because you have them! Or do you wear them because He does?"

"On the contrary, we shave them off—because it seems cleaner and more comfortable."

"Does He wear clothes—in your idea, I mean?"

I was thinking over the pictures of God I had seen—rash advances of the devout mind of man, representing his Omnipotent Deity as an old man in a flowing robe, flowing hair, flowing beard, and in the light of her perfectly frank and innocent questions this concept seemed rather unsatisfying.

I explained that the God of the Christian world was really the ancient Hebrew God, and that we had simply taken over the patriarchal idea—that ancient one which quite inevitably clothed its thought of God with the attributes of the patriarchal ruler, the grandfather.

"I see," she said eagerly, after I had explained the genesis and development of our religious ideals. "They lived in separate groups, with a male head, and he was probably a little—domineering?"

"No doubt of that," I agreed.

"And we live together without any 'head,' in that sense— just our chosen leaders—that *does* make a difference."

"Your difference is deeper than that," I assured her. "It is in your common motherhood. Your children grow up in a world where everybody loves them. They find life made rich and happy for them by the diffused love and wisdom of all mothers. So it is easy for you to think of God in the terms of a similar diffused and competent love. I think you are far nearer right than we are."

"What I cannot understand," she pursued carefully, "is your preservation of such a very ancient state of mind. This patriarchal idea you tell me is thousands of years old?"

"Oh yes—four, five, six thousand—ever so many."

"And you have made wonderful progress in those years— in other things?"

"We certainly have. But religion is different. You see, our religions come from behind us, and are initiated by some great teacher who is dead. He is supposed to have known the whole thing and taught it, finally. All we have to do is believe—and obey."

"Who was the great Hebrew teacher?"

"Oh—there it was different. The Hebrew religion is an accumulation of extremely ancient traditions, some far older than their people, and grew by accretion down the ages. We consider it inspired—'the Word of God.' "

"How do you know it is?"

"Because it says so."

"Does it say so in as many words? Who wrote that in?"

I began to try to recall some text that did say so, and could not bring it to mind.

"Apart from that," she pursued, "what I cannot understand is why you keep these early religious ideas so long. You have changed all your others, haven't you?"

"Pretty generally," I agreed. "But this we call 'revealed religion,' and think it is final. But tell me more about these little temples of yours," I urged. "And these Temple Mothers you run to."

Then she gave me an extended lesson in applied religion, which I will endeavor to concentrate.

They developed their central theory of a Loving Power, and assumed that its relation to them was motherly—that it desired their welfare and especially their development. Their relation to it, similarly, was filial, a loving appreciation and a glad fulfillment of its high purposes. Then, being nothing if not practical, they set their keen and active minds to discover the kind of conduct expected of them. This worked out in a most admirable system of ethics. The principle of Love was universally recognized—and used.

Patience, gentleness, courtesy, all that we call "good breeding," was part of their code of conduct. But where they went far beyond us was in the special application of religious feeling to every field of life. They had no ritual, no little set of performances called "divine service," save those glorious pageants I have spoken of, and those were as much educational as religious, and as much social as either. But they had a clear established connection between everything they did—and God. Their cleanliness, their health, their exquisite order, the rich peaceful beauty of the whole land, the happiness of the children, and above all the constant progress they made—all this was their religion.

They applied their minds to the thought of God, and worked out the theory that such an inner power demanded outward expression. They lived as if God was real and at work within them.

As for those little temples everywhere—some of the women were more skilled, more temperamentally inclined, in this direction, than others. These, whatever their work might be, gave certain hours to the Temple Service, which meant being there with all their love and wisdom and trained thought, to smooth out rough places for anyone who needed it. Sometimes it was a real grief, very rarely a quarrel, most often a perplexity; even in Herland the human soul had its hours of darkness. But all through the country their best and wisest were ready to give help.

If the difficulty was unusually profound, the applicant was directed to someone more specially experienced in that line of thought.

Here was a religion which gave to the searching mind a rational basis in life, the concept of an immense Loving Power working steadily out through them, toward good. It gave to the "soul" that sense of contact with the inmost force, of perception of the uttermost purpose, which we always crave. It gave to the "heart" the blessed feeling of being loved, loved and *understood*. It gave clear, simple, rational directions as to how we should live—and why. And for ritual it gave first those triumphant group demonstrations, when with a union of all the arts, the revivifying combination of great multitudes moved rhythmically with march and dance, song and music, among their own noblest products and the open beauty of their groves and hills. Second, it gave these numerous little centers of wisdom where the least wise could go to the most wise and be helped.

"It is beautiful!" I cried enthusiastically. "It is the most practical, comforting, progressive religion I ever heard of. You *do* have one another—you *do* bear one another's burdens—you *do* realize that a little child is a type of the kingdom of heaven. You are more Christian than any people I ever saw. But—how about death? And the life everlasting? What does your religion teach about eternity?"

"Nothing," said Ellador. "What is eternity?"

What indeed? I tried, for the first time in my life, to get a real hold on the idea.

"It is—never stopping."

"Never stopping?" She looked puzzled.

"Yes, life, going on forever."

"Oh—we see that, of course. Life does go on forever, all about us."

"But eternal life goes on *without dying.* "

"The same person?"

"Yes, the same person, unending, immortal." I was pleased to think that I had something to teach from our religion, which theirs had never promulgated.

"Here?" asked Ellador. "Never to die—here?" I could

see her practical mind heaping up the people, and hurriedly reassured her.

"Oh no, indeed, not here—hereafter. We must die here, of course, but then we 'enter into eternal life.' The soul lives forever."

"How do you know?" she inquired.

"I won't attempt to prove it to you," I hastily continued. "Let us assume it to be so. How does this idea strike you?"

Again she smiled at me, that adorable, dimpling, tender, mischievous, motherly smile of hers. "Shall I be quite, quite honest?"

"You couldn't be anything else," I said, half gladly and half a little sorry. The transparent honesty of these women was a never-ending astonishment to me.

"It seems to me a singularly foolish idea," she said calmly. "And if true, most disagreeable."

Now I had always accepted the doctrine of personal immortality as a thing established. The efforts of inquiring spiritualists, always seeking to woo their beloved ghosts back again, never seemed to me necessary. I don't say I had ever seriously and courageously discussed the subject with myself even; I had simply assumed it to be a fact. And here was the girl I loved, this creature whose character constantly revealed new heights and ranges far beyond my own, this superwoman of a superland, saying she thought immortality foolish! She meant it, too.

"What do you *want* it for?" she asked.

"How can you *not* want it!" I protested. "Do you want to go out like a candle? Don't you want to go on and on—growing and—and—being happy, forever?"

"Why, no," she said. "I don't in the least. I want my child—and my child's child—to go on—and they will. Why should *I* want to?"

"But it means Heaven!" I insisted. "Peace and Beauty and Comfort and Love—with God." I had never been so eloquent on the subject of religion. She could be horrified at Damnation, and question the justice of Salvation, but Immortality—that was surely a noble faith.

"Why, Van," she said, holding out her hands to me. "Why, Van—darling! How splendid of you to feel it so keenly. That's what we all want, of course—Peace and Beauty, and Comfort and Love—with God! And Progress too, remember; Growth, always and always. That is what our religion teaches us to want and to work for, and we do!"

"But that is *here*," I said, "only for this life on earth."

"Well? And do not you in your country, with your beautiful religion of love and service have it here, too—for this life—on earth?"

None of us were willing to tell the women of Herland about the evils of our own beloved land. It was all very well for us to assume them to be necessary and essential, and to criticize—strictly among ourselves—their all-too-perfect civilization, but when it came to telling them about the failures and wastes of our own, we never could bring ourselves to do it.

Moreover, we sought to avoid too much discussion, and to press the subject of our approaching marriages.

Jeff was the determined one on this score.

"Of course they haven't any marriage ceremony or service, but we can make it a sort of Quaker wedding, and have it in the temple—it is the least we can do for them."

It was. There was so little, after all, that we could do for them. Here we were, penniless guests and strangers, with no chance even to use our strength and courage—nothing to defend them from or protect them against.

"We can at least give them our names," Jeff insisted.

They were very sweet about it, quite willing to do whatever we asked, to please us. As to the names, Alima, frank soul that she was, asked what good it would do.

Terry, always irritating her, said it was a sign of possession. "You are going to be Mrs. Nicholson," he said. "Mrs. T. O. Nicholson. That shows everyone that you are my wife."

"What is a 'wife' exactly?" she demanded, a dangerous gleam in her eye.

"A wife is the woman who belongs to a man," he began.

But Jeff took it up eagerly: "And a husband is the man who belongs to a woman. It is because we are monogamous, you know. And marriage is the ceremony, civil and religious, that joins the two together—'until death do us part,' " he finished, looking at Celis with unutterable devotion.

"What make us all feel foolish," I told the girls, "is that

here we have nothing to give you—except, of course, our names."

"Do your women have no names before they are married?" Celis suddenly demanded.

"Why, yes," Jeff explained. "They have their maiden names—their father's names, that is."

"And what becomes of them?" asked Alima.

"They change them for their husbands', my dear," Terry answered her.

"Change them? Do the husbands then take the wives' 'maiden names'?"

"Oh, no," he laughed. "The man keeps his own and gives it to her, too."

"Then she just loses hers and takes a new one—how unpleasant! We won't do that!" Alima said decidedly.

Terry was good-humored about it. "I don't care what you do or don't do so long as we have that wedding pretty soon," he said, reaching a strong brown hand after Alima's, quite as brown and nearly as strong.

"As to giving us things—of course we can see that you'd like to, but we are glad you can't," Celis continued. "You see, we love you just for yourselves—we wouldn't want you to—to pay anything. Isn't it enough to know that you are loved personally—and just as men?"

Enough or not, that was the way we were married. We had a great triple wedding in the biggest temple of all, and it looked as if most of the nation was present. It was very solemn and very beautiful. Someone had written a new song for the occasion, nobly beautiful, about the New Hope for their people—the New Tie with other lands—Brotherhood as well as Sisterhood, and, with evident awe, Fatherhood.

Terry was always restive under their talk of fatherhood. "Anybody'd think we were High Priests of—of Philoprogenitiveness!" he protested. "These women think of *nothing* but children, seems to me! We'll teach 'em!"

He was so certain of what he was going to teach, and Alima so uncertain in her moods of reception, that Jeff and I feared the worst. We tried to caution him—much good that did. The big handsome fellow drew himself up to his full height, lifted that great chest of his, and laughed.

"There are three separate marriages," he said. "I won't interfere with yours—nor you with mine."

So the great day came, and the countless crowds of

women, and we three bridegrooms without any supporting "best men," or any other men to back us up, felt strangely small as we came forward.

Somel and Zava and Moadine were on hand; we were thankful to have them, too—they seemed almost like relatives.

There was a splendid procession, wreathing dances, the new anthem I spoke of, and the whole great place pulsed with feeling—the deep awe, the sweet hope, the wondering expectation of a new miracle.

"There has been nothing like this in the country since our Motherhood began!" Somel said softly to me, while we watched the symbolic marches. "You see, it is the dawn of a new era. You don't know how much you mean to us. It is not only Fatherhood—that marvelous dual parentage to which we are strangers—the miracle of union in life-giving—but it is Brotherhood. You are the rest of the world. You join us to our kind—to all the strange lands and peoples we have never seen. We hope to know them—to love and help them—and to learn of them. Ah! You cannot know!"

Thousands of voices rose in the soaring climax of that great Hymn of The Coming Life. By the great Altar of Motherhood, with its crown of fruit and flowers, stood a new one, crowned as well. Before the Great Over Mother of the Land and her ring of High Temple Counsellors, before that vast multitude of calm-faced mothers and holy-eyed maidens, came forward our own three chosen ones, and we, three men alone in all that land, joined hands with them and made our marriage vows.

11. Our Difficulties

We say, "Marriage is a lottery"; also "Marriages are made in Heaven"—but this is not so widely accepted as the other.

We have a well-founded theory that it is best to marry "in one's class," and certain well-grounded suspicions of international marriages, which seem to persist in the interest of social progress, rather than in those of the contracting parties.

But no combination of alien races, of color, caste, or creed, was ever so basically difficult to establish as that between us, three modern American men, and these three women of Herland.

It is all very well to say that we should have been frank about it beforehand. We had been frank. We had discussed—at least Ellador and I had—the conditions of The Great Adventure, and thought the path was clear before us. But there are some things one takes for granted, supposes are mutually understood, and to which both parties may repeatedly refer without ever meaning the same thing.

The differences in the education of the average man and woman are great enough, but the trouble they make is not mostly for the man; he generally carries out his own views of the case. The woman may have imagined the conditions of married life to be different; but what she imagined, was ignorant of, or might have preferred, did not seriously matter.

I can see clearly and speak calmly about this now, writing after a lapse of years, years full of growth and education, but at the time it was rather hard sledding for all of us—especially for Terry. Poor Terry! You see, in any other imaginable marriage among the peoples of the earth, whether the woman were black, red, yellow, brown, or white; whether she were ignorant or educated, submissive or rebellious, she would have behind her the marriage tradition of our general history. This tradition relates the woman to the man. He goes on with his business, and she adapts herself to him and to it. Even in citizenship, by some strange hocus-pocus, that fact of birth and geography was waved aside, and the woman automatically acquired the nationality of her husband.

Well—here were we, three aliens in this land of women. It was small in area, and the external differences were not so great as to astound us. We did not yet appreciate the differences between the race-mind of this people and ours.

In the first place, they were a "pure stock" of two thousand uninterrupted years. Where we have some long connected lines of thought and feeling, together with a wide range of differences, often irreconcilable, these people were smoothly and firmly agreed on most of the basic principles of their life; and not only agreed in principle, but accustomed for these sixty-odd generations to act on those principles.

This is one thing which we did not understand—had made no allowance for. When in our pre-marital discussions one of those dear girls had said: "We understand it thus and thus," or "We hold such and such to be true," we men, in our own deep-seated convictions of the power of love, and our easy views about beliefs and principles, fondly imagined that we could convince them otherwise. What we imagined, before marriage, did not matter any more than what an average innocent young girl imagines. We found the facts to be different.

It was not that they did not love us; they did, deeply and warmly. But there you are again—what they meant by "love" and what we meant by "love" were so different.

Perhaps it seems rather cold-blooded to say "we" and "they," as if we were not separate couples, with our separate joys and sorrows, but our positions as aliens drove us together constantly. The whole strange experience had made our friendship more close and intimate than it would ever have become in a free and easy lifetime among our own people. Also, as men, with our masculine tradition of far more than two thousand years, we were a unit, small but firm, against this far larger unit of feminine tradition.

I think I can make clear the points of difference without a too painful explicitness. The more external disagreement was in the matter of "the home," and the housekeeping duties and pleasures we, by instinct and long education, supposed to be inherently appropriate to women.

I will give two illustrations, one away up, and the other away down, to show how completely disappointed we were in this regard.

For the lower one, try to imagine a male ant, coming from some state of existence where ants live in pairs, endeavoring to set up housekeeping with a female ant from a highly developed anthill. This female ant might regard him with intense personal affection, but her ideas of parentage and economic management would be on a very different scale from his. Now, of course, if she was a stray female in a country of pairing ants, he might have had his way with her; but if he was a stray male in an anthill—!

For the higher one, try to imagine a devoted and impassioned man trying to set up housekeeping with a lady angel, a real wings-and-harp-and-halo angel, accustomed to fulfilling divine missions all over interstellar space. This angel might love the man with an affection quite beyond his power of return or even of appreciation, but her ideas of service and duty would be on a very different scale from his. Of course, if she was a stray angel in a country of men, he might have had his way with her; but if he was a stray man among angels—!

Terry, at his worst, in a black fury for which, as a man, I must have some sympathy, preferred the ant simile. More of Terry and his special troubles later. It was hard on Terry.

Jeff—well, Jeff always had a streak that was too good for this world! He's the kind that would have made a saintly priest in earlier times. He accepted the angel theory, swallowed it whole, tried to force it on us—with varying effect. He so worshipped Celis, and not only Celis, but what she represented; he had become so deeply convinced of the almost supernatural advantages of this country and people, that he took his medicine like a—I cannot say "like a man," but more as if he wasn't one.

Don't misunderstand me for a moment. Dear old Jeff was no milksop or molly-coddle either. He was a strong, brave, efficient man, and an excellent fighter when fighting was necessary. But there was always this angel streak in him. It was rather a wonder, Terry being so different, that he really loved Jeff as he did; but it happens so sometimes, in spite of the difference—perhaps because of it.

As for me, I stood between. I was no such gay Lothario as Terry, and no such Galahad as Jeff. But for all my limitations I think I had the habit of using my brains in regard to behavior rather more frequently than either of them. I had to use brainpower now, I can tell you.

The big point at issue between us and our wives was, as may easily be imagined, in the very nature of the relation.

"Wives! Don't talk to be about wives!" stormed Terry. "They don't know what the word means."

Which is exactly the fact—they didn't. How could they? Back in their prehistoric records of polygamy and slavery there were no ideals of wifehood as we know it, and since then no possibility of forming such.

"The only thing they can think of about a man is only *Fatherhood!*" said Terry in high scorn. "*Fatherhood!* as if a man was always wanting to be a *father!*"

This also was correct. They had their long, wide, deep, rich experience of Motherhood, and their only perception of the value of a male creature as such was for Fatherhood.

Aside from that, of course, was the whole range of personal love, love which as Jeff earnestly phrased it "passeth the love of women!" It did, too. I can give no idea—either now, after long and happy experience of it, or as it seemed then, in the first measureless wonder—of the beauty and power of the love they gave us.

Even Alima—who had a more stormy temperament than either of the others, and who, heaven knows, had far more provocation—even Alima was patience and tenderness and wisdom personified to the man she loved, until he—but I haven't got to that yet.

These, as Terry put it, "alleged or so-called wives" of ours, went right on with their profession as foresters. We, having no special learnings, had long since qualified as assistants. We had to do something, if only to pass the time, and it had to be work—we couldn't be playing forever.

This kept us out of doors with those dear girls, and more or less together—too much together sometimes.

These people had, it now became clear to us, the highest, keenest, most delicate sense of personal privacy, but not the faintest idea of that *solitude à deux* we are so fond of. They had, every one of them, the "two rooms and a bath" theory realized. From earliest childhood each had a separate bedroom with toilet conveniences, and one of the marks of coming of age was the addition of an outer room in which to receive friends.

Long since we had been given our own two rooms apiece, and as being of a different sex and race, these were in a separate house. It seemed to be recognized that we should breathe easier if able to free our minds in real seclusion.

For food we either went to any convenient eating-house, ordered a meal brought in, or took it with us to the woods, always and equally good. All this we had become used to and enjoyed—in our courting days.

After marriage there arose in us a somewhat unexpected urge of feeling that called for a separate house; but this feeling found no response in the hearts of those fair ladies.

"We *are* alone, dear," Ellador explained to me with gentle patience. "We are alone in these great forests; we may go and eat in any little summer-house—just we two, or have a separate table anywhere—or even have a separate meal in our own rooms. How could we be aloner?"

This was all very true. We had our pleasant mutual solitude about our work, and our pleasant evening talks in their apartments or ours; we had, as it were, all the pleasures of courtship carried right on; but we had no sense of—perhaps it may be called possession.

"Might as well not be married at all," growled Terry, "They only got up that ceremony to please us—please Jeff, mostly. They've no real idea of being married."

I tried my best to get Ellador's point of view, and naturally I tried to give her mine. Of course, what we, as men, wanted to make them see was that there were other, and as we proudly said "higher," uses in this relation than what Terry called "mere parentage." In the highest terms I knew I tried to explain this to Ellador.

"Anything higher than for mutual love to hope to give life, as we did?" she said. "How is it higher?"

"It develops love," I explained. "All the power of beautiful permanent mated love comes through this higher development."

"Are you sure?" she asked gently. "How do you know that it was so developed? There are some birds who love each other so that they mope and pine if separated, and never pair again if one dies, but they never mate except in the mating season. Among your people do you find high and lasting affection appearing in proportion to this indulgence?''

It is a very awkward thing, sometimes, to have a logical mind.

Of course I knew about those monogamous birds and beasts too, that mate for life and show every sign of mutual affection, without ever having stretched the sex relationship beyond its original range. But what of it?

"Those are lower forms of life!" I protested. "They have no capacity for faithful and affectionate, and apparently happy—but oh, my dear! my dear!—what can they know of such a love as draws us together? Why, to touch you—to be near you—to come closer and closer—to lose myself in you—surely you feel it too, do you not?''

I came nearer. I seized her hands.

Her eyes were on mine, tender, radiant, but steady and strong. There was something so powerful, so large and changeless, in those eyes that I could not sweep her off her feet by my own emotion as I had unconsciously assumed would be the case.

It made me feel as, one might imagine, a man might feel who loved a goddess—not a Venus, though! She did not resent my attitude, did not repel it, did not in the least fear it, evidently. There was not a shade of that timid withdrawal or pretty resistance which are so—provocative.

"You see, dearest," she said, "you have to be patient with us. We are not like the women of your country. We are Mothers, and we are People, but we have not specialized in this line.''

"We" and "we" and "we"—it was so hard to get her to be personal. And, as I thought that, I suddenly remembered how we were always criticizing *our* women for *being* so personal.

Then I did my earnest best to picture to her the sweet intense joy of married lovers, and the result in higher stimulus to all creative work.

"Do you mean," she asked quite calmly, as if I was not holding her cool firm hands in my hot and rather quivering ones, "that with you, when people marry, they go right on doing this in season and out of season, with no thought of children at all?''

"They do," I said, with some bitterness. "They are not mere parents. They are men and women, and they love each other.,"

"How long?" asked Ellador, rather unexpectedly.

"How long?" I repeated, a little dashed. "Why as long as they live."

"There is something very beautiful in the idea," she admitted, still as if she were discussing life on Mars. "This climactic expression, which, in all the other life-forms, has but the one purpose, has with you become specialized to higher, purer, nobler uses. It has—I judge from what you tell me—the most ennobling effect on character. People marry, not only for parentage, but for this exquisite interchange—and, as a result, you have a world full of continuous lovers, ardent, happy, mutually devoted, always living on that high tide of supreme emotion which we had supposed to belong only to one season and one use. And you sat it has other results, stimulating all high creative work. That must mean floods, oceans of such work, blossoming from this intense happiness of every married pair! It is a beautiful idea!"

She was silent, thinking.

So was I.

She slipped one hand free, and was stroking my hair with it in a gentle motherly way. I bowed my hot head on her shoulder and felt a dim sense of peace, a restfulness which was very pleasant.

"You must take me there someday, darling," she was saying. "It is not only that I love you so much, I want to see your country—your people—your mother—" she paused reverently. "Oh, how I shall love your mother!"

I had not been in love many times—my experience did not compare with Terry's. But such as I had was so different from this that I was perplexed, and full of mixed feelings: partly a growing sense of common ground between us, a pleasant rested calm feeling, which I had imagined could only be attained in one way; and partly a bewildered resentment because what I found was not what I had looked for.

It was their confounded psychology! Here they were with this profound highly developed system of education so bred into them that even if they were not teachers by profession they all had a general proficiency in it—it was second nature to them.

And no child, stormily demanding a cookie "between meals," was ever more subtly diverted into an interest in house-building than was I when I found an apparently imperative demand had disappeared without my noticing it.

And all the time those tender mother eyes, those keen scientific eyes, noting every condition and circumstance, and learning how to "take time by the forelock" and avoid discussion before occasion arose.

I was amazed at the results. I found that much, very much, of what I had honestly supposed to be a physiological necessity was a psychological necessity—or so believed. I found, after my ideas of what was essential had changed, that my feelings changed also. And more than all, I found this—a factor of enormous weight—these women were not provocative. That made an immense difference.

The thing that Terry had so complained of when we first came—that they weren't "feminine," they lacked "charm," now became a great comfort. Their vigorous beauty was an aesthetic pleasure, not an irritant. Their dress and ornaments had not a touch of the "come-and-find-me" element.

Even with my own Ellador, my wife, who had for a time unveiled a woman's heart and faced the strange new hope and joy of dual parentage, she afterward withdrew again into the same good comrade she had been at first. They were women, *plus,* and so much plus that when they did not choose to let the womanness appear, you could not find it anywhere.

I don't say it was easy for me; it wasn't. But when I made appeal to her sympathies I came up against another immovable wall. She was sorry, honestly sorry, for my distresses, and made all manner of thoughtful suggestions, often quite useful, as well as the wise foresight I have mentioned above, which often saved all difficulty before it arose; but her sympathy did not alter her convictions.

"If I thought it was really right and necessary, I could perhaps bring myself to it, for your sake, dear; but I do not want to—not at all. You would not have a mere submission, would you? That is not the kind of high romantic love you spoke of, surely? It is a pity, of course, that you should have to adjust your highly specialized faculties to our un-specialized ones.''

Confound it! I hadn't married the nation, and I told her so. But she only smiled at her own limitations and explained that she had to ''think in we's.''

Confound it again! Here I'd have all my energies focused on one wish, and before I knew it she'd have them dissipated in one direction or another, some subject of discussion that began just at the point I was talking about and ended miles away.

It must not be imagined that I was just repelled, ignored, left to cherish a grievance. Not at all. My happiness was in the hands of a larger, sweeter womanhood than I had ever imagined. Before our marriage my own ardor had perhaps blinded me to much of this. I was madly in love with not so much what was there as with what I supposed to be there. Now I found an endlessly beautiful undiscovered country to explore, and in it the sweetest wisdom and understanding. It was as if I had come to some new place and people, with a desire to eat at all hours, and no other interests in partic-ular; and as if my hosts, instead of merely saying, ''You shall not eat,'' had presently aroused in me a lively desire for music, for pictures, for games, for exercise, for playing in the water, for running some ingenious machine; and, in the multitude of my satisfactions, I forgot the one point which was not satisfied, and got along very well until meal-time.

One of the cleverest and most ingenious of these tricks was only clear to me many years after, when we were so wholly at one on this subject that I could laugh at my own predicament then. It was this: You see, with us, women are kept as different as possible and as feminine as possible. We men have our own world, with only men in it; we get tired of our ultra-maleness and turn gladly to the ultra-femaleness. Also, in keeping our women as feminine as possible, we see to it that when we turn to them we find the thing we want always in evidence. Well, the atmosphere of this place was anything but seductive. The very numbers of these human women, always in human relation, made them anything but alluring. When, in spite of this, my hereditary instincts and race-traditions made me long for the feminine response in Ellador, instead of withdrawing so that I should want her more, she deliberately gave me a little too much of her society—always de-feminized, as it were. It was awfully funny, really.

Here was I, with an Ideal in mind, for which I hotly longed, and here was she, deliberately obtruding in the foreground of my consciousness a Fact—a fact which I coolly enjoyed, but which actually interfered with what I wanted. I see now clearly enough why a certain kind of man, like Sir Almroth Wright, resents the professional development of women. It gets in the way of the sex ideal; it temporarily covers and excludes femininity.

Of course, in this case, I was so fond of Ellador my friend, of Ellador my professional companion, that I necessarily enjoyed her society on any terms. Only—when I had had her with me in her de-feminine capacity for a sixteen-hour day, I could go to my own room and sleep without dreaming about her.

The witch! If ever anybody worked to woo and win and hold a human soul, she did, great superwoman that she was. I couldn't then half comprehend the skill of it, the wonder. But this I soon began to find: that under all our cultivated attitude of mind toward women, there is an older, deeper, more ''natural'' feeling, the restful reverence which looks up to the Mother sex.

So we grew together in friendship and happiness, Ellador and I, and so did Jeff and Celis.

When it comes to Terry's part of it, and Alima's, I'm sorry—and I'm ashamed. Of course I blame her somewhat. She wasn't as fine a psychologist as Ellador, and what's more, I think she had a far-descended atavistic trace of more marked femaleness, never apparent till Terry called it out. But when all that is said, it doesn't excuse him. I hadn't realized to the full Terry's character—I couldn't, being a man.

The position was the same as with us, of course, only with these distinctions: Alima, a shade more alluring, and several shades less able as a practical psychologist; Terry, a hundredfold more demanding—and proportionately less reasonable.

Things grew strained very soon between them. I fancy at first, when they were together, in her great hope of parentage and his keen joy of conquest—that Terry was inconsiderate. In fact, I know it, from things he said.

''You needn't talk to me,'' he snapped at Jeff one day,

just before our weddings. "There never was a woman yet that did not enjoy being *mastered*. All your pretty talk doesn't amount to a hill o'beans—I *know*." And Terry would hum:

> *I've taken my fun where I found it.*
> *I've rogued and I've ranged in my time,*

and

> *The things that I learned from the yellow and black,*
> *They 'ave helped me a 'eap with the white.*

Jeff turned sharply and left him at the time. I was a bit disquieted myself.

Poor old Terry! The things he'd learned didn't help him a heap in Herland. His idea was to take—he thought that was the way. He thought, he honestly believed, that women like it. Not the women of Herland! Not Alima!

I can see her now—one day in the very first week of their marriage, setting forth to her day's work with long determined strides and hard-set mouth, and sticking close to El lador. She didn't wish to be alone with Terry—you could see that.

But the more she kept away from him, the more he wanted her—naturally.

He made a tremendous row about their separate establishments, tried to keep her in his rooms, tried to stay in hers. But there she drew the line sharply.

He came away one night, and stamped up and down the moonlit road, swearing under his breath. I was taking a walk that night too, but I wasn't in his state of mind. To hear him rage you'd not have believed that he loved Alima at all—you'd have thought that she was some quarry he was pursuing, something to catch and conquer.

I think that, owing to all those differences I spoke of, they soon lost the common ground they had at first, and were unable to meet sanely and dispassionately. I fancy too—this is pure conjecture—that he had succeeded in driving Alima beyond her best judgment, her real conscience, and that after that her own sense of shame, the reaction of the thing, made her bitter perhaps.

They quarreled, really quarreled, and after making it up

once or twice, they seemed to come to a real break—she would not be alone with him at all. And perhaps she was a bit nervous, I don't know, but she got Moadine to come and stay next door to her. Also, she had a sturdy assistant detailed to accompany her in her work.

Terry had his own ideas, as I've tried to show. I daresay he thought he had a right to do as he did. Perhaps he even convinced himself that it would be better for her. Anyhow, he hid himself in her bedroom one night . . .

The women of Herland have no fear of men. Why should they have? They are not timid in any sense. They are not weak; and they all have strong trained athletic bodies. Othello could not have extinguished Alima with a pillow, as if she were a mouse.

Terry put in practice his pet conviction that a woman loves to be mastered, and by sheer brute force, in all the pride and passion of his intense masculinity, he tried to master this woman.

It did not work. I got a pretty clear account of it later from Ellador, but what we heard at the time was the noise of a tremendous struggle, and Alima calling to Moadine. Moadine was close by and came at once; one or two more strong grave women followed.

Terry dashed about like a madman; he would cheerfully have killed them—he told me that, himself—but he couldn't. When he swung a chair over his head one sprang in the air and caught it, two threw themselves bodily upon him and forced him to the floor; it was only the work of a few moments to have him tied hand and foot, and then, in sheer pity for his futile rage, to anesthetize him.

Alima was in a cold fury. She wanted him killed—actually.

There was a trial before the local Over Mother, and this woman, who did not enjoy being mastered, stated her case.

In a court in our country he would have been held quite "within his rights," of course. But this was not our country; it was theirs. They seemed to measure the enormity of the offense by its effect upon a possible fatherhood, and he scorned even to reply to this way of putting it.

He did let himself go once, and explained in definite terms that they were incapable of understanding a man's needs, a man's desires, a man's point of view. He called them neuters, epicenes, bloodless, sexless creatures. He said they could of course kill him—as so many insects could—but that he despised them nonetheless.

And all those stern grave mothers did not seem to mind his despising them, not in the least.

It was a long trial, and many interesting points were brought out as to their views of our habits, and after a while Terry had his sentence. He waited, grim and defiant. The sentence was: ''You must go home!''

12. Expelled

We had all meant to go home again. Indeed we had *not* meant—not by any means—to stay as long as we had. But when it came to being turned out, dismissed, sent away for bad conduct, we none of us really liked it.

Terry said he did. He professed great scorn of the penalty and the trial, as well as all the other characteristics of "this miserable half-country." But he knew, and we knew, that in any "whole" country we should never have been as forgivingly treated as we had been here.

"If the people had come after us according to the directions we left, there'd have been quite a different story!" said Terry. We found out later why no reserve party had arrived. All our careful directions had been destroyed in a fire. We might have all died there and no one at home have ever known our whereabouts.

Terry was under guard now, all the time, known as unsafe, convicted of what was to them an unpardonable sin.

He laughed at their chill horror. "Parcel of old maids!" he called them. "They're all old maids—children or not. They don't know the first thing about Sex."

When Terry said *Sex*, sex with a very large *S*, he meant the male sex, naturally; its special values, its profound conviction of being "the life force," its cheerful ignoring of the true life process, and its interpretation of the other sex solely from its own point of view.

I had learned to see these things very differently since living with Ellador; and as for Jeff, he was so thoroughly Herlandized that he wasn't fair to Terry, who fretted sharply in his restraint.

Moadine, grave and strong, as sadly patient as a mother

with a degenerate child, kept steady watch on him, with enough other women close at hand to prevent an outbreak. He had no weapons, and well knew that all his strength was of small avail against those grim, quiet women.

We were allowed to visit him freely, but he had only his room, and a small high-walled garden to walk in, while the preparations for our departure were under way.

Three of us were to go: Terry, because he must; I, because two were safer for our flyer, and the long boat trip to the coast; Ellador, because she would not let me go without her.

If Jeff had elected to return, Celis would have gone too—they were the most absorbed of lovers; but Jeff had no desire that way.

"Why should I want to go back to all our noise and dirt, our vice and crime, our disease and degeneracy?" he demanded of me privately. We never spoke like that before the women. "I wouldn't take Celis there for anything on earth!" he protested. "She'd die! She'd die of horror and shame to see our slums and hospitals. How can you risk it with Ellador? You'd better break it to her gently before she really makes up her mind."

Jeff was right. I ought to have told her more fully than I did; of all the things we had to be ashamed of. But it is very hard to bridge the gulf of as deep a difference as existed between our life and theirs. I tried to.

"Look here, my dear," I said to her. "If you are really going to my country with me, you've got to be prepared for a good many shocks. It's not as beautiful as this—the cities, I mean, the civilized parts—of course the wild country is."

"I shall enjoy it all," she said, her eyes starry with hope. "I understand it's not like ours. I can see how monotonous our quiet life must seem to you, how much more stirring yours must be. It must be like the biological change you told me about when the second sex was introduced—a far greater movement, constant change, with new possibilities of growth."

I had told her of the later biological theories of sex, and she was deeply convinced of the superior advantages of having two, the superiority of a world with men in it.

"We have done what we could alone; perhaps we have some things better in a quiet way, but you have the whole world—all the people of the different nations—all the long rich history behind you—all the wonderful new knowledge. Oh, I just can't wait to see it!''

What could I do? I told her in so many words that we had our unsolved problems, that we had dishonesty and corruption, vice and crime, disease and insanity, prisons and hospitals; and it made no more impression on her than it would to tell a South Sea Islander about the temperature of the Arctic Circle. She could intellectually see that it was bad to have those things; but she could not *feel* it.

We had quite easily come to accept the Herland life as normal, because it was normal—none of us make any outcry over mere health and peace and happy industry. And the abnormal, to which we are all so sadly well acclimated, she had never seen.

The two things she cared most to hear about, and wanted most to see, were these: the beautiful relation of marriage and the lovely women who were mothers and nothing else; beyond these her keen, active mind hungered eagerly for the world life.

''I'm almost as anxious to go as you are yourself,'' she insisted, ''and you must be desperately homesick.''

I assured her that no one could be homesick in such a paradise as theirs, but she would have none of it.

''Oh, yes—I know. It's like those little tropical islands you've told me about, shining like jewels in the big blue sea—I can't wait to see the sea! The little island may be as perfect as a garden, but you always want to get back to your own big country, don't you? Even if it is bad in some ways?''

Ellador was more than willing. But the nearer it came to our really going, and to my having to take her back to our ''civilization,'' after the clean peace and beauty of theirs, the more I began to dread it, and the more I tried to explain.

Of course I had been homesick at first, while we were prisoners, before I had Ellador. And of course I had, at first, rather idealized my country and its ways, in describing it. Also, I had always accepted certain evils as integral parts of our civilization and never dwelt on them at all. Even when I tried to tell her the worst, I never remembered some things—which, when she came to see them, impressed her at once, as they had never impressed me. Now, in my efforts at explanation, I began to see both ways more keenly than I had before; to see the painful defects of my own land, the marvelous gains of this.

In missing men we three visitors had naturally missed the larger part of life, and had unconsciously assumed that they must miss it too. It took me a long time to realize—Terry never did realize—how little it meant to them. When we say *men, man, manly, manhood,* and all the other masculine derivatives, we have in the background of our minds a huge vague crowded picture of the world and all its activities. To grow up and "be a man," to "act like a man"—the meaning and connotation is wide indeed. That vast background is full of marching columns of men, of changing lines of men, of long processions of men; of men steering their ships into new seas, exploring unknown mountains, breaking horses, herding cattle, ploughing and sowing and reaping, toiling at the forge and furnace, digging in the mine, building roads and bridges and high cathedrals, managing great businesses, teaching in all the colleges, preaching in all the churches; of men everywhere, doing everything—"the world."

And when we say *women,* we think *female*—the sex.

But to these women, in the unbroken sweep of this two-thousand-year-old feminine civilization, the word *woman* called up all that big background, so far as they had gone in social development; and the word *man* meant to them only *male*—the sex.

Of course we could *tell* them that in our world men did everything; but that did not alter the background of their minds. That man, "the male," did all these things was to them a statement, making no more change in the point of view than was made in ours when we first faced the astounding fact—to us—that in Herland women were "the world."

We had been living there more than a year. We had learned their limited history, with its straight, smooth, unpreaching lines, reaching higher and going faster up to the smooth comfort of their present life. We had learned a little of their psychology, a much wider field than the history, but here we could not follow so readily. We were now well used to seeing women not as females but as people; people of all sorts, doing every kind of work.

This outbreak of Terry's, and the strong reaction against it, gave us a new light on their genuine femininity. This was given me with great clearness by both Ellador and Somel. The feeling was the same—sick revulsion and horror, such as would be felt at some climactic blasphemy.

They had no faintest approach to such a thing in their minds, knowing nothing of the custom of marital indulgence among us. To them the one high purpose of motherhood had been for so long the governing law of life, and the contribution of the father, though known to them, so distinctly another method to the same end, that they could not, with all their effort, get the point of view of the male creature whose desires quite ignore parentage and seek only for what we euphoniously term "the joys of love."

When I tried to tell Ellador that women too felt so, with us, she drew away from me, and tried hard to grasp intellectually what she could in no way sympathize with.

"You mean—that with you—love between man and woman expresses itself in that way—without regard to motherhood? To parentage, I mean," she added carefully.

"Yes, surely. It is love we think of—the deep sweet love between two. Of course we want children, and children come—but that is not what we think about."

"But—but—it seems so against nature!" she said. "None of the creatures we know do that. Do other animals—in your country?"

"We are not animals!" I replied with some sharpness. "At least we are something more—something higher. This is a far nobler and more beautiful relation, as I have explained before. Your view seems to us rather—shall I say, practical? Prosaic? Merely a means to an end! With us—oh, my dear girl—cannot you see? Cannot you feel? It is the last, sweetest, highest consummation of mutual love."

She was impressed visibly. She trembled in my arms, as I held her close, kissing her hungrily. But there rose in her eyes that look I knew so well, that remote clear look as if she had gone far away even though I held her beautiful body so close, and was now on some snowy mountain regarding me from a distance.

"I feel it quite clearly," she said to me. "It gives me a deep sympathy with what you feel, no doubt more strongly still. But what I feel, even what you feel, dearest, does not convince me that it is right. Until I am sure of that, of course I cannot do as you wish."

Ellador, at times like this, always reminded me of Epictetus. "I will put you in prison!" said his master. "My body, you mean," replied Epictetus calmly. "I will cut your head off," said his master. "Have I said that my head could not be cut off?" A difficult person, Epictetus.

What is this miracle by which a woman, even in your arms, may withdraw herself, utterly disappear till what you hold is as inaccessible as the face of a cliff?

"Be patient with me, dear," she urged sweetly. "I know it is hard for you. And I begin to see—a little—how Terry was so driven to crime."

"Oh, come, that's a pretty hard word for it. After all, Alima was his wife, you know," I urged, feeling at the moment a sudden burst of sympathy for poor Terry. For a man of his temperament—and habits—it must have been an unbearable situation.

But Ellador, for all her wide intellectual grasp, and the broad sympathy in which their religion trained them, could not make allowance for such—to her—sacrilegious brutality.

It was the more difficult to explain to her, because we three, in our constant talks and lectures about the rest of the world, had naturally avoided the seamy side; not so much from a desire to deceive, but from wishing to put the best foot foremost for our civilization, in the face of the beauty and comfort of theirs. Also, we really thought some things were right, or at least unavoidable, which we could readily see would be repugnant to them, and therefore did not discuss. Again there was much of our world's life which we, being used to it, had not noticed as anything worth describing. And still further, there was about these women a colossal innocence upon which many of the things we did say had made no impression whatever.

I am thus explicit about it because it shows how unexpectedly strong was the impression made upon Ellador when she at last entered our civilization.

She urged me to be patient, and I was patient. You see, I loved her so much that even the restrictions she so firmly established left me much happiness. We were lovers, and there is surely delight enough in that.

Do not imagine that these young women utterly refused "the Great New Hope," as they called it, that of dual parentage. For that they had agreed to marry us, though the marrying part of it was a concession to our prejudices rather than theirs. To them the process was the holy thing—and they meant to keep it holy.

But so far only Celis, her blue eyes swimming in happy tears, her heart lifted with that tide of race-motherhood which was their supreme passion, could with ineffable joy and pride announce that she was to be a mother. "The New Motherhood" they called it, and the whole country knew. There was no pleasure, no service, no honor in all the land that Celis might not have had. Almost like the breathless reverence with which, two thousand years ago, that dwindling band of women had watched the miracle of virgin birth, was the deep awe and warm expectancy with which they greeted this new miracle of union.

All mothers in that land were holy. To them, for long ages, the approach to motherhood has been by the most intense and exquisite love and longing, by the Supreme Desire, the overmastering demand for a child. Every thought they held in connection with the processes of maternity was open to the day, simple yet sacred. Every woman of them placed motherhood not only higher than other duties, but so far higher that there were no other duties, one might almost say. All their wide mutual love, all the subtle interplay of mutual friendship and service, the urge of progressive thought and invention, the deepest religious emotion, every feeling and every act was related to this great central Power, to the River of Life pouring through them, which made them the bearers of the very Spirit of God.

Of all this I learned more and more—from their books, from talk, especially from Ellador. She was at first, for a brief moment, envious of her friend—a thought she put away from her at once and forever.

"It is better," she said to me. "It is much better that it has not come to me yet—to us, that is. For if I am to go with you to your country, we may have 'adventures by sea and land,' as you say [and as in truth we did], and it might not be at all safe for a baby. So we won't try again, dear, till it is safe—will we?"

This was a hard saying for a very loving husband.

"Unless," she went on, "if one is coming, you will leave me behind. You can come back, you know—and I shall have the child."

Then that deep ancient chill of male jealousy of even his own progeny touched my heart.

"I'd rather have you, Ellador, than all the children in the

world. I'd rather have you with me—on your own terms—than not to have you.''

This was a very stupid saying. Of course I would! For if she wasn't there I should want all of her and have none of her. But if she went along as a sort of sublimated sister—only much closer and warmer than that, really—why I should have all of her but that one thing. And I was beginning to find that Ellador's friendship, Ellador's comradeship, Ellador's sisterly affection, Ellador's perfectly sincere love—none the less deep that she held it back on a definite line of reserve—were enough to live on very happily.

I find it quite beyond me to describe what this woman was to me. We talk fine things about women, but in our hearts we know that they are very limited beings—most of them. We honor them for their functional powers, even while we dishonor them by our use of it; we honor them for their carefully enforced virtue, even while we show by our own conduct how little we think of that virtue; we value them, sincerely, for the perverted maternal activities which make our wives the most comfortable of servants, bound to us for life with the wages wholly at our own decision, their whole business, outside of the temporary duties of such motherhood as they may achieve, to meet our needs in every way. Oh, we value them, all right, "in their place,'' which place is the home, where they perform that mixture of duties so ably described by Mrs. Josephine Dodge Daskam Bacon, in which the services of "a mistress'' are carefully specified. She is a very clear writer, Mrs. J. D. D. Bacon, and understands her subject—from her own point of view. But—that combination of industries, while convenient, and in a way economical, does not arouse the kind of emotion commanded by the women of Herland. These were women one had to love "up,'' very high up, instead of down. They were not pets. They were not servants. They were not timid, inexperienced, weak.

After I got over the jar to my pride (which Jeff, I truly think, never felt—he was a born worshipper, and which Terry never got over—he was quite clear in his ideas of "the position of women''), I found that loving "up'' was a very good sensation after all. It gave me a queer feeling, way down deep, as of the stirring of some ancient dim prehistoric consciousness, a feeling that they were right somehow—that this was the way to feel. It was like—coming home to mother. I don't mean the underflannels-and-doughnuts mother, the fussy person that waits on you and spoils you and doesn't really know you. I mean the feeling that a very little child would have, who had been lost—for ever so long. It was a sense of getting home; of being clean and rested; of safety and yet freedom; of love that was always there, warm like sunshine in May, not hot like a stove or a featherbed—a love that didn't irritate and didn't smother.

I looked at Ellador as if I hadn't seen her before. "If you won't go," I said, "I'll get Terry to the coast and come back alone. You can let me down a rope. And if you will go—why you blessed wonder-woman—I would rather live with you all my life—like this—than to have any other woman I ever saw, or any number of them, to do as I like with. Will you come?"

She was keen for coming. So the plans went on. She'd have liked to wait for that Marvel of Celis's, but Terry had no such desire. He was crazy to be out of it all. It made him sick, he said, *sick;* this everlasting mother-mother-mothering. I don't think Terry had what the phrenologists call "the lump of philoprogenitiveness" at all well developed.

"Morbid one-sided cripples," he called them, even when from his window he could see their splendid vigor and beauty; even while Moadine, as patient and friendly as if she had never helped Alima to hold and bind him, sat there in the room, the picture of wisdom and serene strength. "Sexless, epicene, undeveloped neuters!" he went on bitterly. He sounded like Sir Almwroth Wright.

Well—it was hard. He was madly in love with Alima, really; more so than he had ever been before, and their tempestuous courtship, quarrels, and reconciliations had fanned the flame. And then when he sought by that supreme conquest which seems so natural a thing to that type of man, to force her to love him as her master—to have the sturdy athletic furious woman rise up and master him—she and her friends—it was no wonder he raged.

Come to think of it, I do not recall a similar case in all history or fiction. Women have killed themselves rather than submit to outrage; they have killed the outrager; they have escaped; or they have submitted—sometimes seeming to get on very well with the victor afterward. There was that adventure of "false Sextus," for instance, who "found Lucrese combing the fleece, under the midnight lamp." He threatened, as I remember, that if she did not submit he would slay her, slay a slave and place him beside her and say he found him there. A poor device, it always seemed to me. If Mr. Lucretius had asked him how he came to be in his wife's bedroom overlooking her morals, what could he have said? But the point is Lucrese submitted, and Alima didn't.

"She kicked me," confided the embittered prisoner—he had to talk to someone. "I was doubled up with the pain, of course, and she jumped on me and yelled for this old harpy [Moadine couldn't hear him] and they had me trussed up in no time. I believe Alima could have done it alone," he added with reluctant admiration. "She's as strong as a horse. And of course a man's helpless when you hit him like that. No woman with a shade of decency—"

I had to grin at that, and even Terry did, sourly. He wasn't given to reasoning, but it did strike him that an assault like his rather waived considerations of decency.

"I'd give a year of my life to have her alone again," he said slowly, his hands clenched till the knuckles were white.

But he never did. She left our end of the country entirely, went up into the fir-forest on the highest slopes, and stayed there. Before we left he quite desperately longed to see her, but she would not come and he could not go. They watched him like lynxes. (Do lynxes watch any better than mousing cats, I wonder!)

Well—we had to get the flyer in order, and be sure there was enough fuel left, though Terry said we could glide all right, down to that lake, once we got started. We'd have gone gladly in a week's time, of course, but there was a great to-do all over the country about Ellador's leaving them. She had interviews with some of the leading ethicists—wise women with still eyes, and with the best of the teachers. There was a stir, a thrill, a deep excitement everywhere.

Our teaching about the rest of the world has given them all a sense of isolation, of remoteness, of being a little outlying sample of a country, overlooked and forgotten among the family of nations. We had called it "the family of nations," and they liked the phrase immensely.

They were deeply aroused on the subject of evolution; indeed, the whole field of natural science drew them irresistibly. Any number of them would have risked everything to go to the strange unknown lands and study; but we could take only one, and it had to be Ellador, naturally.

We planned greatly about coming back, about establishing a connecting route by water; about penetrating those vast forests and civilizing—or exterminating—the dangerous savages. That is, we men talked of that last—not with the women. They had a definite aversion to killing things.

But meanwhile there was high council being held among the wisest of them all. The students and thinkers who had been gathering facts from us all this time, collating and relating them, and making inferences, laid the result of their labors before the council.

Little had we thought that our careful efforts at concealment had been so easily seen through, with never a word to show us that they saw. They had followed up words of ours on the science of optics, asked innocent questions about glasses and the like, and were aware of the defective eyesight so common among us.

With the lightest touch, different women asking different questions at different times, and putting all our answers together like a picture puzzle, they had figured out a sort of skeleton chart as to the prevalence of disease among us. Even more subtly with no show of horror or condemnation, they had gathered something—far from the truth, but something pretty clear—about poverty, vice, and crime. They even had a goodly number of our dangers all itemized, from asking us about insurance and innocent things like that.

They were well posted as to the different races, beginning with their poison-arrow natives down below and widening out to the broad racial divisions we had told them about. Never a shocked expression of the face or exclamation of revolt had warned us; they had been extracting the evidence without our knowing it all this time, and now were studying with the most devout earnestness the matter they had prepared.

The result was rather distressing to us. They first explained the matter fully to Ellador, as she was the one who purposed visiting the Rest of the World. To Celis they said nothing. She must not be in any way distressed, while the whole nation waited on her Great Work.

Finally Jeff and I were called in. Somel and Zava were there, and Ellador, with many others that we knew.

They had a great globe, quite fairly mapped out from the small section maps in that compendium of ours. They had the different peoples of the earth roughly outlined, and their status in civilization indicated. They had charts and figures and estimates, based on the facts in that traitorous little book and what they had learned from us.

Somel explained: ''We find that in all your historic period, so much longer than ours, that with all the interplay of services, the exchange of inventions and discoveries, and the wonderful progress we so admire, that in this widespread Other World of yours, there is still much disease, often contagious.''

We admitted this at once.

''Also there is still, in varying degree, ignorance, with prejudice and unbridled emotion.''

This too was admitted.

''We find also that in spite of the advance of democracy and the increase of wealth, that there is still unrest and sometimes combat.''

Yes, yes, we admitted it all. We were used to these things and saw no reason for so much seriousness.

''All things considered,'' they said, and they did not say a hundredth part of the things they were considering, ''we are unwilling to expose our country to free communication with the rest of the world—as yet. If Ellador comes back, and we approve her report, it may be done later—but not yet.

''So we have this to ask of you gentlemen [they knew that word was held a title of honor with us], that you promise not in any way to betray the location of this country until permission—after Ellador's return.''

Jeff was perfectly satisfied. He thought they were quite right. He always did. I never saw an alien become naturalized more quickly than that man in Herland.

I studied it awhile, thinking of the time they'd have if some of our contagions got loose there, and concluded they were right. So I agreed.

Terry was the obstacle. ''Indeed I won't!'' he protested. ''The first thing I'll do is to get an expedition fixed up to force an entrance into Ma-land.''

''Then,'' they said quite calmly, ''he must remain an absolute prisoner, always.''

''Anesthesia would be kinder,'' urged Moadine.

"And safer," added Zava.

"He will promise, I think," said Ellador.

And he did. With which agreement we at last left Herland.

Selected Stories

THE UNEXPECTED

I.

"It is the unexpected which happens," says the French proverb. I like the proverb, because it is true—and because it is French.

Edouard Charpentier is my name.

I am an American by birth, but that is all. From infancy, when I had a French nurse; in childhood, when I had a French governess; through youth, passed in a French school; to manhood, devoted to French art, I have been French by sympathy and education.

France—modern France—and French art—modern French art—I adore!

My school is the "pleine-aire," and my master, could I but find him, is M. Duchesne. M. Duchesne has had pictures in the Salon for three years, and pictures elsewhere, eagerly bought, and yet Paris knows not M. Duchesne. We know his house, his horse, his carriage, his servants and his garden-wall, but he sees no one, speaks to no one; indeed, he has left Paris for a time, and we worship afar off.

I have a sketch by this master which I treasure jealously— a pencil sketch of a great picture yet to come. I await it.

M. Duchesne paints from the model, and I paint from the model, exclusively. It is the only way to be firm, accurate, true. Without the model we may have German fantasy or English domesticity, but no modern French art.

It is hard, too, to get models continually when one is but a student after five years' work, and one's pictures bring francs indeed, but not dollars.

Still, there is Georgette!

There, also, were Emilie and Pauline. But now it is Georgette, and she is adorable!

'Tis true, she has not much soul; but, then, she has a charming body, and 'tis that I copy.

Georgette and I get on together to admiration. How much better is this than matrimony for an artist! How wise is M. Daudet!

Antoine is my dearest friend. I paint with him, and we are happy. Georgette is my dearest model. I paint from her, and we are happy.

Into this peaceful scene comes a letter from America, bringing much emotion.

It appears I had a great-uncle there, in some northeastern corner of New England. Maine? No; Vermont.

And it appears, strangely enough, that this northeastern great-uncle was seized in his old age with a passion for French art; at least I know not how else to account for his hunting me up through a lawyer and leaving me some quarter of a million when he died.

An admirable great-uncle!

But I must go home and settle the property; that is imperative. I must leave Paris, I must leave Antoine, I must leave Georgette!

Could anything be further from Paris than a town in Vermont? No, not the Andaman Islands.

And could anything be further from Antoine and Georgette than the family of great-cousins I find myself among?

But one of them, ah, Heaven! some forty-seventh cousin who is so beautiful that I forget she is an American, I forget Paris, I forget Antoine—yes, and even Georgette! Poor Georgette! But this is fate.

This cousin is not like the other cousins. I pursue, I inquire, I ascertain.

Her name is Mary D. Greenleaf. I shall call her Marie.

And she comes from Boston.

But, beyond the name, how can I describe her? I have seen beauty, yes, much beauty, in maid, matron and model, but I never saw anything to equal this country girl. What a figure!

No, not a "figure"—the word shames her. She has a body, the body of a young Diana, and a body and a figure are two very different things. I am an artist, and I have lived in Paris, and I know the difference.

The lawyers in Boston can settle that property, I find.

The air is delightful in northern Vermont in March. There are mountains, clouds, trees. I will paint here a while. Ah, yes; and I will assist this shy young soul!

"Cousin Marie," say I, "come, let me teach you to paint!"

"It would be too difficult for you, Mr. Carpenter—it would take too long!"

"Call me Edouard!" I cry. "Are we not cousins? Cousin Edouard, I beg of you! And nothing is difficult when you are with me, Marie—nothing can be too long at your side!"

"Thanks, cousin Edward, but I think I will not impose on your good nature. Besides, I shall not stay here. I go back to Boston, to my aunt."

I find the air of Boston is good in March, and there are places of interest there, and rising American artists who deserve encouragement. I will stay in Boston a while to assist the lawyers in settling my property; it is necessary.

I visit Marie continually. Am I not a cousin?

I talk to her of life, of art, of Paris, of M. Duchesne. I show her my precious sketch.

"But," says she, "I am not wholly a wood nymph, as you seem fondly to imagine. I have been to Paris myself—with my uncle—years since."

"Fairest cousin," say I, "if you had not been even to Boston, I should still love you! Come and see Paris again—with me!" And then she would laugh at me and send me away. Ah, yes! I had come even to marriage, you see!

I soon found she had the usual woman's faith in those conventions. I gave her "Artists' Wives." She said she had read it. She laughed at Daudet and me!

I talked to her of ruined geniuses I had known myself, but she said a ruined genius was no worse than a ruined woman! One cannot reason with young girls!

Do not believe I succumbed without a struggle. I even tore myself away and went to New York. It was not far enough, I fear. I soon came back.

She lived with an aunt—my adorable little precisian!—with a horrible strong-minded aunt, and such a life as I led between them for a whole month!

I call continually. I bury her in flowers. I take her to the theatre, aunt and all. And at this the aunt seemed greatly surprised, but I disapprove of American familiarities. No;

my wife—and wife she must be—shall be treated with punctilious respect.

Never was I so laughed at and argued with in my life as I was laughed at by that dreadful beauty, and argued with by that dreadful aunt.

The only rest was in pictures. Marie would look at pictures always, and seemed to have a real appreciation of them, almost an understanding, of a sort. So that I began to hope—dimly and faintly to hope—that she might grow to care for mine. To have a wife who would care for one's art, who would come to one's studio—but, then, the models! I paint from the model almost entirely, as I said, and *I* know what women are about models, without Daudet to tell me!

And this prudish New England girl! Well, she might come to the studio on stated days, and perhaps in time I might lead her gently to understand.

That I should ever live to commit matrimony!

But Fate rules all men.

I think that girl refused me nine times. She always put me off with absurd excuses and reasons: said I didn't know her yet; said we should never agree; said I was French and she was American; said I cared more for art than I did for her! At that I earnestly assured her that I would become an organ-grinder or a bank-clerk rather than lose her—and then she seemed downright angry, and sent me away again.

Women are strangely inconsistent!

She always sent me away, but I always came back.

After about a month of this torture, I chanced to find her, one soft May twilight, without the aunt, sitting by a window in the fragrant dusk.

She had flowers in her hand—flowers I had sent her—and sat looking down at them, her strong, pure profile clear against the saffron sky.

I came in quietly, and stood watching, in a rapture of hope and admiration. And while I watched I saw a great pearl tear roll down among my violets.

That was enough.

I sprang forward, I knelt beside her, I caught her hands in mine, I drew her to me, I cried, exultantly: "You love me! And I—ah, God! how I love you!"

Even then she would have put me from her. She insisted that I did not know her yet, that she ought to tell me—but

I held her close and kissed away her words, and said: "You love me, perfect one, and I love you. The rest will be right."

Then she laid her white hands on my shoulders, and looked deep into my eyes.

"I believe that is true," said she; "and I will marry you, Edward."

She dropped her face on my shoulder then—that face of fire and roses—and we were still.

II.

It is but two months' time from then; I have been married a fortnight. The first week was heaven—and the second was hell! O my God! my wife! That young Diana to be but—! I have borne it a week. I have feared and despised myself. I have suspected and hated myself. I have discovered and cursed myself. Aye, and cursed her, and *him*, whom this day I shall kill!

It is now three o'clock. I cannot kill him until four, for he comes not till then.

I am very comfortable here in this room opposite—very comfortable; and I can wait and think and remember.

Let me think.

First, to kill him. That is simple and easily settled.

Shall I kill her?

If she lived, could I ever see her again? Ever touch that hand—those lips—that, within two weeks of marriage—? No, she shall die!

And, if she lived, what would be before her but more shame, and more, till she felt it herself?

Far better that she die!

And I?

Could I live to forget her? To carry always in my heart a black stone across that door? To rise and rise, and do great work—*alone?*

Never! I cannot forget her!

Better die with her, even now.

Hark! Is that a step on the stair? Not yet.

My money is well bestowed. Antoine is a better artist than I, and a better man, and the money will widen and lighten a noble life in his hands.

And little Georgette is provided for. How long ago, how

faint and weak, that seems! But Georgette loved me, I believe, at least for a time—longer than a week.

To wait—until four o'clock!

To think—I have thought; it is all arranged!

These pistols, that she admired but day before yesterday, that we practised with together, both loaded full. What a shot she is! I believe she can do everything!

To wait—to think—to remember.

Let me remember.

I knew her a week, wooed her a month, have been married a fortnight.

She always said I didn't know her. She was always on the point of telling me something, and I would not let her. She seemed half repentant, half in jest—I preferred to trust her. Those clear, brown eyes—clear and bright, like brook water with the sun through it! And she would smile so! 'Tis not that I must remember.

Am I sure? Sure! I laugh at myself.

What would you call it, you—any man? A young woman steals from her house, alone, every day, and comes privately, cloaked and veiled, to this place, this den of Bohemians, this building of New York studios! Painters? I know them—I am a painter myself.

She goes to this room, day after day, and tells me nothing.

I say to her gently: "What do you do with your days, my love?"

"Oh, many things," she answers; "I am studying art—to please you!"

That was ingenious. She knew she might be watched.

I say, "Cannot I teach you?" and she says, "I have a teacher I used to study with. I must finish. I want to surprise you!" So she would soothe me—to appearance.

But I watch and follow, I take this little room. I wait, and I see.

Lessons? Oh, perjured one! There is no tenant of that room but yourself, and to it *he* comes each day.

Is that a step? Not yet. I watch and wait. This is America, I say, not France. This is my wife. I will trust her. But the man comes every day. He is young. He is handsome—handsome as a fiend.

I cannot bear it. I go to the door. I knock. There is no response. I try the door. It is locked. I stoop and look through the keyhole. What do I see? Ah, God! The hat and cloak of that man upon a chair, and then only a tall screen. Behind that screen, low voices!

I did not go home last night. I am here today—with these!

That is a step. Yes! Softly, now. He has gone in. I heard her speak. She said: "You are late, Guillaume!"

Let me give them a little time.

Now—softly—I come, friends. *I* am not late!

III.

Across the narrow passage I steal, noiselessly. The door is unlocked this time. I burst in.

There stands my young wife, pale, trembling, startled, unable to speak.

There is the handsome Guillaume—behind the screen. My fingers press the triggers. There is a sharp double report. Guillaume tumbles over, howling, and Marie flings herself between us.

"Edward! One moment! Give me a moment for my life! The pistols are harmless, dear—blank cartridges. I fixed them myself. I saw you suspected. But you've spoiled my surprise. I shall have to tell you now. This is my studio, love. Here is the picture you have the sketch of. *I* am 'M. Duchesne'— Mary Duchesne Greenleaf Carpenter—and this is my model!"

IV.

We are very happy in Paris, with our double studio. We sometimes share our models. We laugh at M. Daudet.

MY POOR AUNT

"Belle," said my mother, in tones bordering on despair, "what shall I do with you?"

"What would you like to do with me?" I inquired, with some acerbity.

"Oh, my dear, if I could only see you safely married."

My mother was a singularly inconsistent person, even for a woman. Her one governing ambition was to see me married, and yet she refused to take any steps toward this event, or to let me!

She had the most rigid notions of what was feminine and fitting, and had spent all her small resources in giving me an expensive, first-class, well-nigh useless, education. Two years I had spent at my rich aunt's in New York, going to a very select school. My mother had some vague idea that I would form friendships there which would be "useful" to me.

What she meant by "useful" I never could find out, for she always refused to allow me to visit any of the girls, or accept any of their invitations.

"No, dear," she would say, "I cannot afford to dress you now according to your station—you must wait till you are older."

I was older now. I was one-and-twenty. I had been at home for a year, and seemed likely to stay there. And as schoolgirl friendships do not thrive on long snubbing, nor home friendships on long absence, I was singularly alone.

Mother, having spent all she had on my education, now took boarders; and on the boarders and the little farm we subsisted. At present we had only one boarder, and, in point of fact, he supported the family. That he knew this as well as I, was painfully evident; but mother could not be led to see it. When the other boarders left he kept on taking their rooms, till now he occupied and paid for all four, and used ostentatiously to walk about in them at all hours to prove his claims.

Mother thought this was perfectly natural, but to me it seemed the most insulting charity, and, now that the house was almost empty, he used to talk a great deal at the table, and often ask if he might spend the evening with us. Mother always said yes, and I did not really care, for, bad as he was, he was better than nothing.

But what I did object to was the way mother consulted him about me, for he was only a young man, and she never minded whether I was present or not. She used to shake her head dismally and ask him what opening he thought best for young women who were driven to depend on their own exertions; and he would answer, in a way that I personally resented, that it depended on the capacity of the girl, and that a well-endowed young woman could hold her own almost anywhere nowadays.

How he held *his* own was a mystery to me, for, though he pretended to be a journalist and dependent on his work, he did very little that I could see, and always seemed to have plenty of money. I do despise these mysterious people with airs of disguised superiority!

He was an uncommonly homely man, too.

My troubles began to culminate. We had a long visit from Aunt Ellen. She was my rich aunt from New York.

"Not married yet!" she asked, with a resigned air. "I should like to know, Lucy Bennett, how you expect to marry Kate in this benighted town!" My mother sat up with some show of animosity. "I'm sure you were married here yourself, Ellen, and so was I; and if poor Kate had been, it might have been better for her!"

This Kate was my other aunt, of whom I had heard often in the course of my life, but little that was good. I had been named for her in early days, when the family was united; but she, the youngest of three sisters and the last to wed, had broken bonds that proved intolerable, and fled to the great West. Not a word had we heard from her since, but she still served as a terrible example wherewith to intimidate and restrain my rebellious youth. Forever was I checked and warned and covered with abasement by the dreadful statement, "That is just like your poor aunt!"

But of late years, since leaving school and city life, since being so much alone and listening so often to the revolutionary remarks of our boarder, I had sometimes dared to wonder whether "my poor aunt's" conduct had been wholly inexcusable after all.

My mother was the oldest of the sisters. She had married at eighteen, and was now forty. But she looked twenty years older. Of all her children I alone remained to her, the first and the last. My father was a pious, well-meaning man, but I had not lived with Aunt Ellen for two years without learning to pity his struggling, ineffectual life, and dear mama's uninterrupted trials and disappointments.

The six little babies, the five little graves, the slow, downward path from easy competence to genteel poverty, the loss of health and hope and ambition—it was a pathetic story, and often kept me patient when mother was most absurd.

"She used to be so clever and ambitious!" said Aunt Ellen. "She taught school here, and had some splendid offers to teach in town. I daresay she might have been a college professor if she had kept on. But Marcus Bennett wanted to marry her, and marry her he would. He was well off then, 'twas too good a chance to lose—teaching is uncertain, you know!"

Aunt Ellen would sigh in a general way and add: "Oh, Kate! Do be sure and marry well!"

I used to think Aunt Ellen had all the cream, and my poor mother the bluest of skim milk; but as I grew older and mother more confidential, I learned otherwise.

"She used to be so sweet and lovable!" said mother. "She had a beautiful future, I am sure, but she would marry James Gallup! He was a promising young man, too, but he went to the city and rose in the world, and—oh, dear!— there are worse troubles in life, Kate, than poverty or even death!" and then mother would descant on my father's endless domestic virtues, and hint things about Uncle James till I began to understand Aunt Ellen's sad, drawn face and gray hair, and pity her from the bottom of my heart; and mother would add in the same way: "Oh, Kate! Do be sure and marry well!"

"What kind of a husband did Aunt Kate marry?" I inquired. But mother pursed her lips and shook her head and answered. "I cannot talk to you about your poor aunt."

But I put this and that together and made out quite a story.

Aunt Kate was well remembered by me—she was but ten years older than I, ten years younger than mother. I was yet a mere child, when she went to the city to visit Aunt Ellen, married and settled there, and after a stormy year or two simply ran away! She went West. I knew, and got a divorce, I knew, but that was all.

Mother never would say what the matter was, nor would Aunt Ellen; but whenever I grew restive under their careful rule they would shake their heads and murmur: "Just like her poor aunt!"

So I had grown up with a dim, unpleasant sense of naughtiness about Aunt Kate, and regarded her, in spite of my inward sympathy, as an epitome of all iconoclasm and unwomanly rebellion.

And now, when Aunt Ellen asked if I were not married yet, and mother shook her head and looked as if I were to blame for it, I quite blazed up and said I did not care if I never was married! I wanted to earn my own living and be independent! They quite jumped in their chairs, and mother said: "Don't let me ever hear you speak like that again! Do you wish to follow your poor aunt?"

"I don't know where she is," I replied, spitefully, "or I might be tempted to!"

Mother had a special grievance against me because I had repressed a young minister in the village—a pallid, narrow-chested person whom she declared to have every Christian virtue, and whom I declared to have neither brain nor muscle.

Aunt Ellen, too, had a special grievance against me because I had refused a young society man whose father was extremely wealthy—a flushed, weak-legged youth, whom she declared to have everything in prospect, and whom I declared to have nothing at present.

And, what is much worse, they were not united in a common grievance against me, because they were, for a wonder, agreed on a new candidate for my hand, and I was holding out against all three of them.

"Kate, you are flying in the face of Providence!" said my mother.

"Kate, you are a goose!" said my aunt.

"He has a noble character," said my mother.

"He has a splendid position," said my aunt.

"What have you against him?" asked both.

"I don't love him," said I.

"Love!" said mother, sadly, "that's not everything!"

"Love!" said Aunt Ellen, bitterly, "that don't last long!"

"I don't care," I answered; "I won't marry without it!"

This dreadful man was coming for a final answer, he said, and they were pressing me very hard.

I tried to cajole mother a little—usually an easy task. "How can you want me to go and leave you, mother dear?" I pleaded.

"Now, don't try to make out I hinder you," she responded. "I am more than willing you should leave me for your own welfare. To know you were provided for would do me more good than anything in life."

"And she won't be left alone, either," said Aunt Ellen; "for as soon as you go she is coming to live with me. I can't take you both permanently, but your mother I could, and the rent from the farm will take care of her."

"There's nothing in the way but your own foolish obstinacy," said mother.

I really began to feel desperate. To be sure, the man was personally repulsive to me, but I could learn to bear that—I hadn't lived in the house with that horrid boarder of ours for nothing!

My pecuniary prospects were dismal at best, since mother would not let me go away to earn anything. I did not know what I could look forward to but this or some other marriage; and, as far as I had seen, there was small choice and no certainty in marriages. It is true, I had been writing furtively for some Western papers and magazines for a year past, but the profits were exceeding small; there was no encouragement to depend on that business. I didn't pretend to be a genius, but had always a strong leaning toward the press. Still, what could I do? This suitor of mine was decent enough—a well-meaning sort of person, and heartily attached to me, I had reason to believe. He was pigheaded and conservative, but there might be worse qualities than those—perhaps! And mother was so feeble. This life of want and worry and anxiety about me was ageing her visibly. She wouldn't let me leave her on any other terms, and Aunt

Ellen couldn't take us both—even if I should go there on charity, which I wouldn't.

So I began to weaken. And yet—and yet—oh, he was horrid! I mean I didn't like him, I hated to have him touch me. I resented to my last fiber his masterful airs. We had a time of it, I assure you.

And that wretched boarder of ours had not enough sense of decency to keep out of it, but sat around more than ever! He made himself very agreeable to Aunt Ellen; and mother thought everything of him, as I have said.

He spoke very highly of this hovering incubus of mine. "A fine man," he remarked. "A manly man. A man who would support a family, and control a family on the good old plan!"

He had a peculiarly uncivil way of saying things which dear mother took for solemn earnest, and then smiling a little under his moustache. He knew they were all sarcastic, and so did I. But he praised this man so that I was fairly bewildered.

At last mother took a step which drove me to despair. She actually asked that boarder to reason with me about accepting Mr. Boon!

I thought she was looking unusually nervous, and Aunt Ellen unusually distracted, but I never imagined what was coming till the boarder drew a chair up near mine and said, with the utmost solemnity:

"Miss Bennett, your mother has asked me to use what little influence I may possess to modify your persistent rashness in refusing Mr. Boon's honorable proposals."

I gave one jump, and then sat still, looking at mother in a way that ought to have made her ashamed and sorry.

But she only said: "Now do, Kate, listen to Mr. Jameson. You won't hear reason from us. Perhaps a man can represent things better."

Mr. Jameson bowed to her and said he would do his humble best. I gave him a single glance but his eyes laughed so that I turned all one blush, I was so angry and ashamed! To think that my own mother should have exposed me to this!

The boarder leaned back in his chair and put the tips of his fingers together. He looked as magisterial and severe as a Supreme Judge, all but the eyes.

"Miss Bennett," said he, "as I understand this question, it has three sides: first, the economic; second, the dutiful;

third, the affectionate. On the economic side the case is invincible. You are at present—if you will pardon me—of limited means, and show no special talent or capacity for adding to them. I do not mean that you are not possessed of feminine qualities and personal charms attractive in the last degree; but, for fighting the cold and cruel world, you have no better equipment than the majority of your sex. Here is a position offered you in which you can obtain all the necessaries, most of the comforts and some of the luxuries of life, by no exertion save of those feminine qualities and charms above mentioned. The position is lucrative, and, in every sense of the word, honorable!''

I wished in my heart that I had a brother who would throw this man out of the house. But I hadn't, and, with some wild hope that even mother would resent his impudence, I sat still.

He went on, calmly:

"At best it is an uncertain and precarious life for a woman to face the world alone—especially a young and handsome woman; but in the holy estate of matrimony you are sheltered, protected, provided for, made happy. Marriage, of course, is woman's true career. I understand the gentleman who asks your hand to be possessed of ample means, and therefore fully qualified to fulfil his share of the engagement.''

I looked at mother again, but she was drinking it in, and nodding to Aunt Ellen, and glancing triumphantly at me, as much as to say, "You never can withstand this!''

"For the second clause, the call of duty, there is also a clear case,'' pursued Mr. Jameson. "The claim of a parent who has sacrificed her health and strength—her life, one might say—on the altar of maternal devotion, is a claim which can never exact too much return. To gratify the wish of such a parent''—mother was actually crying in her handkerchief—''no sacrifice is too great. In the present instance no sacrifice is exacted. Your own interests will be amply provided for, and your mother made comfortable for life by this step. Her welfare depends upon it!

"Now, as to the third or affectional clause''—the horrid creature was looking me calmly in the eye all this time—''there seems to be some disagreement. You claim, do you not, that you do not love this man?''

Aunt Ellen sniffed at this question, and even mother

looked a little less satisfied; but, as I vouchsafed no reply, he went on:

"I will grant, for purposes of argument, that you do not love this man. But I maintain that it has very little to do with the case. Of course, in a selfish light, merely as a matter of personal gratification, it does add a transient glow to human happiness. But human happiness"—here he cast up his eyes devoutly—"is uncertain at best. I have seen families where this species of affection existed rendered miserable from other causes; and I have seen families where it did not exist, flourish and prosper notwithstanding!"

Both mother and aunt shook their heads in dismal acquiescence.

"Now, I ask you as an adult human being—you are of age I believe?—and as a reasonable human being—you are reasonable, I believe?—whether it does not seem to you a clear duty to ignore a childish prejudice and become this man's wife for the sake of your provision in life and your mother's?"

I rose to my feet. I never had been so angry in all my life. This man's insulting eyes and tones and manner, his evident assurance of overruling me in this easy way, his complacent air of success, quite maddened me. So I spoke.

"Mr. Jameson," said I, "you have reminded me of two things which I had utterly forgotten: that I am a reasonable being, and legally of age. Under the first head I deny your arguments in toto. Under the second I refuse to be coerced. I know more of life than you seem to suppose, Mr. Jameson, and I know that there is nothing more wicked and base—more cowardly, too, under its cloak of respectability—than a loveless marriage!

"Suppose I were now dead? Aunt Ellen would take mother, and the world would go on without me very well. It can go on without me now. I utterly refuse to marry this man, and, what is more, I refuse to stay longer in this condition of childish dependence! I claim my right as an individual, and leave this house tomorrow to earn my own living, even if it be as a maid-of-all-work!"

I was very hot and excited. Mother and Aunt Ellen were images of horror, and even the boarder had sprung to his feet and was looking extremely queer, when we were greeted by a burst of applause from the open hall door, and into the room came a woman, young, handsome, well-dressed—the picture of health, happiness, and success.

Mother sprang forward with a scream; Aunt Ellen dropped into a chair with a gasp; but I knew the newcomer in an instant, and cried: "Aunt Kate!"

"So glad I happened in just now!" said she, pleasantly. "Ellen, I think Lucy would be much happier with you than here alone; and Kate can do worlds for her soon. Kate, my dear, I'm owner and editor of the *Nebraska Morning Star.* I've had some of your little things in it, and I offer you the position of assistant editor, with a salary of eight hundred a year to begin with. Afterward it will be more. Will you take it?"

I fell into her arms literally and metaphorically.

With what infinite satisfaction did I look upon a woman who was sufficient to herself and a little over!

Of course it was not till afterward that I learned to really know her, and to love and honor her more with every year of knowledge.

Brave and patient had she been at first, till she found the shame and injury heaped upon her by the scoundrel she had so trustfully married too much for a woman to bear in honor. Then she had thrown off the yoke, gone to new fields of work, and won for herself an honest name and an honest living by clear desert and effort and common sense. She had now come back to see her sisters, and perhaps save her niece and namesake from the dreary dangers of her own youth.

I feasted my eyes upon her. Was this hale, bright, blooming creature only ten years younger than my gray and feeble mother, only five years younger than sad-eyed Aunt Ellen with her bitter wrinkles and cheeks of unchanging pink?

She gave me hope and strength and courage with every breath.

To live like that! To be strong and brave and glad and independent!

"Aunt Kate," said I, "I am of age, and I will go with you as soon as you please!"

"Aunt Kate," said the boarder, "may I go too?"

I shouldn't have known that man: he looked so pleased and proud—fairly handsome—almost agreeable!

And he did go, too.

THE YELLOW WALLPAPER

It is very seldom that mere ordinary people like John and myself secure ancestral halls for the summer.

A colonial mansion, a hereditary estate, I would say a haunted house and reach the height of romantic felicity—but that would be asking too much of fate!

Still I will proudly declare that there is something queer about it.

Else, why should it be let so cheaply? And why have stood so long untenanted?

John laughs at me, of course, but one expects that.

John is practical in the extreme. He has no patience with faith, an intense horror of superstition, and he scoffs openly at any talk of things not to be felt and seen and put down in figures.

John is a physician, and *perhaps*—(I would not say it to a living soul, of course, but this is dead paper and a great relief to my mind)—*perhaps* that is one reason I do not get well faster.

You see, he does not believe I am sick! And what can one do?

If a physician of high standing, and one's own husband, assures friends and relatives that there is really nothing the matter with one but temporary nervous depression—a slight hysterical tendency—what is one to do?

My brother is also a physician, and also of high standing, and he says the same thing.

So I take phosphates or phosphites—whichever it is—and tonics, and air and exercise, and journeys, and am absolutely forbidden to "work" until I am well again.

Personally, I disagree with their ideas.

Personally, I believe that congenial work, with excitement and change, would do me good.

But what is one to do?

I did write for a while in spite of them; but it *does* exhaust me a good deal—having to be so sly about it, or else meet with heavy opposition.

I sometimes fancy that in my condition, if I had less opposition and more society and stimulus—but John says the very worst thing I can do is to think about my condition, and I confess it always makes me feel bad.

So I will let it alone and talk about the house.

The most beautiful place! It is quite alone, standing well back from the road, quite three miles from the village. It makes me think of English places that you read about, for there are hedges and walls and gates that lock, and lots of separate little houses for the gardeners and people.

There is a *delicious* garden! I never saw such a garden—large and shady, full of box-bordered paths, and lined with long grape-covered arbors with seats under them.

There were greenhouses, but they are all broken now.

There was some legal trouble, I believe, something about the heirs and co-heirs; anyhow, the place has been empty for years.

That spoils my ghostliness, I am afraid, but I don't care—there is something strange about the house—I can feel it.

I even said so to John one moonlight evening, but he said what I felt was a draught, and shut the window.

I get unreasonably angry with John sometimes. I'm sure I never used to be so sensitive. I think it is due to this nervous condition.

But John says if I feel so I shall neglect proper self-control; so I take pains to control myself—before him, at least, and that makes me very tired.

I don't like our room at bit. I wanted one downstairs that opened onto the piazza and had roses all over the window, and such pretty old-fashioned chintz hangings! But John would not hear of it.

He said there was only one window and not room for two beds, and no near room for him if he took another.

He is very careful and loving, and hardly lets me stir without special direction.

I have a schedule prescription for each hour in the day;

he takes all care from me, and so I feel basely ungrateful not to value it more.

He said he came here solely on my account, that I was to have perfect rest and all the air I could get. "Your exercise depends on your strength, my dear," said he, "and your food somewhat on your appetite; but air you can absorb all the time." So we took the nursery at the top of the house.

It is a big, airy room, the whole floor nearly, with windows that look all ways, and air and sunshine galore. It was nursery first, and then playroom and gymnasium, I should judge, for the windows are barred for little children, and there are rings and things in the walls.

The paint and paper look as if a boys' school had used it. It is stripped off—the paper—in great patches all around the head of my bed, about as far as I can reach, and in a great place on the other side of the room low down. I never saw a worse paper in my life. One of those sprawling, flamboyant patterns committing every artistic sin.

It is dull enough to confuse the eye in following, pronounced enough constantly to irritate and provoke study, and when you follow the lame uncertain curves for a little distance they suddenly commit suicide—plunge off at outrageous angles, destroy themselves in unheard-of contradictions.

The color is repellent, almost revolting: a smouldering unclean yellow, strangely faded by the slow-turning sunlight. It is a dull yet lurid orange in some places, a sickly sulphur tint in others.

No wonder the children hated it! I should hate it myself if I had to live in this room long.

There comes John, and I must put this away—he hates to have me write a word.

We have been here two weeks, and I haven't felt like writing before, since that first day.

I am sitting by the window now, up in this atrocious nursery, and there is nothing to hinder my writing as much as I please, save lack of strength.

John is away all day, and even some nights when his cases are serious.

I am glad my case is not serious!

But these nervous troubles are dreadfully depressing.

John does not know how much I really suffer. He knows there is no reason to suffer, and that satisfies him.

Of course it is only nervousness. It does weigh on me so not to do my duty in any way!

I meant to be such a help to John, such a real rest and comfort, and here I am a comparative burden already!

Nobody would believe what an effort it is to do what little I am able—to dress and entertain, and order things.

It is fortunate Mary is so good with the baby. Such a dear baby!

And yet I *cannot* be with him, it makes me so nervous.

I suppose John never was nervous in his life. He laughs at me so about this wallpaper!

At first he meant to repaper the room, but afterward he said that I was letting it get the better of me, and that nothing was worse for a nervous patient than to give way to such fancies.

He said that after the wallpaper was changed it would be the heavy bedstead, and then the barred windows, and then that gate at the head of the stairs, and so on.

"You know the place is doing you good," he said, "and really, dear, I don't care to renovate the house just for a three months' rental."

"Then do let us go downstairs," I said. "There are such pretty rooms there."

Then he took me in his arms and called me a blessed little goose, and said he would go down cellar, if I wished, and have it whitewashed into the bargain.

But he is right enough about the beds and windows and things.

It is as airy and comfortable a room as anyone need wish, and, of course, I would not be so silly as to make him uncomfortable just for a whim.

I'm really getting quite fond of the big room, all but that horrid paper.

Out of one window I can see the garden—those mysterious deep-shaded arbors, the riotous old-fashioned flowers, and bushes and gnarly trees.

Out of another I get a lovely view of the bay and a little private wharf belonging to the estate. There is a beautiful shaded lane that runs down there from the house. I always fancy I see people walking in these numerous paths and arbors, but John has cautioned me not to give way to fancy in the least. He says that with my imaginative power and habit of story-making, a nervous weakness like mine is sure to lead to all manner of excited fancies, and that I ought to use my will and good sense to check the tendency. So I try.

I think sometimes that if I were only well enough to write a little it would relieve the press of ideas and rest me.

But I find I get pretty tired when I try.

It is so discouraging not to have any advice and companionship about my work. When I get really well, John says we will ask Cousin Henry and Julia down for a long visit; but he says he would as soon put fireworks in my pillowcase as to let me have those stimulating people about now.

I wish I could get well faster.

But I must not think about that. This paper looks to me as if it *knew* what a vicious influence it had!

There is a recurrent spot where the pattern lolls like a broken neck and two bulbous eyes stare at you upside down.

I get positively angry with the impertinence of it and the everlastingness. Up and down and sideways they crawl, and those absurd unblinking eyes are everywhere. There is one place where two breadths didn't match, and the eyes go all up and down the line, one a little higher than the other.

I never saw so much expression in an inanimate thing before, and we all know how much expression they have! I used to lie awake as a child and get more entertainment and terror out of blank walls and plain furniture than most children could find in a toy store.

I remember what a kindly wink the knobs of our big old bureau used to have, and there was one chair that always seemed like a strong friend.

I used to feel that if any of the other things looked too fierce I could always hop into that chair and be safe.

The furniture in this room is no worse than inharmonious, however, for we had to bring it all from downstairs. I suppose when this was used as a playroom they had to take the nursery things out, and no wonder! I never saw such ravages as the children have made here.

The wallpaper, as I said before, is torn off in spots, and it sticketh closer than a brother—they must have had perseverance as well as hatred.

Then the floor is scratched and gouged and splintered, the plaster itself is dug out here and there, and this great heavy bed, which is all we found in the room, looks as if it had been through the wars.

But I don't mind it a bit—only the paper.

There comes John's sister. Such a dear girl as she is, and so careful of me! I must not let her find me writing.

She is a perfect and enthusiastic housekeeper, and hopes for no better profession. I verily believe she thinks it is the writing which made me sick!

But I can write when she is out, and see her a long way off from these windows.

There is one that commands the road, a lovely shaded winding road, and one that just looks off over the country. A lovely country, too, full of great elms and velvet meadows.

This wallpaper has a kind of sub-pattern in a different shade, a particularly irritating one, for you can only see it in certain lights, and not clearly then.

But in the places where it isn't faded and where the sun is just so—I can see a strange, provoking, formless sort of figure that seems to skulk about behind that silly and conspicuous front design.

There's sister on the stairs!

Well, the Fourth of July is over! The people are all gone, and I am tired out. John thought it might do me good to see a little company, so we just had Mother and Nellie and the children down for a week.

Of course I didn't do a thing. Jennie sees to everything now.

But it tired me all the same.

John says if I don't pick up faster he shall send me to Weir Mitchell in the fall.

But I don't want to go there at all. I had a friend who was in his hands once, and she says he is just like John and my brother, only more so!

Besides, it is such an undertaking to go so far.

I don't feel as if it was worthwhile to turn my hand over for anything, and I'm getting dreadfully fretful and querulous.

I cry at nothing, and cry most of the time.

Of course I don't when John is here, or anybody else, but when I am alone.

And I am alone a good deal just now. John is kept in town very often by serious cases, and Jennie is good and lets me alone when I want her to.

So I walk a little in the garden or down that lovely lane, sit on the porch under the roses, and lie down up here a good deal.

I'm getting really fond of the room in spite of the wallpaper. Perhaps *because* of the wallpaper.

It dwells in my mind so!

I lie here on this great immovable bed—it is nailed down, I believe—and follow that pattern about by the hour. It is as good as gymnastics, I assure you. I start, we'll say, at the bottom, down in the corner over there where it has not been touched, and I determine for the thousandth time that I *will* follow that pointless pattern to some sort of a conclusion.

I know a little of the principle of design, and I know this thing was not arranged on any laws of radiation, or alternation, or repetition, or symmetry, or anything else that I ever heard of.

It is repeated, of course, by the breadths, but not otherwise.

Looked at in one way, each breadth stands alone; the bloated curves and flourishes—a kind of "debased Romanesque" with delirium tremens—go waddling up and down in isolated columns of fatuity.

But, on the other hand, they connect diagonally, and the sprawling outlines run off in great slanting waves of optic horror, like a lot of wallowing seaweeds in full chase.

The whole thing goes horizontally, too, at least it seems so, and I exhaust myself trying to distinguish the order of its going in that direction.

They have used a horizontal breadth for a frieze, and that adds wonderfully to the confusion.

There is one end of the room where it is almost intact, and there, when the crosslights fade and the low sun shines directly upon it, I can almost fancy radiation after all—the interminable grotesque seems to form around a common center and rush off in headlong plunges of equal distraction.

It makes me tired to follow it. I will take a nap, I guess.

I don't know why I should write this.

I don't want to.

I don't feel able.

And I know John would think it absurd. But I *must* say what I feel and think in some way—it is such a relief!

But the effort is getting to be greater than the relief.

Half the time now I am awfully lazy, and lie down ever so much. John says I mustn't lose my strength, and has me take cod liver oil and lots of tonics and things, to say nothing of ale and wine and rare meat.

Dear John! He loves me very dearly, and hates to have me sick. I tried to have a real earnest reasonable talk with him the other day, and tell him how I wish he would let me go and make a visit to Cousin Henry and Julia.

But he said I wasn't able to go, nor able to stand it after I got there; and I did not make out a very good case for myself, for I was crying before I had finished.

It is getting to be a great effort for me to think straight. Just this nervous weakness, I suppose.

And dear John gathered me up in his arms, and just carried me upstairs and laid me on the bed, and sat by me and read to me till it tired my head.

He said I was his darling and his comfort and all he had, and that I must take care of myself for his sake, and keep well.

He says no one but myself can help me out of it, that I must use my will and self-control and not let any silly fancies run away with me.

There's one comfort—the baby is well and happy, and does not have to occupy this nursery with the horrid wallpaper.

If we had not used it, that blessed child would have! What a fortunate escape! Why, I wouldn't have a child of mine, an impressionable little thing, live in such a room for worlds.

I never thought of it before, but it is lucky that John kept me here after all; I can stand it so much easier than a baby, you see.

Of course I never mention it to them any more—I am too wise—but I keep watch for it all the same.

There are things in that wallpaper that nobody knows about but me, or ever will.

Behind that outside pattern the dim shapes get clearer every day.

It is always the same shape, only very numerous.

And it is like a woman stooping down and creeping about behind that pattern. I don't like it a bit. I wonder—I begin to think—I wish John would take me away from here!

It is so hard to talk with John about my case, because he is so wise, and because he loves me so.

But I tried it last night.

It was moonlight. The moon shines in all around just as the sun does.

I hate to see it sometimes, it creeps so slowly, and always comes in by one window or another.

John was asleep and I hated to waken him, so I kept still and watched the moonlight on that undulating wallpaper till I felt creepy.

The faint figure behind seemed to shake the pattern, just as if she wanted to get out.

I got up softly and went to feel and see if the paper *did* move, and when I came back John was awake.

"What is it, little girl?" he said. "Don't go walking about like that—you'll get cold."

I thought it was a good time to talk, so I told him that I really was not gaining here, and that I wished he would take me away.

"Why, darling!" said he. "Our lease will be up in three weeks, and I can't see how to leave before.

"The repairs are not done at home, and I cannot possibly leave town just now. Of course, if you were in any danger, I could and would, but you really are better, dear, whether you can see it or not. I am a doctor, dear, and I know. You are gaining flesh and color, your appetite is better, I feel really much easier about you."

"I don't weigh a bit more," said I, "nor as much; and my appetite may be better in the evening when you are here but it is worse in the morning when you are away!"

"Bless her little heart!" said he with a big hug. "She shall be as sick as she pleases! But now let's improve the shining hours by going to sleep, and talk about it in the morning!"

"And you won't go away?" I asked gloomily.

"Why, how can I, dear? It is only three weeks more and then we will take a nice little trip of a few days while Jennie is getting the house ready. Really, dear, you are better!"

"Better in body perhaps—" I began, and stopped short, for he sat up straight and looked at me with such a stern, reproachful look that I could not say another word.

"My darling," said he, "I beg of you, for my sake and for our child's sake, as well as for your own, that you will never for one instant let that idea enter your mind! There is nothing so dangerous, so fascinating, to a temperament like yours. It is a false and foolish fancy. Can you not trust me as a physician when I tell you so?''

So of course I said no more on that score, and we went to sleep before long. He thought I was asleep first, but I wasn't, and lay there for hours trying to decide whether that front pattern and the back pattern really did move together or separately.

On a pattern like this, by daylight, there is a lack of sequence, a defiance of law, that is a constant irritant to a normal mind.

The color is hideous enough, and unrealizable enough, and infuriating enough, but the pattern is torturing.

You think you have mastered it, but just as you get well under way in following, it turns a back-somersault and there you are. It slaps you in the face, knocks you down, and tramples upon you. It is like a bad dream.

The outside pattern is a florid arabesque, reminding one of a fungus. If you can imagine a toadstool in joints, an interminable string of toadstools, budding and sprouting in endless convolutions—why, that is something like it.

That is, sometimes!

There is one marked peculiarity about this paper, a thing nobody seems to notice but myself, and that is that it changes as the light changes.

When the sun shoots in through the east window—I always watch for that first long, straight ray—it changes so quickly that I never can quite believe it.

That is why I watch it always.

By moonlight—the moon shines in all night when there is a moon—I wouldn't know it was the same paper.

At night in any kind of light, in twilight, candlelight, lamplight, and worst of all by moonlight, it becomes bars! The outside pattern, I mean, and the woman behind it is as plain as can be.

I didn't realize for a long time what the thing was that showed behind, that dim sub-pattern, but now I am quite sure it is a woman.

By daylight she is subdued, quiet. I fancy it is the pattern that keeps her so still. It is so puzzling. It keeps me quiet by the hour.

I lie down ever so much now. John says it is good for me, and to sleep all I can.

Indeed he started the habit by making me lie down for an hour after each meal.

It is a very bad habit, I am convinced, for you see, I don't sleep.

And that cultivates deceit, for I don't tell them I'm awake—oh, no!

The fact is I am getting a little afraid of John.

He seems very queer sometimes, and even Jennie has an inexplicable look.

It strikes me occasionally, just as a scientific hypothesis, that perhaps it is the paper!

I have watched John when he did not know I was looking, and come into the room suddenly on the most innocent excuses, and I've caught him several times *looking at the paper!* And Jennie too. I caught Jennie with her hand on it once.

She didn't know I was in the room, and when I asked her in a quiet, a very quiet voice, with the most restrained manner possible, what she was doing with the paper, she turned around as if she had been caught stealing, and looked quite angry—asked me why I should frighten her so!

Then she said that the paper stained everything it touched, that she had found yellow smooches on all my clothes and John's and she wished we would be more careful!

Did not that sound innocent? But I know she was studying that pattern, and I am determined that nobody shall find it out but myself!

Life is very much more exciting now than it used to be. You see, I have something more to expect, to look forward to, to watch. I really do eat better, and am more quiet than I was.

John is so pleased to see me improve! He laughed a little the other day, and said I seemed to be flourishing in spite of my wallpaper.

I turned it off with a laugh. I had no intention of telling him it was *because* of the wallpaper—he would make fun of me. He might even want to take me away.

I don't want to leave now until I have found it out. There is a week more, and I think that will be enough.

I'm feeling so much better!

I don't sleep much at night, for it is so interesting to watch developments; but I sleep a good deal during the daytime.

In the daytime it is tiresome and perplexing.

There are always new shoots on the fungus, and new shades of yellow all over it. I cannot keep count of them, though I have tried conscientiously.

It is the strangest yellow, that wallpaper! It makes me think of all the yellow things I ever saw—not beautiful ones like buttercups, but old, foul, bad yellow things.

But there is something else about that paper—the smell! I noticed it the moment we came into the room, but with so much air and sun it was not bad. Now we have had a week of fog and rain, and whether the windows are open or not, the smell is here.

It creeps all over the house.

I find it hovering in the dining room, skulking in the parlor, hiding in the hall, lying in wait for me on the stairs.

It gets into my hair.

Even when I go to ride, if I turn my head suddenly and surprise it—there is that smell!

Such a peculiar odor, too! I have spent hours in trying to analyze it, to find what it smelled like.

It is not bad—at first—and very gentle, but quite the subtlest, most enduring odor I ever met.

In this damp weather it is awful. I wake up in the night and find it hanging over me.

It used to disturb me at first. I thought seriously of burning the house—to reach the smell.

But now I am used to it. The only thing I can think of that it is like is the *color* of the paper! A yellow smell.

There is a very funny mark on this wall, low down, near the mopboard. A streak that runs round the room. It goes behind every piece of furniture, except the bed, a long, straight, even *smooch*, as if it had been rubbed over and over.

I wonder how it was done and who did it, and what they did it for. Round and round and round—round and round and round—it makes me dizzy!

I really have discovered something at last.

Through watching so much at night, when it changes so, I have finally found out.

The front pattern *does* move—and no wonder! The woman behind shakes it!

Sometimes I think there are a great many women behind, and sometimes only one, and she crawls around fast, and her crawling shakes it all over.

Then in the very bright spots she keeps still, and in the very shady spots she just takes hold of the bars and shakes them hard.

And she is all the time trying to climb through. But nobody could climb through that pattern—it strangles so; I think that is why it has so many heads.

They get through, and then the pattern strangles them off and turns them upside down, and makes their eyes white!

If those heads were covered or taken off it would not be half so bad.

I think that woman gets out in the daytime!

And I'll tell you why—privately—I've seen her!

I can see her out of every one of my windows!

It is the same woman, I know, for she is always creeping, and most women do not creep by daylight.

I see her in that long shaded lane, creeping up and down. I see her in those dark grape arbors, creeping all around the garden.

I see her on that long road under the trees, creeping along, and when a carriage comes she hides under the blackberry vines.

I don't blame her a bit. It must be very humiliating to be caught creeping by daylight!

I always lock the door when I creep by daylight. I can't do it at night, for I know John would suspect something at once.

And John is so queer now that I don't want to irritate him. I wish he would take another room! Besides, I don't want anybody to get that woman out at night but myself.

I often wonder if I could see her out of all the windows at once.

But, turn as fast as I can, I can only see out of one at one time.

And though I always see her, she *may* be able to creep faster than I can turn! I have watched her sometimes away off in the open country, creeping as fast as a cloud shadow in a wind.

If only that top pattern could be gotten off from the under one! I mean to try it, little by little.

I have found out another funny thing, but I shan't tell it this time! It does not do to trust people too much.

There are only two more days to get this paper off, and I believe John is beginning to notice. I don't like the look in his eyes.

And I heard him ask Jennie a lot of professional questions about me. She had a very good report to give.

She said I slept a good deal in the daytime.

John knows I don't sleep very well at night, for all I'm so quiet!

He asked me all sorts of questions, too, and pretended to be very loving and kind.

As if I couldn't see through him!

Still, I don't wonder he acts so, sleeping under this paper for three months.

It only interests me, but I feel sure John and Jennie are affected by it.

Hurrah! This is the last day, but it is enough. John is to stay in town over night, and won't be out until this evening.

Jennie wanted to sleep with me—the sly thing; but I told her I should undoubtedly rest better for a night all alone.

That was clever, for really I wasn't alone a bit! As soon as it was moonlight and that poor thing began to crawl and shake the pattern, I got up and ran to help her.

I pulled and she shook. I shook and she pulled, and before morning we had peeled off yards of that paper.

A strip about as high as my head and half around the room.

And then when the sun came and that awful pattern began to laugh at me, I declared I would finish it today!

We go away tomorrow, and they are moving all my furniture down again to leave things as they were before.

Jennie looked at the wall in amazement, but I told her merrily that I did it out of pure spite at the vicious thing.

She laughed and said she wouldn't mind doing it herself, but I must not get tired.

How she betrayed herself that time!

But I am here, and no person touches this paper but Me—not *alive!*

She tried to get me out of the room—it was too patent!

But I said it was so quiet and empty and clean now that I believed I would lie down again and sleep all I could, and not to wake me even for dinner—I would call when I woke.

So now she is gone, and the servants are gone, and the things are gone, and there is nothing left but that great bedstead nailed down, with the canvas mattress we found on it.

We shall sleep downstairs tonight, and take the boat home tomorrow.

I quite enjoy the room, now it is bare again.

How those children did tear about here!

This bedstead is fairly gnawed!

But I must get to work.

I have locked the door and thrown the key down into the front path.

I don't want to go out, and I don't want to have anybody come in, till John comes.

I want to astonish him.

I've got a rope up here that even Jennie did not find. If that woman does get out, and tried to get away, I can tie her!

But I forgot I could not reach far without anything to stand on!

This bed will *not* move!

I tried to lift and push it until I was lame, and then I got so angry I bit off a little piece at one corner—but it hurt my teeth.

Then I peeled off all the paper I could reach standing on the floor. It sticks horribly and the pattern just enjoys it! All those strangled heads and bulbous eyes and waddling fungus growths just shriek with derision!

I am getting angry enough to do something desperate. To jump out of the window would be admirable exercise, but the bars are too strong even to try.

Besides I wouldn't do it. Of course not. I know well enough that a step like that is improper and might be misconstrued.

I don't like to *look* out of the windows even—there are so many of those creeping women, and they creep so fast.

I wonder if they all come out of that wallpaper as I did?

But I am securely fastened now by my well-hidden rope—you don't get *me* out in the road there!

I suppose I shall have to get back behind the pattern when it comes night, and that is hard!

It is so pleasant to be out in this great room and creep around as I please!

I don't want to go outside. I won't, even if Jennie asks me to.

For outside you have to creep on the ground, and everything is green instead of yellow.

But here I can creep smoothly on the floor, and my shoulder just fits in that long smooch around the wall, so I cannot lose my way.

Why, there's John at the door!

It is no use, young man, you can't open it!

How he does call and pound!

Now he's crying to Jennie for an axe.

It would be a shame to break down that beautiful door!

"John, dear!" said I in the gentlest voice. "The key is down by the front steps, under a plantain leaf!"

That silenced him for a few moments.

Then he said, very quietly indeed, "Open the door, my darling!"

"I can't," said I. "The key is down by the front door under a plantain leaf!" And then I said it again, several times, very gently and slowly, and said it so often that he had to go and see, and he got it of course, and came in. He stopped short by the door.

"What is the matter?" he cried. "For God's sake, what are you doing!"

I kept on creeping just the same, but I looked at him over my shoulder.

"I've got out at last," said I, "in spite of you and Jane. And I've pulled off most of the paper, so you can't put me back!"

Now why should that man have fainted? But he did, and right across my path by the wall, so that I had to creep over him every time!

THREE THANKSGIVINGS

Andrew's letter and Jean's letter were in Mrs. Morrison's lap. She had read them both, and sat looking at them with a varying sort of smile, now motherly and now unmotherly.

"You belong with me," Andrew wrote. "It is not right that Jean's husband should support my mother. I can do it easily now. You shall have a good room and every comfort. The old house will let for enough to give you quite a little income of your own, or it can be sold and I will invest the money where you'll get a deal more out of it. It is not right that you should live alone there. Sally is old and liable to accident. I am anxious about you. Come on for Thanksgiving—and come to stay. Here is the money to come with. You know I want you. Annie joins me in sending love. ANDREW."

Mrs. Morrison read it all through again, and laid it down with her quiet, twinkling smile. Then she read Jean's.

"Now, mother, you've got to come to us for Thanksgiving this year. Just think! You haven't seen the baby since he was three months old! And have never seen the twins. You won't know him—he's such a splendid big boy now. Joe says for you to come, of course. And, mother, why won't you come and live with us? Joe wants you, too. There's the little room upstairs; it's not very big, but we can put in a Franklin stove for you and make you pretty comfortable. Joe says he should think you ought to sell that white elephant of a place. He says he could put the money into his store and pay you good interest. I wish you would, mother. We'd just love to have you here. You'd be such a comfort to me, and such a help with the babies. And Joe just loves you. Do come now, and stay with us. Here is the money for the trip.—Your affectionate daughter,

JEANNIE.''

Mrs. Morrison laid this beside the other, folded both, and placed them in their respective envelopes, then in their several well-filled pigeon-holes in her big, old-fashioned desk. She turned and paced slowly up and down the long parlor, a tall woman, commanding of aspect, yet of a winningly attractive manner, erect and light-footed, still imposingly handsome.

It was now November, the last lingering boarder was long since gone, and a quiet winter lay before her. She was alone, but for Sally; and she smiled at Andrew's cautious expression, ''liable to accident.'' He could not say ''feeble'' or ''ailing,'' Sally being a colored lady of changeless aspect and incessant activity.

Mrs. Morrison was alone, and while living in the Welcome House she was never unhappy. Her father had built it, she was born there, she grew up playing on the broad green lawns in front, and in the acre of garden behind. It was the finest house in the village, and she then thought it the finest in the world.

Even after living with her father at Washington and abroad, after visiting hall, castle and palace, she still found the Welcome House beautiful and impressive.

If she kept on taking boarders she could live the year through, and pay interest, but not principal, on her little mortgage. This had been the one possible and necessary thing while the children were there, though it was a business she hated.

But her youthful experience in diplomatic circles, and the years of practical management in church affairs, enabled her to bear it with patience and success. The boarders often confided to one another, as they chatted and tatted on the long piazza, that Mrs. Morrison was ''certainly very refined.''

Now Sally whisked in cheerfully, announcing supper, and Mrs. Morrison went out to her great silver tea-tray at the lit end of the long, dark mahogany table, with as much dignity as if twenty titled guests were before her.

Afterward Mr. Butts called. He came early in the evening, with his usual air of determination and a somewhat unusual spruceness. Mr. Peter Butts was a florid, blonde person, a little stout, a little pompous, sturdy and immovable in the attitude of a self-made man. He had been a poor boy when she was a rich girl; and it gratified him much to realize—and to call upon her to realize—that their positions had changed. He meant no unkindness, his pride was honest and unveiled. Tact he had none.

She had refused Mr. Butts, almost with laughter, when he proposed to her in her gay girlhood. She had refused him, more gently, when he proposed to her in her early widowhood. He had always been her friend, and her husband's friend, a solid member of the church, and had taken the small mortgage on the house. She refused to allow him at first, but he was convincingly frank about it.

"This has nothing to do with my wanting you, Delia Morrison," he said. "I've always wanted you—and I've always wanted this house, too. You won't sell, but you've got to mortgage. By and by you can't pay up, and I'll get it—see? Then maybe you'll take me—to keep the house. Don't be a fool, Delia. It's a perfectly good investment."

She had taken the loan. She had paid the interest. She would pay the interest if she had to take boarders all her life. And she would not, at any price, marry Peter Butts.

He broached the subject again that evening, cheerful and undismayed. "You might as well come to it, Delia," he said. "Then we could live right here just the same. You aren't so young as you were, to be sure; I'm not, either. But you are as good a housekeeper as ever—better—you've had more experience."

"You are extremely kind, Mr. Butts," said the lady, "but I do not wish to marry you."

"I know you don't," he said. "You've made that clear. You don't, but I do. You've had your way and married the minister. He was a good man, but he's dead. Now you might as well marry me."

"I do not wish to marry again, Mr. Butts; neither you nor anyone."

"Very proper, very proper, Delia," he replied. "It wouldn't look well if you did—at any rate, if you showed it. But why shouldn't you? The children are gone now—you can't hold them up against me any more."

"Yes, the children are both settled now, and doing nicely," she admitted.

"You don't want to go and live with them—either one of them—do you?" he asked.

"I should prefer to stay here," she answered.

"Exactly! And you can't! You'd rather live here and be a grandee—but you can't do it. Keepin' house for boarders isn't any better than keepin' house for me, as I see. You'd much better marry me."

"I should prefer to keep the house without you, Mr. Butts."

"I know you would. But you can't, I tell you. I'd like to know what a woman of your age can do with a house like this—and no money? You can't live eternally on hens' eggs and garden truck. That won't pay the mortgage."

Mrs. Morrison looked at him with her cordial smile, calm and noncommittal. "Perhaps I can manage it," she said.

"That mortgage falls due two years from Thanksgiving, you know."

"Yes—I have not forgotten."

"Well, then, you might just as well marry me now, and save two years of interest. It'll be my house, either way—but you'll be keepin' it just the same."

"It is very kind of you, Mr. Butts. I must decline the offer none the less. I can pay the interest, I am sure. And perhaps—in two years' time—I can pay the principal. It's not a large sum."

"That depends on how you look at it," said he. "Two thousand dollars is considerable money for a single woman to raise in two years—*and* interest."

He went away, as cheerful and determined as ever; and Mrs. Morrison saw him go with a keen light in her fine eyes, a more definite line to that steady, pleasant smile.

Then she went to spend Thanksgiving with Andrew. He was glad to see her. Annie was glad to see her. They proudly installed her in "her room," and said she must call it "home" now.

This affectionately offered home was twelve by fifteen, and eight feet high. It had two windows, one looking at some pale gray clapboards within reach of a broom, the other giving a view of several small fenced yards occupied by cats, clothes and children. There was an ailanthus tree under the window, a lady ailanthus tree. Annie told her how profusely it bloomed. Mrs. Morrison particularly disliked the smell of ailanthus flowers. "It doesn't bloom in November," said she to herself. "I can be thankful for that!"

Andrew's church was very like the church of his father, and Mrs. Andrew was doing her best to fill the position of minister's wife—doing it well, too—there was no vacancy for a minister's mother.

Besides, the work she had done so cheerfully to help her husband was not what she most cared for, after all. She liked the people, she liked to manage, but she was not strong on doctrine. Even her husband had never known how far her views differed from his. Mrs. Morrison had never mentioned what they were.

Andrew's people were very polite to her. She was invited out with them, waited upon and watched over and set down among the old ladies and gentlemen—she had never realized so keenly that she was no longer young. Here nothing recalled her youth, every careful provision anticipated age. Annie brought her a hot-water bag at night, tucking it in at the foot of the bed with affectionate care. Mrs. Morrison thanked her, and subsequently took it out—airing the bed a little before she got into it. The house seemed very hot to her, after the big, windy halls at home.

The little dining room, the little round table with the little round fern-dish in the middle, the little turkey and the little carving-set—game-set she would have called it—all made her feel as if she was looking through the wrong end of an opera-glass.

In Annie's precise efficiency she saw no room for her assistance; no room in the church, no room in the small, busy town, prosperous and progressive, and no room in the house. "Not enough to turn round in!" she said to herself. Annie, who had grown up in a city flat, thought their little parsonage palatial. Mrs. Morrison grew up in the Welcome House.

She stayed a week, pleasant and polite, conversational, interested in all that went on.

"I think your mother is just lovely," said Annie to Andrew.

"Charming woman, your mother," said the leading church member.

"What a delightful old lady your mother is!" said the pretty soprano.

And Andrew was deeply hurt and disappointed when she

announced her determination to stay on for the present in her old home. "Dear boy," she said, "you mustn't take it to heart. I love to be with you, of course, but I love my home, and want to keep it is long as I can. It is a great pleasure to see you and Annie so well settled, and so happy together. I am most truly thankful for you."

"My home is open to you whenever you wish to come, mother," said Andrew. But he was a little angry.

Mrs. Morrison came home as eager as a girl, and opened her own door with her own key, in spite of Sally's haste.

Two years were before her in which she must find some way to keep herself and Sally, and to pay two thousand dollars and the interest to Peter Butts. She considered her assets. Here was the house—the white elephant. It *was* big— very big. It was profusely furnished. Her father had entertained lavishly like the Southern-born, hospitable gentleman he was; and the bedrooms ran in suites—somewhat deteriorated by the use of boarders, but still numerous and habitable. Boarders—she abhorred them. They were people from afar, strangers and interlopers. She went over the place from garret to cellar, from front gate to backyard fence.

The garden had great possibilities. She was fond of gardening, and understood it well. She measured and estimated.

"This garden," she finally decided, "with the hens, will feed us two women and sell enough to pay Sally. If we make plenty of jelly, it may cover the coal bill, too. As to clothes— I don't need any. They last admirably. I can manage. I can *live*—but two thousand dollars—*and* interest!"

In the great attic was more furniture, discarded sets put there when her extravagant young mother had ordered new ones. And chairs—uncounted chairs. Senator Welcome used to invite numbers to meet his political friends—and they had delivered glowing orations in the wide, double parlors, the impassioned speakers standing on a temporary dais, now in the cellar; and the enthusiastic listeners disposed more or less comfortably on these serried rows of "folding chairs," which folded sometimes, and let down the visitor in scarlet confusion to the floor.

She sighed as she remembered those vivid days and glittering nights. She used to steal downstairs in her little pink wrapper and listen to the eloquence. It delighted her young soul to see her father rising on his toes, coming down sharply on his heels, hammering one hand upon the other; and then to hear the fusillade of applause.

Here were the chairs, often borrowed for weddings, funerals, and church affairs, somewhat worn and depleted, but still numerous. She mused upon them. Chairs—hundreds of chairs. They would sell for very little.

She went through her linen room. A splendid stock in the old days; always carefully washed by Sally; surviving even the boarders. Plenty of bedding, plenty of towels, plenty of napkins and tablecloths. "It would make a good hotel—but I *can't* have it so—I *can't!* Besides, there's no need of another hotel here. The poor little Haskins House is never full."

The stock in the china closet was more damaged than some other things, naturally; but she inventoried it with care. The countless cups of crowded church receptions were especially prominent. Later additions these, not very costly cups, but numerous, appallingly.

When she had her long list of assets all in order, she sat and studied it with a clear and daring mind. Hotel—boardinghouse—she could think of nothing else. School! A girl's school! A boarding school! There was money to be made at that, and fine work done. It was a brilliant thought at first, and she gave several hours, and much paper and ink, to its full consideration. But she would need some capital for advertising; she must engage teachers—adding to her definite obligation; and to establish it, well, it would require time.

Mr. Butts, obstinate, pertinacious, oppressively affectionate, would give her no time. He meant to force her to marry him for her own good—and his. She shrugged her fine shoulders with a little shiver. Marry Peter Butts! Never! Mrs. Morrison still loved her husband. Some day she meant to see him again—God willing—and she did not wish to have to tell him that at fifty she had been driven into marrying Peter Butts.

Better live with Andrew. Yet when she thought of living with Andrew, she shivered again. Pushing back her sheets of figures and lists of personal property, she rose to her full graceful height and began to walk the floor. There was plenty of floor to walk. She considered, with a set deep thoughtfulness, the town and the townspeople, the surrounding country, the hundreds upon hundreds of women whom she knew—and liked, and who liked her.

It used to be said of Senator Welcome that he had no enemies; and some people, strangers, maliciously disposed, thought it no credit to his character. His daughter had no enemies, but no one had ever blamed her for her unlimited friendliness. In her father's wholesale entertainments the whole town knew and admired his daughter; in her husband's popular church she had come to know the women of the countryside about them. Her mind strayed off to these women, farmers' wives, comfortably off in a plain way, but starving for companionship, for occasional stimulus and pleasure. It was one of her joys in her husband's time to bring together these women—to teach and entertain them.

Suddenly she stopped short in the middle of the great high-ceiled room, and drew her head up proudly like a victorious queen. One wide, triumphant, sweeping glance she cast at the well-loved walls—and went back to her desk, working swiftly, excitedly, well into the hours of the night.

Presently the little town began to buzz, and the murmur ran far out into the surrounding country. Sunbonnets wagged over fences; butcher carts and pedlar's wagon carried the news farther; and ladies visiting found one topic in a thousand houses.

Mrs. Morrison was going to entertain. Mrs. Morrison had invited the whole feminine population, it would appear, to meet Mrs. Isabelle Carter Blake, of Chicago. Even Haddleton had heard of Mrs. Isabelle Carter Blake. And even Haddleton had nothing but admiration for her.

She was known the world over for her splendid work for children—for the school children and the working children of the country. Yet she was known also to have lovingly and wisely reared six children of her own—and made her husband happy in his home. On top of that she had lately written a novel, a popular novel, of which everyone was talking; and on top of that she was an intimate friend of a certain conspicuous Countess—an Italian.

It was even rumored, by some who knew Mrs. Morrison better than others—or thought they did—that the Countess was coming, too! No one had known before that Delia Welcome was a schoolmate of Isabelle Carter, and a lifelong friend; and that was ground for talk in itself.

The day arrived, and the guests arrived. They came in hundreds upon hundreds, and found ample room in the great white house.

The highest dream of the guests was realized—the Countess had come, too. With excited joy they met her, receiving impressions that would last them for all their lives, for those large widening waves of reminiscence which delight us the more as years pass. It was an incredible glory—Mrs. Isabelle Carter Blake, *and* a Countess!

Some were moved to note that Mrs. Morrison looked the easy peer of these eminent ladies, and treated the foreign nobility precisely as she did her other friends.

She spoke, her clear quiet voice reaching across the murmuring din, and silencing it.

"Shall we go into the east room? If you will all take chairs in the east room, Mrs. Blake is going to be so kind as to address us. Also perhaps her friend—"

They crowded in, sitting somewhat timorously on the unfolded chairs.

Then the great Mrs. Blake made them an address of memorable power and beauty, which received vivid sanction from that imposing presence in Parisian garments on the platform by her side. Mrs. Blake spoke to them of the work she was interested in, and how it was aided everywhere by the women's clubs. She gave them the number of these clubs, and described with contagious enthusiasm the inspiration of their great meetings. She spoke of the women's clubhouses, going up in city after city, where many associations meet and help one another. She was winning and convincing and most entertaining—an extremely attractive speaker.

Had they a women's club there? They had not.

Not *yet*, she suggested, adding that it took no time at all to make one.

They were delighted and impressed with Mrs. Blake's speech, but its effect was greatly intensified by the address of the Countess.

"I, too, am American," she told them; "born here, reared in England, married in Italy." And she stirred their hearts with a vivid account of the women's clubs and associations all over Europe, and what they were accomplishing. She was going back soon, she said, the wiser and happier for this visit to her native land, and she should remember particularly this beautiful, quiet town, trusting that if she came to it again it would have joined the great sisterhood of women, "whose hands were touching around the world for the common good."

It was a great occasion.

The Countess left next day, but Mrs. Blake remained, and spoke in some of the church meetings, to an ever widening circle of admirers. Her suggestions were practical.

"What you need here is a 'Rest and Improvement Club,' " she said. "Here are all you women coming in from the country to do your shopping—and no place to go to. No place to lie down if you're tired, to meet a friend, to eat your lunch in peace, to do your hair. All you have to do is organize, pay some small regular due, and provide yourself with what you want."

There was a volume of questions and suggestions, a little opposition, much random activity.

Who was to do it? Where was there a suitable place? They would have to hire someone to take charge of it. It would only be used once a week. It would cost too much.

Mrs. Blake, still practical, made another suggestion. "Why not combine business with pleasure, and make use of the best place in town, if you can get it? I *think* Mrs. Morrison could be persuaded to let you use part of her house; it's quite too big for one woman."

Then Mrs. Morrison, simple and cordial as ever, greeted with warm enthusiasm by her wide circle of friends.

"I have been thinking this over," she said. "Mrs. Blake has been discussing it with me. My house is certainly big enough for all of you, and there am I, with nothing to do but entertain you. Suppose you formed such a club as you speak of—for Rest and Improvement. My parlors are big enough for all manner of meetings; there are bedrooms in plenty for resting. If you form such a club I shall be glad to help with my great, cumbersome house, shall be delighted to see so many friends there so often; and I think I could furnish accommodations more cheaply than you could manage in any other way."

Then Mrs. Blake gave them facts and figures, showing how much clubhouses cost—and how little this arrangement would cost. "Most women have very little money, I know," she said, "and they hate to spend it on themselves when they have; but even a little money from each goes a long way when it is put together. I fancy there are none of us so poor we could not squeeze out, say ten cents a week. For a hundred women that would be ten dollars. Could you feed a hundred tired women for ten dollars, Mrs. Morrison?''

Mrs. Morrison smiled cordially. ''Not on chicken pie,'' she said. ''But I could give them tea and coffee, crackers and cheese for that, I think. And a quiet place to rest, and a reading room, and a place to hold meetings.''

Then Mrs. Blake quite swept them off their feet by her wit and eloquence. She gave them to understand that if a share in the palatial accommodation of the Welcome House, and as good tea and coffee as old Sally made, with a place to meet, a place to rest, a place to talk, a place to lie down, could be had for ten cents a week each, she advised them to clinch the arrangement at once before Mrs. Morrison's natural good sense had overcome her enthusiasm.

Before Mrs. Isabelle Carter Blake had left, Haddleton had a large and eager women's club, whose entire expenses, outside of stationery and postage, consisted of ten cents a week *per capita*, paid to Mrs. Morrison. Everybody belonged. It was open at once for charter members, and all pressed forward to claim that privileged place.

They joined by hundreds, and from each member came this tiny sum to Mrs. Morrison each week. It was very little money, taken separately. But it added up with silent speed. Tea and coffee, purchased in bulk, crackers by the barrel, and whole cheeses—these are not expensive luxuries. The town was full of Mrs. Morrison's ex-Sunday-school boys, who furnished her with the best they had—at cost. There was a good deal of work, a good deal of care, and room for the whole supply of Mrs. Morrison's diplomatic talent and experience. Saturdays found the Welcome House as full as it could hold, and Sundays found Mrs. Morrison in bed. But she liked it.

A busy, hopeful year flew by, and then she went to Jean's for Thanksgiving.

The room Jean gave her was about the same size as her haven in Andrew's home, but one flight higher up, and with a sloping ceiling. Mrs. Morrison whitened her dark hair upon it, and rubbed her head confusedly. Then she shook it with renewed determination.

The house was full of babies. There was little Joe, able to get about, and into everything. There were the twins, and there was the new baby. There was one servant, over-worked

and cross. There was a small, cheap, totally inadequate
nursemaid. There was Jean, happy but tired, full of joy,
anxiety and affection, proud of her children, proud of her
husband, and delighted to unfold her heart to her mother.

By the hour she babbled of their cares and hopes, while
Mrs. Morrison, tall and elegant, in her well-kept old black
silk, sat holding the baby or trying to hold the twins. The
old silk was pretty well finished by the week's end. Joseph
talked to her also, telling her how well he was getting on,
and how much he needed capital, urging her to come and
stay with them; it was such a help to Jeannie; asking questions about the house.

There was no going visiting here. Jeannie could not leave
the babies. And few visitors; all the little suburb being full
of similarly overburdened mothers. Such as called found
Mrs. Morrison charming. What she found them, she did not
say. She bade her daughter an affectionate good-bye when
the week was up, smiling at their mutual contentment.

"Good-bye, my dear children," she said. "I am so glad
for all your happiness. I am thankful for both of you."

But she was more thankful to get home.

Mr. Butts did not have to call for his interest this time,
but he called none the less.

"How on earth'd you get it, Delia?" he demanded.
"Screwed it out o' these club-women?"

"Your interest is so moderate, Mr. Butts, that it is easier
to meet than you imagine," was her answer. "Do you know
the average interest they charge in Colorado? The women
vote there, you know."

He went away with no more personal information than
that; and no nearer approach to the twin goals of his desire
than the passing of the year.

"One more year, Delia," he said; "then you'll have to
give in."

"One more year!" she said to herself, and took up her
chosen task with renewed energy.

The financial basis of the undertaking was very simple,
but it would never have worked so well under less skilful
management. Five dollars a year these country women could
not have faced, but ten cents a week was possible to the
poorest. There was no difficulty in collecting, for they
brought it themselves; no unpleasantness in receiving, for

old Sally stood at the receipt of custom and presented the covered cashbox when they came for their tea.

On the crowded Saturdays the great urns were set going, the mighty array of cups arranged in easy reach, the ladies filed by, each taking her refection and leaving her dime. Where the effort came was in enlarging the membership and keeping up the attendance; and this effort was precisely in the line of Mrs. Morrison's splendid talents.

Serene, cheerful, inconspicuously active, planning like the born statesman she was, executing like a practical politician, Mrs. Morrison gave her mind to the work, and thrived upon it. Circle within circle, and group within group, she set small classes and departments at work, having a boys' club by and by in the big room over the woodshed, girls' clubs, reading clubs, study clubs, little meetings of every sort that were not held in churches, and some that were—previously.

For each and all there was, if wanted, tea and coffee, crackers and cheese; simple fare, of unvarying excellence, and from each and all, into the little cashbox, ten cents for these refreshments. From the club members this came weekly; and the club members, kept up by a constant variety of interests, came every week. As to numbers, before the first six months were over The Haddleton Rest and Improvement Club numbered five hundred women.

Now, five hundred times ten cents a week is twenty-six hundred dollars a year. Twenty-six hundred dollars a year would not be very much to build or rent a large house, to furnish five hundred people with chairs, lounges, books and magazines, dishes and service; and with food and drink even of the simplest. But if you are miraculously supplied with a clubhouse, furnished, with a manager and servant on the spot, then that amount of money goes a long way.

On Saturdays Mrs. Morrison hired two helpers for half a day, for half a dollar each. She stocked the library with many magazines for fifty dollars a year. She covered fuel, light, and small miscellanies with another hundred. And she fed her multitude with the plain viands agreed upon, at about four cents apiece.

For her collateral entertainments, her many visits, the various new expenses entailed, she paid as well; and yet at the end of the first year she had not only her interest, but a solid thousand dollars of clear profit. With a calm smile she surveyed it, heaped in neat stacks of bills in the small safe in the wall behind her bed. Even Sally did not know it was there.

The second season was better than the first. There were difficulties, excitements, even some opposition, but she rounded out the year triumphantly. "After that," she said to herself, "they may have the deluge if they like."

She made all expenses, made her interest, made a little extra cash, clearly her own, all over and above the second thousand dollars.

Then did she write to son and daughter, inviting them and their families to come home to Thanksgiving, and closing each letter with joyous pride: "Here is the money to come with."

They all came, with all the children and two nurses. There was plenty of room in the Welcome House, and plenty of food on the long mahogany table. Sally was as brisk as a bee, brilliant in scarlet and purple; Mrs. Morrison carved her big turkey with queenly grace.

"I don't see that you're overrun with club-women, mother," said Jeannie.

"It's Thanksgiving, you know; they're all at home. I hope they are all as happy, as thankful for their homes as I am for mine," said Mrs. Morrison.

Afterward Mr. Butts called. With dignity and calm unruffled, Mrs. Morrison handed him his interest—and principal.

Mr. Butts was almost loath to receive it, though his hand automatically grasped the crisp blue check.

"I didn't know you had a bank account," he protested, somewhat dubiously.

"Oh, yes; you'll find the check will be honored, Mr. Butts."

"I'd like to know how you got this money. You *can't* 'a' skinned it out o' that club of yours."

"I appreciate your friendly interest, Mr. Butts; you have been most kind."

"I believe some of these great friends of yours have lent it to you. You won't be any better off, I can tell you."

"Come, come Mr. Butts! Don't quarrel with good money. Let us part friends."

And they parted.

HER HOUSEKEEPER

On the top floor of a New York boarding-house lived a particularly attractive woman who was an actress. She was also a widow, not divorcée, but just plain widow; and she persisted in acting under her real name, which was Mrs. Leland. The manager objected, but her reputation was good enough to carry the point.

"It will cost you a great deal of money, Mrs. Leland," said the manager.

"I make money enough," she answered.

"You will not attract so many—admirers," said the manager.

"I have admirers enough," she answered; which was visibly true.

She was well under thirty, even by daylight—and about eighteen on the stage; and as for admirers—they apparently thought Mrs. Leland was a carefully selected stage name.

Besides being a widow she was a mother, having a small boy of about five years; and this small boy did not look in the least like a "stage child," but was a brown-skinned, healthy little rascal of the ordinary sort.

With this boy, an excellent nursery governess, and a maid, Mrs. Leland occupied the top floor above mentioned, and enjoyed it. She had a big room in front, to receive in; and a small room with a skylight, to sleep in. The boy's room and the governess' room were at the back, with sunny south windows, and the maid slept on a couch in the parlor. She was a colored lady, named Alice, and did not seem to care where she slept, or if she slept at all.

"I never was so comfortable in my life," said Mrs. Leland to her friends. "I've been here three years and mean to stay. It is not like any boarding-house I ever saw, and it is not like any home I ever had. I have the privacy, the detachment, the carelessness of a boarding-house, and 'all the comforts of a home.' Up I go to my little top flat as private as you like. My Alice takes care of it—the house-maids only come in when I'm out. I can eat with the others downstairs if I please; but mostly I don't please; and up come my little meals on the dumbwaiter—hot and good.''

''But—having to flock with a lot of promiscuous boarders!'' said her friends.

''I don't flock, you see; that's just it. And besides, they are not promiscuous—there isn't a person in the house now who isn't some sort of a friend of mine. As fast as a room was vacated I'd suggest somebody—and here we all are. It's great.''

''But do you *like* a skylight room?'' Mrs. Leland's friends further inquired of her?''

''By no means!'' she promptly replied. ''I hate it. I feel like a mouse in a pitcher!''

''Then why in the name of reason—?''

''Because I can sleep there! *Sleep!*—It's the only way to be quiet in New York, and I have to sleep late if I sleep at all. I've fixed the skylight so that I'm drenched with air—and not drenched with rain!—and there I am. Johnny is gagged and muffled as it were, and carried downstairs as early as possible. He gets his breakfast, and the unfortunate Miss Merton has to go out and play with him—in all weathers—except kindergarten time. Then Alice sits on the stairs and keeps everybody away till I ring.''

Possibly it was owing to the stillness and the air and the sleep till near lunchtime that Mrs. Leland kept her engaging youth, her vivid uncertain beauty. At times you said of her, ''She has a keen intelligent face, but she's not pretty.'' Which was true. She was not pretty. But at times again she overcame you with her sudden loveliness.

All of which was observed by her friend from the second floor who wanted to marry her. In this he was not alone; either as a friend, of whom she had many, or as lover, of whom she had more. His distinction lay first in his oppor-tunities, as a co-resident, for which he was heartily hated by all the more and some of the many; and second in that he remained a friend in spite of being a lover, and remained a lover in spite of being flatly refused.

His name in the telephone book was given "Arthur Olmstead, real estate"; office this and residence that—she looked him up therein after their first meeting. He was rather a short man, heavily built, with a quiet kind face, and a somewhat quizzical smile. He seemed to make all the money he needed, occupied the two rooms and plentiful closet space of his floor in great contentment, and manifested most improper domesticity of taste by inviting friends to tea. "Just like a woman!" Mrs. Leland told him.

"And why not? Women have so many attractive ways— why not imitate them?" he asked her.

"A man doesn't want to be feminine, I'm sure," struck in a pallid, overdressed youth, with openwork socks on his slim feet, and perfumed handkerchief.

Mr. Olmstead smiled a broad friendly smile. He was standing near the young man, a little behind him, and at this point he put his hands just beneath the youth's arms, lifted and set him aside as if he were an umbrella-stand. "Excuse me, Mr. Masters," he said gravely, "but you were standing on Mrs. Leland's gown."

Mr. Masters was too much absorbed in apologizing to the lady to take umbrage at the method of his removal; but she was not so oblivious. She tried doing it to her little boy afterward and found him very heavy.

When she came home from her walk or drive in the early winter dusk, this large quietly furnished room, the glowing fire, the excellent tea and delicate thin bread and butter were most restful. "It is two more stories up before I can get my own"; she would say—"I must stop a minute."

When he began to propose to her the first time she tried to stop him. "O please don't!" she cried. *"Please* don't! There are no end of reasons why I will not marry anybody again. Why can't some of you men be nice to me and not— that! Now I can't come in to tea any more!"

"I'd like to know why not," said he calmly. "You don't have to marry me if you don't want to; but that's no reason for cutting my acquaintance, is it?"

She gazed at him in amazement.

"I'm not threatening to kill myself, am I? I don't intend going to the devil. I'd like to be your husband, but if I can't—mayn't I be a brother to you?"

She was inclined to think he was making fun of her, but no—his proposal had had the real ring in it. "And you're not, you're not going to—?'' It seemed the baldest assumption to think that he was going to, he looked so strong and calm and friendly.

"Not going to annoy you? Not going to force an undesired affection on you and rob myself of a most agreeable friendship? Of course not. Your tea is cold, Mrs. Leland— let me give you another cup. And do you think Miss Rose is going to do well as 'Angelina'?''

So presently Mrs. Leland was quite relieved in her mind, and free to enjoy the exceeding comfortableness of this relation. Little Johnny was extremely fond of Mr. Olmstead; who always treated him with respect, and who could listen to his tales of strife and glory more intelligently than either mother or governess. Mr. Olmstead kept on hand a changing supply of interesting things; not toys—never, but real things not intended for little boys to play with. No little boy would want to play with dolls for instance; but what little boy would not be fascinated by a small wooden lay figure, capable of unheard-of contortions. Tin soldiers were common, but the flags of all nations—real flags, and true stories about them, were interesting. Noah's arks were cheap and unreliable scientifically; but Barye lions, ivory elephants, and Japanese monkeys in didactic groups of three, had unfailing attraction. And the books this man had—great solid books that could be opened wide on the floor, and a little boy lie down to in peace and comfort!

Mrs. Leland stirred her tea and watched them until Johnny was taken upstairs.

"Why don't you smoke?'' she asked suddenly. "Doctor's orders?''

"No—mine," he answered. "I never consulted a doctor in my life.''

"Nor a dentist, I judge,'' said she.

"Nor a dentist.''

"You'd better knock on wood!'' she told him.

"And cry 'Uncle Reuben'?'' he asked smilingly.

"You haven't told me why you don't smoke!'' said she suddenly.

"Haven't I?'' he said. "That was very rude of me. But look here. There's a thing I wanted to ask you. Now I'm not pressing any sort of inquiry as to myself; but as a brother, would you mind telling me some of those numerous reasons why you will not marry anybody?''

She eyed him suspiciously, but he was as solid and calm as usual, regarding her pleasantly and with no hint of ulterior purpose. ''Why—I don't mind,'' she began slowly. ''First—I have been married—and was very unhappy. That's reason enough.''

He did not contradict her; but merely said, ''That's one,'' and set it down in his notebook.

''Dear me, Mr. Olmstead! You're not a reporter, are you!''

''O no— But I wanted to have them clear and think about them,'' he explained. ''Do you mind?'' And he made as if to shut his little book again.

''I don't know as I mind,'' she said slowly. ''But it looks so—businesslike.''

''This is a very serious business, Mrs. Leland, as you must know. Quite aside from any personal desire of my own, I am truly 'your sincere friend and well-wisher,' as the Complete Letter Writer has it; and there are so many men wanting to marry you.''

This she knew full well, and gazed pensively at the toe of her small flexible slipper, poised on a stool before the fire.

Mr. Olmstead also gazed at the slipper toe with appreciation.

''What's the next one?'' he said cheerfully.

''Do you know you are a real comfort,'' she told him suddenly. ''I never knew a man before who could—well leave off being a man for a moment and just be a human creature.''

''Thank you, Mrs. Leland,'' he said in tones of pleasant sincerity. ''I want to be a comfort to you if I can. Incidentally wouldn't you be more comfortable on this side of the fire—the light falls better—don't move.'' And before she realized what he was doing he picked her up, chair and all, and put her down softly on the other side, setting the footstool as before, and even daring to place her little feet upon it—but with so busineslike an air that she saw no opening for rebuke. It is a difficult matter to object to a man's doing things like that when he doesn't look as if he was doing them.

''That's better,'' said he cheerfully, taking the place where she had been. ''Now, what's the next one?''

"The next one is my boy."

"Second—Boy," he said, putting it down. "But I should think he'd be a reason the other way. Excuse me—I wasn't going to criticize—yet! And the third?"

"Why should you criticize at all, Mr. Olmstead?"

"I shouldn't—on my own account. But there may come a man you love." He had a fine baritone voice. When she heard him sing Mrs. Leland always wished he were taller, handsomer, more distinguished looking; his voice sounded as if he were. "And I should hate to see these reasons standing in the way of your happiness," he continued.

"Perhaps they wouldn't," said she in a revery.

"Perhaps they wouldn't—and in that case it is no possible harm that you tell me the rest of them. I won't cast it up at you. Third?"

"Third, I won't give up my profession for any man alive."

"Any man alive would be a fool to want you to," said he setting down—"Third—Profession."

"Fourth—I like *Freedom!*" she said with sudden intensity. You don't know!—they kept me so tight!—so *tight!*— when I was a girl! Then—I was left alone, with a very little money, and I began to study for the stage—that was like heaven! And then—O what *idiots* women are!" She said the word not tragically, but with such hard-pointed intensity that it sounded like a gimlet. "Then I married, you see—I gave up all my new-won freedom to *marry!*—and he kept me tighter than ever." She shut her expressive mouth in level lines—stood up suddenly and stretched her arms wide and high. "I'm free again, free—I can do exactly as I please!" The words were individually relished. "I have the work I love. I can earn all I need—am saving something for the boy. I'm perfectly independent!"

"And perfectly happy!" he cordially endorsed her. "I don't blame you for not wanting to give it up."

"O well—happy!" she hesitated. "There are times, of course, when one isn't happy. But then—the other way I was unhappy all the time."

"He's dead—unfortunately," mused Mr. Olmstead.

"Unfortunately?—Why?"

He looked at her with his straightforward, pleasant smile. "I'd have liked the pleasure of killing him," he said regretfully.

She was startled, and watched him with dawning alarm.

But he was quite quiet—even cheerful. "Fourth—Freedom," he wrote. "Is that all?"

"No—there are two more. Neither of them will please you. You won't think so much of me any more. The worst one is this. I like—lovers! I'm very much ashamed of it, but I do! I try not to be unfair to them—some I really try to keep away from me—but honestly I like admiration and lots of it."

"What's the harm of that?" he asked easily, setting down, "Fifth—Lovers."

"No harm, so long as I'm my own mistress," said she defiantly. "I take care of my boy, I take care of myself—let them take care of themselves! Don't blame me too much!"

"You're not a very good psychologist, I'm afraid," said he.

"What do you mean?" she asked rather nervously.

"You surely don't expect a man to blame you for being a woman, do you?"

"All women are not like that," she hastily asserted. "They are too conscientious. Lots of my friends blame me severely."

"Women friends," he ventured.

"Men, too. Some men have said very hard things of me."

"Because you turned 'em down. That's natural."

"You don't!"

"No, I don't. I'm different."

"How different?" she asked.

He looked at her steadily. His eyes were hazel, flecked with changing bits of color, deep, steady, with a sort of inner light that grew as she watched till presently she thought it well to consider her slipper again; and continued, "The sixth is as bad as the other almost. I hate—I'd like to write a dozen tragic plays to show how much I hate—Housekeeping! There! That's all!"

"Sixth—Housekeeping," he wrote down, quite unmoved. "But why should anyone blame you for that—it's not your business."

"No—thank goodness, it's not! And never will be! I'm *free*, I tell you and I stay free!—But look at the clock!" And she whisked away to dress for dinner.

He was not at table that night—not at home that night—not at home for some days—the landlady said he had gone out of town; and Mrs. Leland missed her afternoon tea.

She had it upstairs, of course, and people came in—both friends and lovers; but she missed the quiet and coziness of the green and brown room downstairs.

Johnny missed his big friend still more. "Mama, where's Mr. Olmstead? Mama, why don't Mr. Olmstead come back? Mama! When is Mr. Olmstead coming back? Mama! Why don't you write to Mr. Olmstead and tell him to come back? Mama!—can't we go in there and play with his things?"

As if in answer to this last wish she got a little note from him saying simply, "Don't let Johnny miss the lions and monkeys—he and Miss Merton and you, of course, are quite welcome to the whole floor. Go in at any time."

Just to keep the child quiet she took advantage of this offer, and Johnny introduced her to all the ins and outs of the place. In a corner of the bedroom was a zinc-lined tray with clay in it, where Johnny played rapturously at "making country." While he played his mother noted the quiet good taste and individuality of the place.

"It smells so clean!" she said to herself. "There! he hasn't told me yet why he doesn't smoke. I never told him I didn't like it."

Johnny tugged at bureau drawer. "He keeps the water in here!" he said, and before she could stop him he had out a little box with bits of looking-glass in it, which soon became lakes and rivers in his clay continent.

Mrs. Leland put them back afterward, admiring the fine quality and goodly number of garments in that drawer, and their perfect order. Her husband had been a man who made a chowder of his bureau drawers, and who expected her to find all his studs and put them in for him.

"A man like this would be no trouble at all," she thought for a moment—but then remembered other things and set her mouth hard. "Not for mine!" she said determinedly.

By and by he came back, serene as ever, friendly and unpresuming.

"Aren't you going to tell me why you don't smoke?" she suddenly demanded of him on another quiet dusky afternoon when tea was before them.

He seemed so impersonal, almost remote, though nicer than ever to Johnny; and Mrs. Leland rather preferred the personal note in conservation.

"Why of course I am," he replied cordially. "That's easy," and he fumbled in his inner pocket.

"Is that where you keep your reasons?" she mischievously inquired.

"It's where I keep yours," he promptly answered, producing the little notebook. "Now look here—I've got these all answered—you won't be able to hold to one of 'em after this. May I sit by you and explain?"

She made room for him on the sofa amiably enough, but defied him to convince her. "Go ahead," she said cheerfully.

"'First,'" he read off, "'Previous Marriage. This is not a sufficient objection. Because you have been married you now know what to choose and what to avoid. A girl is comparatively helpless in this matter; you are armed. That your first marriage was unhappy is a reason for trying it again. It is not only that you are better able to choose, but that by the law of chances you stand to win next time. Do you admit the justice of this reasoning?"

"I don't admit anything," she said. "I'm waiting to ask you a question."

"Ask it now."

"No—I'll wait till you are all through. Do go on."

"'Second—The Boy,'" he continued. "Now Mrs. Leland, solely on the boy's account I should advise you to marry again. While he is a baby a mother is enough, but the older he grows the more he will need a father. Of course you should select a man the child could love—a man who could love the child."

"I begin to suspect you of deep double-dyed surreptitious designs, Mr. Olmstead. You know Johnny loves you dearly. And you know I won't marry you," she hastily added.

"I'm not asking you to—now, Mrs. Leland. I did, in good faith, and I would again if I thought I had the shadow of a chance—but I'm not at present. Still, I'm quite willing to stand as an instance. Now, we might resume, on that basis. Objection one does not really hold against me—now does it?"

He looked at her cheerily, warmly, openly; and in his clean, solid strength and tactful kindness he was so unspeakably different from the dark, fascinating slender man who had become a nightmare to her youth, that she felt in her heart he was right—so far. "I won't admit a thing," she said sweetly. "But pray go on."

He went on, unabashed. "'Second—Boy.' Now if you

married me I should consider the boy as an added attraction. Indeed—if you do marry again—someone who doesn't want the boy—I wish you'd give him to me. I mean it. I think he loves me, and I think I could be of real service to the child.''

He seemed almost to have forgotten her, and she watched him curiously.

"Now, to go on," he continued. " 'Third—Profession.' As to your profession," said he slowly, clasping his hands over one knee and gazing at the dark soft-colored rug, "if you married me, and gave up your profession I should find it a distinct loss. I should lose my favorite actress.''

She gave a little start of surprise.

"Didn't you know how much I admire your work?" he said. "I don't hang around the stage entrance—there are plenty of chappies to do that; and I don't always occupy a box and throw bouquets—I don't like a box anyhow. But I haven't missed seeing you in any part you've played yet— some of 'em I've seen a dozen times. And you're growing— you'll do better work still. It is sometimes a little weak in the love parts—seemed as if you couldn't quite take it seriously—couldn't let yourself go—but you'll grow. You'll do better—I really think—after you're married.''

She was rather impressed by this, but found it rather difficult to say anything; for he was not looking at her at all. He took up his notebook again with a smile.

"So—if you married me, you would be more than welcome to go on with your profession. I wouldn't stand in your way any more than I do now. 'Fourth—Freedom,' he read slowly. "That is easy, in one way—hard in another. If you married me,''—She stirred resentfully at this constant reference to their marriage; but he seemed purely hypothetical in tone; "*I* wouldn't interfere with your freedom any. Not of my own will. But if you ever grew to love me—or if there were children—it would make *some* difference. Not much. There mightn't be any children, and it isn't likely you'd ever love me enough to have that stand in your way. Otherwise than that you'd have freedom—as much as now. A little more; because if you wanted to take a foreign tour, or anything like that, I'd take care of Johnny. 'Fifth—Lovers.' " Here he paused leaning forward with his chin in his hands, his eyes bent down. She could see the broad heavy shoulders, the smooth fit of the well-made coat, the spotless collar, and the fine, strong, clean-cut neck. As it happened she particularly disliked the neck of the average man—either the cordy, the beefy or the adipose, and particularly liked this kind, firm and round like a Roman's, with the hair coming to a clean-cut edge and stopping there.

"As to lovers," he went on—"I hesitate a little as to what to say about that. I'm afraid I shall shock you. Perhaps I'd better leave out that one."

"As insuperable?" she mischievously asked.

"No, as too easy," he answered.

"You'd better explain," she said.

"Well then—it's simply this: as a man—I myself admire you more because so many other men admire you. I don't sympathize with them, any!—Not for a minute. Of course, if you loved any one of them you wouldn't be my wife. But if you were my wife—"

"Well?" said she, a little breathlessly. "You're very irritating! What would you do? Kill 'em all? Come—If I were your wife?—"

"If you were my wife—" he turned and faced her squarely, his deep eyes blazing steadily into hers, "In the first place the more lovers you had that you didn't love the better I'd be pleased."

"And if I did?" she dared him.

"If you were my wife," he pursued with perfect quietness, "you would never love anyone else."

There was a throbbing silence.

" 'Sixth—Housekeeping,' " he read.

At this she rose to her feet as if released. "Sixth and last and all-sufficient!" she burst out, giving herself a little shake as if to waken. "Final and conclusive and admitting no reply!—I will not keep house for any man. Never! Never!! Never!!!"

"Why should you?" he said, as he had said it before; "Why not board?"

"I wouldn't board on any account!"

"But you are boarding now. Aren't you comfortable here?"

"O yes, perfectly comfortable. But this is the only boarding-house I ever saw that was comfortable."

"Why not go on as we are—if you married me?"

She laughed shrilly. "With the other boarders round them and a whole floor laid between," she parodied gaily. "No, sir! *If* I ever married again—and I won't—I'd want a home of my own—a whole house—and have it run as smoothly and perfectly as this does. With no more care than I have now!''

''If I could give you a whole house, like this, and run it for you as smoothly and perfectly as this one—then would you marry me?'' he asked.

''O, I dare say I would,'' she said mockingly.

''My dear,'' said he, ''I have kept this house—for you— for three years.''

''What do you mean?'' she demanded, flushingly.

''I mean that it is my business,'' he answered serenely. ''Some men run hotels and some restaurants: I keep a number of boarding-houses and make a handsome income from them. All the people are comfortable—I see to that. I planned to have you use these rooms, had the dumbwaiter run to the top so you could have meals comfortably there. You didn't much like the first housekeeper. I got one you liked better; cooks to please you, maids to please you. I have most seriously tried to make you comfortable. When you didn't like a boarder I got rid of him—or her—they are mostly your friends now. Of course if we were married, we'd fire 'em all.'' His tone was perfectly calm and businesslike. ''You should keep your special apartments on top; you should also have the floor above this, a larger bedroom, drawingroom, and bath, and private parlor for you;—I'd stay right here as I am now—and when you wanted me—I'd be here.''

She stiffened a little at this rather tame ending. She was stirred, uneasy, dissatisfied. She felt as if something had been offered and withdrawn; something was lacking.

''It seems such a funny business—for a man,'' she said.

''Any funnier than Delmonico's?'' he asked. ''It's a business that takes some ability—witness the many failures. It is certainly useful. And it pays—amazingly.''

''I thought it was real estate,'' she insisted.

''It is. I'm in a real estate office. I buy and sell houses— that's how I came to take this up!''

He rose up, calmly and methodically, walked over to the fire, and laid his notebook on it. ''There wasn't any strength in any of those objections, my dear,'' said he. ''Especially the first one. Previous marriage, indeed! You have never been married before. You are going to be—now.''

* * *

It was some weeks after that marriage that she suddenly turned upon him—as suddenly as one can turn upon a person whose arms are about one—demanding.

"And why don't you smoke?—You never told me!"

"I shouldn't like to kiss you so well if you smoked!"—said he.

"I never had any idea," she ventured after a while, "that it could be—like this."

WHEN I WAS A WITCH

If I had understood the terms of that one-sided contract with Satan, the Time of Witching would have lasted longer—you may be sure of that. But how was I to tell? It just happened, and has never happened again, though I've tried the same preliminaries as far as I could control them.

The thing began all of a sudden, one October midnight—the 30th, to be exact. It had been hot, really hot, all day, and was sultry and thunderous in the evening; no air stirring, and the whole house stewing with that ill-advised activity which always seems to move the steam radiator when it isn't wanted.

I was in a state of simmering rage—hot enough, even without the weather and the furnace—and I went up on the roof to cool off. A top-floor apartment has that advantage, among others—you can take a walk without the mediation of an elevator boy!

There are things enough in New York to lose one's temper over at the best of times, and on this particular day they seemed to all happen at once, and some fresh ones. The night before, cats and dogs had broken my rest, of course. My morning paper was more than usually mendacious; and my neighbor's morning paper—more visible than my own as I went down town—was more than usually salacious. My cream wasn't cream—my egg was a relic of the past. My "new" napkins were giving out.

Being a woman, I'm supposed not to swear; but when the motorman disregarded my plain signal, and grinned as he rushed by; when the subway guard waited till I was just about to step on board and then slammed the door in my face—standing behind it calmly for some minutes before the bell rang to warrant his closing—I desired to swear like a mule-driver.

At night it was worse. The way people paw one's back in the crowd! The cow-puncher who packs the people in or jerks them out—the men who smoke and spit, law or no law—the women whose saw-edged cart-wheel hats, swashing feathers and deadly pins, add so to one's comfort inside.

Well, as I said, I was in a particularly bad temper, and went up on the roof to cool off. Heavy black clouds hung low overhead, and lightning flickered threateningly here and there.

A starved, black cat stole from behind a chimney and mewed dolefully. Poor thing! She had been scalded.

The street was quiet for New York. I leaned over a little and looked up and down the long parallels of twinkling lights. A belated cab drew near, the horse so tired he could hardly hold his head up.

Then the driver, with a skill born of plenteous practice, flung out his long-lashed whip and curled it under the poor beast's belly with a stinging cut that made me shudder. The horse shuddered too, poor wretch, and jingled his harness with an effort at a trot.

I leaned over the parapet and watched that man with a spirit of unmitigated ill-will.

"I wish," said I, slowly—and I did wish it with all my heart—"that every person who strikes or otherwise hurts a horse unnecessarily, shall feel the pain intended—and the horse not feel it!"

It did me good to say it, anyhow, but I never expected any result. I saw the man swing his great whip again, and lay on heartily. I saw him throw up his hands—heard him scream—but I never thought what the matter was, even then.

The lean, black cat, timid but trustful, rubbed against my skirt and mewed.

"Poor Kitty!" I said; "poor Kitty! It is a shame!" And I thought tenderly of all the thousands of hungry, hunted cats who slink and suffer in a great city.

Later, when I tried to sleep, and up across the stillness rose the raucous shrieks of some of these same sufferers, my pity turned cold. "Any fool that will try to keep a cat in a city!" I muttered, angrily.

Another yell—a pause—an ear-torturing, continuous cry.

"I wish," I burst forth, "that every cat in the city was comfortably dead!"

A sudden silence fell, and in course of time I got to sleep.

Things went fairly well next morning, till I tried another egg. They were expensive eggs, too.

"I can't help it!" said my sister, who keeps house.

"I know you can't," I admitted. "But somebody could help it. I wish the people who are responsible had to eat their old eggs, and never get a good one till they sold good ones!"

"They'd stop eating eggs, that's all," said my sister, "and eat meat."

"Let 'em eat meat!" I said, recklessly. "The meat is as bad as the eggs! It's so long since we've had a clean, fresh chicken that I've forgotten how they taste!"

"It's cold storage," said my sister. She is a peaceable sort; I'm not.

"Yes, cold storage!" I snapped. "It ought to be a blessing—to tide over shortages, equalize supplies, and lower prices. What does it do? Corner the market, raise prices the year round, and make all the food bad!"

My anger rose. "If there was any way of getting at them!" I cried. "The law don't touch 'em. They need to be cursed somehow! I'd like to do it! I wish the whole crowd that profit by this vicious business might taste their bad meat, their old fish, their stale milk—whatever they ate. Yes, and feel the prices as we do!"

"They couldn't, you know; they're rich," said my sister.

"I know that," I admitted, sulkily. "There's no way of getting at 'em. But I wish they could. And I wish they knew how people hated 'em, and felt that, too—till they mended their ways!"

When I left for my office I saw a funny thing. A man who drove a garbage cart took his horse by the bits and jerked and wrenched brutally. I was amazed to see him clap his hands to his own jaws with a moan, while the horse philosophically licked his chops and looked at him.

The man seemed to resent his expression, and struck him on the head, only to rub his own poll and swear amazedly, looking around to see who had hit him. The horse advanced a step, stretching a hungry nose toward a garbage pail crowned with cabbage leaves, and the man, recovering his sense of proprietorship, swore at him and kicked him in the ribs. That time he had to sit down, turning pale and weak. I watched with growing wonder and delight.

A market wagon came clattering down the street; the hard-faced young ruffian fresh for his morning task. He gathered the ends of the reins and brought them down on the horse's back with a resounding thwack. The horse did not notice this at all, but the boy did. He yelled!

I came to a place where many teamsters were at work hauling dirt and crushed stone. A strange silence and peace hung over the scene where usually the sound of the lash and sight of brutal blows made me hurry by. The men were talking together a little, and seemed to be exchanging notes. It was too good to be true. I gazed and marvelled, waiting for my car.

It came, merrily running along. It was not full. There was one not far ahead, which I had missed in watching the horses; there was no other near it in the rear.

Yet the coarse-faced person in authority who ran it, went gaily by without stopping, though I stood on the track almost, and waved my umbrella.

A hot flush of rage surged to my face. "I wish you felt the blow you deserve," said I, viciously, looking after the car. "I wish you'd have to stop, and back to here, and open the door and apologize. I wish that would happen to all of you, every time you play that trick."

To my infinite amazement, that car stopped and backed till the front door was before me. The motorman opened it, holding his hand to his cheek. "Beg your pardon, madam!" he said.

I passed in, dazed, overwhelmed. Could it be? Could it possibly be that—that what I wished came true. The idea sobered me, but I dismissed it with a scornful smile. "No such luck!" said I.

Opposite me sat a person in petticoats. She was of a sort I particularly detest. No real body of bones and muscles, but the contours of grouped sausages. Complacent, gaudily dressed, heavily wigged and ratted, with powder and perfume and flowers and jewels—and a dog.

A poor, wretched, little, artificial dog—alive, but only so by virtue of man's insolence; not a real creature that God made. And the dog had clothes on—and a bracelet! His fitted jacket had a pocket—and a pocket-handkerchief! He looked sick and unhappy.

I meditated on his pitiful position, and that of all the other poor chained prisoners, leading unnatural lives of enforced celibacy, cut off from sunlight, fresh air, the use of their limbs; led forth at stated intervals by unwilling servants, to defile our streets; over-fed, under-exercised, nervous and unhealthy.

"And we say we love them!" said I, bitterly to myself. "No wonder they bark and howl and go mad. No wonder they have almost as many diseases as we do! I wish——" Here the thought I had dismissed struck me again. "I wish that all the unhappy dogs in cities would die at once!"

I watched the sad-eyed little invalid across the car. He dropped his head and died. She never noticed it till she got off; then she made fuss enough.

The evening papers were full of it. Some sudden pestilence had struck both dogs and cats, it would appear. Red headlines struck the eye, big letters, and columns were filled out of the complaints of those who had lost their "pets," of the sudden labors of the board of health, and interviews with doctors.

All day, as I went through the office routine, the strange sense of this new power struggled with reason and common knowledge. I even tried a few furtive test "wishes"—wished that the waste basket would fall over, that the inkstand would fill itself; but they didn't.

I dismissed the idea as pure foolishness, till I saw those newspapers, and heard people telling worse stories.

One thing I decided at once—not to tell a soul. "Nobody'd believe me if I did," said I to myself. "And I won't give 'em the chance. I've scored on cats and dogs, anyhow—and horses."

As I watched the horses at work that afternoon, and thought of all their unknown sufferings from crowded city stables, bad air and insufficient food, and from the wearing strain of asphalt pavements in wet and icy weather, I decided to have another try on horses.

"I wish," said I, slowly and carefully, but with a fixed intensity of purposes, "that every horse owner, keeper, hirer and driver or rider, might feel what the horse feels, when he suffers at our hands. Feel it keenly and constantly till the case is mended."

I wasn't able to verify this attempt for some time; but the effect was so general that it got widely talked about soon;

and this "new wave of humane feeling" soon raised the status of horses in our city. Also it diminished their numbers. People began to prefer motor drays—which was a mighty good thing.

Now I felt pretty well assured in my own mind, and kept my assurance to myself. Also I began to make a list of my cherished grudges, with a fine sense of power and pleasure.

"I must be careful," I said to myself; "very careful; and, above all things, 'make the punishment fit the crime.' "

The subway crowding came to my mind next; both the people who crowd because they have to, and the people who make them. "I mustn't punish anybody for what they can't help," I mused. "But when it's pure meanness!" Then I bethought me of the remote stockholders, of the more immediate directors, of the painfully prominent officials and insolent employees—and got to work.

"I might as well make a good job of it while this lasts," said I to myself. "It's quite a responsibility, but lots of fun." And I wished that every person responsible for the condition of our subways might be mysteriously compelled to ride up and down in them continuously during rush hours.

This experiment I watched with keen interest, but for the life of me I could see little difference. There were a few more well-dressed persons in the crowds, that was all. So I came to the conclusion that the general public was mostly to blame, and carried their daily punishment without knowing it.

For the insolent guards and cheating ticket-sellers who give you short change, very slowly, when you are dancing on one foot and your train is there, I merely wished that they might feel the pain their victims would like to give them, short of real injury. They did, I guess.

Then I wished similar things for all manner of corporations and officials. It worked. It worked amazingly. There was a sudden conscientious revival all over the country. The dry bones rattled and sat up. Boards of directors, having troubles enough of their own, were aggravated by innumerable communications from suddenly sensitive stockholders.

In mills and mines and railroads, things began to mend. The country buzzed. The papers fattened. The churches sat up and took credit to themselves. I was incensed at this; and, after brief consideration, wished that every minister would preach to his congregation exactly what he believed and what he thought of them.

I went to six services the next Sunday—about ten minutes each, for two sessions. It was most amusing. A thousand pulpits were emptied forthwith, refilled, re-emptied, and so on, from week to week. People began to go to church; men largely—women didn't like it as well. They had always supposed the ministers thought more highly of them than now appeared to be the case.

One of my oldest grudges was against the sleeping-car people; and I now began to consider them. How often I had grinned and borne it—with other thousands—submitting helplessly.

Here is a railroad—a common carrier—and you have to use it. You pay for your transportation, a good round sum.

Then if you wish to stay in the sleeping car during the day, they charge you another two dollars and a half for the privilege of sitting there, whereas you have paid for a seat when you bought your ticket. That seat is now sold to another person—twice sold. Five dollars for twenty-four hours in a space six feet by three by three at night, and one seat by day; twenty-four of these privileges to a car—$120 a day for the rent of the car—and the passengers to pay the porter besides. That makes $44,800 a year.

Sleeping cars are expensive to build, they say. So are hotels; but they do not charge at such a rate. Now, what could I do to get even? Nothing could ever put back the dollars into the millions of pockets; but it might be stopped now, this beautiful process.

So I wished that all persons who profited by this performance might feel a shame so keen that they would make public avowal and apology, and, as partial restitution, offer their wealth to promote the cause of free railroads!

Then I remembered parrots. This was lucky, for my wrath flamed again. It was really cooling, as I tried to work out responsibility and adjust penalties. But parrots! Any person who wants to keep a parrot should go and live on an island alone with their preferred conversationalist!

There was a huge, squawky parrot right across the street from me, adding its senseless, rasping cries to the more necessary evils of other noises.

I had also an aunt with a parrot. She was a wealthy, ostentatious person, who had been an only child and inherited her money.

Uncle Joseph hated the yelling bird, but that didn't make any difference to Aunt Mathilda.

I didn't like this aunt, and wouldn't visit her, lest she think I was truckling for the sake of her money; but after I had wished this time, I called at the time set for my curse to work; and it did work with a vengeance. There sat poor Uncle Joe, looking thinner and meeker than ever; and my aunt, like an overripe plum, complacent enough.

"Let me out!" said Polly, suddenly. "Let me out to take a walk!"

"The clever thing!" said Aunt Mathilda. "He never said that before."

She let him out. Then he flapped up on the chandelier and sat among the prisms, quite safe.

"What an old pig you are, Mathilda!" said the parrot.

She started to her feet—naturally.

"Born a Pig—trained a Pig—a Pig by nature and education!" said the parrot. "Nobody'd put up with you, except for your money; unless it's this long-suffering husband of yours. He wouldn't, if he hadn't the patience of Job!"

"Hold your tongue!" screamed Aunt Mathilda. "Come down from there! Come here!"

Polly cocked his head and jingled the prisms. "Sit down, Mathilda!" he said, cheerfully. "You've got to listen. You are fat and homely and selfish. You are a nuisance to everybody about you. You have got to feed me and take care of me better than ever—and you've got to listen to me when I talk. Pig!"

I visited another person with a parrot the next day. She put a cloth over his cage when I came in.

"Take it off!" said Polly. She took it off.

"Won't you come into the other room?" she asked me, nervously.

"Better stay here!" said her pet. "Sit still—sit still!"

She sat still.

"Your hair is mostly false," said pretty Poll. "And your teeth—and your outlines. You eat too much. You are lazy. You ought to exercise, and don't know enough. Better apologize to this lady for backbiting! You've got to listen."

The trade in parrots fell off from that day; they say there

is no call for them. But the people who kept parrots, keep them yet—parrots live a long time.

Bores were a class of offenders against whom I had long borne undying enmity. Now I rubbed my hands and began on them, with this simple wish: That every person whom they bored should tell them the plain truth.

There is one man whom I have specially in mind. He was blackballed at a pleasant club, but continues to go there. He isn't a member—he just goes; and no one does anything to him.

It was very funny after this. He appeared that very night at a meeting, and almost every person present asked him how he came there. "You're not a member, you know," they said. "Why do you butt in? Nobody likes you."

Some were more lenient with him. "Why don't you learn to be more considerate of others, and make some real friends?" they said. "To have a few friends who do enjoy your visits ought to be pleasanter than being a public nuisance."

He disappeared from that club, anyway.

I began to feel very cocky indeed.

In the food business there was already a marked improvement; and in transportation. The hubbub of reformation waxed louder daily, urged on by the unknown sufferings of all the profiters by iniquity.

The papers thrived on all this; and as I watched the loud-voiced protestations of my pet abomination in journalism, I had a brilliant idea, literally.

Next morning I was down town early, watching the men open their papers. My abomination was shamefully popular, and never more so than this morning. Across the top was printed in gold letters:

All intentional lies, in adv., editorial, news, or any other column.. Scarlet
All malicious matter..................................... Crimson
All careless or ignorant mistakes .... Pink
All for direct self-interest of owner.............. Dark green
All mere bait—to sell the paper .... Bright green
All advertising, primary or secondary .... Brown
All sensational and salacious matter.................. Yellow
All hired hypocrisy.. Purple

Good fun, instruction and entertainment .... Blue
True and necessary news and honest
editorials .... Ordinary print

You never saw such a crazy quilt of a paper. They were
bought like hot cakes for some days; but the real business
fell off very soon. They'd have stopped it all if they could;
but the papers looked all right when they came off the press.
The color scheme flamed out only to the bona fide reader.

I let this work for about a week, to the immense joy of
all the other papers; and then turned it on to them, all at
once. Newspaper reading became very exciting for a little,
but the trade fell off. Even newspaper editors could not keep
on feeding a market like that. The blue printed and ordinary
printed matter grew from column to column and page to
page. Some papers—small, to be sure, but refreshing—began
to appear in blue and black alone.

This kept me interested and happy for quite a while; so
much so that I quite forgot to be angry at other things. There
was *such* a change in all kinds of business, following the
mere printing of truth in the newspapers. It began to appear
as if we had lived in a sort of delirium—not really knowing
the facts about anything. As soon as we really knew the
facts, we began to behave very differently, of course.

What really brought all my enjoyment to an end was
women. Being a woman, I was naturally interested in them,
and could see some things more clearly than men could. I
saw their real power, their real dignity, their real responsibility in the world; and then the way they dress and behave
used to make me fairly frantic. 'Twas like seeing archangels
playing jackstraws—or real horses only used as rocking-
horses. So I determined to get after them.

How to manage it! What to hit first! Their hats, their ugly,
inane, outrageous hats—that is what one thinks of first. Their
silly, expensive clothes—their diddling beads and jewelry—
their greedy childishness—mostly of the women provided
for by rich men.

Then I thought of all the other women, the real ones, the
vast majority, patiently doing the work of servants without
even a servant's pay—and neglecting the noblest duties of
motherhood in favor of house-service; the greatest power
on earth, blind, chained, untaught, in a treadmill. I thought

of what they might do, compared to what they did do, and my heart swelled with something that was far from anger.

Then I wished—with all my strength—that women, all women, might realize Womanhood at last; its power and pride and place in life; that they might see their duty as mothers of the world—to love and care for everyone alive; that they might see their duty to men—to choose only the best, and then to bear and rear better ones; that they might see their duty as human beings, and come right out into the full life and work and happiness!

I stopped, breathless, with shining eyes. I waited, trembling, for things to happen.

Nothing happened.

You see, this magic which had fallen on me was black magic—and I had wished white.

It didn't work at all, and, what was worse, it stopped all the other things that were working so nicely.

Oh, if I had only thought to wish permanence for those lovely punishments! If only I had done more while I could do it, had half appreciated my privileges when I was a Witch!

MARTHA'S MOTHER

It was nine feet long.

It was eight feet high.

It was six feet wide.

There was a closet, actually!—a closet one foot deep—that was why she took this room. There was the bed, and the trunk, and just room to open the closet door part way—that accounted for the length. There was the bed and the bureau and the chair—that accounted for the width. Between the bedside and the bureau and chair side was a strip extending the whole nine feet. There was room to turn around by the window. There was room to turn round by the door. Martha was thin.

One, two, three, four—turn.

One, two, three, four—turn.

She managed it nicely.

"It is a stateroom," she always said to herself. "It is a luxurious, large, well-furnished stateroom with a real window. It is *not* a cell."

Martha had a vigorous constructive imagination. Sometimes it was the joy of her life, her magic carpet, her Aladdin's lamp. Sometimes it frightened her—frightened her horribly, it was so strong.

The cell idea had come to her one gloomy day, and she had foolishly allowed it to enter—played with it a little while. Since then she had to keep a special bar on that particular intruder, so she had arranged a stateroom "set," and forcibly kept it on hand.

Martha was a stenographer and typewriter in a real estate office. She got $12 a week, and was thankful for it. It was steady pay, and enough to live on. Seven dollars she paid for board and lodging, ninety cents for her six lunches, ten a day for carfare, including Sundays; seventy-five for laundry; one for her mother—that left one dollar and sixty-five cents for clothes, shoes, gloves, everything. She had tried cheaper board, but made up the cost in doctor's bills; and lost a good place by being ill.

"Stone walls do not a prison make, nor hall bedrooms a cage," said she determinedly. "Now then—here is another evening—what shall I do?" Library? No. My eyes are tired. Besides, three times a week is enough. 'Tisn't club night. Will *not* sit in the parlor. Too wet to walk. Can't sew, worse'n reading—O good *land!* I'm almost ready to go with Basset!"

She took herself and paced up and down again.

Prisoners form the habit of talking to themselves—this was the suggestion that floated through her mind—that cell idea again.

"I've got to get out of this!" said Martha, stopping short. "It's enough to drive a girl crazy!"

The driving process was stayed by a knock at the door. "Excuse me for coming up," said a voice. "It's Mrs. MacAvelly."

Martha knew this lady well. She was a friend of Miss Podder at the Girls' Trade Union Association. "Come in. I'm glad to see you!" she said hospitably. "Have the chair— or the bed's really more comfortable!"

"I was with Miss Podder this evening and she was anxious to know whether your union has gained any since the last meeting—I told her I'd find out—I had nothing else to do. Am I intruding?"

"Intruding!" Martha gave a short laugh. "Why, it's a godsend, Mrs. MacAvelly! If you knew how dull the evenings are to us girls!"

"Don't you—go out much? To—to theaters—or parks?" The lady's tone was sympathetic and not inquisitive.

"Not very much," said Martha, rather sardonically. "Theaters—two girls, two dollars, and twenty cents carfare. Parks, twenty cents—walk your feet off, or sit on the benches and be stared at. Museums—not open evenings."

"But don't you have visitors—in the parlor here?"

"Did you see it?" asked Martha.

Mrs. MacAvelly had seen it. It was cold and also stuffy. It was ugly and shabby and stiff. Three tired girls sat there, two trying to read by a strangled gaslight overhead; one trying to entertain a caller in a social fiction of privacy at the other end of the room.

"Yes, we have visitors—but mostly they ask us out. And some of us don't go," said Martha darkly.

"I see, I see!" said Mrs. MacAvelly, with a pleasant smile; and Martha wondered whether she did see, or was just being civil.

"For instance, there's Mr. Basset," the girl pursued, somewhat recklessly; meaning that her visitor should understand her.

"Mr. Basset?"

"Yes, 'Pond & Basset'—one of my employers."

Mrs. MacAvelly looked pained. "Couldn't you—er— avoid it?" she suggested.

"You mean shake him?" asked Martha. "Why, yes—I could. Might lose my job. Get another place—another Basset, probably."

"I see!" said Mrs. MacAvelly again. "Like the Fox and the Swarm of Flies! There ought to be a more comfortable way of living for all you girls! And how about the union— I have to be going back to Miss Podder."

Martha gave her the information she wanted, and started to accompany her downstairs. They heard the thin jangle of the door-bell, down through the echoing halls, and the dragging feet of the servant coming up. A kinky black head was thrust in the door.

"Mr. Basset, callin' on Miss Joyce," was announced formally.

Martha stiffened. "Please tell Mr. Basset I am not feeling well tonight—and beg to be excused."

She looked rather defiantly at her guest, as Lucy clattered down the long stairs; then stole to the railing and peered down the narrow well. She heard the message given with pompous accuracy, and then heard the clear, firm tones of Mr. Basset:

"Tell Miss Joyce that I will wait."

Martha returned to her room in three long steps, slipped off her shoes and calmly got into bed. "Good-night, Mrs. MacAvelly," she said. "I'm so sorry but my head aches and I've gone to bed! Would you be so very good as to tell Lucy so as you're going down."

Mrs. MacAvelly said she would, and departed, and Martha lay conscientiously quiet till she heard the door shut far below.

She was quiet, but she was not contented.

Yet the discontent of Martha was as nothing to the discontent of Mrs. Joyce, her mother, in her rural home. Here was a woman of fifty-three, alert, vigorous, nervously active; but an automobile-agitated horse had danced upon her, and her usefulness, as she understood it, was over. She could not get about without crutches, nor use her hands for needlework, though still able to write after a fashion. Writing was not her *forte*, however, at the best of times.

She lived with a widowed sister in a little, lean dusty farmhouse by the side of the road; a hill road that went nowhere in particular, and was too steep for those who were going there.

Brisk on her crutches, Mrs. Joyce hopped about the little house, there was nowhere else to hop to. She had talked her sister out long since—Mary never had much to say. Occasionally they quarreled and then Mrs. Joyce hopped only in her room, a limited process.

She sat at the window one day, staring greedily out at the lumpy rock-ribbed road; silent, perforce, and tapping the arms of her chair with nervous intensity. Suddenly she called out, "Mary! Mary Ames! Come here quick! There's somebody coming up the road!"

Mary came in, as fast as she could with eggs in her apron. "It's Mrs. Holmes!" she said. "And a boarder, I guess."

"No, it ain't," said Mrs. Joyce, eagerly. "It's that woman that's visiting the Holmes—she was in church last week, Myra Slater told me about her. Her name's MacDowell, or something."

"It ain't MacDowell," said her sister. "I remember; it's MacAvelly."

This theory was borne out by Mrs. Holmes' entrance and introduction of her friend.

"Have you any eggs for us, Mrs. Ames?" she said.

"Set down—set down," said Mrs. Ames cordially. "I was just getting in my eggs—but here's only about eight yet. How many was you wantin'?"

"I want all you can find," said Mrs. Holmes. "Two dozen, three dozen—all I can carry."

"There's two hens layin' out—I'll go and look them up.

And I ain't been in the woodshed chamber yet. I'll go'n hunt. You set right here with my sister." And Mrs. Ames bustled off.

"Pleasant view you have here," said Mrs. MacAvelly politely, while Mrs. Holmes rocked and fanned herself.

"Pleasant! Glad you think so, ma'am. Maybe you city folks wouldn't think so much of views if you had nothing clse to look at!"

"What would you like to look at?"

"Folks!" said Mrs. Joyce briefly. "Lots of folks! Somethin' doin'."

"You'd like to live in the city?"

"Yes, ma'am—I would so! I worked in the city once when I was a girl. Waitress. In a big restaurant. I got to be cashier—in two years! I like the business!"

"And then you married a farmer?" suggested Mrs. Holmes.

"Yes, I did. And I never was sorry, Mrs. Holmes. David Joyce was a mighty good man. We was engaged before I left home—I was workin' to help earn, so 't we could marry."

"There's plenty of work on a farm, isn't there?" Mrs. MacAvelly inquired.

Mrs. Joyce's eager eyes kindled. "There is *so!*" she agreed. "Lots to do. And lots to manage! We kept help then, and the farm hands, and the children growin' up. And some seasons we took boarders."

"Did you like that?"

"I did. I liked it first rate. I like lots of people, and to do for 'em. The best time I ever had was one summer I ran a hotel."

"Ran a hotel! How interesting!"

"Yes'm—it was interesting! I had a cousin who kept a summer hotel up here in the mountains a piece—and he was short-handed that summer and got me to go up and help him out. Then he was taken sick, and I had the whole thing on my shoulders! I just enjoyed it! And the place cleared more that summer'n it ever did! He said 'twas owin' to his advantageous buyin'. Maybe 'twas! But I could 'a bought more advantageous than he did—I could 'a told him that. Point o' fact, I did tell him that—and hc wouldn't have me again."

"That was a pity!" said Mrs. Holmes. "And I suppose

if it wasn't for your foot you would do that now—and enjoy it!''

"Of course I could!'' protested Mrs. Joyce. ''Do it better 'n ever, city or country! But her I am, tied by the leg! And dependent on my sister and children! It galls me terribly!''

Mrs. Holmes nodded sympathetically. ''You are very brave, Mrs. Joyce,'' she said. ''I admire your courage, and—'' she couldn't say patience, so she said, ''cheerfulness.''

Mrs. Ames came in with more eggs. ''Not enough, but some,'' she said, and the visitors departed therewith.

Toward the end of the summer, Miss Podder at the Girls' Trade Union Association, sweltering in the little office, was pleased to receive a call from her friend, Mrs. MacAvelly.

"I'd no idea you were in town,'' she said.

"I'm not, officially,'' answered her visitor, ''just stopping over between visits. It's hotter than I thought it would be, even on the upper west side.'

"Think what it is on the lower east side!'' answered Miss Podder, eagerly. ''Hot all day—and hot all night! My girls do suffer so! They are so crowded!''

"How do the clubs get on?'' asked Mrs. MacAvelly. ''Have your girls any residence clubs yet?''

"No—nothing worth while. It takes somebody to run it right, you know. The girls can't; the people who work for money can't meet our wants—and the people who work for love, don't work well as a rule.''

Mrs. MacAvelly smiled sympathetically. ''You're quite right about that,'' she said. ''But really—some of those 'Homes' are better than others, aren't they?''

"The girls hate them,'' answered Miss Podder. ''They'd rather board—even two or three in a room. They like their independence. You remember Martha Joyce?''

Mrs. MacAvelly remembered. ''Yes,'' she said, ''I do— I met her mother this summer.''

"She's a cripple, isn't she?'' asked Miss Podder. ''Martha's told me about her.''

"Why, not exactly. She's what a Westerner might call 'crippled up some,' but she's livelier than most well persons.'' And she amused her friend with a vivid rehearsal of Mrs. Joyce's love of the city and her former triumphs in restaurant and hotel.

"She'd be a fine one to run such a house for the girls, wouldn't she?" suddenly cried Miss Podder.

"Why—if she could," Mrs. MacAvelly admitted slowly.

"Could! Why not? You say she gets about easily enough. All she'd have to do is *manage,* you see. She could order by 'phone and keep the servants running!"

"I'm sure she'd like it," said Mrs. MacAvelly. "But don't such things require capital?"

"Miss Podder was somewhat daunted. "Yes—some; but I guess we could raise it. If we could find the right house!"

"Let's look in the paper," suggested her visitor. "I've got a *Herald.* "

"There's one that reads all right," Miss Podder presently proclaimed. "The location's good, and it's got a lot of rooms—furnished. I suppose it would cost too much."

Mrs. MacAvelly agreed, rather ruefully.

"Come," she said, "it's time to close here, surely. Let's go and look at that house, anyway. It's not far."

They got their permit and were in the house very shortly. "I remember this place," said Miss Podder. "It was for sale earlier in the summer."

It was one of those once spacious houses, not of "old," but at least of "middle-aged" New York; with large rooms arbitrarily divided into smaller ones.

"It's been a boarding-house, that's clear," said Mrs. MacAvelly.

"Why, of course!" Miss Podder answered, cagerly plunging about and examining everything. "Anybody could see that! But it's been done over—most thoroughly. The cellar's all whitewashed, and there's a new furnace, and new range, and look at this ice-box!" It was an ice-closet, as a matter of fact, of large capacity, and a most sanitary aspect.

"Isn't it too big?" Mrs. MacAvelly inquired.

"Not for a boarding-house, my dear," Miss Podder enthusiastically replied. "Why, they could buy a side of beef with that ice-box! And look at the extra ovens! Did you ever see a place better furnished—for what we want? It looks as if it had been done on purpose!"

"It does, doesn't it?" said Mrs. MacAvelly.

Miss Podder, eager and determined, let no grass grow under her feet. The rent of the place was within reason.

"If they had twenty boarders—and some "mealers," I

believe it could be done!'' she said. ''It's a miracle—this house. Seems as if somebody had done it just for us!''

Armed with a list of girls who would agree to come, for six and seven dollars a week, Miss Podder made a trip to Willettville, and laid the matter before Martha's mother.

''What an outrageous rent!'' said that lady.

''Yes—New York rents *are* rather inconsiderate,'' Miss Podder admitted. ''But see, here's a guaranteed income if the girls stay—and I'm sure they will; and if the cooking's good you could easily get table boarders besides.''

Mrs. Joyce hopped to the bureau and brought out a hard, sharp-pointed pencil, and a lined writing tablet.

''Let's figger it out,'' said she. ''You say that house rents furnished at $3,200. It would take a cook and a chamber-maid!''

''And a furnace man,'' said Miss Podder. ''They come to about fifty a year. The cook would be thirty a month, the maid twenty-five, if you got first-class help, and you'd need it.''

''That amounts to $710 altogether,'' stated Mrs. Joyce.

''Fuel and light and such things would be $200,'' Miss Podder estimated, ''and I think you ought to allow $200 more for breakage and extras generally.''

''That's $4,310 already,'' said Mrs. Joyce.

''Then there's the food,'' Miss Podder went on. ''How much do you think it would cost to feed twenty girls, two meals a day, and three Sundays?''

''And three more,'' Mrs. Joyce added, ''with me, and the help, twenty-three. I could do it for $2.00 a week apiece.''

''Oh!'' said Miss Podder. ''*Could* you? At New York prices?''

''See me do it!'' said Mrs. Joyce.

''That makes a total expense of $6,710 a year. Now, what's that income, ma'am?''

The income was clear—if they could get it. Ten girls at $6.00 and ten at $7.00 made $130.00 a week—$6,760.00 a year.

''There you are!'' said Mrs. Joyce triumphantly. ''And the 'mealers'—if my griddle-cakes don't fetch 'em I'm mistaken! If I have ten—at $5.00 a week and clear $3.00 off 'em—that'll be another bit—$1,560.00 more. Total income

$8,320.00. More'n one thousand clear! Maybe I can feed 'em a little higher—or charge less.''

The two women worked together for an hour or so; Mrs. Ames drawn in later with demands as to butter, eggs, and "eatin' chickens."

"There's an ice-box as big as a closet," said Miss Podder.

Mrs. Joyce smiled triumphantly. "Good!" she said. "I can buy my critters of Judson here and have him freight 'em down. I can get apples here and potatoes, and lots of stuff."

"You'll need, probably, a little capital to start with," suggested Miss Podder. "I think the Association could—"

"It don't have to, thank you just the same," said Mrs. Joyce. "I've got enough in my stocking to take me to New York and get some fuel. Besides, all my boarders is goin' to pay in advance—that's the one sure way. The mealers can buy tickets!"

Her eyes danced. She fairly coursed about the room on her nimble crutches. "My!" she said, "it will seem good to have my girl to feed again."

The house opened in September, full of eager girls with large appetites long unsatisfied. The place was new-smelling, fresh-painted, beautifully clean. The furnishing was cheap, but fresh, tasteful, with minor conveniences dear to the hearts of women.

The smallest rooms were larger than hall bedrooms, the big ones were shared by friends. Martha and her mother had a chamber with two beds and space to spare!

The dining room was very large, and at night the tables were turned into "settles" by the wall and the girls could dance to the sound of a hired pianola. So could the "mealers," when invited; and there was soon a waiting list of both sexes.

"I guess I can make a livin'," said Mrs. Joyce, "allowin' for bad years."

"I don't understand how you feed us so well—for so little," said Miss Podder, who was one of the boarders.

" 'Sh!" said Mrs. Joyce, privately. "Your breakfast don't really cost more'n ten cents—nor your dinner fifteen—not the way I order! Things taste good 'cause they're *cooked* good—that's all."

"And you have no troubles with your help?"

" 'Sh!" said Mrs. Joyce again, more privately. "I work 'em hard—and pay 'em a bonus—a dollar a week extra, as long as they give satisfaction. It reduces my profits some—but it's worth it."

"It's worth it to us, I'm sure!" said Miss Podder.

Mrs. MacAvelly called one evening in the first week, with warm interest and approval. The tired girls were sitting about in comfortable rockers and lounges, under comfortable lights, reading and sewing. The untired ones were dancing in the dining room, to the industrious pianola, or having games of cards in the parlor.

"Do you think it'll be a success?" she asked her friend.

"It *is* a success!" Miss Podder triumphantly replied. "I'm immensely proud of it!"

"I should think you would be," said Mrs. MacAvelly.

The doorbell rang sharply.

Mrs. Joyce was hopping through the hall at the moment, and promptly opened it."

"Does Miss Martha Joyce board here?" inquired a gentleman.

"She does."

"I should like to see her," said he, handing in his card.

Mrs. Joyce read the card and looked at the man, her face setting in hard lines. She had heard that name before.

"Miss Joyce is engaged," she replied curtly, still holding the door.

He could see past her into the bright, pleasant rooms. He heard the music below, the swing of dancing feet, Martha's gay laugh from the parlor.

The little lady on crutches blocked his path.

"Are you the housekeeper of this place?" he asked sharply.

"I'm more'n that!" she answered. "I'm Martha's mother."

Mr. Basset concluded he would not wait.

THE BOYS AND THE
BUTTER

Young Holdfast and J. Edwards Fernald sat grimly at their father's table, being seen and not heard, and eating what was set before them, asking no questions for conscience' sake, as they had been duly reared. But in their hearts were most unchristian feelings toward a venerable guest, their mother's aunt, by name Miss Jane McCoy.

They knew, with the keen observation of childhood, that it was only a sense of hospitality, and duty to a relative, which made their father and mother polite to her—polite, but not cordial.

Mr. Fernald, as a professed Christian, did his best to love his wife's aunt, who came as near being an "enemy" as anyone he knew. But Mahala, his wife, was of a less saintly nature, and made no pretense of more than decent courtesy.

"I don't like her and I won't pretend to; it's not honest!" she protested to her husband, when he remonstrated with her upon her want of natural affection. "I can't help her being my aunt—we are not commanded to honor our aunts and uncles, Jonathan E."

Mrs. Fernald's honesty was of an iron hardness and heroic mould. She would have died rather than have told a lie, and classed as lies any form of evasion, deceit, concealment or even artistic exaggeration.

Her two sons, thus starkly reared, found their only imaginative license in secret converse between themselves, sacredly guarded by a pact of mutual faith, which was stronger than any outward compulsion. They kicked each other under the table, while enduring this visitation, exchanged dark glances concerning the object of their common dislike, and discussed her personal peculiarities with caustic comment later, when they should have been asleep.

Miss McCoy was not an endearing old lady. She was heavily built, and gobbled her food, carefully selecting the best. Her clothing was elaborate, but not beautiful, and on close approach aroused a suspicion of deferred laundry bills.

Among many causes for dislike for her aunt, Mrs. Fernald cherished this point especially. On one of these unwelcome visits she had been at some pains to carry up hot water for the Saturday evening bath, which was all the New England conscience of those days exacted, and the old lady had neglected it not only once but twice.

"Goodness sake, Aunt Jane! aren't you ever going to take a bath?"

"Nonsense!" replied her visitor. "I don't believe in all this wetting and slopping. The Scripture says, 'Whoso washeth his feet, his whole body shall be made clean.'"

Miss McCoy had numberless theories for other people's conduct, usually backed by well-chosen texts, and urged them with no regard to anybody's feelings. Even the authority of parents had no terrors for her.

Sipping her tea from the saucer with deep swattering inhalations, she fixed her prominent eyes upon the two boys as they ploughed their way through their bread and butter. Nothing must be left on the plates in the table ethics of that time. The meal was simple in the extreme. A New Hampshire farm furnished few luxuries, and the dish of quince preserves had already been depleted by her.

"Mahala," she said with solemn determination, "those boys eat too much butter."

Mrs. Fernald flushed up to the edging of her cap. "I think I must be the judge of what my children eat at my table, Aunt Jane," she answered, not too gently.

Here Mr. Fernald interposed with a "soft answer." (He had never lost faith in the efficacy of these wrath turners, even on long repeated failure. As a matter of fact, to his wife's temper, a soft answer, especially an intentionally soft answer, was a fresh aggravation.) "The missionary, now, he praised our butter; said he never got any butter in China, or wherever 'tis he lives."

"He is a man of God," announced Miss McCoy. "If there is anybody on this poor earth deserving reverence, it is a missionary. What they endure for the Gospel is a lesson for us all. When I am taken I intend to leave all I have to the Missionary Society. You know that.''

They knew it and said nothing. Their patience with her was in no way mercenary.

"But what I am speaking of is children," she continued, not to be diverted from her fell purpose. "Children ought not to eat butter."

"They seem to thrive on it," Mrs. Fernald replied tartly. And in truth both the boys were sturdy little specimens of humanity, in spite of their luxurious food.

"It's bad for them. Makes them break out. Bad for the blood. And self-denial is good for children. 'It is better to bear the yoke in thy youth.' "

The youth in question spread its butter more thickly, and ate it with satisfaction, saying nothing.

"Look here, boys!" she suddenly assailed them. "If you will go without butter for a year—a whole year, till I come round again—I'll give each of you fifty dollars!"

This was an overwhelming proposition.

Butter was butter—almost the only alleviation of a dry and monotonous bill of fare, consisting largely of bread. Bread without butter! Brown bread without butter! No butter on potatoes! No butter on anything! The young imagination recoiled. And this measureless deprivation was to cover a whole year. A ninth or an eleventh of a lifetime to them respectively. About a fifth of all they could really remember. Countless days, each having three meals; weeks, months, the long dry butterless vista stretched before them like Siberian exile to a Russian prisoner.

But, on the other hand, there was the fifty dollars. Fifty dollars would buy a horse, a gun, tools, knives—a farm, maybe. It could be put in the bank and drawn on for life, doubtless. Fifty dollars at that time was like five hundred today, and to a child it was a fortune.

Even their mother wavered in her resentment as she considered the fifty dollars, and the father did not waver at all, but thought it a Godsend.

"Let 'em choose," said Miss McCoy.

Stern is the stock of the Granite State. Self-denial is the essence of their religion; and economy, to give it a favorable name, is for them Nature's first law.

The struggle was brief. Holdfast laid down his thick-spread slice. J. Edwards laid down his. "Yes, ma'am," said one after the other. "Thank you, ma'am. We'll do it."

It was a long year. Milk did not take the place of it. Gravy and drippings, freely given by their mother, did not take the place of it, nor did the infrequent portions of preserves. Nothing met the same want. And if their health was improved by the abstinence it was in no way visible to the naked eye. They were well, but they were well before.

As to the moral effect—it was complex. An extorted sacrifice has not the same odor of sanctity as a voluntary one. Even when made willingly, if the willingness is purchased, the effect seems somewhat confused. Butter was not renounced, only postponed, and as the year wore on the young ascetics, in their secret conferences, indulged in wild visions of oleaginous excess so soon as the period of dearth should be over.

But most they refreshed their souls with plans for the spending and the saving of the hard-earned wealth that was coming to them. Holdfast was for saving his, and being a rich man—richer than Captain Briggs or Deacon Holbrook. But at times he wavered, spurred by the imagination of J. Edwards, and invested that magic sum in joys unnumbered.

The habit of self-denial was perhaps being established, but so was the habit of discounting the future, of indulging in wild plans of self-gratification when the ship came in.

Even for butterless boys, time passes, and the endless year at last drew to a close. They counted the months, they counted the weeks, they counted the days. Thanksgiving itself shone pale by contrast with this coming festival of joy and triumph. As it drew nearer and nearer their excitement increased, and they could not forget it even in the passing visit of a real missionary, a live one, who had been to those dark lands where the heathen go naked, worship idols and throw their children to the crocodiles.

They were taken to hear him, of course, and not only so, but he came to supper at their house and won their young hearts by the stories he told them. Gray of hair and beard was the preacher and sternly devout; but he had a twinkling eye none the less, and told tales of wonder and amazement that were sometimes almost funny and always interesting.

"Do not imagine, my young friends," he said, after filling them with delicious horror at the unspeakable wickedness of those "godless lands," "that the heathen are wholly without morality. The Chinese, among whom I have labored for many years, are more honest than some Christians. Their business honor is a lesson to us all. But works alone cannot save." And he questioned them as to their religious state, receiving satisfactory answers.

The town turned out to hear him; and, when he went on his circuit, preaching, exhorting, describing the hardships and dangers of missionary life, the joys of soul-saving, and urging his hearers to contribute to this great duty of preaching the Gospel to all creatures, they had a sort of revival season; and arranged for a great missionary church meeting with a special collection when he should return.

The town talked missionary and thought missionary; dreamed missionary, it might well be; and garrets were ransacked to make up missionary boxes to send to the heathen. But Holdfast and J. Edwards mingled their interest in those unfortunate savages with a passionate desire for butter, and a longing for money such as they had never known before.

Then Miss McCoy returned.

They knew the day, the hour. They watched their father drive down to meet the stage, and tormented their mother with questions as to whether she would give it to them before supper or after.

"I'm sure I don't know!" she snapped at last. "I'll be thankful when it's over and done with, I'm sure! A mighty foolish business, I think!"

Then they saw the old chaise turn the corner. What? Only one in it! The boys rushed to the gate—the mother, too.

"What is it, Jonathan? Didn't she come?"

"Oh, father!"

"Where is she, father?"

"She's not coming," said Mr. Fernald. "Says she's going to stay with Cousin Sarah, so's to be in town and go to all the missionary doin's. But she's sent it."

Then he was besieged, and as soon as the horse was put up, by three pairs of busy hands, they came to the supper table, whereon was a full two pounds of delicious butter, and sat down with tingling impatience.

The blessing was asked in all due form—a blessing ten miles long, it seemed to the youngsters, and then the long, fat envelope came out of Mr. Fernald's pocket.

"She must have written a lot," he said, taking out two folded papers, and then a letter.

"My dear great-nephews," ran this epistle, "as your parents have assured me that you have kept your promise, and denied yourselves butter for the space of a year, here is the fifty dollars I promised to each of you—wisely invested."

Mr. Fernald opened the papers. To Holdfast Fernald and to J. Edwards Fernald, duly made out, receipted, signed and sealed, were two $50 life memberships in the Missionary Society!

Poor children! The younger one burst into wild weeping. The older seized the butter dish and cast it on the floor, for which he had to be punished, of course, but the punishment added nothing to his grief and rage.

When they were alone at last, and able to speak for sobbing, those gentle youths exchanged their sentiments; and these were of the nature of blasphemy and rebellion against God. They had learned at one fell blow the hideous lesson of human depravity. People lied—grown people—religious people—they lied! You couldn't trust them! They had been deceived, betrayed, robbed! They had lost the actual joy renounced, and the potential joy promised and withheld. The money they might some day earn, but not heaven itself could give back that year of butter. And all this in the name of religion—and of missionaries! Wild, seething outrage filled their hearts at first; slower results would follow.

The pious enthusiasm of the little town was at its height. The religious imagination, rather starved on the bald alternatives of Calvinism, found rich food in these glowing tales of danger, devotion, sometimes martyrdom; while the spirit of rigid economy, used to daylong saving from the cradle to the grave, took passionate delight in the success of these noble evangelists who went so far afield to save lost souls.

Out of their narrow means they had scraped still further; denied themselves necessaries where no pleasures remained; and when the crowning meeting was announced, the big collection meeting, with the wonderful brother from the Church in Asia to address them again, the meeting house was packed in floor and gallery.

Hearts were warm and open, souls were full of enthusiasm for the great work, wave on wave of intense feeling streamed through the crowded house.

Only in the Fernalds' pew was a spirit out of tune.

Mr. Fernald, good man though he was, had not yet forgiven. His wife had not tried.

"Don't talk to me!" she had cried passionately, when he had urged a reconciliation. "Forgive your enemies! Yes, but she hasn't done any harm to *me!* It's my boys she's hurt! It don't say one word about forgiving other people's enemies!"

Yet Mrs. Fernald, for all her anger, seemed to have some inner source of consolation, denied her husband, over which she nodded to herself from time to time, drawing in her thin lips, and wagging her head decisively.

Vengeful bitterness and impotent rage possessed the hearts of Holdfast and J. Edwards.

This state of mind in young and old was not improved when, on arriving at the meeting a little late, they had found the head of the pew was occupied by Miss McCoy.

It was neither the time nor the place for a demonstration. No other seats were vacant, and Mrs. Fernald marched in and sat next to her, looking straight at the pulpit. Next came the boys, and murder was in their hearts. Last, Mr. Fernald, inwardly praying for a more Christian spirit, but not getting it.

Holdfast and young J. Edwards dared not speak in church or make any protest; but they smelled the cardamum seeds in the champing jaws beyond their mother, and they cast black looks at each other and very secretly showed clenched fists, held low.

In fierce inward rebellion they sat through the earlier speeches, and when the time came for the address of the occasion, even the deep voice of the brother from Asia failed to stir them. Was he not a missionary, and were not missionaries and all their works proved false?

But what was this?

The address was over; the collection, in cash, was in the piled plates at the foot of the pulpit. The collection in goods was enumerated and described with full names given.

Then the hero of the hour was seen to confer with the other reverend brothers, and to rise and come forward, raising his hand for silence.

"Dearly beloved brethren and sisters," he said, "in this time of thanksgiving for gifts spiritual and temporal I wish to ask your patience for a moment more, that we may do justice. There has come to my ears a tale concerning one of our recent gifts which I wish you to hear, that judgment may be done in Israel.

"One among us has brought to the House of the Lord a tainted offering—an offering stained with cruelty and falsehood. Two young children of our flock were bribed a year ago to renounce one of the scant pleasures of their lives, for a year's time—a whole long year of a child's life. They were bribed with a promise—a promise of untold wealth to a child, of fifty dollars each."

The congregation drew a long breath.

Those who knew of the Fernald boys' endeavor (and who in that friendly radius did not?) looked at them eagerly. Those who recognized Miss McCoy looked at her, too, and they were many. She sat, fanning herself, with a small, straight-handled palmleaf fan, striving to appear unconscious.

"When the time was up," the clear voice went on remorselessly, "the year of struggle and privation, and the eager hearts of childhood expected the reward; instead of keeping the given word, instead of the money promised, each child was given a paid life membership in our society!"

Again the house drew in its breath. Did not the end justify the means?

He went on:

"I have conferred with my fellow members, and we are united in our repudiation of this gift. The money is not ours. It was obtained by a trick which the heathen themselves would scorn."

There was a shocked pause. Miss McCoy was purple in the face, and only kept her place for fear of drawing more attention if she strove to escape.

"I name no names," the speaker continued, "and I regret the burden laid upon me to thus expose this possibly well-meant transaction, but what we have at stake tonight is not this handful of silver, nor the feelings of one sinner, but two children's souls. Are we to have their sense of justice outraged in impressionable youth? Are they to believe with the Psalmist that all men are liars? Are they to feel anger and blame for the great work to which our lives are given because in its name they were deceived and robbed? No, my brothers, we clear our skirts of this ignominy. In the name of the society, I shall return this money to its rightful owners. 'Whoso offendeth one of these little ones, it were better that a millstone be hanged about his neck and he cast into the depths of the sea.' ''

MAKING A LIVING

"There won't be any litigation and chicanery to help you out, young man. I've fixed that. Here are the title deeds of your precious country-place; you can sit in that handmade hut of yours and make poetry and crazy inventions the rest of your life! The water's good—and I guess you can live on the chestnuts!"

"Yes, sir," said Arnold Blake, rubbing his long chin dubiously. "I guess I can."

His father surveyed him with entire disgust. "If you had wit enough you might rebuild that old saw-mill and make a living off it!"

"Yes, sir," said Arnold again. "I had thought of that."

"You had, had you?" sneered his father. "Thought of it because it rhymed, I bet you! Hill and mill, eh? Hut and nut, trees and breeze, waterfall—beat-'em-all? I'm something of a poet myself, you see! Well,—there's your property. And with what your Mother left you will buy books and writing paper! As for my property—that's going to Jack. I've got the papers for that too. Not being an idiot I've saved out enough for myself—no Lear business for mine! Well, boy—I'm sorry you're a fool. But you've got what you seem to like best."

"Yes, sir," said Arnold once more. "I have, and I'm really much obliged to you, Father, for not trying to make me take the business."

Then young John Blake, pattern and image of his father, came into possession of large assets and began to use them in the only correct way; to increase and multiply without end.

Then old John Blake, gazing with pride on his younger

son, whose acumen almost compensated him for the bitter disappointment of being father to a poet; set forth for a season of rest and change.

"I'm going to see the world! I never had time before!" quoth he; and started off for Europe, Asia, and Africa.

Then Arnold Blake, whose eyes were the eyes of a poet, but whose mouth had a touch of resemblance to his father's betook himself to his Hill.

But the night before they separated, he and his brother both proposed to Ella Sutherland; John because he had made up his mind that it was the proper time for him to marry, and this was the proper woman; and Arnold because he couldn't help it.

John got to work first. He was really very fond of Ella; and made hot love to her. It was a painful surprise to him to be refused. He argued with her. He told her how much he loved her.

"There are others!" said Miss Ella.

He told her how rich he was.

"That isn't the point," said Ella,

He told her how rich he was going to be.

"I'm not for sale!" said Ella, "even on futures!"

Then he got angry and criticized her judgment.

"It's a pity, isn't it," she said, "for me to have such poor judgment—and for you to have to abide by it!"

"I won't take your decision," said John. "You're only a child yet. In two years' time you'll be wiser. I'll ask you again then."

"All right," said Ella. "I'll answer you again then."

John went away, angry, but determined.

Arnold was less categorical.

"I've no right to say a word," he began, and then said it. Mostly he dilated on her beauty and goodness—and his overmastering affection for her.

"Are you offering marriage?" she inquired, rather quizzically.

"Why yes—of course!" said he, "only—only I've nothing to offer."

"There's you!" said Ella.

"But that's so little!" said Arnold. "O! if you will wait for me!—I will work!—"

"What will you work at?" said Ella.

Arnold laughed. Ella laughed. "I love to camp out!" said she.

"Will you wait for me a year?" said Arnold.

"Ye-es," said Ella. "I'll even wait two—if I have to. But no longer!"

"What will you do then?" asked Arnold miserably.

"Marry you," said Ella.

So Arnold went off to his Hill.

What was one hill among so many? There they arose about him, far green, farther blue, farthest purple, rolling away to the real peaks of the Catskills. This one had been part of his mother's father's land; a big stretch, coming down to them from an old Dutch grant. It ran out like a promontory into the winding valley below; the valley that had been a real river when the Catskills were real mountains. There was some river there yet, a little sulky stream, fretting most of the year in its sunken stony bed, and losing its temper altogether when the spring floods came.

Arnold did not care much for the river—he had a brook of his own; an ideal brook, beginning with an over-flowing spring; and giving him three waterfalls and a lake on his own land. It was a very little lake and handmade. In one place his brook ran through a narrow valley or valleyette— so small it was; and a few weeks of sturdy work had dammed the exit and made a lovely pool. Arnold did that years ago, when he was a great hulking brooding boy, and used to come up there with his mother in summer; while his father stuck to the office and John went to Bar Harbor with his chums. Arnold could work hard even if he was a poet.

He quarried stone from his Hill—as everyone did in those regions; and built a small solid house, adding to it from year to year; that was a growing joy as long as the dear mother lived.

This was high up, near the dark, clear pool of the spring; he had piped the water into the house—for his mother's comfort. It stood on a level terrace, fronting south-westward; and every season he did more to make it lovely. There was a fine smooth lawn there now and flowering vines and bushes; every pretty wild thing that would grow and bloom of itself in that region, he collected about him.

That dear mother had delighted in all the plants and trees; she studied about them and made observations, while he enjoyed them—and made poems. The chestnuts were their common pride. This hill stood out among all the others in the flowering time, like a great pompon, and the odor of it was by no means attractive—unless you happened to like it, as they did.

The chestnut crop was tremendous; and when Arnold found that not only neighboring boys, but business expeditions from the city made a practice of rifling his mountain garden, he raged for one season and acted the next. When the first frost dropped the great burrs, he was on hand, with a posse of strong young fellows from the farms about. They beat and shook and harvested, and sack upon sack of glossy brown nuts were piled on wagons and sent to market by the owner instead of the depredator.

Then he and his mother made great plans, the eager boy full of ambition. He studied forestry and arboriculture; and grafted the big fat foreign chestnut on his sturdy native stocks, while his father sneered and scolded because he would not go into the office.

Now he was left to himself with his plans and hopes. The dear mother was gone, but the Hill was there—and Ella might come some day; there was a chance.

"What do you think of it?" he said to Patsy. Patsy was not Irish. He was an Italian from Tuscany; a farmer and forester by birth and breeding, a soldier by compulsion, an American citizen by choice.

"Fine!" said Patsy. "Fine. Ver' good. You do well."

They went over the ground together. "Could you build a little house here?" said Arnold. "Could you bring your wife? Could she attend to my house up there?—and could you keep hens and a cow and raise vegetables on this patch here—enough for all of us?—you to own the house and land—only you cannot sell it except to me?"

Then Patsy thanked his long neglected saints, imported his wife and little ones, took his eldest daughter out of the box factory, and his eldest son out of the printing office; and by the end of the summer they were comfortably established and ready to attend to the chestnut crop.

Arnold worked as hard as his man. Temporarily he hired other sturdy Italians, mechanics of experience; and spent his little store of capital in a way that would have made his father swear and his brother jeer at him.

When the year was over he had not much money left, but he had by his second waterfall a small electrical plant, with a printing office attached; and by the third a solid little mill, its turbine wheel running merrily in the ceaseless pour. Millstones cost more money than he thought, but there they were—brought up by night from the Hudson River—that his neighbors might not laugh too soon. Over the mill were large light rooms, pleasant to work in; with the shade of mighty trees upon the roof; and the sound of falling water in the sun.

By next summer this work was done, and the extra workmen gone. Whereat our poet refreshed himself with a visit to his Ella, putting in some lazy weeks with her at Gloucester, happy and hopeful, but silent.

"How's the chestnut crop?" she asked him.

"Fine. Ver' good," he answered. "That's what Patsy says—and Patsy knows."

She pursued her inquiries. "Who cooks for you? Who keeps your camp in order? Who washes your clothes?"

"Mrs. Patsy," said he. "She's a good a cook as anybody need want."

"And how is the prospect?" asked Ella.

Arnold turned lazily over, where he lay on the sand at her feet, and looked at her long and hungrily. "The prospect," said he "is divine."

Ella blushed and laughed and said he was a goose; but he kept on looking.

He wouldn't tell her much, though. "Don't, dear," he said when she urged for information. "It's too serious. If I should fail—"

"You won't fail!" she protested. "You can't fail! And if you do—why—as I told you before, I like to camp out!"

But when he tried to take some natural advantage of her friendliness she teased him—said he was growing to look just like his father! Which made them both laugh.

Then Arnold returned and settled down to business. He purchased stores of pasteboard, of paper, of printers ink, and a little machine to fold cartons. Thus equipped he retired to his fastness, and set dark-eyed Caterlina to work in a little box factory of his own; while clever Giuseppe ran the printing press, and Mafalda pasted. Cartons, piled flat, do not take up much room, even in thousands.

Then Arnold loafed deliberately.

"Why not your Mr. Blake work no more?" inquired Mrs. Patsy of her spouse.

"O he work—he work hard," replied Patsy. "You women—you not understand work!"

Mrs. Patsy tossed her head and answered in fluent Italian, so that her husband presently preferred out of doors occupation; but in truth Arnold Blake did not seem to do much that summer. He loafed under his great trees, regarding them lovingly; he loafed by his lonely upper waterfall, with happy dreaming eyes; he loafed in his little blue lake—floating face to the sky, care free and happy as a child. And if he scribbled a great deal—at any sudden moment when the fit seized him, why that was only his weakness as a poet.

Toward the end of September, he invited an old college friend up to see him; now a newspaper man—in the advertising department. These two seemed to have merry times together. They fished and walked and climbed, they talked much; and at night were heard roaring with laughter by their hickory fire.

"Have you got any money left?" demanded his friend.

"About a thou—" said Arnold. "And that's got to last me till next spring, you know."

"Blow it in—blow in every cent—it'll pay you. You can live through the winter somehow. How about transportation?"

"Got a nice electric dray—light and strong. Runs down hill with the load to tidewater, you see, and there's the old motorboat to take it down. Brings back supplies."

"Great!—It's simply great! Now you save out enough to eat till spring—and give me the rest. Send me your stuff, all of it! and as soon as you get in a cent above expenses—send me that—I'll 'tend to the advertising!"

He did. He had only $800.00 to begin with. When the first profits began to come in he used them better; and as they rolled up he still spent them. Arnold began to feel anxious, to want to save money; but his friend replied: "You furnish the meal—I'll furnish the market!" And he did.

He began it in the subway in New York; that place of misery where eyes, ears, nose, and common self-respect are all offended, and even an advertisement is some relief.

"Hill" said the first hundred dollars, on a big blank space for a week. "Mill" said the second. "Hill Mill Mcal," said the third.

The fourth was more explicit. "When tired of every cereal Try our new material—

Hill Mill Meal.''

The fifth—''Ask your grocer if you feel An interest in Hill Mill Meal.

Samples free.''

The sixth—''A paradox! Surprising! True! Made of chestnuts but brand new!

Hill Mill Meal.''

And the seventh—''Solomon said it couldn't be done, There wasn't a new thing under the sun—

He never ate Hill Mill Meal!''

Seven hundred dollars went in this one method only; and meanwhile diligent young men in automobiles were making arrangements and leaving circulars and samples with the grocer. Anybody will take free samples and everybody likes chestnuts. Are they not the crown of luxury in turkey stuffing? The gem of the confection as *marrons glacés?* The sure profit of the corner-merchant with his little charcoal stove, even when they are half scorched and half cold? Do we not all love them, roast, or boiled—only they are so messy to peel.

Arnold's only secret was his process; but his permanent advantage was in the fine quality of his nuts, and his exquisite care in manufacture. In dainty, neat, easily opened cartons (easily shut, too, so they were not left gaping to gather dust), he put upon the market a sort of samp, chestnuts perfectly shelled and husked, roasted and ground, both coarse and fine. Good? You stood and ate half a package, out of your hand, just tasting of it. Then you sat down and ate the other half.

He made pocket-size cartons, filled with whole ones, crafty man! And they became ''The Business Man's Lunch'' forthwith. A pocketful of roast chestnuts—and no mess nor trouble! And when they were boiled—well, we all know how good boiled chestnuts are. As to the meal, a new variety of mush appeared, and gems, muffins, and pancakes that made old epicures feel young again in the joys of a fresh taste, and gave America new standing in the eyes of France.

The orders rolled in and the poetry rolled out. The market for a new food is as wide as the world; and Jim Chamberlin was mad to conquer it, but Arnold explained to him that his total output was only so many bushels a year.

''Nonsense!'' said Jim. ''You're a—a—well, a *poet!* Come! Use your imagination! Look at these hills about you—they could grow chestnuts to the horizon! Look at this valley, that rattling river, a bunch of mills could run here! You can support a fine population—a whole village of people—there's no end to it, I tell you!"

"And where would my privacy be then and the beauty of the place?" asked Arnold. "I love this green island of chestnut trees, and the winding empty valley, just freckled with a few farms. I'd hate to support a village!"

"But you can be a Millionaire!" said Jim.

"I don't want to be a Millionaire," Arnold cheerfully replied.

Jim gazed at him, opening and shutting his mouth in silence. "You—confounded old—*poet!*" he burst forth at last.

"I can't help that," said Arnold.

"You'd better ask Miss Sutherland about it, I think," his friend drily suggested.

"To be sure! I had forgotten that—I will," the poet replied.

Then he invited her to come up and visit his Hill, met her at the train with the smooth, swift, noiseless, smell-less electric car, and held her hand in blissful silence as they rolled up the valley road. They wound more slowly up his graded avenue, green-arched by chestnut boughs.

He showed her the bit of meadowy inlet where the mill stood, by the heavy lower fall; the broad bright packing rooms above, where the busy Italian boys and girls chattered gaily as they worked. He showed her the second fall, with his little low-humming electric plant; a bluestone building, vine-covered, lovely, a tiny temple to the flower-god.

"It does our printing," said Arnold, "gives us light, heat and telephones. And runs the cars."

Then he showed her the shaded reaches of his lake, still, starred with lilies, lying dark under the curving boughs of water maples, doubling the sheer height of flower-crowned cliffs.

She held his hand tighter as they wound upward, circling the crown of the hill that she might see the splendid range of outlook; and swinging smoothly down a little and out on the green stretch before the house.

Ella gasped with delight. Gray, rough and harmonious, hung with woodbine and wildgrape, broad-porched and wide-windowed, it faced the setting sun. She stood looking,

looking, over the green miles of tumbling hills, to the blue billowy far-off peaks swimming in soft light.

"There's the house," said Arnold, "furnished—there's a new room built on—for you, dear; I did it myself. There's the hill—and the little lake and one waterfall all for us! And the spring, and the garden, and some very nice Italians. And it will earn—my Hill and my Mill, about three or four thousand dollars a year—above *all* expenses!"

"How perfectly splendid!" said Ella. "But there's one thing you've left out!"

"What's that?" he asked, a little dashed.

"*You!*" she answered. "Arnold Blake! My Poet!"

"Oh, I forgot," he added, after some long still moments. "I ought to ask you about this first. Jim Chamberlain says I can cover all these hills with chestnuts, fill this valley with people, string that little river with a row of mills, make breakfast for all the world—and be a Millionaire. Shall I?"

"For goodness sake—*No!*" said Ella. "Millionaire, indeed! And spoil the most perfect piece of living I ever saw or heard of!"

Then there was a period of bliss, indeed there was enough to last indefinitely.

But one pleasure they missed. They never saw even the astonished face, much less the highly irritated mind, of old John Blake, when he first returned from his two years of travel. The worst of it was he had eaten the stuff all the way home—and liked it! They told him it was Chestnut Meal—but that meant nothing to him. Then he began to find the jingling advertisements in every magazine; things that ran in his head and annoyed him.

> *When corn or rice no more are nice,*
> *When oatmeal seems to pall,*
> *When cream of wheat's no longer sweet*
> *And you abhor them all—*

"I do abhor them all!" the old man would vow, and take up a newspaper, only to read:

> *Better than any food that grows*
> *Upon or in the ground,*
> *Strong, pure and sweet*

> And good to eat
> Our tree-born nuts are found.

"Bah!" said Mr. Blake, and tried another, which only showed him:

> Good for mother, good for brother,
>   Good for child;
> As for father—well, rather!
>   He's just wild.

He was. But the truth never dawned upon him until he came to this one:

> About my hut
> There grew a nut
>   Nutritious;
> I could but feel
> 'Twould make a meal
>   Delicious.

> I had a Hill,
> I built a Mill
>   Upon it.
> And hour by hour
> I sought for power
>   To run it.

> To burn my trees
> Or try the breeze
>   Seemed crazy;
> To use my arm
> Had little charm—
>   I'm lazy!

> The nuts are here,
> But coal!—Quite dear
>   We find it!
> We have the stuff,
> Where's power enough
>   To grind it?

> *What force to find*
> *My nuts to grind?—*
>   *I've found it!*
> *The Water-fall*
> *Could beat 'em all—*
>   *And ground it!*

PETER POETICUS

"Confound your impudence!" he wrote to his son. "And confound your poetic stupidity in not making a Big Business now you've got a start. But I understand you do make a living, and I'm thankful for that."

Arnold and Ella, watching the sunset from their hammock, laughed softly together, and lived.

OLD MRS. CROSLEY

Mrs. Crosley's son was married and gone for good. There was no criticism to make of his marriage. Ella was all that a girl should be—all that a bride should be—promised all that a wife and mother should be. She was healthy. She was practical. She was skilled in all the arts and crafts of housewifery, from its scientific base to its decorative appendages. She had had a course in kindergartening, too. No one could find fault with Ella.

Her perfections seemed to promise well for Houston Crosley's happiness; but they satisfied him so perfectly that he had no longer any need of his mother.

Not for Ella were the painful references to "mother's biscuits," and "mother's jelly," and "mother's pies." The pies and jellies and biscuits of young Mrs. Crosley were better than those of her mother-in-law, and instead of regarding his mother as the standard of excellence, Houston grew to entertain for her a sense of pitying affection, as for one who had tried hard and long, but whose success was limited. This was not quite pleasant for old Mrs. Crosley.

How she did hate that name. She overheard it at the sewing circle one day—"Do you mean young Mrs. Crosley?" "No, I mean old Mrs. Crosley, Mrs. Hale."

A woman who spends her life in the flat glitter of "society"; who is in constant competition with "buds" and blossoms of all stages; whose "coming out" is counted against her like a birthday—she knows full well that she is growing older. She hates it. She fights it with all those guileless ostrich arts by which rich women insist that to-day is still yesterday morning. But at least it is no surprise to her.

But a woman who is married young and placed in the honored position of wife, housekeeper, and mother; whose husband loves her with gentle continuity, and whose friends and neighbors are similarly situated, does not realize the passing of years for herself. She sees her children grow and change, but her own growth and change is unconscious—she is not thinking of herself.

Old Mrs. Crosley! And she was only fifty-two! She went home from that sewing circle early, walking slowly by herself, and thinking hard. She did not want to go home, and hesitated at the gate when she reached it.

There was the comfortable home which had been the scene of her life and labors for thirty years. She knew every inch of it, inside and out; and loved it—within bounds.

There was no more conscientious woman in Elliston than Mrs. Crosley—Old Mrs. Crosley—and she had done her duty unhesitatingly and uncomplainingly all her life. Now that life seemed to be done. Both her daughters were gone; one married and settled in a distant city, the other unmarried and settled in another city—a teacher of manual training. They did not need her. They did not want her. Mrs. Crosley had no illusions about her children. She loved them all; she had been faithful to her tasks, and had done all she knew to "raise a family" as a family should be raised; but as she looked back on her years of motherhood they seemed to be thick strewn with mistakes and failures; and, though they never said as much, she felt sure the children saw them too.

Houston had been the nearest to her; the dearest in many ways. He had never been critical, had never said "Oh, *Mother!*" in that despairing sort of way; had seemed to need her, and to be satisfied with her. And now he was gone—gone forever—and another woman was taking better care of him than she had!

When his children came, and Ella firmly and proudly exhibited her trained skill in their care and management, he too would realize that his mother had made mistakes—many of them. And neither Houston with his children, nor May with her children, nor Joanna with her manual training, would have any further use for Old Mrs. Crosley.

She opened the gate and walked down the path slowly. At least Hall needed her. Hall was two years her senior. He was fifty-four. But no one called him Old Mr. Crosley.

They might call Houston "young Crosley," but his father "H. D."—not "old."

She found a telephone message from him; he would not be home till late—a matter of politics. Hall had only recently taken up politics. He liked it. It had opened new vistas of life to him. His business was well established and running smoothly, his family all provided for, and he had launched out on this new field of endeavor with all the enthusiasm of youth.

Did he need her? She was no help to him in his business. She was no help to him in his politics—no one had ever credited Mrs. Crosley with "the social gift." As to the house, though herself a most inadequate domestic functionary she had long ago learned to depute her tasks to others better fitted. She could not vie with her neighbors in layer cake and crocheted lace, or in the successful and inexpensive concoction of beautiful dresses; but she did feel a pleasant sense of superiority when they began to complain of their servants, actual or potential. She never had any trouble with servants. Out of the sullen rows in the intelligence office she would unerringly select the best material; out of that material she presently developed efficiency and contentment; and no changes convulsed her household until the damsels tearfully left her for some venture in matrimony.

At present they had two; a hard-featured cook, a widow with a deep-seated distrust of men, and a daughter at school for whom she toiled and saved; and a maid of more youthful and attractive appearance, but equal skill in her work.

The cook was caterer as well, ordering for the household with far more inventive genius than her mistress ever possessed. The two did all the work of the house between them, including the laundry, and had hours of quiet relaxation on their shady porch, in their common parlor with its books and pictures and sewing machine; or in the comfortable seclusion of their several bedchambers.

They ran the house. They kept Mr. Crosley comfortable. "Of what earthly use am I?" was the bitter persistent thought of old Mrs. Crosley.

She ate the excellent little supper before her, with a word of approval for her maids, and faced an enemy—with herself. It was not a pleasant evening. She tried to read, but the insistent gnawing thought that her life was done, and not very well done at that, appeared on every page. She tried to sew—but the work she had at hand was unsatisfactory. "It's only another failure!" she said to herself, and laid it down.

She had no fancy work. If her books failed her she was lonely indeed.

For a while she pitied herself because her husband had not come home; but she was too honest to hide behind a fallacy. "That's not what's the matter," she owned to herself. "If he was there reading the paper it wouldn't alter the facts any. I'm an old woman. I've lived my life—rather poorly, it appears—but I'm not dead yet. There may be twenty years before me yet."

When the doorbell rang she was pleased. Anything, anybody, was better than that dreary prospect; and when the new minister came in she was more than pleased—delighted. He seemed only a boy to her, but such a nice boy. She had known his mother years ago, and admired her much.

"Good evening, Mrs. Crosley," he said. "This is a pastoral call—the real thing. This impertinent youngster has come to say 'how do you do' to your soul.' "

"It's very poorly, thank you, John. You don't mind my calling you John, do you?"

"Not a bit—not the least bit in the world. If you don't mind my being a kid. I wish you'd tell me about it."

"I've just found out that I'm 'Old Mrs. Crosley,' " she said. "I'd never thought of it before, but it's so. The children are all grown up and gone—and—what's the worst of all, I shan't make even a valuable grandma!"

She laughed a little sadly. "You hear all manner of complaints from all manner of foolish women, I know; but I don't believe any of them own to being failures."

"No," said he, grimly. "I wish they did. There'd be more hopes of them. Nothing like 'conviction of sin' as a preliminary, Mrs. Crosley! Do go on."

"Why—that's about all. I am fifty-two, and a strong woman yet; likely to last another twenty years, as—as—'Old Mrs. Crosley.' "

He studied her with earnest eyes, boyish in their fresh cleanness, mature with thought and work.

"You know I don't believe in all these barriers of age and sex, Mrs. Crosley," he said. "You and I might talk now as 'man to man'—as one human soul to another. Can you stand it?''

"I'll try," she answered.

"Just forget that I'm Nell Fairmount's boy—or man. This is a matter of practical psychology. I may have to be a little harsh, but I do think I know what's the trouble—and how to help it."

"I wish you may, John; I wish you may! Say what you please."

"The trouble with you is that you have not done your duty," he began.

She flushed painfully. "I know it. That is what I said. But I have tried—"

He smiled his frank, cheery smile, and shook his head. "No—you have not even tried! You have done what you thought was your duty, like a well-intentioned racehorse trying to plow, and not plowing well for all its efforts. But you have not used the best powers God gave you for their best purpose."

"Go on and expound, John—I don't see what you mean yet."

"What do you think is your chief ability?" he asked. "What can you do best—and therefore like best to do?"

Mrs. Crosley smiled rather sadly. "I can enumerate my failures. Perhaps by a process of elimination we may arrive at something. I'm not very good with children. I'm a poor needle-woman, I can't cook, I hate to sweep and dust and scrub, I'm a poor accountant, I'm not a good buyer, I have no 'gifts' of any sort. No, John, if you can show me the talent I've buried in a napkin, I'll be obliged to you."

The young man looked around the pleasant, well-appointed room with its faint odor of continuous cleanliness. "You seem to be a good housekeeper," he said. "And I remember many a good meal here. Delicious and well-served."

Again she colored a little. "It's no credit to me," she answered. "I have excellent servants—they run the house for me. I don't even order the meals, unless I want something very special."

John Fairmount leaned back in his chair and thrust his hands deep into his clerical trousers pockets, watching her with a slowly widening smile. "Well?" he said, "Don't you get any light yet?"

She shook her head.

"I visit a good bit in this town, Mrs. Crosley, and many women come to me with their troubles. Perhaps you do not know that you are the only woman in Elliston who has 'excellent servants.' "

"I know I've always been fortunate in that way," she agreed, "and I'm deeply thankful. I never could have got along at all but for that."

The young man threw back his head and laughed. "You exquisite type of perfect humility!" he said. "You have a rare and invaluable talent—and don't even know it! There are thousands of women who can cook and sew and clean to one who can manage servants."

"I'm sure I'm glad if I have it," she said.

He took her up sharply. "Yes, you have it; but what have you done with it? What use have you made of it? What good has it done to anyone in the world but you and yours?"

She turned a puzzled face upon him. "What could I do with it?" she asked.

"Prepare for extreme severity, Mrs. Crosley," said the young minister. "For an ecclesiastical drubbing. You have perhaps noticed that there are other women in Elliston beside yourself? And that one of the major troubles in their lives is difficulty with servants? You, with your special ability, should use it as all human abilities are meant to be used—for the good of the community. You should run a really intelligent intelligence office, with a training school attached. You should raise the grade of domestic service in Elliston, and show the way to all the rest of the world. You should lift one of the heaviest burdens of life from your neighbors' shoulders—not from the suffering employer, but the suffering employee. You should furnish not only permanent help, but transient; trained service by the hour—one of the needs of the age. You should run an experiment station, laundry and cook shop, to exercise your transients. You should raise the standard of service, the standard of food, the standard of comfort and economy; for the town, the state, the world. Incidentally you should make a comfortable independent income. *That's* what you should do, Mrs. Crosley. And now is the time to begin!"

She sat silent, gripping the arm of her chair, staring at him, large-eyed.

"It is not only a possibility, and perhaps a pleasure, as

one's true work always is, but it is a plain duty. If you don't do it—" he set his jaws firmly and looked her square in the eye, "it will be no longer due to ignorance, but to selfishness and cowardice."

He saw the tears rise, the dark flush; but she faced him bravely.

"Forgive me!" he said. "I know I'm severe. But it's a big step, and something has to happen to make you see it. It will take a lot of strength, a lot of courage, a lot of real love of God and man. And I believe you've got it, Mrs. Crosley."

They were silent for a while. Then she said slowly, "I think you are right, John."

The real beginning of any great new step in life is to see the truth and make up one's mind. But it is only a beginning. The work comes after—and the opposition.

Her children were solidly and violently opposed to it, especially Houston.

What? Mother going to work? *Their* mother?

She having always figured in their minds as "mother," they were naturally unable to credit her with any previous, subsequent, or at any time different existence. But they were gone, all of them. May and Joanna wrote letters that hurt; hurt so cruelly that they weakened their own purpose, rousing a feeling that was almost anger in her maternal heart. She remembered the years of life she had experienced and enjoyed before these new persons appeared upon the scene. She thought of the years probably before her, after they had left it.

"Do they think I have no place in life but to sit down and remember that I have been a mother?" she said to herself.

Houston was even worse. Her boy—her baby—always her friend and champion, now showed the man, the man's pride and prejudice. He felt that it "reflected on him" to have "his mother" go into business.

To Ella it was anathema.

As to Mr. Crosley, Sr, and his attitude, Mrs. Crosley never gave out all "the particulars." She showed that it would cost him nothing, that it would not detract from "the comfort of his home" in the least degree, that she would be at home with him in the evenings—which was all that he ever saw of her after breakfast.

These considerations did not convince him. She showed,

or tried to show, what it would mean to her. The new life, new hope, new interests, new duties, new pleasures, and possibly new pains. This did not appeal to him. She modestly hinted of the possible value of such work in the community. He was annoyed, hurt, angry. "A woman's place is to be a wife and mother!" he said.

"I am your wife, Hall dear, and shall keep on being so. I have been a mother; that is accomplished. I can't spend all my waking hours writing letters to the girls, or visiting Houston."

"You have your housekeeping!" he insisted.

"To care for two people, by means of two good servants, cannot occupy all a woman's time, Hale."

"It will hurt me politically!" he protested. But she came to the conclusion that he could stand it if it did. That her work was as important as his politics.

In all the protest and opposition of her family she grew to realize, with a sickening pain, that none of them cared for *her*, the individual—Mary Crosley. They loved the wife—housekeeper—mother—"in her place"; but the happiness of Mary Crosley seemed to be entirely negligible. Whatsoever there might be to her outside of these functional activities, to them was non-existent.

John Fairmount held up her hands. He consoled and encouraged, spurred and stimulated. He used his influence with the other women to excellent advantage. He helped in some of the business details in starting the enterprise.

It began modestly enough.

"I won't have my name on it!" stormed her husband.

"Your name?" she said, "I thought you gave it to me! Have I no name of my own?" And she took one for trade purposes, calling it "The Newcome Agency." Strangers called her "Mrs. Newcome," which did not trouble her at all.

The thing grew surely to assured success, and all the women of the place rose up and called her blessed—or most of them. So, in some measure, did the men, as better food and service, with smaller bills, made its impression on their consciousness.

With her steady and growing income she found, to her surprise, that "mother" now commanded a new respect, and won new gratitude and affection. Her husband's anger slowly died away for lack of fuel. The political injury he dreaded did not materialize. Where he was vilified and ridiculed by some he was honored and praised by others as a public-spirited, progressive citizen. He grew quite proud of being called "progressive."

His home was as smoothly comfortable as ever, and brighter with new life and stimulus. The patient eyes of his wife had a new light in them. Her small captiousness gave way to a broader, more genial temper, as her experience widened. She looked fresher, handsomer; was far better dressed.

"How young Mrs. Crosley is looking!" they said in the sewing circle.

"Mrs. Houston?"

"No, Mrs. Hale."

TURNED

In her soft-carpeted, thick-curtained, richly furnished chamber, Mrs. Marroner lay sobbing on the wide, soft bed.

She sobbed bitterly, chokingly, despairingly; her shoulders heaved and shook convulsively; her hands were tight-clenched. She had forgotten her elaborate dress, the more elaborate bedcover; forgotten her dignity, her self-control, her pride. In her mind was an overwhelming, unbelievable horror, an immeasurable loss, a turbulent, struggling mass of emotion.

In her reserved, superior, Boston-bred life, she had never dreamed that it would be possible for her to feel so many things at once, and with such trampling intensity.

She tried to cool her feelings into thoughts; to stiffen them into words; to control herself—and could not. It brought vaguely to her mind an awful moment in the breakers at York Beach, one summer in girlhood when she had been swimming under water and could not find the top.

In her uncarpeted, thin-curtained, poorly furnished chamber on the top floor, Gerta Petersen lay sobbing on the narrow, hard bed.

She was of larger frame than her mistress, grandly built and strong; but all her proud young womanhood was prostrate now, convulsed with agony, dissolved in tears. She did not try to control herself. She wept for two.

If Mrs. Marroner suffered more from the wreck and ruin of a longer love—perhaps a deeper one; if her tastes were finer, her ideals loftier; if she bore the pangs of bitter jealousy and outraged pride, Gerta had personal shame to meet, a hopeless future, and a looming present which filled her with unreasoning terror.

She had come like a meek young goddess into that perfectly ordered house, strong, beautiful, full of goodwill and eager obedience, but ignorant and childish—a girl of eighteen.

Mr. Marroner had frankly admired her, and so had his wife. They discussed her visible perfections and as visible limitations with that perfect confidence which they had so long enjoyed. Mrs. Marroner was not a jealous woman. She had never been jealous in her life—till now.

Gerta had stayed and learned their ways. They had both been fond of her. Even the cook was fond of her. She was what is called "willing," was unusually teachable and plastic; and Mrs. Marroner, with her early habits of giving instruction, tried to educate her somewhat.

"I never saw anyone so docile," Mrs. Marroner had often commented. "It is perfection in a servant, but almost a defect in character. She is helpless and confiding."

She was precisely that: a tall, rosy-cheeked baby; rich womanhood without, helpless infancy within. Her braided wealth of dead-gold hair, her grave blue eyes, her mighty shoulders and long, firmly moulded limbs seemed those of a primal earth spirit; but she was only an ignorant child, with a child's weakness.

When Mr. Marroner had to go abroad for his firm, unwillingly, hating to leave his wife, he had told her he felt quite safe to leave her in Gerta's hands—she would take care of her.

"Be good to your mistress, Gerta," he told the girl that last morning at breakfast. "I leave her to you to take care of. I shall be back in a month at latest."

Then he turned, smiling, to his wife. "And you must take care of Gerta, too," he said. "I expect you'll have her ready for college when I get back."

This was seven months ago. Business had delayed him from week to week, from month to month. He wrote to his wife, long, loving, frequent letters, deeply regretting the delay, explaining how necessary, how profitable it was, congratulating her on the wide resources she had, her well-filled, well-balanced mind, her many interests.

"If I should be eliminated from your scheme of things, by any of those 'acts of God' mentioned on the tickets, I do not feel that you would be an utter wreck," he said. "That is very comforting to me. Your life is so rich and wide that no one loss, even a great one, would wholly cripple you. But nothing of the sort is likely to happen, and I shall be home again in three weeks—if this thing gets settled. And you will be looking so lovely, with that eager light in your eyes and the changing flush I know so well—and love so well! My dear wife! We shall have to have a new honeymoon—other moons come every month, why shouldn't the mellifluous kind?"

He often asked after "little Gerta," sometimes enclosed a picture postcard to her, joked his wife about her laborious efforts to educate "the child," was so loving and merry and wise—

All this was racing through Mrs. Marroner's mind as she lay there with the broad, hemstitched border of fine linen sheeting crushed and twisted in one hand, and the other holding a sodden handkerchief.

She had tried to teach Gerta, and had grown to love the patient, sweet-natured child, in spite of her dullness. At work with her hands, she was clever, if not quick, and could keep small accounts from week to week. But to the woman who held a Ph.D., who had been on the faculty of a college, it was like baby-tending.

Perhaps having no babies of her own made her love the big child the more, though the years between them were but fifteen.

To the girl she seemed quite old, of course; and her young heart was full of grateful affection for the patient care which made her feel so much at home in this new land.

And then she had noticed a shadow on the girl's bright face. She looked nervous, anxious, worried. When the bell rang, she seemed startled, and would rush hurriedly to the door. Her peals of frank laughter no longer rose from the area gate as she stood talking with the always admiring tradesmen.

Mrs. Marroner had labored long to teach her more reserve with men, and flattered herself that her words were at last effective. She suspected the girl of homesickness, which was denied. She suspected her of illness, which was denied also. At last she suspected her of something which could not be denied.

For a long time she refused to believe it, waiting. Then

she had to believe it, but schooled herself to patience and understanding. "The poor child," she said. "She is here without a mother—she is so foolish and yielding—I must not be too stern with her." And she tried to win the girl's confidence with wise, kind words.

But Gerta had literally thrown herself at her feet and begged her with streaming tears not to turn her away. She would admit nothing, explain nothing, but frantically promised to work for Mrs. Marroner as long as she lived—if only she would keep her.

Revolving the problem carefully in her mind, Mrs. Marroner thought she would keep her, at least for the present. She tried to repress her sense of ingratitude in one she had so sincerely tried to help, and the cold, contemptuous anger she had always felt for such weakness.

"The thing to do now," she said to herself, "is to see her through this safely. The child's life should not be hurt any more than is unavoidable. I will ask Dr. Bleet about it—what a comfort a woman doctor is! I'll stand by the poor, foolish thing till it's over, and then get her back to Sweden somehow with her baby. How they do come where they are not wanted—and don't come where they are wanted!" And Mrs. Marroner, sitting alone in the quiet, spacious beauty of the house, almost envied Gerta.

Then came the deluge.

She had sent the girl out for needed air toward dark. The late mail came; she took it in herself. One letter for her— her husband's letter. She knew the postmark, the stamp, the kind of typewriting. She impulsively kissed it in the dim hall. No one would suspect Mrs. Marroner of kissing her husband's letters—but she did, often.

She looked over the others. One was for Gerta, and not from Sweden. It looked precisely like her own. This struck her as a little odd, but Mr. Marroner had several times sent messages and cards to the girl. She laid the letter on the hall table and took hers to her room.

"My poor child," it began. What letter of hers had been sad enough to warrant that?

"I am deeply concerned at the news you send." What news to so concern him had she written? "You must bear it bravely, little girl. I shall be home soon, and will take care of you, of course. I hope there is not immediate anxiety— you do not say. Here is money, in case you need it. I expect to get home in a month at latest. If you have to go, be sure to leave your address at my office. Cheer up—be brave—I will take care of you.''

The letter was typewritten, which was not unusual. It was unsigned, which was unusual. It enclosed an American bill—fifty dollars. It did not seem in the least like any letter she had ever had from her husband, or any letter she could imagine him writing. But a strange, cold feeling was creeping over her, like a flood rising around a house.

She utterly refused to admit the ideas which began to bob and push about outside her mind, and to force themselves in. Yet under the pressure of these repudiated thoughts she went downstairs and brought up the other letter—the letter to Gerta. She laid them side by side on a smooth dark space on the table; marched to the piano and played, with stern precision, refusing to think, till the girl came back. When she came in, Mrs. Marroner rose quietly and came to the table. ''Here is a letter for you,'' she said.

The girl stepped forward eagerly, saw the two lying together there, hesitated, and looked at her mistress.

''Take yours, Gerta. Open it, please.''

The girl turned frightened eyes upon her.

''I want you to read it, here,'' said Mrs. Marroner.

''Oh, ma'am—No! Please don't make me!''

''Why not?''

There seemed to be no reason at hand, and Gerta flushed more deeply and opened her letter. It was long; it was evidently puzzling to her; it began ''My dear wife.'' She read it slowly.

''Are you sure it is your letter?'' asked Mrs. Marroner. ''Is not this one yours? Is not that one—mine?''

She held out the other letter to her.

''It is a mistake,'' Mrs. Marroner went on, with a hard quietness. She had lost her social bearings somehow, lost her usual keen sense of the proper thing to do. This was not life; this was a nightmare.

''Do you not see? Your letter was put in my envelope and my letter was put in your envelope. Now we understand it.''

But poor Gerta had no antechamber to her mind, no trained forces to preserve order while agony entered. The thing swept over her, resistless, overwhelming. She cowered before the outraged wrath she expected; and from some hidden cavern that wrath arose and swept over her in pale flame.

"Go and pack your trunk," said Mrs. Marroner. "You will leave my house tonight. Here is your money."

She laid down the fifty-dollar bill. She put with it a month's wages. She had no shadow of pity for those anguished eyes, those tears which she heard drop on the floor.

"Go to your room and pack," said Mrs. Marroner. And Gerta, always obedient, went.

Then Mrs. Marroner went to hers, and spent a time she never counted, lying on her face on the bed.

But the training of the twenty-eight years which had elapsed before her marriage; the life at college, both as student and teacher; the independent growth which she had made, formed a very different background for grief from that in Gerta's mind.

After a while Mrs. Marroner arose. She administered to herself a hot bath, a cold shower, a vigorous rubbing. "Now I can think," she said.

First she regretted the sentence of instant banishment. She went upstairs to see if it had been carried out. Poor Gerta! The tempest of her agony had worked itself out at last as in a child, and left her sleeping, the pillow wet, the lips still grieving, a big sob shuddering itself off now and then.

Mrs. Marroner stood and watched her, and as she watched she considered the helpless sweetness of the face; the defenseless, unformed character; the docility and habit of obedience which made her so attractive—and so easily a victim. Also she thought of the mighty force which had swept over her; of the great process now working itself out through her; of how pitiful and futile seemed any resistance she might have made.

She softly returned to her own room, made up a little fire, and sat by it, ignoring her feelings now, as she had before ignored her thoughts.

Here were two women and a man. One woman was a wife: loving, trusting, affectionate. One was a servant: loving, trusting, affectionate—a young girl, an exile, a dependent; grateful for any kindness; untrained, uneducated, childish. She ought, of course, to have resisted temptation; but Mrs. Marroner was wise enough to know how difficult temptation is to recognize when it comes in the guise of friendship and from a source one does not suspect.

Gerta might have done better in resisting the grocer's clerk; had, indeed, with Mrs. Marroner's advice, resisted several. But where respect was due, how could she criticize? Where obedience was due, how could she refuse—with ignorance to hold her blinded—until too late?

As the older, wiser woman forced herself to understand and extenuate the girl's misdeed and foresee her ruined future, a new feeling rose in her heart, strong, clear, and overmastering: a sense of measureless condemnation for the man who had done this thing. He knew. He understood. He could fully foresee and measure the consequences of his act. He appreciated to the full the innocence, the ignorance, the grateful affection, the habitual docility, of which he deliberately took advantage.

Mrs. Marroner rose to icy peaks of intellectual apprehension, from which her hours of frantic pain seemed far indeed removed. He had done this thing under the same roof with her—his wife. He had not frankly loved the younger woman, broken with his wife, made a new marriage. That would have been heart-break pure and simple. This was something else.

That letter, that wretched, cold, carefully guarded, unsigned letter, that bill—far safer than a check—these did not speak of affection. Some men can love two women at one time. This was not love.

Mrs. Marroner's sense of pity and outrage for herself, the wife, now spread suddenly into a perception of pity and outrage for the girl. All that splendid, clean young beauty, the hope of a happy life, with marriage and motherhood, honorable independence, even—these were nothing to that man. For his own pleasure he had chosen to rob her of her life's best joys.

He would "take care of her," said the letter. How? In what capacity?

And then, sweeping over both her feelings for herself, the wife, and Gerta, his victim, came a new flood, which literally lifted her to her feet. She rose and walked, her head held high. "This is the sin of man against woman," she said. "The offense is against womanhood. Against motherhood. Against—the child."

She stopped.

The child. His child. That, too, he sacrificed and injured—doomed to degradation.

Mrs. Marroner came of stern New England stock. She was not a Calvinist, hardly even a Unitarian, but the iron of Calvinism was in her soul: of that grim faith which held that most people had to be damned "for the glory of God."

Generations of ancestors who both preached and practiced stood behind her; people whose lives had been sternly moulded to their highest moments of religious conviction. In sweeping bursts of feeling, they achieved "conviction," and afterward they lived and died according to that conviction.

When Mr. Marroner reached home a few weeks later, following his letters too soon to expect an answer to either, he saw no wife upon the pier, though he had cabled, and found the house closed darkly. He let himself in with his latch-key, and stole softly upstairs, to surprise his wife.

No wife was there.

He rang the bell. No servant answered it.

He turned up light after light, searched the house from top to bottom; it was utterly empty. The kitchen wore a clean, bald, unsympathetic aspect. He left it and slowly mounted the stairs, completely dazed. The whole house was clean, in perfect order, wholly vacant.

One thing he felt perfectly sure of—she knew.

Yet was he sure? He must not assume too much. She might have been ill. She might have died. He started to his feet. No, they would have cabled him. He sat down again.

For any such change, if she had wanted him to know, she would have written. Perhaps she had, and he, returning so suddenly, had missed the letter. The thought was some comfort. It must be so. He turned to the telephone and again hesitated. If she had found out—if she had gone—utterly gone, without a word—should he announce it himself to friends and family?

He walked the floor; he searched everywhere for some letter, some word of explanation. Again and again he went to the telephone—and always stopped. He could not bear to ask: "Do you know where my wife is?"

The harmonious, beautiful rooms reminded him in a dumb, helpless way of her—like the remote smile on the face of the dead. He put out the lights, could not bear the darkness, turned them all on again.

It was a long night—

In the morning he went early to the office. In the accumulated mail was no letter from her. No one seemed to know of anything unusual. A friend asked after his wife—"Pretty glad to see you, I guess?" He answered evasively.

About eleven a man came to see him: John Hill, her lawyer. Her cousin, too. Mr. Marroner had never liked him. He liked him less now, for Mr. Hill merely handed him a letter, remarked, "I was requested to deliver this to you personally," and departed, looking like a person who is called on to kill something offensive.

"I have gone. I will care for Gerta. Good-bye. Marion."

That was all. There was no date, no address, no postmark, nothing but that.

In his anxiety and distress, he had fairly forgotten Gerta and all that. Her name aroused in him a sense of rage. She had come between him and his wife. She had taken his wife from him. That was the way he felt.

At first he said nothing, did nothing, lived on alone in his house, taking meals where he chose. When people asked him about his wife, he said she was traveling—for her health. He would not have it in the newspapers. Then, as time passed, as no enlightenment came to him, he resolved not to bear it any longer, and employed detectives. They blamed him for not having put them on the track earlier, but set to work, urged to the utmost secrecy.

What to him had been so blank a wall of mystery seemed not to embarrass them in the least. They made careful inquiries as to her "past," found where she had studied, where taught, and on what lines; that she had some little money of her own, that her doctor was Josephine L. Bleet, M.D., and many other bits of information.

As a result of careful and prolonged work, they finally told him that she had resumed teaching under one of her old professors, lived quietly, and apparently kept boarders; giving him town, street, and number, as if it were a matter of no difficulty whatever.

He had returned in early spring. It was autumn before he found her.

A quiet college town in the hills, a broad, shady street, a pleasant house standing in its own lawn, with trees and flowers about it. He had the address in his hand, and the number showed clear on the white gate. He walked up the straight gravel path and rang the bell. An elderly servant opened the door.

"Does Mrs. Marroner live here?"

"No, sir."

"This is number twenty-eight?"

"Yes, sir."

"Who does live here?"

"Miss Wheeling, sir."

Ah! Her maiden name. They had told him, but he had forgotten.

He stepped inside. "I would like to see her," he said.

He was ushered into a still parlor, cool and sweet with the scent of flowers, the flowers she had always loved best. It almost brought tears to his eyes. All their years of happiness rose in his mind again—the exquisite beginnings; the days of eager longing before she was really his; the deep, still beauty of her love.

Surely she would forgive him—she must forgive him. He would humble himself; he would tell her of his honest remorse—his absolute determination to be a different man.

Through the wide doorway there came in to him two women. One like a tall Madonna, bearing a baby in her arms.

Marion, calm, steady, definitely impersonal, nothing but a clear pallor to hint of inner stress.

Gerta, holding the child as a bulwark, with a new intelligence in her face, and her blue, adoring eyes fixed on her friend—not upon him.

He looked from one to the other dumbly.

And the woman who had been his wife asked quietly:

"What have you to say to us?"

MAKING A
CHANGE

"Wa-a-a-a-a! Waa-a-a-aaa!"

Frank Gordins set down his coffee cup so hard that it spilled over into the saucer.

"Is there no way to stop that child crying?" he demanded.

"I do not know of any," said his wife, so definitely and politely that the words seemed cut off by machinery.

"*I do,*" said his mother with even more definiteness, but less politeness.

Young Mrs. Gordins looked at her mother-in-law from under her delicate level brows, and said nothing. But the weary lines about her eyes deepened; she had been kept awake nearly all night, and for many nights.

So had he. So, as a matter of fact, had his mother. She had not the care of the baby—but lay awake wishing she had.

"There's no use talking about it," said Julia. "If Frank is not satisfied with the child's mother, he must say so— perhaps we can make a change."

This was ominously gentle. Julia's nerves were at the breaking point. Upon her tired ears, her sensitive mother's heart, the grating wail from the next room fell like a lash— burnt in like fire. Her ears were hypersensitive, always. She had been an ardent musician before her marriage, and had taught quite successfully on both piano and violin. To any mother a child's cry is painful; to a musical mother it is torment.

But if her ears were sensitive, so was her conscience. If her nerves were weak, her pride was strong. The child was her child, it was her duty to take care of it, and take care

of it she would. She spent her days in unremitting devotion
to its needs and to the care of her neat flat; and her nights
had long since ceased to refresh her.

Again the weary cry rose to a wail.

"It does seem to be time for a change of treatment,"
suggested the older woman acidly.

"Or a change of residence," offered the younger, in a
deadly quiet voice.

"Well, by Jupiter! There'll be a change of some kind,
and p.d.q.!" said the son and husband, rising to his feet.

His mother rose also, and left the room, holding her head
high and refusing to show any effects of that last thrust.

Frank Gordins glared at his wife. His nerves were raw,
too. It does not benefit anyone in health or character to be
continuously deprived of sleep. Some enlightened persons
use that deprivation as a form of torture.

She stirred her coffee with mechanical calm, her eyes sul-
lenly bent on her plate.

"I will not stand having Mother spoken to like that," he
stated with decision.,

"I will not stand having her interfere with my methods
of bringing up children."

"Your methods! Why, Julia, my mother knows more
about taking care of babies than you'll ever learn! She has
the real love of it—and the practical experience. Why can't
you *let* her take care of the kid—and we'll all have some
peace!"

She lifted her eyes and looked at him; deep inscrutable
wells of angry light. He had not the faintest appreciation of
her state of mind. When people say they are "nearly crazy"
from weariness, they state a practical fact. The old phrase
which describes reason as "tottering on her throne" is also
a clear one.

Julia was more near the verge of complete disaster than
the family dreamed. The conditions were so simple, so
usual, so inevitable.

Here was Frank Gordins, well brought up, the only son
of a very capable and idolatrously affectionate mother. He
had fallen deeply and desperately in love with the exalted
beauty and fine mind of the young music teacher, and his
mother had approved. She too loved music and admired
beauty.

Her tiny store in the savings bank did not allow of a separate home, and Julia had cordially welcomed her to share in their household.

Here was affection, propriety, and peace. Here was a noble devotion on the part of the young wife, who so worshipped her husband that she used to wish she had been the greatest musician on earth—that she might give it up for him! She had given up her music, perforce, for many months, and missed it more than she knew.

She bent her mind to the decoration and artistic management of their little apartment, finding her standards difficult to maintain by the ever-changing inefficiency of her help. The musical temperament does not always include patience, nor, necessarily, the power of management.

When the baby came, her heart overflowed with utter devotion and thankfulness; she was his wife—the mother of his child. Her happiness lifted and pushed within till she longed more than ever for her music, for the free-pouring current of expression, to give forth her love and pride and happiness. She had not the gift of words.

So now she looked at her husband, dumbly, while wild visions of separation, of secret flight—even of self-destruction—swung dizzily across her mental vision. All she said was, "All right, Frank. We'll make a change. And you shall have—some peace."

"Thank goodness for that, Jule! You do look tired, girlie—let Mother see to His Nibs, and try to get a nap, can't you?"

"Yes," she said. "Yes . . . I think I will." Her voice had a peculiar note in it. If Frank had been an alienist, or even a general physician, he would have noticed it. But his work lay in electric coils, in dynamos and copper wiring—not in women's nerves—and he did not notice it.

He kissed her and went out, throwing back his shoulders and drawing a long breath of relief as he left the house behind him and entered his own world.

"This being married—and bringing up children—is not what it's cracked up to be." That was the feeling in the back of his mind. But it did not find full admission, much less expression.

When a friend asked him, "All well at home?" he said, "Yes, thank you—pretty fair. Kid cries a good deal—but that's natural, I suppose."

He dismissed the whole matter from his mind and bent

his faculties to a man's task—how he can earn enough to support a wife, a mother, and a son.

At home his mother sat in her small room, looking out of the window at the ground-glass one just across the "well," and thinking hard.

By the disorderly little breakfast table his wife remained motionless, her chin in her hands, her big eyes staring at nothing, trying to formulate in her weary mind some reliable reason why she should not do what she was thinking of doing. But her mind was too exhausted to serve her properly.

Sleep—sleep—sleep—that was the one thing she wanted. Then his mother could take care of the baby all she wanted to, and Frank could have some peace. . . . Oh, dear! It was time for the child's bath.

She gave it to him mechanically. On the stroke of the hour, she prepared the sterilized milk and arranged the little one comfortably with his bottle. He snuggled down, enjoying it, while she stood watching him.

She emptied the tub, put the bath apron to dry, picked up all the towels and sponges and varied appurtenances of the elaborate performance of bathing the first-born, and then sat staring straight before her, more weary than ever, but growing inwardly determined.

Greta had cleared the table, with heavy heels and hands, and was now rattling dishes in the kitchen. At every slam, the young mother winced, and when the girl's high voice began a sort of doleful chant over her work, young Mrs. Gordins rose to her feet with a shiver and made her decision.

She carefully picked up the child and his bottle, and carried him to his grandmother's room.

"Would you mind looking after Albert?" she asked in a flat, quiet voice. "I think I'll try to get some sleep."

"Oh, I shall be delighted," replied her mother-in-law. She said it in a tone of cold politeness, but Julia did not notice. She laid the child on the bed and stood looking at him in the same dull way for a little while, then went out without another word.

Mrs. Gordins, senior, sat watching the baby for some long moments. "He's a perfectly lovely child!" she said softly, gloating over his rosy beauty. "There's not a *thing* the matter with him! It's just her absurd ideas. She's so irregular with him! To think of letting that child cry for an hour! He is nervous because she is. And of course she couldn't feed him till after his bath—of course not!''

She continued in these sarcastic meditations for some time, taking the empty bottle away from the small wet mouth, that sucked on for a few moments aimlessly and then was quiet in sleep.

''I could take care of him so that he'd *never* cry!'' she continued to herself, rocking slowly back and forth. ''And I could take care of twenty like him—and enjoy it! I believe I'll go off somewhere and do it. Give Julia a rest. Change of residence, indeed!''

She rocked and planned, pleased to have her grandson with her, even while asleep.

Greta had gone out on some errand of her own. The rooms were very quiet. Suddenly the old lady held up her head and sniffed. She rose swiftly to her feet and sprang to the gas jet—no, it was shut off tightly. She went back to the dining room—all right there.

''That foolish girl has left the range going and it's blown out!'' she thought, and went to the kitchen. No, the little room was fresh and clean, every burner turned off.

''Funny! It must come in from the hall.'' She opened the door. No, the hall gave only its usual odor of diffused basement. Then the parlor—nothing there. The little alcove called by the renting agent ''the music room,'' where Julia's closed piano and violin case stood dumb and dusty—nothing there.

''It's in her room—and she's asleep!'' said Mrs. Gordins, senior; and she tried to open the door. It was locked. She knocked—there was no answer; knocked louder—shook it—rattled the knob. No answer.

Then Mrs. Gordins thought quickly. ''It may be an accident, and nobody must know. Frank mustn't know. I'm glad Greta's out. I *must* get in somehow!'' She looked at the transom, and the stout rod Frank had himself put up for the portieres Julia loved.

''I believe I can do it, at a pinch.''

She was a remarkably active woman of her years, but no memory of earlier gymnastic feats could quite cover the exercise. She hastily brought the step-ladder. From its top she could see in, and what she saw made her determine recklessly.

Grabbing the pole with small strong hands, she thrust her light frame bravely through the opening, turning clumsily but successfully, and dropping breathlessly and somewhat bruised to the floor, she flew to open the windows and doors.

When Julia opened her eyes she found loving arms around her, and wise, tender words to soothe and reassure.

"Don't say a thing, dearie—I understand. I *understand,* I tell you! Oh, my dear girl—my precious daughter! We haven't been half good enough to you, Frank and I! But cheer up now—I've got the *loveliest* plan to tell you about! We *are* going to make a change! Listen now!"

And while the pale young mother lay quiet, petted and waited on to her heart's content, great plans were discussed and decided on.

Frank Gordins was pleased when the baby "outgrew his crying spells." He spoke of it to his wife.

"Yes," she said sweetly. "He has better care."

"I knew you'd learn," said he, proudly.

"I have!" she agreed. "I've learned—ever so much!"

He was pleased, too, vastly pleased, to have her health improve rapidly and steadily, the delicate pink come back to her cheeks, the soft light to her eyes; and when she made music for him in the evening, soft music, with shut doors—not to waken Albert—he felt as if his days of courtship had come again.

Greta the hammer-footed had gone, and an amazing French matron who came in by the day had taken her place. He asked no questions as to this person's peculiarities, and did not know that she did the purchasing and planned the meals, meals of such new delicacy and careful variance as gave him much delight. Neither did he know that her wages were greater than her predecessor's. He turned over the same sum weekly, and did not pursue details.

He was pleased also that his mother seemed to have taken a new lease of life. She was so cheerful and brisk, so full of little jokes and stories—as he had known her in his boyhood; and above all she was so free and affectionate with Julia, that he was more than pleased.

"I tell you what it is!" he said to a bachelor friend. "You fellows don't know what you're missing!" And he brought one of them home to dinner—just to show him.

"Do you do all that on thirty-five a week?" his friend demanded.

"That's about it," he answered proudly.

"Well, your wife's a wonderful manager—that's all I can say. And you've got the best cook I ever saw, or heard of, or ate of—I suppose I might say—for five dollars."

Mrs. Gordins was pleased and proud. But he was neither pleased nor proud when someone said to him, with displeasing frankness, "I shouldn't think you'd want your wife to be giving music lessons, Frank!"

He did not show surprise nor anger to his friend, but saved it for his wife. So surprised and so angry was he that he did a most unusual thing—he left his business and went home early in the afternoon. He opened the door of his flat. There was no one in it. He went through every room. No wife; no child; no mother; no servant.

The elevator boy heard him banging about, opening and shutting doors, and grinned happily. When Mr. Gordins came out, Charles volunteered some information.

"Young Mrs. Gordins is out, sir; but old Mrs. Gordins and the baby—they're upstairs. On the roof, I think."

Mr. Gordins went to the roof. There he found his mother, a smiling, cheerful nursemaid, and fifteen happy babies.

Mrs. Gordins, senior, rose to the occasion promptly.

"Welcome to my baby-garden, Frank," she said cheerfully. "I'm so glad you could get off in time to see it."

She took his arm and led him about, proudly exhibiting her sunny roof-garden, her sand-pile and big, shallow, zinc-lined pool, her flowers and vines, her seesaws, swings, and floor mattresses.

"You see how happy they are," she said. "Celia can manage very well for a few moments." And then she exhibited to him the whole upper flat, turned into a convenient place for many little ones to take their naps or to play in if the weather was bad.

"Where's Julia?" he demanded first.

"Julia will be in presently," she told him, "by five o'clock anyway. And the mothers come for the babies by then, too. I have them from nine or ten to five."

He was silent, both angry and hurt.

"We didn't tell you at first, my dear boy, because we knew you wouldn't like it, and we wanted to make sure it would go well. I rent the upper flat, you see—it is forty dollars a month, same as ours—and pay Celia five dollars a week, and pay Dr. Holbrook downstairs the same for looking over my little ones every day. She helped me to get them, too. The mothers pay me three dollars a week each, and don't have to keep a nursemaid. And I pay ten dollars a week board to Julia, and still have about ten of my own.''

"And she gives music lessons?''

"Yes, she gives music lessons, just as she used to. She loves it, you know. You must have noticed how happy and well she is now—haven't you? And so am I. And so is Albert. You can't feel very badly about a thing that makes us all happy, can you?''

Just then Julia came in, radiant from a brisk walk, fresh and cheery, a big bunch of violets at her breast.

"Oh, Mother,'' she cried, "I've got tickets and we'll all go to hear Melba—if we can get Celia to come in for the evening.''

She saw her husband, and a guilty flush rose to her brow as she met his reproachful eyes.

"Oh, Frank!'' she begged, her arms around his neck. "Please don't mind! Please get used to it! Please be proud of us! Just think, we're all so happy, and we earn about a hundred dollars a week—all of us together. You see, I have Mother's ten to add to the house money, and twenty or more of my own!''

They had a long talk together that evening, just the two of them. She had told him, at last, what a danger had hung over them—how near it came.

"And Mother showed me the way out, Frank. The way to have my mind again—and not lose you! She is a different woman herself now that she has her heart and hands full of babies. Albert does enjoy it so! And *you've* enjoyed it—till you found it out!

"And dear—my own love—I don't mind it now at all! I love my home, I love my work, I love my mother, I love you. And as to children—I wish I had six!''

He looked at her flushed, eager, lovely face, and drew her close to him.

"If it makes all of you as happy as that,'' he said, "I guess I can stand it.''

And in after years he was heard to remark, "This being married and bringing up children is as easy as can be—when you learn how!''

A MISCHIEVOUS RUDIMENT

"A woman—a real woman—needs to be mastered!" said Hugh Wyndam with decision, jamming tobacco into his pipe with a forceful thumb. "She likes it. She loves the man who can *make* her love him—against her will!"

"What's your authority for that?" inquired Billy Weston from the other side of the billiard room. He did not smoke, but as he never criticized those who did, they tolerated him—with commiseration.

"Authority?" Wyndam turned and looked at the speaker as if he was a tiresome child. "All life's authority for that. Better study it a little."

"Modern life—or ancient history?" persisted Weston, unabashed.

"Don't irritate Wyndam any more," urged Ned Richmond, pacifically, "he's on the verge of a tantrum now. What's wrong with you Wyndam, anyhow? Have you found one you can't master?"

The upholder of masculine violence seemed little pleased by this interference.

"It's a perfectly discussible subject, if Weston wants to discuss it," he said. "But if he imagines that modern life is any different from ancient history in the relations of men and women, he's mistaken. We've got a lot of neurotic, introspective, denatured modern women, I admit; but even at that, if a real man is fool enough to care for one of them, and will simply ignore all this new nonsense and seize her with the strong hand, she'll respond fast enough."

The speaker was a big heavy fellow, with the square redoubtable chin beloved of novelists, thick eyebrows, and eyes that had lost their first luster. He was conspicuously in love with Ria Bland. But so were the other visitors; and there was a waiting list also.

Ria was a pale quiet girl; not remarkably beautiful, but with a puzzling attractiveness. "A girl you wouldn't look twice at" young Richmond had said; but he looked the second time to make sure, and was still looking. His touring car, his limousine, and his runabout were all at her service—even his racer, if she wanted it. But beyond the limits of open friendship she had not allowed him.

Wyndam had set her down for one of these modern neurasthenics, but found she played an excellent game of tennis, danced well, and differed with him on so many grounds, with so slight and ill-pursued advantage that he was always arguing further in the hope of establishing his points. One does not like to break a butterfly upon the wheel, but if the butterfly is obdurately evasive, it provokes him.

Young Weston made no secret of his devotion, and no virtue of it. "Why, we're all in love with her," he said, cheerfully. "What's the use of pretending? And she won't look at one of us. Why should she?"

This modest view of their respective or collective merits met no agreement. Mr. Richmond bought a new car of another make, and tried that on her. His imagination was limited, but his financial resources were not.

And Mr. Wyndam untiringly exerted his mighty muscles and his alert intellect to dazzle and subdue.

Mr. Weston was too modest in his judgment. Miss Bland was, as a matter of fact, looking at them all most carefully, and weighing their respective claims with an attempt at fair judgment. To judge wisely and impartially among many lovers is not easy, at twenty-five. By a process of exclusion she had gradually eliminated many of the less desirable, and in this little house-party that she had persuaded her Aunt Isabel to give, she had temporarily isolated these three, to study at close quarters.

Being a grass-orphan, she had less than the ordinary illusions about marriage; having a comfortable income of her own, besides a small fortune in her mother's diamonds, she was early forced to admit that the affection of man is not always disinterested. And then, as years slipped by, as travel, study and varied experience added to her wisdom, she became difficult to suit and doubtful of ever attaining "happiness."

"A reasonable marriage" was about what she looked forward to; for she had no desire for a career, and by no means wished to spend her life without children.

The millions of Mr. Richmond gave him the advantage of disinterestedness; the splendid vigor of Mr. Wyndam had a stronger charm than she even admitted to herself; and Mr. Weston's quiet good manners and keen intelligence gave her so much pleasure that she was definitely striving to hold his friendship.

She knew that he felt more than that, though he made few advances; for once or twice she had caught a look in his steady eyes that no woman could mistake; and she had counted him in on this occasion to widen her problem.

"I have three to choose from—that's the regulation number," she said to herself. "You never were a beauty, Ria,— though I will admit you are attractive, somehow, but you're not so young, remember. If you want *my* advice you marry Ned Richmond and be *thankful.*"

The girl's quiet beauty, her grace and tact and social charm, appealed to the young millionaire intensely; he was a simple soul, patient with the inevitable attack of many willing maidens; and finding in this different one a restful satisfaction.

With heavy boxes of bonbons, gorgeously beribboned; with roses that stood five feet high upon their sturdy stems, and violets in purple balls as big as cabbages he pursued his attentions.

She was very gentle with him. "I do not love you, Ned," she explained. "I like you—I hate to send you away, but honestly, I do not know my own mind yet."

"I'll wait," he said, "I'm not as smart as Weston—he's got a good mind, that fellow, he'll make his mark; and I don't trot in the same class with Wyndham, he's a record breaker, all right. But I'm awfully fond of you—and if you could make up your mind to marry me, I won't demand very much,—I'll be too happy,—you shall have things your own way."

She meditated upon this; and was not wholly pleased Wyndham swam with her and she could not but admire the smooth strength and poise of him, he rowed with her in easy power that never tired, and beat all comers at outdoor games.

He stopped the canoe mid-lake, one moonlight evening, with decisive paddle, and demanded the answer she had deferred indefinitely.

"I am not sure, yet," she protested, "I must have time to decide."

"How much time? How long do you expect a man to hang between heaven and earth and say nothing?" He laid down the paddle and approached her.

"Oh, please don't!" she cried, "Don't! It'll tip over!"

"No, it won't" he said grimly. "Besides, if it does, I could rescue you in fine style. And then you'd have to marry me!"

"I wouldn't," she protested. "And I won't—in any case—if you don't sit down!"

"I am sitting down," said he, and he adjusted his sinewy length, so as to balance the frail shell and yet lie close beside her. She had no place of withdrawal, unless it were the lake, and that looked chilly; rippling and glittering under the moon.

"Stop it," she said. "This is ridiculous!—Do you want me to scream?"

"Indeed I do not," he said. "And what's more, I don't believe you will. I want you to sit still, and give me that little hand—and say you will marry me."

He took the little hand in question—took both, indeed—and kissed them severally and together.

"Will you marry me?" he asked again in a low insistent voice. "I love you— as you know. I don't say I never loved before—that's foolishness—and it doesn't matter anyhow—I love—*you*—*now*—enough for both of us! Say yes, my darling! say yes—or shall I come near and make you?"

His words were violent, but his voice was wooing, thrilling, all-persuasive, and his whole strong being seemed to come forward and envelop her.

She did cry out—but it was a faint sound, and he laughed and took her in his arms.

Then another canoe suddenly shot out into the light and ran up behind them.

"I beg your pardon, if I intrude, Miss Bland, but I thought I heard you call. Have you lost your paddle?"

"You do intrude, Mr. Weston, most abominably," said

Wyndham in a low tense voice; but the girl reached out and seized the edge of his canoe."

"Not in the least, Mr. Weston," said she. "I think Mr. Wyndham has a cramp—or something—he's stopped paddling and I was afraid we'd tip over. Tow us in, won't you?"

To this ignominy, Mr. Wyndham was forced to submit; but he bided his time, not ill-pleased with his progress. She avoided him somewhat thereafter, but this too did not displease him.

"If she did not care, I'd be helpless," he said to himself, "but she does—she can't deny it! I'll have her! *I must have her!*"

Her views on his behavior she did not share with anyone; but she did turn from him, and show more favor to both the others. Richmond was dumbly grateful, Weston always pleasant, efficient, courteous, but faintly irritating in his sustained attitude of friendliness. This was what she asked, but perhaps its coolness contrasted unfavorably with the warmth of the others.

He met her perfectly in the discussions she loved, was familiar with many of the books she had read and more that she had not; by no means agreeing with all her views, but opposing them fairly and with consideration. Richmond hated discussion; he had read little, and had no gift of speech; argument was to him mere quarreling; and Wyndham, while always ready to debate, was overbearing and dictatorial. They sat by the ever-welcome evening fire one night, and the girl dropped an apple of discord among them by referring to what she described as "the renaissance of primevalism" in modern fiction.

"Just as we are really growing wiser," she said, "as women are enjoying a much broader, sounder education, and men getting more—reasonable—here all this Jack-Kipling school begins again in the old note of brute force!"

"I quite agree with you," Richmond hastened to admit; but her soft eyes rested on him for a moment with faint disapproval.

"I completely disagree with you," contradicted Wyndham. "Kipling and his imitators rest their work on unchanging natural laws. No amount of 'education' and 'sweet reasonableness' alters the fact that man is stronger than woman and that in her heart she knows it and she likes it."

He looked at her daringly, but she gazed into the fire.

"What do you think, Mr. Weston?" she asked. "Is not the cave-man in modern literature a mischievous rudiment?"

"I think the kind of writing you speak of appeals to the prevalent sentiment among men, just as a lot of emotional stuff appeals to the prevalent sentiment among women—and therefore is marketable," he replied.

"But do you think it is true? True to life?" she persisted. "Do you really think women like the cave-man attitude?"

"They seem to like to read about it, that's the real answer. Just as they like to read detective stories and adventure stories which they would not enjoy figuring in."

"Then you think these men write all these tales of gore and gunpowder merely to sell?"

"Of course they do," agreed Richmond.

"Not in the least!" protested Wyndham. "They write because they are artists and see life as it is."

"As they think it is, perhaps; that may be true of the most honest of them. I think Kipling has a most sincere conviction of the permanent truth and social value of his antique standards. But as to what modern women really like—suppose you tell us, Miss Bland," and Mr. Weston, leaning far back in his big chair, looked at her steadfastly out of the shadow.

Wyndham rose and stood before the fire, an imposing figure, looming dark against the leaping light.

"This is all nonsense," he said; "just talk about talk— Wait till there's an opportunity to *do* something."

There came an opportunity presently for the ever-assiduous Mr. Richmond to be of service.

An invitation arrived for them both to an especially splendid and expensive entertainment at the "camp" of a mutual friend. It was a towering timber palace, as luxurious as a Newport "cottage," but she called it a "camp" because it was in the mountains.

"Let's motor over," he said. "I'll take you myself. Do let me, Miss Bland."

They were to start by daylight immediately after dinner, and return by the late half moon, a poor second to the blinding acetylene lamps.

The car sat purring at the door. She had taken her seat and was waiting for him, her aunt had not come down, when Mr. Wyndham stepped forward and took the driver's place.

They were off so suddenly and so fast that she was scarce able to object, beyond a mere protesting cry; whizzing around the curves and out of the gate so that the car rocked dangerously. They turned to the left instead of the right and sped madly down hill and out into the open country. She looked at him cautiously, fearing he was intoxicated; but no, his face was set in a calm triumphant smile, his fixed steady eyes on the road ahead, his hands firm on the steering wheel. After some flying miles she rose without a word and stepped over the seat back into the tonneau.

They had reached a smooth straight sandy stretch and he slowed a little, turned and looked at her.

"Better come back," he said, "I like you near me." She made no answer. He only smiled again over his shoulder. "You are too proud to ask questions but I will allay your natural curiosity none the less. We are going over the border to the home of a priest I know, who will marry us." She gave a little, derisive laugh. "I recognize the incredulity in your heart," he went on, "or rather in your mind, in your heart you know he will.

"Because, you see, we can in no way get back before tomorrow, and the priest is better than the newspapers—don't you think so? Also to make all sure, I left a note for Richmond to say that we had planned the elopement, and if he wanted to keep the affair decent and quiet, he'd better sit tight."

She laughed again, this time an appreciative giggle. "Poor Mr. Richmond," she said, "and his car, too."

"I thought you'd see the ingenuity of it," he remarked, and they sped smoothly on.

Suddenly she cried out in real distress. "Oh, Mr. Wyndham! My jewel case! I must have lost it when I came back here!"

He stopped, but turned and looked at her. She was searching anxiously. "Please bring one of the lamps," she said. "It may be inside yet."

"What on earth were you doing with your jewels?" he demanded.

"I was taking them to wear at Mrs. Vastor's, of course."

He was still incredulous, but she showed irritated impatience.

"I assure you, Mr. Wyndham, that I would much rather

marry you with a third of my fortune in my hands than to leave it on these Adirondack roads.''

He searched the car assiduously, but in vain. "You lose more time searching than you would in going back for it," she said. "it was only a little way back—and we can't miss it with those lamps! I'll come in front and look."

He turned, though still suspicious, and they went slowly back, both sharply examining the road. She saw it first. "There it is!" she said. "Look—we've passed it!"

He looked back, still doubting, and saw the small brown jewel case by the side of the road, and with a relieved expression he stopped and ran back to get it.

It was only a few steps, but in that moment she sprang into his seat, threw on full speed, and the great car leaped forward like a mad thing. He turned with a shout and made a rush for it, but after several gasping moments saw that it was a useless chase; and turned his steps slowly in the other direction.

The jewel case still lay in the road. He picked it up, grimly enough, and put it in his pocket. Presently he took it out again—yes, it was unlocked. He opened it. It was quite empty.

Though late in arriving, Miss Bland's diamonds were greatly admired at Mrs. Vastor's ball, and Mr. Richmond was easily convinced that Mr. Wyndham's note had no foundation.

When they returned next day, Mr. Weston announced his intention of leaving at once, much to the satisfaction of Aunt Isabel, but not of her niece. If he was gone, and never came back, how could she endure life?

She sought him in the garden where he walked alone.

"Why do you go so suddenly, Mr. Weston?"

He turned and looked at her, the look that was unmistakable.

"Because I have to," he said. "There's no use in my staying here."

"There might be," she suggested.

He turned sharply away. "No use!" he repeated, "no use. I'm not that kind."

Then she took her life bravely in her hands. "If you won't,

I will,'' she said. ''It's leap year, any way. Mr. Weston, I have grown to care for you very much. Will you marry me?''

He raised her hand to his lips, and kissed it as if it were a queen's.

''You are the sweetest, bravest woman in the world—and I love you with my whole heart. I shall be proud and glad to marry you—when my income is equal to yours. It may take me two or three years—will you wait for me?''

And she waited.

MRS. ELDER'S IDEA

Did you ever repeat a word or phrase so often that it lost all meaning to you?

Did you ever eat at the same table, of the same diet, till the food had no taste to you?

Did you ever feel a sudden overmastering wave of revolt against the ceaseless monotony of your surroundings till you longed to escape anywhere at any cost?

That was the way Mrs. Elder felt on this gray, muggy morning, toward the familiar objects about her dining room, the familiar dishes on the table, even, for the moment, at the familiar figure at the other end of it.

It was Mr. Elder's idea of a pleasant breakfast to set up his preferred newspaper against the water pitcher, and read it as long as he could continue eating and drinking. Other people were welcome to do the same, he argued; *he* had no objection. It is true that there was but one newspaper.

Mrs. Elder was a woman naturally chatty, but skilled in silence. One cannot long converse with an absorbed opposing countenance which meets one's choicest anecdote, some minutes after the event, with a testy ''What's that?''

She sat still, stirring her cool coffee, waiting to ring for it, hot, when he wanted more, and studying his familiar outlines with a dull fascination. She knew every line and tint, every curve and angle, every wrinkle in the loose-fitting coat, every moderate change in expression. They were only moderate, nowadays. Never any more did she see the looks she remembered so well, over twenty years ago; looks of admiration, of approval, of interest, of desire to please; looks with a deep kindling fire in them—

"I would thou wert either cold or hot," she was half consciously repeating to herself.

O yes, he was kind to her in most things; he was fond of her, even, she could admit that. He missed her, when she was not there, or would miss her—she seldom had a chance to test it. They had no quarrel, no complaint against each other; only a long, slow cooling, as of lava beds; the gradual evaporation of a fine fervor; the process of torpid, tepid, mutual accommodation which is complacently referred to by the worldly wise as "settling down."

"Had she no children?" will demand those whose psychological medicine closets hold but a few labels.

"For a Woman: A Husband, Home and Children. Good for whatever ails her.

"For a Man: Success, Money, A Good Wife.

"For a Child: Proper Care, Education, A Good Bringing Up."

There are no other persons to be doctored, and no other remedies.

Now Mrs. Elder had had children, four, fulfilling the formula announced by Mr. Grant Allen, some years since, that each couple must have four children, merely to preserve the balance of the population; two to replace their parents, and two to die. Two of hers had accordingly, died; and two, living, were now ready to replace their parents; that is they were grown up.

Theodore was of age, and had gone into business already, at a distance. Alice was of age, too; the lesser age allowed the weaker vessel, and also away from home. She was staying with an aunt in Boston, a wealthy aunt who insisted in maintaining her in luxury; but the girl insisted equally upon studying at the Institute of Technology, and threatened an early departure into the proud freedom of self support.

Mrs. Elder was fond of children, but these young persons were not children any more. She would have been glad to continue her ministrations; but however motherhood may seek to prolong its period of usefulness, childhood is evanescent; and youth, modern youth, serenely rebellious. The cycle which is supposed to so perfectly round out a woman's life, was closed for the present.

Mr. Elder projected a cup, without looking at it, or her; and Mrs. Elder rang, poured his coffee, modified it to his liking, and handed it back to him. She even took a fresh cup for herself, but found she did not want it.

There was a heavier shadow than usual between them this morning. As a general thing there was not a real cloud, only the bluish mist of distance in thick air; but now they had had a "difference," a decided difference.

Mr. Elder's concerns in life had never been similar to his wife's. She had tried, as is held to be the duty of wives, to interest herself in his, but with only a measurable success. Her own preferences had never amounted to more than topics of conversation, to him, and distasteful topics, at that. What was the use of continually talking about things, if you could not have them and ought not to want to?

She loved the city, thick and bustling, the glitter and surge of the big shops with their kaleidoscope exhibition of color and style, that changed even as you looked.

Her fondness for shopping was almost a passion; to her an unending delight; to him, a silly vice.

This attitude was reversed in the matter of tobacco; to him, an unending delight; to her, a silly vice.

They had had arguments upon these lines, but that was years ago.

One of the reasons for Mrs. Elder's hard-bitted silence was Mr. Elder's extreme dislike of argument. Why argue, when you could not help yourself? that was his position; and not to be able to help herself was hers. How could she shop, to any advantage, when they lived an hour from town, and she had to ask for money to go with, or at least for money to shop with.

Just once in her life had Mrs. Elder had an orgy of shopping. A widowed aunt of Mr. Elder, who had just paid them a not too agreeable visit, surprised her beyond words with a Christmas present of a hundred dollars. "It is conditional," she said grimly, holding the amazing yellow-backed treasure in her bony and somewhat purple hand. "You're not to tell Herbert a word about it till it's spent. You're to go in town, early in January, some day when the sales are on, and spend it all. And half of it you're to spend on yourself. Promise, now."

Mrs. Elder had promised, but the last condition was a little stretched. She swore she had wanted the movable electric drop light and the little music machine, but Herbert and the children seemed to use them more than she did. Anyhow she had a day's shopping, which was the solace of barren years.

She liked the theater, too, but that had been so wholly out of the question for so long that it did not trouble her, much.

As for Mr. Elder, he had to work in the city to maintain his family, but what he liked above everything else was the country; the real, wild, open country, where you could count your visible neighbors on your fingers, and leave them, visible, but not audible. They had compromised for twenty-two years, by living in Highvale, which was enough like a city to annoy him, and enough like the country to annoy her. She hated the country, it "got on her nerves."

Which brings us to the present difference between them.

Theodore being grown up and earning his living; Alice being well on the way to it, and a small expense at present; Mr. Elder had concluded that his financial resources would allow of the realization of his fondest hope—retirement. A real retirement, not only officially, from business, and its hated environment; but physically, into the remote and lonely situation which his soul loved. So he had sold his business and bought a farm.

They had talked about it all last evening; at least she had. Mr. Elder, as has been stated, was not much of a talker. He had seemed rather more preoccupied than usual during dinner; possibly he did realize in a dim way that the change would be extremely unwelcome to his wife. Then as they settled down to their usual quiet evening, wherein he was supremely comfortable in house-coat, slippers, cigars of the right sort, the books he loved, and a good light at the left back corner of his leather-cushioned chair; and wherein she read as long as she could stand it, sewed as long as she could stand it, and talked as long as he could stand it.

This time, he had, after strengthening himself with a preliminary cigar, heaved a sigh, and faced the inevitable.

"Oh, Grace," he said, laying down his book, as if this was a minor incident which had just occurred to him, "I've sold out the business."

She dropped her work, and looked at him, startled. He went on, wishing to make all clear at once—he did hate discussion.

"Given up for good. It don't cost us much to live, now the children are practically off our hands. You know I've always hated office work; it's a great relief to be done with it, I assure you. . . . And I've bought that farm on Warren Hill. . . . We'll move out by October. I'd have left it till spring—but I had a splendid chance to sell—and then I didn't dare wait lest I lose the farm. . . . No use keeping up two places. . . . Our lease is out in October, you know.''

He had left little gaps of silence between these blows, not longer than those required to heave up the axe, for its full swing; and when he finished Mrs. Elder felt as if her head verily rolled in the basket. She moistened her lips, and looked at him rather piteously, saying nothing at first. She could not say anything.

He arose from the easy depth of the chair, and came round the table, giving her a cursory kiss, and a reassuring pat on the shoulder.

''I know you won't like it at first, Grace, but it will do you good—good for your nerves—open air—rest—and a garden. You can have a lovely garden—and'' (this was a carefully thought out boon, really involving some intent of sacrifice) ''and company, in summer. Have your friends come out!''

He sat down again feeling that the subject had been fully, fairly and finally discussed. She thought differently. There arose in her a slow, boiling flood of long-suppressed rebellion. He could speak like this—he could do a thing like that—and she was expected to say ''Yes, Herbert'' to what amounted to penal servitude for life—to her.

But the habit of a score of years is strong, to say nothing of the habit of several scores of centuries, and out of that surging sea of resistance came only fatuous protests, and inefficacious pleas.

Mr. Elder had been making up his mind to take this step for many years, and it was now a fact accomplished. He had decided that is would be good for his wife even if she did not like it; and that conviction gave him added strength.

Against this formidable front of fact and theory she had nothing to advance save a pathetic array of likes and dislikes; feeble neglected things, weak from disuse. But he had generously determined to ''let her talk it out'' for that one evening; so she had talked from hour to hour—till she had at last realized that all this talk reached nowhere—the thing was done.

A dull cloud oppressed her dreams; she woke with a sense

of impending calamity, and as the remembrance grew, into awakening pain. There was constraint between them at the breakfast table; a cold response from her when he went, with a fine effect of being cheerful and affectionate; and then Mrs. Elder was left alone to consider her future.

She was a woman of forty-two, in excellent health, and would have been extremely good-looking if she could have "dressed the part." Some women look best in evening dress, some in house gowns, some in street suits; the last was her kind.

She gave her orders for the day listlessly, noting with weary patience the inefficiency of the suburban maid, and then suddenly thinking of how much worse the servant question would become on Warren Hill.

"Perhaps he expects me to do the housework," she grimly remarked to herself. "And have company. Company!"

As a matter of fact, Mrs. Elder did not enjoy household visitors. They were to her a care, an added strain upon her housekeeping skill. Her idea of company was "seeing people"; the chance meeting in the street, the friendly face in a theater crowd, the brisk easily-ended chatter of a "call," and now and then a real party—where one could dance. Should she ever dance again?

Mrs. Elder always considered it a special providence that brought Mrs. Gaylord, a neighbor, in to see her that day; and with her a visiting friend, Mrs. MacAvelly, rather a silent person, but sympathetic and suggestive. Mrs. Gaylord was profusely interested and even angry at Mr. Elder's heartlessness, as she called it; but Mrs. MacAvelly had merely assisted in the conversation, by gentle references to this and that story, book and play. Had she seen this? Had she read that? Did she think so and so was right to do what she did?

After they left, Mrs. Elder went down town, and bought a magazine or two which had been mentioned, and got a book from the little library.

She read, she was amazed, shocked, fascinated; she read more, and after a week of this inoculation, a strange light dawned upon her mind, quite suddenly and clearly.

"Why not?" she said to herself. And again, "Why not?" Even in the night she woke and lay smiling, while heavy breathing told of sleep beside her; saying inwardly, "Why not?"

It was only the end of August; there was a month yet.

She made plans, rapidly but quietly; consulting at length with several of her friends in Highvale, women with large establishments, large purses, and profoundly domestic tastes.

Mrs. Gaylord was rapturously interested, introducing her to other friends, and Mrs. MacAvelly wrote a little note from the city, mentioning several more; from more than one of these came large encouragement.

She wrote to her daughter also, and her son, whose business brought him to Boston that season. They had a talk in the soft-colored little parlor; Mrs. Elder smiling, flushed, eager and excited as a girl, as she announced her plans, under pledge of strictest secrecy.

"I don't care whether you agree or not!" she stoutly proclaimed. "But I'm going to do it. And you mustn't say one word. He never said word till it was all done."

None the less she looked a little anxiously at Theodore. He soon reassured her. "Bully for you, Mama," he said. "You look about sixteen! Go ahead—I'll back you up."

Alice was profoundly pleased.

"How perfectly splendid, Mama! I'm so proud of you! What glorious times we'll have, won't we just?" And they discussed her plans with enthusiasm and glee.

Toward the middle of September Mr. Elder, immersed though he was in frequent visits to that idol of his heart, the farm, began to notice the excitement in his wife's manner. "I hope you're not tiring yourself too much, packing," he said, and added, quite affectionately, "You won't hate it so much after a while, my dear."

"No, I won't," she admitted, with an ambiguous smile. "I think I might even like it, a little while, in summer."

About the twentieth of the month she made up her mind to tell him, finding it harder than she had anticipated in the first proud moments of determination.

It was evening again, and he had settled luxuriously into his big chair, surrounded by The Country Gentleman, The Fruit-Grower, and The Breeder and Sportsman. She let him have one cigar, and then—"Herbert."

He was a moment or two in answering—coming up from the depths of his studies in "The Profits of Making Honey" with appropriate slowness. "Yes, Grace, what is it?"

"I am not going with you to the farm."

He smiled a little wearily. "Oh, yes you are, my dear; don't make a fuss about the inevitable."

She flushed at that and gathered courage. "I have made other arrangements," she said calmly. "I am going to board in Boston. I've rented a furnished floor. Theodore is going to hire one room, and Alice one. And we take our meals out. She is to have a position this year. They both approve——" She hesitated a moment, and added breathlessly, "I'm to be a professional shopper! I've got a lot of orders ahead. I can see my way half through the season already!"

She paused. So did he. He was not good at talking. "You seem to have it all arranged," he said drily.

"I have," she eagerly agreed. "It's all planned out."

"Where do I come in?" he asked, after a little.

She took him seriously. "There is plenty of room for you, dear, and you'll always be welcome. You might like it awhile—in winter."

This time it was Mr. Elder who spent some hours in stating his likes and dislikes; but she explained how easily he could hire some one to pack and move for him—and how much happier he would be, when once well settled on the farm.

"You can get a nice housekeeper, you see—for I shan't be costing you *anything* now!"

"I'm going to town next week," she added, "and we hope to see you by Christmas, at latest."

They did.

They had an unusually happy Christmas, and an unusually happy summer following. From sullen rage, Mr. Elder, in serene rural solitude, simmered down to a grieved state of mind. When he did come to town, he found an eagerly delighted family; and a wife so roguishly young, so attractively dressed, so vivacious and happy and amusing, that the warmth of a sudden Indian summer fell upon his heart.

Alice and Theodore chuckled in corners. "Just see Papa making love to Mama! Isn't it impressive?"

Mrs. Elder was certainly much impressed by it; and Mr. Elder found that two half homes and half a happy wife, were really more satisfying than one whole home, and a whole unhappy wife, withering in discontent.

In her new youth and gaiety of spirit, and her half-remorseful tenderness for him, she grew ever more desirable, and presently the Elder family maintained a city flat and a country home; and spent their happy years between them.

HER BEAUTY

Amaryllis was her name.

She used bitterly to reflect, chin on hands, eyes staring gloomily into the ill-natured little mirror—a dull, green-tinted, worse than truthful mirror—that her name was the only beautiful thing about her.

Amaryllis Delong! Some remote Huguenot refugee ancestor put that "de" into this American family; and an immediate one, her mother, in fact, had insisted on calling her Amaryllis, in the face of the whole town.

A dull face that town had, green-tinted like the old looking-glass, brown and gray of fence and house, though prosperous enough, and contented enough, for the most part.

Not so Amaryllis. She was "congenitally discontented" her school teacher said—the one that came from Wellesley. She was "rebellious against Providence" her minister said. She was "a hard child to bring up" her mother said. She was the most miserable girl alive, she said to herself, lowering into her little glass, which lowered back at her.

It was no use. She had tried every arrangement of that mirror, every angle, every sort of light, from the pink dawn to the pale moon radiance, with two candles and a kerosene lamp as special experiment. She had arranged her hair in every way she knew how; she had tried every costume and combination of costumes she possessed, and as much lack of costume as her conscience permitted—and it was no use. Never once could she bring into that mirror the thing she longed for—beauty.

"Amaryllis is dreadful fond of pretty things," her mother said discerningly. "It's a pity she's so plain!"

It was a pity. It grieved her childhood, darkened her girl-hood, and now it had crushed and ruined her womanhood.

Because her name was Amaryllis, probably, she had attracted the attention of Weldon Thomas for a little while—the only time of soul-stirring happiness she had ever known. He had asked to be introduced to Miss Amaryllis Delong on the wide foot-worn steps of the First Church after prayer meeting; had talked with her there a moment; had walked home with her; had asked if he might call.

That was all in an evening, a summer evening, when lights were soft and flickering among leaf shadows, and the young face flushing and smiling under the wide hat, had at least the charm of mystery. She must have pleased him then, for he had come to see her once or twice, and the close-blinded parlor, the shaded lamp, the girl's bright, wistful pleasure and happy talk still seemed to hold. Then he asked her to a picnic, and there, alas, she met not only the full daylight, but competition. Among other girls, girls who were round and rosy, soft, alluring and dressed with prompt submission to the prevailing style, Amaryllis was never seen to advantage.

After that he went away on some visit or vacation. After that he only bowed or spoke briefly as they met. After that again he went with Bessy Sharpless and Myra Hall—and now it was all over. He had married Myra.

Myra was undeniably handsome. No one denied it, least of all beauty-worshipping Amaryllis. Myra was smooth and plump; Myra had bright hair that fluffed and curled and blew about her face bewitchingly; Myra had white, regular, shiny teeth, and a round little chin, dimpled hands, small feet in smaller shoes whose high heels captivated the eye—most eyes, that is. And Weldon, who loved beauty almost as well as Amaryllis, who even wrote verses about it, which were printed in The Plainville Watchman, was carried off his feet with a rush. Besides, Myra had practically all the unattached men of the little town at those dapper little feet of hers, and rivalry has charms.

The hope of love died in the heart of Amaryllis, died and was buried under a heavy weight of reticence, a quiet but effective monument of dumb pride.

But the love of beauty did not die. She decided, away out there in middle-western Plainville, to search for beauty and to find it. The only avenues then open to her were books, the books in the little public library, in the minister's library, in the traveling libraries of the Woman's Club. But "love will find out a way," more than one kind of love; a girl of eighteen, with a strong character and a heavy disappointment, can do a great deal.

With all the resignation of a nun, she abandoned the thought of happiness, and determined on a life of devotion to her heart's idol, beauty. For right appreciation of this education was required. She determined to go to college. She went to college forthwith, her father rather approving.

"She'll have to teach, I expect," he said. "Her face is not her fortune, sure." And he worked hard to help her.

The girl was proud, and intended to help herself. She took a summer course in dressmaking and worked her way through the last years by helping the girls with their wardrobes.

Teaching was no part of her ambition. When college was over she took a position in a good dressmaking establishment and gained experience if not money. Then she got up a co-operative affair with three other girls, gained more experience, and more money.

In ten years' time Amaryllis was recognized by all Plainville, when they saw her, as an old maid. Even her parents admitted it.

"She's doin' real well, Amaryllis is," her mother boasted. "She's sent back to her father all it cost him to start her in college, and pretty nearly clothes me, let alone supportin' herself."

The clothes of Mrs. Delong had indeed waxed in elegance and beauty till her best friends, in the confidence of private friendship, whispered that she was "a little too dressy."

In Plainville only young girls, on special occasions, were admired for being "dressy." For other persons and seasons any noticeable beauty of apparel was condemned as inappropriate, also as "conspicuous." Yet these same people would gladly surround their homes with Canna Indicus and Golden Glow; yes, and with Poinsettias if they would have grown there.

On an ocean steamer a keen young face looked out from hood and rugs and watched the flying, interminable waves with eager eyes. Amaryllis had "done" better than her parents knew. The dressmaking business, rightly handled, is a gold mine. With garments well made and effective, with a ten percent discount for cash and prepayment for all materials required, she had lost no sleep nor cash income from unpaid bills, and her bank account had grown with her reputation. Now she could leave her forewoman, as a sort of partner, in charge of the business, and go to represent the Parisian end.

She knew the language; she had been there often on buying and observing trips, but this time she was to live there, and, at last, to study art. There was no misguided ambition to be a painter. She was no painter, no draughtsman, no artist really, except in the negative sense of appreciation and delight; one may study music without being a musician, surely.

Her trained eye, her business experience, enabled her to send to the home shop its share of Parisian novelties and triumphs, and this required small part of Amaryllis' time. Her real purpose was like that of some rapt "Bather," the laying aside of unneeded cumbering things, the stepping into a wide, warm, shimmering sea.

From year to year her business steadied and grew, not a great business, but a small, solid, well-established one, with its full time, its regular patrons, and its waiting list of transient customers. She was able to travel, to study to her heart's content, to meet people, to hear lectures, to read books, to see pictures, to attend plays, to feed her soul with knowledge, and to enjoy as far as it exists in the modern world, the beauty she desired.

On one of her ocean voyages she saw at the captain's table a face that seemed familiar. A woman's face it was, large, overblown, like a La France rose a day too old; a woman's form, strenuously conventionalized by the last violence of corsets. It was Myra Hall—that was; Myra Thomas now, of course, and Amaryllis watched her with a strange sinking of the heart. Where was Weldon? Was he—could he be— no, Myra was not in black.

She spoke to her, and the stout matron was unfeignedly glad to see her.

"Why, Amaryllis! How stylish you do look! I've heard you were doing wonders, and now I believe it. Did you make that? Will you make me one? How much would it cost—between friends, you know!"

She smiled archly. The round little chin was rounder, larger, manifold; it was, in fact, two chins, and might have been more but for the uncompromising pressure of an ear-lifting lace stock, with "stiffeners" full four inches long. The small white teeth were much the worse for wear. Her hands were dimpled still, conspicuously so, as the soft tissues expanded; her small feet not so small, however.

"Can't wear my old sizes now, I tell you," she cheerfully agreed. "Had a bad case of dropped arch—have to wear these awful things now—doctor's orders!" And she exhibited a pair of those fearsome shoes with which modern science seeks to improve on nature and force reluctant toes to curve and straddle as they never intended.

The bright flying hair was mostly gone, but in its place had come seven other devils worse than the first; a swelling mattress effect, puffs suggestive of upholstery—abundance certainly, but never again the golden shine.

Again Amaryllis' heart sank for Weldon, but not for his life. Myra assured her that he was well, and working hard. "He's a newspaper man, you see. They can't leave, ever. Yes, Weldon works hard. But he likes it. What? Poetry?" she laughed. "I guess not. Weldon outgrew that long ago. Guess I laughed him out of it a good deal."

Amaryllis bade farewell to Myra, who was taking a vacation, she said, and returned to her work in Paris. The cable about her mother's illness brought her home in time only to say good-bye. Her father seemed helpless and lonely after that. In a year's time Amaryllis was alone again, with the old place on her hands. Quite a sum of money awaited her, too; they had had no interest in life but saving, for these last few years.

To her own surprise she felt a deep resurgence of love for the home of her childhood. With eyes trained now in larger views, she saw that the weary ugliness of the town was superficial and transient, while the beauty of the countryside was strong and pure beneath it all. Their own house stood near the road; dust defaced it, noise affronted it, only a few whitened trees and stiff, narrow flowerbeds between their windows and the fence. At the back of the long yard were trees, large trees and old, elms, a walnut, water maples, and beyond the maples flowed a wide, quiet river.

A flame kindled in her eyes. She walked the big place over from corner to corner, from end to end, studying, thinking, looking, with her eyes half shut, her head thrown back as she tried this view and the other.

The island was theirs, too, and the river pasture across. Far over the swale meadow, the low-rolling hills, the sun set even more gloriously than she remembered.

Amaryllis consulted the old lawyer who had been her father's friend; she reckoned up her inheritance, consulted her bank account, and sent for two friends from Boston to come and visit her. One was an architect of growing fame.

Weldon Thomas at forty was frankly considered a failure by his brothers of the press. Newspaper men, however, are not invariably right. He had lost his job on one big daily after another. "He hasn't snap enough." "Lacks ginger." "Does good work, but too slow." "Trouble with Thomas is he's too old."

He was, in fact, forty-two. An expensive wife and a residence in New York are not conducive of thrift. The severest economy of one member of the family cannot counterbalance many pleasant indulgences by the party of the second part. Weldon's twenty years in New York left him barely enough to buy a controlling interest in The Plainville Watchman. His city friends thought it a miserable comedown. "Too bad about old Thomas. He's had to give up work and go down to the country. Bought a rube sheet, I believe. It's a shame."

He did not feel wholly of that mind as he took up his new duties in the old place. The quiet streets rested him. The arching trees rested him. The cool silence of the nights unutterably rested him. He renewed his acquaintance gradually, more with the place than with the people.

Walking one golden afternoon along the outskirts of the little town he came to a new wall, new to the place he was sure, but softly old to the eye. Above it blossoming boughs curved richly; the gateway gave full view of a deep lawn, far back on which a low, wide house, serene in outline, beautifully white, waited invitingly.

He remembered. "That Delong girl," they had told him, had "fixed up the old place so't you wouldn't know it; tore down the old house and built the queerest thing you ever saw. She must have earned a lot of money, dressmakin'."

He remembered Amaryllis and what he had heard of her work—he would drop in and see her.

The path curved a little, enough to rest the eye, not enough to annoy the feet. It was only a hundred yards or so, but he stopped more than once to admire the softly changing picture about him, and at the doorstep turned back for a good look. How a mere "front yard," however large, could have changed to such a pleasance he could not understand, but the effect had an uplifting sweetness to which his city-starved soul responded with grateful joy.

The house itself was so quiet in its gentle beauty, so restrained and calm, that he made no attempts at analysis, just smiled at the white façade of it, and rang the bell. A soft-voiced colored maid opened the door to him, motioned him to a seat in the broad, hospitable hall, and took his card. Presently she returned to say that he was to come in, and opened a door.

He stopped in the entrance, a quick sigh of pleasure escaping him. A long room, a wide room, a room of just proportions, gracious spaces, blending colors, that were like warmth and flowers and wine, and opposite him a window that was a mighty picture, deep-framed by the broad cushioned seat, the dark casings, the rich hangings. In that picture the river lived before him, veiled here and there by trees; beyond the river beautiful farmland, curving hills, dark woods, the softening splendor of the sun.

A little laugh of pleasure greeted him:

"You like my window."

He turned to her with a start of pleased surprise. Her kind, clear-cut face glowed with hospitable warmth, perhaps with something more. She reached white hands to him, delicate but strong. Her soft robe swept down from the straight shoulders full of a gentle womanly grace and a discerning color sense; it suited not only her, but the room. She spoke harmony in every tint and line, in the grace of her movements, the stately repose of her quiet beauty, the well-modulated tones of her voice.

The tired man stood and gazed at her, as one drinking thirstily. His soul was stirred and comforted first by that broad stretch of garden ground, then by the gracious house, then by this satisfying restful room, with its windows into heaven, and now he felt in her something like all of them, and something better still.

"Why, Amaryllis! How beautiful you are!"

She laughed merrily.

"You always were a poet, Weldon—and good at pretty speeches. Sit down, won't you?"

He would not let go her hand.

"I feel as if I'd been on a horrible long journey," he told her, "and this—" he hesitated, and glanced about him with the same satisfaction, concluding:

"I'd just like to sit and look at you for hours!"

"And what would Myra say to that?" she asked him, smiling.

"Didn't you know?" he said. "I lost her a year ago. May I look at you now?"

IF I WERE
A MAN

"If I were a man, . . ." that was what pretty little Mollie Mathewson always said when Gerald would not do what she wanted him to—which was seldom.

That was what she said this bright morning, with a stamp of her little high-heeled slipper, just because he had made a fuss about that bill, the long one with the "account rendered," which she had forgotten to give him the first time and been afraid to the second—and now he had taken it from the postman himself.

Mollie was "true to type." She was a beautiful instance of what is reverentially called "a true woman." Little, of course—no true woman may be big. Pretty, of course—no true woman could possibly be plain. Whimsical, capricious, charming, changeable, devoted to pretty clothes and always "wearing them well," as the esoteric phrase has it. (This does not refer to the clothes—they do not wear well in the least—but to some special grace of putting them on and carrying them about, granted to but few, it appears.)

She was also a loving wife and a devoted mother possessed of "the social gift" and the love of "society" that goes with it, and, with all these was fond and proud of her home and managed it as capably as—well, as most women do.

If ever there was a true woman it was Mollie Mathewson, yet she was wishing heart and soul she was a man.

And all of a sudden she was!

She was Gerald, walking down the path so erect and square-shouldered, in a hurry for his morning train, as usual, and, it must be confessed, in something of a temper.

Her own words were ringing in her ears—not only the

"last word," but several that had gone before, and she was holding her lips tight shut, not to say something she would be sorry for. But instead of acquiescence in the position taken by that angry little figure on the veranda, what she felt was a sort of superior pride, a sympathy as with weakness, a feeling that "I must be gentle with her," in spite of the temper.

A man! Really a man—with only enough subconscious memory of herself remaining to make her recognize the differences.

At first there was a funny sense of size and weight and extra thickness, the feet and hands seemed strangely large, and her long, straight, free legs swung forward at a gait that made her feel as if on stilts.

This presently passed, and in its place, growing all day, wherever she went, came a new and delightful feeling of being *the right size*.

Everything fitted now. Her back snugly against the seat-back, her feet comfortably on the floor. Her feet? . . . His feet! She studied them carefully. Never before, since her early school days, had she felt such freedom and comfort as to feet—they were firm and solid on the ground when she walked; quick, springy, safe—as when, moved by an unrecognizable impulse, she had run after, caught, and swung aboard the car.

Another impulse fished in a convenient pocket for change—instantly, automatically, bringing forth a nickel for the conductor and a penny for the newsboy.

These pockets came as a revelation. Of course she had known they were there, had counted them, made fun of them, mended them, even envied them; but she never had dreamed of how it *felt* to have pockets.

Behind her newspaper she let her consciousness, that odd mingled consciousness, rove from pocket to pocket, realizing the armored assurance of having all those things at hand, instantly get-at-able, ready to meet emergencies. The cigar case gave her a warm feeling of comfort—it was full; the firmly held fountain pen, safe unless she stood on her head; the keys, pencils, letters, documents, notebook, checkbook, bill folder—all at once, with a deep rushing sense of power and pride, she felt what she had never felt before in all her life—the possession of money, of her own earned money—hers to give or to withhold, not to beg for, tease for, wheedle for—hers.

That bill—why, if it had come to her—to him, that is—he would have paid it as a matter of course, and never mentioned it—to her.

Then, being he, sitting there so easily and firmly with his money in his pockets, she wakened to his life-long consciousness about money. Boyhood—its desires and dreams, ambitions. Young manhood—working tremendously for the wherewithal to make a home—for her. The present years with all their net of cares and hopes and dangers; the present moment, when he needed every cent for special plans of great importance, and this bill, long overdue and demanding payment, meant an amount of inconvenience wholly unnecessary if it had been given him when it first came; also, the man's keen dislike of that "account rendered."

"Women have no business sense!" she found herself saying. "And all that money just for hats—idiotic, useless, ugly things!"

With that she began to see the hats of the women in the car as she had never seen hats before. The men's seemed normal, dignified, becoming, with enough variety for personal taste, and with distinction in style and in age, such as she had never noticed before. But the women's—

With the eyes of a man and the brain of a man; with the memory of a whole lifetime of free action wherein the hat, close-fitting on cropped hair, had been no handicap; she now perceived the hats of women.

The massed fluffed hair was at once attractive and foolish, and on that hair, at every angle, in all colors, tipped, twisted, tortured into every crooked shape, made of any substance chance might offer, perched these formless objects. Then, on their formlessness the trimmings—these squirts of stiff feathers, these violent outstanding bows of glistening ribbon, these swaying, projecting masses of plumage which tormented the faces of bystanders.

Never in all her life had she imagined that this idolized millinery could look, to those who paid for it, like the decorations of an insane monkey.

And yet, when there came into the car a little woman, as foolish as any, but pretty and sweet-looking, up rose Gerald Mathewson and gave her his seat. And, later, when there came in a handsome red-cheeked girl, whose hat was wilder, more violent in color and eccentric in shape than any other—when she stood nearby and her soft curling plumes swept his cheek once and again—he felt a sense of sudden pleasure at the intimate tickling touch—and she, deep down within, felt such a wave of shame as might well drown a thousand hats forever.

When he took his train, his seat in the smoking car, she had a new surprise. All about him were the other men, commuters too, and many of them friends of his.

To her, they would have been distinguished as "Mary Wade's husband," "the man Belle Grant is engaged to," "that rich Mr. Shopworth," or "that pleasant Mr. Beale." And they would all have lifted their hats to her, bowed, made polite conversation if near enough—especially Mr. Beale.

Now came the feeling of open-eyed acquaintance, of knowing men—as they were. The mere amount of this knowledge was a surprise to her—the whole background of talk from boyhood up, the gossip of barber-shop and club, the conversation of morning and evening hours on trains, the knowledge of political affiliation, of business standing and prospects, of character—in a light she had never known before.

They came and talked to Gerald, one and another. He seemed quite popular. And as they talked, with this new memory and new understanding, an understanding which seemed to include all these men's minds, there poured in on the submerged consciousness beneath a new, a startling knowledge—what men really think of women.

Good, average, American men were there; married men for the most part, and happy—as happiness goes in general. In the minds of each and all there seemed to be a two-story department, quite apart from the rest of their ideas, a separate place where they kept their thoughts and feelings about women.

In the upper half were the tenderest emotions, the most exquisite ideals, the sweetest memories, all lovely sentiments as to "home" and "mother," all delicate admiring adjectives, a sort of sanctuary, where a veiled statue, blindly adored, shared place with beloved yet commonplace experiences.

In the lower half—here that buried consciousness woke to keen distress—they kept quite another assortment of ideas.

Here, even in this clean-minded husband of hers, was the memory of stories told at men's dinners, of worse ones overheard in street or car, of base traditions, coarse epithets, gross experiences—known, though not shared.

And all these in the department "woman," while in the rest of the mind—here was new knowledge indeed.

The world opened before her. Not the world she had been reared in—where Home had covered all the map, almost, and the rest had been "foreign," or "unexplored country," but the world as it was—man's world, as made, lived in, and seen, by men.

It was dizzying. To see the houses that fled so fast across the car window, in terms of builders' bills, or of some technical insight into materials and methods; to see a passing village with lamentable knowledge of who "owned it" and of how its Boss was rapidly aspiring in state power, or of how that kind of paving was a failure; to see shops, not as mere exhibitions of desirable objects, but as business ventures, many mere sinking ships, some promising a profitable voyage—this new world bewildered her.

She—as Gerald—had already forgotten about that bill, over which she—as Mollie—was still crying at home. Gerald was "talking business" with this man, "talking politics" with that, and now sympathizing with the carefully withheld troubles of a neighbor.

Mollie had always sympathized with the neighbor's wife before.

She began to struggle violently with this large dominant masculine consciousness. She remembered with sudden clearness things she had read, lectures she had heard, and resented with increasing intensity this serene masculine preoccupation with the male point of view.

Mr. Miles, the little fussy man who lived on the other side of the street, was talking now. He had a large complacent wife; Mollie had never liked her much, but had always thought him rather nice—he was so punctilious in small courtesies.

And here he was talking to Gerald—such talk!

"Had to come in here," he said. "Gave my seat to a dame who was bound to have it. There's nothing they won't get when they make up their minds to it—eh?"

"No fear!" said the big man in the next seat. "They

haven't much mind to make up, you know—and if they do, they'll change it.''

"The real danger," began the Rev. Alfred Smythe, the new Episcopal clergyman, a thin, nervous, tall man with a face several centuries behind the times, "is that they will overstep the limits of their God-appointed sphere."

"Their natural limits ought to hold 'em, I think," said cheerful Dr. Jones. "You can't get around physiology, I tell you."

"I've never seen any limits, myself, not to what they want, anyhow," said Mr. Miles. "Merely a rich husband and a fine house and no end of bonnets and dresses, and the latest thing in motors, and a few diamonds—and so on. Keeps us pretty busy."

There was a tired gray man across the aisle. He had a very nice wife, always beautifully dressed, and three unmarried daughters, also beautifully dressed—Mollie knew them. She knew he worked hard, too, and she looked at him now a little anxiously.

But he smiled cheerfully.

"Do you good, Miles," he said. "What else would a man work for? A good woman is about the best thing on earth."

"And a bad one's the worst, that's sure," responded Miles.

"She's a pretty weak sister, viewed professionally," Dr. Jones averred with solemnity, and the Rev. Alfred Smythe added, "She brought evil into the world."

Gerald Mathewson sat up straight. Something was stirring in him which he did not recognize—yet could not resist.

"Seems to me we all talk like Noah," he suggested drily. "Or the ancient Hindu scriptures. Women have their limitations, but so do we, God knows. Haven't we known girls in school and college just as smart as we were?"

"They cannot play our games," coldly replied the clergyman.

Gerald measured his meager proportions with a practiced eye.

"I never was particularly good at football myself," he modestly admitted, "but I've known women who could outlast a man in all-round endurance. Besides—life isn't spent in athletics!"

This was sadly true. They all looked down the aisle where a heavy ill-dressed man with a bad complexion sat alone. He had held the top of the columns once, with headlines and photographs. Now he earned less than any of them.

"It's time we woke up," pursued Gerald, still inwardly urged to unfamiliar speech. "Women are pretty much *people,* seems to me. I know they dress like fools—but who's to blame for that? We invent all those idiotic hats of theirs, and design their crazy fashions, and, what's more, if a woman is courageous enough to wear common-sense clothes—and shoes—which of us wants to dance with her?

"Yes, we blame them for grafting on us, but are we willing to let our wives work? We are not. It hurts our pride, that's all. We are always criticizing them for making mercenary marriages, but what do we call a girl who marries a chump with no money? Just a poor fool, that's all. And they know it.

"As for Mother Eve—I wasn't there and can't deny the story, but I will say this. If she brought evil into the world, we men have had the lion's share of keeping it going ever since—how about that?"

They drew into the city, and all day long in his business, Gerald was vaguely conscious of new views, strange feelings, and the submerged Mollie learned and learned.

SPOKEN TO

"It's no use, mother. I'm of age. I'm self-supporting. I think it is right; I'm going to do it."

This, not aggressively, but with quiet decision, by Miss Lucille Wright. Apropos of which name it may be here remarked that she hated it, and demanded all her friends that they call her Luke. Further on the subject, in instance of the well-known sweetness and smoothness of family relation, her brother accused her of wishing only to "look right," called her an "edition de looks," "luke warm," and similar merry plays upon her preferred title.

This same brother now lazily took part in the discussion wherein she had so emphatically laid down the affirmative.

" 'Too much ego in your cosmos,' Lucy. Can't you squeeze in a few more I's—just to make it clearer?"

Mrs. Wright looked from one to the other with loving pathetic eyes.

"It's very hard, daughter,—" (that was her compromise between the "Lucille" she loved and the "Luke" she hated) "—to have my little girl grow up and go out into the world so soon—I can't get used to it. And this going out nights—alone—I never *heard* of such a thing—for a young girl! If your father was only here—"

"I wish he was, mother darling. Then it wouldn't be so hard on you to have me grow up. He would console you for my evil behavior. But—he couldn't stop me!"

This was too much for Aunt Marie—not a real aunt, but so old a friend of Mrs. Wright's as to have long held the courtesy title. She was a French woman, though resident in America for twenty years; a competent teacher of languages, supporting herself and caring for a very old father with loving efficiency, while maintaining with all her force the theory of the weakness and dependence of women.

As an aunt, though only be election, she now asserted herself.

"I am astonished, Louise! To hear a young girl speak so to her mother! To have such ideas—to even think of going about alone at night—it is shocking! You do not know the dangers you so recklessly court."

"What are they?" asked the girl. "If there are dangers you know and I don't, I think you ought to tell me."

"Why you might—you might be *spoken to,*" her mother answered.

"Why not?" the girl inquired. "That's not fatal, is it?"

"It is enough that we protect you," pursued Aunt Marie. "You should accept that with gratitude and without explanation. Your brother ought to convince you of that."

Lucille looked at Hervey and smiled. He looked at her, and grinned. He was two years younger, a slim, delicate lad, and of a naturally timid disposition. All through their childhood "Big Sister" had guarded and defended "Little Brother," and the position was not easily reversed on a technicality. His deepest interest and chosen work was painting, watercolor preferred. Hers was physical culture, and she had just secured a position as teacher in a girls' gymnasium.

The one thing he could beat her in was running, but to this she would cheerfully retort that she didn't have to run— she preferred to stand her ground.

Still he now took up the offered suggestion with solemnity.

"You are quite right, Aunt Marie. I ought to convince her. She ought to let me convince her. Man—" he expanded his chest to its slender utmost. "Man is woman's natural protector!" But he winked at Lucille.

Aunt Marie agreed with him in good faith. "Hervey is quite right. A true man is always willing to accompany a lady in the evening to protect her."

"Against what?" asked Lucille.

"Stubborn girl!" protested her brother. "Against the untrue men, of course!"

Mrs. Wright was unmoved by the laughter of her children or the annoyance of her friend. She felt only a maternal terror and that deep-seated dread of the unconventional which to so many women is stronger than the fear of hell.

"It's not *safe,* daughter," she insisted. "I just can't bear it—to think of my little girl being out at night—alone!"

"Mother dear—." Lucille came and sat down at her feet, dropping softly to the floor, cross-legged, as easily as a child. "You are only forty-two—do you know it? I'm twenty-one. We hope—we confidently expect—that you will live as long as the rest of the family. Grandma, as you know, is as lively as a kitten, at sixty. Great-grandma is only seventy-eight. Great-great-grandma lived to be nearly a hundred.

"Now what I want to ask is—at what age are you willing your little girl shall be allowed to go out alone—at night?"

Mrs. Wright laughed in spite of herself, and gave her daughter a resigned kiss.

"The worst of this generation is that it is so—so terribly *reasonable.* A rebellious child is easier to handle than an argumentative one."

"I think it is scandalous, Lucille," persisted Aunt Marie, "both that you should oppose your dear mother and that you should even want to be out alone at night. Think how it looks!"

Lucille laid her head on her mother's knee, and nestled close to her. "I love my mother dearly, and she knows it, Aunty. And I've been a good girl up to now—haven't I?"

Her mother bent and kissed her again. "You've been the best possible daughter—always. That's why I can't understand why you should be willing to hurt me now."

Lucille rose up—as softly and swiftly as she had settled down. "Sorry!" she said. "Awfully sorry! But the unnatural child has now Grown Up. Also I am self-supporting—I pay my board. I'm a Person and I have Views—and I'm going to live up to them. By all the shades of my stern, stubborn ('Pigheaded,' interpolated Hervey) Puritan ancestors, I swear it! See my door-key!"

"Where'd you get that?" her mother asked, a little sharply.

"Borrowed brother's and had it made—paid for it—cost a quarter," the girl explained cheerfully. "Are you going to cast me from your door because I've got a key to it?"

When a person is inflexibly determined, prompt and ingenious in argument, perfectly goodnatured, and all the time affectionate and serviceable, it is very difficult to quarrel with such.

Aunt Marie poured forth a long and somewhat biting lecture, protesting that in this country everything was upside down—that no one knew what we were coming to, that if Lucille were in France she would see!

"In my country, you foolish child, no young girl of any birth and breeding is allowed to go out alone, even in daylight. What could you do, you poor misguided child, if some terrible man were to insult you?"

"Can't tell till the time comes," answered the girl, with unabated cheerfulness. "Thanks to your splendid teaching, I could understand him, even in France!" Lucille was very fond of Aunt Marie.

Hervey did not try to assume the position of a "Protector," much less of a Sovereign Power, but used what weapons of ridicule he could muster, his attacks being parried and returned so efficiently that he made small progress.

And Mrs. Wright gradually—very gradually, became used to her tall daughter's going out in the evening to visit friends, to read in the Public Library, to attend meetings or lectures, and letting herself in at about ten o'clock with what she called "the Palladium of Woman's Liberty"—the latchkey.

At first it was a constant terror to the mother heart, but gradually she became accustomed to it. Nothing ever happened to Lucille. She met neither insult nor danger, though sometimes the apparent opening for adventure.

There was the time, by daylight this, when she was walking on a lonely road at the edge of the town, a long high wall on one side, open fields on the other, some trees and bushes near. She had noticed a man in the neighboring meadows whose path appeared to be converging with the road, and when she stopped to pick up a useful-looking stick—a stout stick is always handy on a walk—she saw another man some distance behind her. Now appeared a third, in front, loafing along, as if waiting for her; trampish looking fellows, all.

Lucille did not alter her firm swinging gait, and presently caught up with the front one. He came forward and "spoke to her"—innocently enough.

"Can you tell me what time it is, Miss?"

"Certainly," said Lucille, with prompt goodwill. She

stopped and looked at her watch—a cheap silver-plated one. "It is quarter to four."

She smiled and resumed her walk, neither faster nor slower, turning no eyes behind her. Ears were enough, if she was followed. But nothing happened.

Then there was one occasion, at night, when a man in shirt sleeves loafed out of a dark side street and stood on the corner waiting for her. It was a quiet place, wide open unbuilt lots, few houses, no one else in sight. But Lucille, seeing that he wished to speak to her, drew up and turned her friendly face to him.

He seemed a little surprised and somewhat lamely asked the way to the best known street in the vicinity, a question she answered with careful explicitness and resumed her walk.

Then there were boys sometimes, rude ignorant fellows, strong in numbers, who called out minor impertinences with great bravado, that always amused the girl, as she steadily pursued her way.

"The poor geese!" she thought. "They think that is such a fine thing to do, and most women think they are killed if they are 'spoken to.' Goodness! What harm does it do!"

It surely did none to her; and as she proceeded to enjoy the only leisure her busy life allowed, she felt more and more pity for the housebound, timid ones, who were quite shut in after dark—unless some commiserating, or admiring, man would "take them out."

The sense of ease and freedom was extremely pleasant, but quite beyond that she enjoyed what most women never experience in all their lives—the still wonder of being alone with the stars. There was the high shining moon she could stop and gaze at as long as she wished; the slim silver crescent that sailed so lightly among feathery clouds; the sagging old moon, yellow and heavy. There were the soft cloudy nights permeated with diffused light if the moon was there; velvet dark sometimes, moist with rain, and sweet, poignantly sweet, with lilac and syringa; or tugging at one's heartstrings with the odor of wet leaves.

Near her home was an open block crossed by a footpath; in the middle rose a big boulder, and when that lot was white with unbroken snow and the sky above black-blue, endlessly deep, and all one blaze and glitter of crowding stars, Lucille loved to sit on that rock, alone, and feel only earth and sky and—God.

"When you go to Paris you *must* do differently," said Aunt Marie.

This was a few years later. Hervey had failed to get through the college he hated, and was now, thanks to a small windfall of a legacy, allowed to study the art he loved.

He had been a year abroad; he had a lofty, uncomfortable, but altogether fascinating studio in Paris; and now Lucille was coming over to visit him—accompanied by Aunt Marie. That patient soul, having lost her beloved father, was now the proud possessor of two years' savings, the larger because she had become a "paying guest" at the home of her old friends.

To her it was a joy unmeasured to see again the land she loved, the city she adored, the friends and relatives who were still left to her. In her happiness she bubbled over with confidences, telling Lucille a thousand things she should know about Paris; chattering in her swift-flowing French which the girl knew almost as her mother tongue.

"But oh, my dear—remember! You must *not* go alone in the streets of Paris. It is not safe. It is not—respectable. I am here—your brother is here—you must have company."

Lucille did not contradict her. She was too happy in this new world to explore.

Then the older lady told her, with bated breath, of an adventure she had had some twenty years before.

"It is so terrible, my dear, that I never could bring myself to speak of it before. In America it does not matter so much—but here! You do not know! My dear—I was out alone! It was only once. I was about your age. I had no one to ask and there was an errand I thought I *must* do—so I dared to go.

"I was hurrying along, looking at no one, on the Rue de Matin near Claron's, and there stepped up from behind—a man! He was close—almost touching my elbow, and he—spoke to me! He said—I cannot bring myself to tell you what he said! Oh, it was terrible! And he lifted his hat with a mock courtesy. A finely dressed man he was, a soldier I think, for he had a long white scar down one cheek. I shall never forget his terrible face—handsome as the devil, my dear, beautifully dressed, with a cloak-overcoat, with an ebony and gold stick; with a waxed moustache, an imperial, eyes of an infinite audacity! Oh, my shame!''

"But what did you *do*, dear Aunt Marie—he didn't touch you, did he?''

"Oh—touch me! Surely I had been insulted enough. What could I do? I blushed—I am sure I blushed from head to foot! I shall never forget it.'' And the good lady, now of some fifty odd years, blushed again even at the memory. "And I heard since—from my father, that this man is well known in Paris. He has a reputation most terrible. And it is one of his—amusements—to make women blush. He boasts of it! He lays wagers on it! No young girl is safe in Paris, my dear. Do be warned by me.''

Lucille thanked her for her kind warning; as she grew older she was more considerate, though no less independent. Being now twenty-four she considered herself quite full grown, and equal to the dangers of Paris or any other place.

Hervey was more than delighted to see them. There were for them two tiny rooms connecting with his atelier; he slept on the none too comfortable lounge in the big room, and insisted that he enjoyed it.

Aunt Marie exhibited a discretion in purchasing and a skill in cooking which filled both the young people with inexpressible admiration.

As for Lucille, her cup of happiness was full—save for a certain limitation to her freedom of movement. They were so kind she could not decline such affectionate attention. Aunt Marie was never too tired to go farther, to accompany her anywhere, and Hervey vowed he had not seen her for so long that he wasn't going to lose a minute of her society if he could help it. So she was escorted by one or by both, to everything she wanted to see and some that she did not, and began to long intensely for her well loved amusement of strolling "broadcast," as she phrased it, going where the spirit moved.

Then one day an unhoped-for opportunity occurred. Aunt Marie had gone to do some necessary shopping, and Lucille preferred to finish a delectable novel she was reading. Then a neighboring student had rushed in, and begged Hervey to accompany him at once—help rescue a newly arrived American of an unwise temper who had sent a messenger begging for two identifiers to save him from arrest.

"You're all right, Sis? I won't be long," Hervey had hurriedly explained—and gone.

Then arose Lucille as briskly as if no novel had ever held her attention, donned her hat and a short jacket with pockets in which she could plunge her hands—another bad habit; saw that she had some money with her, and her card-case with her brother's address; hastily wrote a note to allay their fears: "Have gone for a little walk—will be back before five," and set forth.

It felt good, very good. The whole city looked fresher, now she saw it in the light of freedom. She took a 'bus to the shopping region—she too had some little errands, and it was such fun to stroll and look about, all by herself.

And then there happened one of those coincidences which are too absurd to occur except in real life.

Aunt Marie came out of Claron's, her purchases accomplished, and was joined most unexpectedly by Hervey on his way homeward.

Together they saw coming toward them Lucille, head up, a happy smile on her face, tramping gaily along as if she were in Omaha.

And then, of a sudden, a gentleman approached her with studied grace, came close, very close, murmured something in her ear, and swept off his glossy hat with a magnificent air.

He was a little bald, and of soldierly bearing. He wore a cape-coat, carried an ebony and gold cane; his very black moustache was waxed to stiff perfection; his imperial as accurately trimmed, and across his cheek ran a long white scar.

Aunt Marie gave a gasp of voiceless horror, and clung to Hervey's arm. He stood still, quite willing to have a little joke on the always sufficient Lucille, and to rush to her rescue when necessary.

A little group of well-dressed men drew near, with meaning smiles, their eyes on the girl's face.

And Lucille?

She halted promptly, as the gentleman spoke, took in his whole impressive appearance with one lightning glance; heard, and fully understood, the unmeasured insult of his whispered words; gazed on him with eyes of unmoved cheerfulness; drew from her pocket one well-gloved hand—and put two cents in his hat.

She passed on, quite undisturbed, as one who has performed a good action.

He stood there, the center of many eyes, of much laughter, and from the edge of his white collar to the top of his bald head the slow color rose—pink—red—purple. If he had never blushed before, he was blushing now.

And Lucille was given the freedom of the city.

DR. CLAIR'S PLACE

"You must count your mercies," said her friendly adviser. "There's no cloud so dark but it has a silver lining, you know,—count your mercies."

She looked at her with dull eyes that had known no hope for many years. "Perhaps you will count them for me: Health—utterly broken and gone since I was twenty-four. Youth gone too—I am thirty-eight. Beauty—I never had it. Happiness—buried in shame and bitterness these fourteen years. Mother-hood—had and lost. Usefulness—I am too weak even to support myself. I have no money. I have no friends. I have no home. I have no work. I have no hope in life." Then a dim glow of resolution flickered in those dull eyes. "And what is more I don't propose to bear it much longer."

It is astonishing what people will say to strangers on the cars. These two sat on the seat in front of me, and I had heard every syllable of their acquaintance, from the "Going far?" of the friendly adviser to this confidence as to pro-posed suicide. The offerer of cheerful commonplaces left before long, and I took her place, or rather the back-turned seat facing it, and studied the Despairing One.

Not a bad looking woman, but so sunk in internal misery that her expression was that of one who had been in prison for a lifetime. Her eyes had that burned out look, as hope-less as a cinder heap; her voice a dreary grating sound. The muscles of her face seemed to sag downward. She looked at the other passengers as if they were gray ghosts and she another. She looked at the rushing stretches we sped past as if the window were ground glass. She looked at me as if I were invisible.

"This," said I to myself, "is a case for Dr. Clair."

It was not difficult to make her acquaintance. There was no more protective tissues about her than about a skeleton. I think she would have showed the utter wreck of her life to any who asked to look, and not have realized their scrutiny. In fact it was not so much that she exhibited her misery, as that she was nothing but misery—whoever saw her, saw it.

I was a "graduate patient" of Dr. Clair, as it happened; and had the usual enthusiasms of the class. Also I had learned some rudiments of the method, as one must who has profited by it. By the merest touch of interest and considerate attention I had the "symptoms"—more than were needed; by a few indicated "cases I had known" I touched that spring of special pride in special misery which seems to be co-existent with life; and then I had an account which would have been more than enough for Dr. Clair to work on.

Then I appealed to that queer mingling of this pride and of the deep instinct of social service common to all humanity, which Dr. Clair had pointed out to me, and asked her—

"If you had an obscure and important physical disease you'd be glad to leave your body to be of service to science, wouldn't you?" She would—anyone would, of course.

"You can't leave your mind for an autopsy very well, but there's one thing you can do—if you will; and that is, give this clear and prolonged self-study you have made, to a doctor I know who is profoundly interested in neurasthenia—melancholia—all that kind of thing. I really think you'd be a valuable—what shall I say—exhibit."

She gave a little muscular smile, a mere widening of the lips, the heavy gloom of her eyes unaltered.

"I have only money enough to go where I am going," she said. "I have just one thing to do there—that ought to be done before I—leave."

There was no air of tragedy about her. She was merely dead, or practically so.

"Dr. Clair's is not far from there, as it happens, and I know her well enough to be sure she'd be glad to have you come. You won't mind if I give you the fare up there—purely as a scientific experiment? There are others who may profit by it, you see."

She took the money, looking at it as if she hardly knew

what it was, saying dully: "All right—I'll go." And, after a pause, as if she had half forgotten it, "Thank you."

And some time later she added: "My name is Octavia Welch."

Dr. Willy Clair—she was Southern, and really named Willy—was first an eager successful young teacher, very young. Then she spent a year or two working with atypical children. Then, profoundly interested, she plunged into the study of medicine and became as eager and successful a doctor as she had been a teacher. She specialized in psychopathic work, developed methods of her own, and with the initial aid of some of her numerous "G. P.'s" established a sanatorium in Southern California. There are plenty of such for "lungers," but this was of quite another sort.

She married, in the course of her full and rich career, one of her patients, a young man who was brought to her by his mother—a despairing ruin. It took five years to make him over, but it was done, and then they were married. He worshipped her; and she said he was the real mainstay of the business—and he was, as far as the business part of it went.

Dr. Clair was about forty when I sent Octavia Welch up there. She had been married some six years, and had, among her other assets, two splendid children. But other women have husbands and children, also splendid—no one else had a psycho-sanatorium. She didn't call it that; the name on the stationery was just "The Hills."

On the southern face of the Sierra Madres she had bought a high-lying bit of mesa-land and steep-sided arroyo, and gradually added to it both above and below, until it was now quite a large extent of land. Also she had her own water; had built a solid little reservoir in her deepest canyon; had sunk an artesian well far up in the hills behind, ran a windmill to keep the water up, and used the overflow for power as well as for irrigation. That had made the whole place such garden land as only Southern California knows. From year to year, the fame of the place increased, and its income also, she built and improved; and now it was the most wonderful combination of peaceful, silent wilderness and blossoming fertility.

The business end of it was very simply managed. On one of the steep flat-topped mesas, the one nearest the town that lay so pleasantly in the valley below, she had built a comfortable, solid little Center surrounded by small tent-houses.

Here she took ordinary patients, and provided them not only with good medical advice but with good beds and good food, and further with both work and play.

"The trouble with Sanatoriums," said Dr. Clair to me—we were friends since the teaching period, and when I broke down at my teaching I came to her and was mended—"is that the sick folks have nothing to do but sit about and think of themselves and their 'cases.' Now I let the relatives come too; some well ones are a resource; and I have one or more regularly engaged persons whose business it is to keep them busy—and amused."

She did. She had for the weakest ones just chairs and hammocks; but these were moved from day to day so that the patient had new views. There was an excellent library, and all manner of magazines and papers. There were picture-puzzles too, with little rimmed trays to set them up in—they could be carried here and there, but not easily lost. Then there were all manner of easy things to learn to do; basket-work, spinning, weaving, knitting, embroidery; it cost very little to the patients and kept them occupied. For those who were able there was gardening and building—always some new little place going up, or a walk or something to make. Her people enjoyed life every day. All this was not compulsory, of course, but they mostly liked it.

In the evenings there was music, and dancing too, for those who were up to it; cards and so on, at the Center; while the others went off to their quiet little separate rooms. Everyone of them had a stove in it; they were as dry and warm as need be—which is more than you can say of most California places.

People wanted to come and board—well people, I mean—and from year to year she ran up more cheap comfortable little shacks, each with its plumbing, electric lights and heating—she had water-power, you see—and a sort of cafeteria place where they could eat together or buy food and take to their homes. I tell you it was popular. Mr. Wolsey (that's her husband, but she kept on as Dr. Clair) ran all this part of it, and ran it well. He had been a hotel man.

All this was only a foundation for her real work with the psychopathic cases. But it was a good foundation, and it paid in more ways than one. She not only had the usual string of Grateful Patients, but another group of friends among those boarders. And there's one thing she did which is well worth the notice of other people who are trying to help humanity—or to make money—in the same way.

You know how a hotel will have a string of "rules and regulations" strung up in every room? She had that—and more. She had a "Plain Talk With Boarders" leaflet, which was freely distributed—a most amusing and useful document. I haven't one here to quote directly, but it ran like this:

> You come here of your own choice, for your own health and pleasure, freely; and are free to go when dissatisfied. The comfort and happiness of such a place depends not only on the natural resources, on the quality of the accommodations, food, service and entertainment, but on the behavior of the guests.
>
> Each visitor is requested to put in a complaint at the office, not only of fault in the management, but of objectionable conduct on the part of patrons.
>
> Even without such complaint any visitor who is deemed detrimental in character or behavior will be requested to leave.

She did it too. She made the place so attractive, so *comfortable,* in every way so desirable, that there was usually a waiting list; and if one of these fault-finding old women, or noisy, disagreeable young men, or desperately flirtatious persons got in, Dr. Clair would have it out with them.

"I am sorry to announce that you have been black-balled by seven of your fellow guests. I have investigated the complaints and find them well founded. We herewith return your board from date (that was always paid in advance) and shall require your room tomorrow."

People didn't like to own to a thing like that—not and tell the truth. They did tell all manner of lies about the place, of course; but she didn't mind—there were far more people to tell the truth. I can tell you a boarding-place that is as beautiful, as healthful, as exquisitely clean and comfortable, and as reasonable as hers in price, is pretty popular. Then, from year to year, she enlarged and developed her plan till she had, I believe, the only place in the world where a sick soul could go and be sure of help.

Here's what Octavia Welch wrote about it. She showed it to me years later:

I was dead—worse than dead—buried—decayed—gone to foul dirt. In my body I still walked heavily—but out of accumulated despair I had slowly gathered about enough courage to drop that burden. Then I met the Friend on the train who sent me to Dr Clair. . . .

I sent the postcard, and was met at the train, by motor. We went up and up—even I could see how lovely the country was—up into the clear air, close to those shaggy, steep dry mountains.

We passed from ordinary streets with pretty homes through a region of pleasant groups of big and little houses which the driver said was the "boarding section," through a higher place where he said there were "lungers and such," on to "Dr. Clair's Place."

The Place was apparently just out of doors. I did not dream then of all the cunningly contrived walks and seats and shelters, the fruits and flowers just where they were wanted, the marvellous mixture of natural beauty and ingenious loving-kindness, which make this place the wonder it is. All I saw was a big beautiful wide house, flower-hung, clean and quiet, and this nice woman, who received me in her office, just like any doctor, and said:

"I'm glad to see you, Mrs. Welch. I have the card announcing your coming, and you can be of very great service to me, if you are willing. Please understand—I do not undertake to cure you; I do not criticize in the least your purpose to leave an unbearable world. That I think is the last human right—to cut short unbearable and useless pain. But if you are willing to let me study you awhile and experiment on you a little—it won't hurt, I assure you—"

Sitting limp and heavy, I looked at her, the old slow tears rolling down as usual. "You can do anything you want to," I said. "Even hurt—what's a little more pain?—if it's any use."

She made a thorough physical examination, blood-test and all. Then she let me tell her all I wanted to about myself, asking occasional questions, making notes, setting it all down on a sort of chart. "That's enough to show me the way for a start," she said. "Tell me—do you dread anaesthetics?"

"No," said I, "so that you give me enough."

"Enough to begin with," she said cheerfully. "May I show you your room?"

It was the prettiest room I had ever seen, as fair and shining as the inside of a shell.

"You are to have the bath treatment first," she said, "then a sleep—then food—I mean to keep you very busy for a while."

So I was put through an elaborate course of bathing, shampoo, and massage, and finally put to bed, in that quiet fragrant rosy room, so physically comfortable that even my corroding grief and shame were forgotten, and I slept.

It was late next day when I woke. Someone had been watching all the time, and at any sign of waking a gentle anaesthetic was given, quite unknown to me. My special attendant, a sweet-faced young giantess from Sweden, brought me a tray of breakfast and flowers, and asked if I liked music.

"It is here by your bed," she said. "Here is the card—you ask for what you like, and just regulate the sound as you please."

There was a light moveable telephone, with a little megaphone attached to the receiver, and a long list of records. I had only to order what I chose, and listen to it as close or as far off as I desired. Between certain hours there was a sort of "table d'hôte" to which we could listen or not as we liked, and these other hours wherein we called for favorites. I found it very restful. There were books and magazines, if I chose, and a rose-draped balcony with a hammock where I could sit or lie, taking my music there if I preferred. I was bathed and oiled and rubbed and fed; I slept better than I had for years, and more than I knew at the time, for when the restless misery came up they promptly put me to sleep and kept me there.

Dr. Clair came in twice a day, with notebook and pencil, asking me many careful questions; not as a physician to a patient, but as an inquiring scientific searcher for valuable truths. She told me about other cases, somewhat similar to my own, consulted me in a way, as to this or that bit of analysis she had made; and again and again as to certain points in my own case. Insensibly under her handling this grew more and more objective, more as if it were someone else who was suffering, and not myself.

"I want you to keep a record, if you will," she said, "when the worst paroxysms come, the overwhelming waves of despair, or that slow tidal ebb of misery—here's a little chart by your bed. When you feel the worst will you be so good as to try either of these three things, and note the result. The Music, as you have used it, noting the effect of the different airs. The Color—we have not introduced you to the color treatment yet—see here—"

She put in my hand a little card of buttons, as it were, with wire attachments. I pressed one; the room was darkened, save for the tiny glow by which I saw the color list. Then, playing on the others, I could fill the room with any lovely hue I chose, and see them driving, mingling, changing as I played.

"There," she said, "I would much like to have you make a study of these effects and note it for me. Then—don't laugh!—I want you to try tastes, also. Have you never noticed the close connection between a pleasant flavor and a state of mind?"

For this experiment I had a numbered set of little sweetmeats, each delicious and all beneficial, which I was to deliberately use when my misery was acute or wearing. Still further, she had a list of odors for similar use.

This bedroom and balcony treatment lasted a month, and at the end of that time I was so much stronger physically that Dr. Clair said, if I could stand it, she wanted to use certain physical tests on me. I almost hated to admit how much better I felt, but told her I would do anything she said. Then I was sent out with my attending maiden up the canyon to a certain halfway house. There I spent another month of physical enlargement. Part of it was slowly graduated mountain climbing; part was bathing and swimming in a long narrow pool. I grew gradually to feel the delight of mere ascent, so that every hilltop called me, and the joy of plain physical exhaustion and utter rest. To come down from a day on the mountain, to dip deep in that pure water and be rubbed by my ever careful masseuse; to eat heartily of the plain but delicious food, and sleep—out of doors now, on a pine needle bed—that was new life.

My misery and pain and shame seemed to fade into a remote past, as a wholesome rampart of bodily health grew up between me and it.

Then came the People.

This was her Secret. She had People there who were better than Music and Color and Fragrance and Sweetness,—People who lived up there with work and interests of their own, some teachers, some writers, some makers of various things, but all Associates in her wonderful cures.

It was the People who did it. First she made my body as strong as might be, and rebuilt my worn-out nerves with sleep—sleep—sleep. Then I had the right Contact, Soul to Soul.

And now? Why now I am still under forty; I have a little cottage up here in these heavenly hills; I am a well woman; I earn my living by knitting and teaching it to others. And out of the waste and wreck of my life—which is of small consequence to me, I can myself serve to help new-comers. I am an Associate—even I! And I am Happy!

JOAN'S DEFENDER

Joan's mother was a poor defense. Her maternal instinct did not present that unbroken front of sterling courage, that measureless reserve of patience, that unfailing wisdom which we are taught to expect of it. Rather a broken reed was Mrs. Marsden, broken in spirit even before her health gave way, and her feeble nerves were unable to stand the strain of adjudicating the constant difficulties between Joan and Gerald.

"Mother! Mo-o-ther!" would rise a protesting wail from the little girl. "Gerald's pulling my hair!"

"Cry baby!" her brother would promptly retort. "Tell tale! Run to mother—do!"

Joan did—there was no one else to run to—but she got small comfort.

"One of you is as much to blame as the other," the invalid would proclaim. And if this did not seem to help much: "If he teases you, go into another room!"

Whether Mrs. Marsden supposed that her daughter was a movable body and her son a fixed star as it were, did not appear, but there was small comfort to be got from her.

"If you can't play nicely together you must be separated. If I hear anything more from you, I'll send you to your room—now be quiet!"

So Joan sulked, helplessly, submitted to much that was painful and more that was contumelious, and made little remonstrance. There was, of course, a last court of appeal, or rather a last threat—that of telling father.

"I'll tell father! I'll tell father! Then you'll be sorry!" her tormentor would chant, jumping nimbly about just out of reach, if she had succeeded in any overt act of vengeance.

"I shall have to tell your father!" was the last resource of the mother on the sofa.

If father was told, no matter by whom, the result was always the same—he whipped them both. Not so violently, to be sure, and Joan secretly believed less violently in Gerald's case than in hers, but it was an ignominious and unsatisfying punishment which both avoided.

"Can't you manage to keep two children in order?" he would demand of his wife. "My mother managed eleven—and did the work of the house too."

"I wish I could, Bert, dear," she would meekly reply. "I do try—but they are so wearying. Gerald is too rough, I'm afraid. Joan is always complaining."

"I should think she was!" Mr. Marsden agreed irritably. "Trust a woman for that!"

And Joan, though but nine years old, felt that life was not worth living, being utterly unjust. She was a rather large-boned, meager child, with a whiney voice, and a habit of crying, "Now stop!" whenever Gerald touched her. Her hair was long, fine and curly, a great trouble to her as well as to her mother. Both were generally on edge for the day, before those curls were all in order, and their principal use appeared to be as handles for Gerald, who was always pulling them. He was a year and a half older than Joan, but not much bigger, and of a somewhat puny build.

Their father, a burly, loud-voiced man, heavy of foot and of hand, looked at them both with ill-concealed disapproval, and did not hesitate to attribute the general deficiencies of his family wholly to their feeble mother and her "side of the house."

"I'm sure I was strong as a girl, Bert—you remember how I used to play tennis, and I could dance all night."

"Oh I remember," he would answer. "Blaming your poor health on me, I suppose—that seems to be the way nowadays. I don't notice that other women give out just because they're married and have two children—*two!*" he repeated scornfully, as if Mrs. Marsden's product were wholly negligible. "And one of them a girl!"

"Girls are no good!" Gerald quickly seconded. "Girls can't fight or climb or do anything. And they're always hollering. Huh! I wouldn't be a girl——!" Words failed him.

Such was their case, as it says so often in the *Arabian Nights,* and then something pleasant happened. Uncle Arthur came for a little visit, and Joan liked him. He was mother's brother, not father's. He was big, like father, but gentle and pleasant, and he had such a nice voice, jolly but not loud.

Uncle Arthur was a western man, with a ranch, and a large family of his own. He had begun life as a physician, but weak lungs drove him into the open. No one would ever think of him now as ever having been an invalid.

He stayed for a week or so, having some business to settle which dragged on for more days than had been counted on, and gave careful attention to the whole family.

Joan was not old enough, nor Mrs. Marsden acute enough, to note the gradual disappearance of topic after topic from the conversation between Uncle Arthur and his host. But Mr. Marsden's idea of argument was volume of sound, speed in repetition, and a visible scorn for those who disagreed with him, and as Arthur Warren did not excel in these methods he sought for subjects of agreement. Not finding any, he contented himself with telling stories, or listening—for which there was large opportunity.

He bought sweetmeats for the children, and observed that Gerald got three-quarters, if not more; brought them presents, and found that if Gerald did not enjoy playing with Joan's toys, he did enjoy breaking them.

He sounded Gerald, as man to man, in regard to these habits, but that loyal son, who believed his father to be a type of all that was worthy, and who secretly had assumed the attitude of scorn adopted by that parent toward his visitor, although civil enough, was little moved by anything his uncle might say.

Dr. Warren was not at all severe with him. He believed in giving a child the benefit of every doubt, and especially the benefit of time.

"How can the youngster help being a pig?" he asked himself, sitting quite silent and watching Gerald play ball with a book just given to Joan, who cried "Now sto-op!" and tried to get it away from him.

"Madge Warren Marsden!" he began very seriously, when the children were quarreling mildly in the garden, and the house was quiet: "Do you think you're doing right by

Joan—let alone Gerald? Is there no way that boy can be made to treat his sister decently?"

"Of course you take her part—I knew you would," she answered fretfully. "You always were partial to girls—having so many of your own, I suppose. But you've no idea how irritating Joan is, and Gerald is extremely sensitive—she gets on his nerves. As for *my* nerves! I have none left! Of course those children ought to be separated. By and by when we can afford it, we mean to send Gerald to a good school; he's a very bright boy—you must have noticed that?"

"Oh yes, he's bright enough," her brother agreed. "And so is Joan, for that matter. But look here, Madge—this thing is pretty hard on you, isn't it—having these two irreconcilables to manage all the time?"

The ready tears rose and ran over. "Oh, Arthur, it's awful! I do my best—but I never was good with children—and with my nerves—*you* know, being a doctor."

He did know, rather more than she gave him credit for. She had responded to his interest with interminable details as to her symptoms and sensations, and while he sat patiently listening he had made a diagnosis which was fairly accurate. Nothing in particular was the matter with his sister except the fretful temper she was born with, idle habits, and the effects of an overbearing husband.

The temper he could not alter, the habits he could not change, nor the husband either, so he gave her up—she was out of his reach.

But Joan was a different proposition. Joan had his mother's eyes, his mother's smile—when she did smile; and though thin and nervous, she had no serious physical disability as yet.

"Joan worries you even more than Gerald, doesn't she?" he ventured. "It's often so with mothers."

"How well you understand, Arthur. Yes, indeed, I feel as if I knew just what to do with my boy, but Joan is a puzzle. She is so—unresponsive."

"Seems to me you would be much stronger if you were less worried over the children."

"Of course—but what can I do? It is my duty and I hope I can hold out."

"For the children's sake you ought to be stronger, Madge. See here, suppose you lend me Joan for a long visit. It would be no trouble at all to us—we have eight, you know, and all outdoors for them to romp in. I think it would do the child good.''

The mother looked uncertain. ''It's a long way to let her go——'' she said.

''And it would do Gerald good, I verily believe,'' her brother continued. ''I've often heard you say that she irritates him.''

He could not bring himself to advance this opinion, but he could quote it.

''She does indeed, Arthur. I think Gerald would give almost no trouble if he was alone.''

''And you are of some importance,'' he continued cheerfully. ''How about that? Let me borrow Joan for a year—you'll be another woman when you get rested.''

There was a good deal of discussion, and sturdy opposition from Mr. Marsden, who considered the feelings of a father quite outraged by the proposal; but as Dr. Warren did not push it, and as his wife suggested that in one way it would be an advantage—they could save toward Gerald's schooling—adding that her brother meant to pay all expenses, including tickets—he finally consented.

Joan was unaccountably reluctant. She clung to her mother, who said, ''There! There!'' and kissed her with much emotion. ''It's only a visit, dearie—you'll be back to mother bye and bye!''

She kissed her father, who told her to be a good girl and mind her uncle and aunt. She would have kissed Gerald, but he said: ''Oh shucks!'' and drew away from her.

It was a silently snivelling little girl who sat by the window, with Uncle Arthur reading the paper beside her, a little girl who felt as if nobody loved her in the whole wide world. He put a big arm around her and drew her to him. She snuggled up with a long sigh of relief. He took her in his lap, held her close, and told her interesting things about the flying landscape. She nestled close to him, and then, starting up suddenly to look at something, her hair caught on his buttons and pulled sharply.

She cried, as was her habit, while he disentangled it.

''How'd you like to have it cut off?'' he asked.

''I'd like it—but mother won't let me. She says it's my only beauty. And father won't let me either—says I want to be a tom-boy.''

"Well, I'm in loco parentis now," said Uncle Arthur, "and I'll let you. Furthermore, I'll do it forthwith, before it gets tangled up tonight."

He produced a pair of sharp little scissors, and a pocket-comb, and in a few minutes the small head looked like one of Sir Joshua Reynolds' cherubs.

"You see I know how," he explained, as he snipped cautiously, "because I cut my own youngsters' on the ranch. I think you look prettier short than long," he told her, and she found the little mirror between the windows quite a comfort.

Before the end of that long journey the child was more quietly happy with her uncle than she had ever been with either father or mother, and as for Gerald—the doctor's wise smile deepened.

"Irritated *him,* did she!" he murmured to himself. "The little skate! Why, I can just see her *heal* now she's escaped."

A big, high-lying California ranch, broad, restful sweeps of mesa and plain, purple hills rising behind. Flowers beyond dreams of heaven, fruit of every kind in gorgeous abundance. A cheerful Chinese cook and houseboy, who did their work well and seemed to enjoy it. The uncle she already loved, and an aunt who took her to her motherly heart at once.

Then the cousins—here was terror. And four of them boys—four! But which four? There they all were in a row, giggling happily, standing up to be counted, and to be introduced to their new cousin. All had short hair. All had bare feet. All had denim knickerbockers. And all had been racing and tumbling and turning somersaults on the cushiony Bermuda grass as Joan and her uncle drove up.

The biggest one was a girl, tall Hilda, and the baby was a girl, a darling dimpled thing, and two of the middle ones. But the four boys were quite as friendly as Hilda, and seeing that their visitor was strangely shy, Jack promptly proposed to show her his Belgian hares, and Harvey to exhibit his Angora goats, and the whole of them trooped off hilariously.

"What a forlorn child!" said Aunt Belle. "I'm glad you brought her, dear. Ours will do her good."

"I knew you'd mother her, Blessing," he said with a grateful kiss. "And if ever a poor kid needed mothering, it's that one. You see, my sister has married a noisy pig of a man—and doesn't seem to mind it much. But she's become an invalid—one of these sofa women; I don't know as she'll ever get over it. And the other child's rather a mean cuss, I'm afraid. They love him the best. So I thought we'd educate Joan a bit.''

Joan's education was largely physical. A few weeks of free play, and then a few moments every day of the well-planned exercises Dr. Warren had invented for his children. There were two ponies to ride; there were hills to climb; there was work to do in the well-irrigated garden. There were games, and I am obliged to confess, fights. Every one of those children was taught what we used to grandiloquently call ''the noble art of self-defense''; not only the skilled management of their hands, with swift ''foot-work,'' but the subtler methods of jiu-jitsu.

''I took the course on purpose,'' the father explained to his friends, ''and the kids take to it like ducks to water.''

To her own great surprise, and her uncle's delight, Joan showed marked aptitude in her new studies. In the hours of definite instruction, from books or in nature study and laboratory work, she was happy and successful, but the rapture with which she learned to use her body was fine to see.

The lower reservoir made a good sized swimming pool, and there she learned to float and dive. The big barn had a little simple apparatus for gymnastics in the rainy season, and the jolly companionship of all those bouncing cousins was an education in itself.

Dr. Warren gave her special care, watched her food, saw to it that she was early put to bed on the wide sleeping porch, and trained her as carefully as if she had some tremendous contest before her. He trained her mind as well as her body. Those children were taught to reason, as well as to remember; taught to think for themselves, and to see through fallacious arguments. In body and mind she grew strong.

At first she whimpered a good deal when things hurt her, but finding that the other children did not, and that, though patient with her, they evidently disliked her doing it, she learned to take her share of the casualties of vigorous childhood without complaint.

At the end of the year Dr. Warren wrote to his brother-in-law that it was not convenient for him to furnish the return ticket, or to take the trip himself, but if they could spare the child a while longer he would bring her back as agreed—that she was doing finely in all ways.

It was nearly two years when Joan Marsden, aged eleven, returned to her own home, a very different looking child from the one who left it so mournfully. She was much taller, larger, with a clear color, a light, firm step, a ready smile.

She greeted her father with no shadow of timidity, and rushed to her mother so eagerly as well-nigh to upset her.

"Why, child!" said the mother. "Where's your beautiful hair? Arthur—how could you?"

"It is much better for her health," he solemnly assured her. "You see how much stronger she looks. Better keep it short till she's fourteen or fifteen."

Gerald looked at his sister with mixed emotions. He had not grown as much. She was certainly as big as he was now. With her curls gone she was not so easy to hurt. However, there were other places. As an only child his disposition had not improved, and it was not long before that disposition led him to derisive remarks and then to personal annoyance, which increased as days passed.

She met him cheerfully. She met him patiently. She gave him fair warning. She sought to avoid his attacks, and withdrew herself to the far side of the garage, but he followed her.

"It's not fair, Gerald, and you know it," said Joan. "If you hurt me again I shall have to do something to you."

"Oh you will, will you?" he jeered, much encouraged by her withdrawal, much amused by her threat. "Let's see you do it—smarty! 'Fraid cat!" and he struck her again, a blow neatly planted, where the deltoid meets the biceps and the bone is near the surface.

Joan did not say, "Now *stop!*" She did not whine, *"Please* don't!" She did not cry. She simply knocked him down.

And when he got up and rushed at her, furious, meaning to reduce this rebellious sister to her proper place, Joan set her teeth and gave him a clean thrashing.

"Will you give up?"

He did. He was glad to.

"Will you promise to behave? To let me alone?"

He promised.

She let him up, and even brushed off his dusty clothes.

"If you're mean to me any more, I'll do it again," she said calmly. "And if you want to tell mother—or father— or anybody—that I licked you, you may."

But Gerald did not want to.

MRS. BEAZLEY'S DEEDS

Mrs. William Beazley was crouching on the floor of her living room over the store in a most peculiar attitude. It was what a doctor would call the "knee-chest position"; and the woman's pale, dragged out appearance quite justified the idea.

She was as one scrubbing a floor and then laying her cheek to it, a rather undignified little pile of bones, albeit discreetly covered with stringy calico.

A hard voice from below suddenly called "Maria!" and when she jumped nervously, and hurried downstairs in answer, the cause of the position became apparent—she had been listening at a stove-pipe hole.

In the store sat Mr. Beazley, quite comfortable in his back-tilted chair, enjoying a leisurely pipe and as leisurely conversation with another smoking, back-tilting man, beside the empty stove.

"This lady wants some cotton elastic," said he; "you know where those dewdabs are better'n I do."

A customer, also in stringy calico, stood at the counter. Mrs. Beazley waited on her with the swift precision of long practice, and much friendliness besides, going with her to the wagon afterward, and standing there to chat, her thin little hand on the wheel as if to delay it.

"Maria!" called Mr. Beazley.

"Oh, good land!" said Mrs. Janeway, gathering up the reins.

"Well—good-bye, Mrs. Janeway—do come around when you can; I can't seem to get down to Rockwell."

"Maria!" She hurried in. "Ain't supper ready yet?" inquired Mr. Beazley.

"It'll be ready at six, same as it always is," she replied wearily, turning again to the door. But her friend had driven off and she went slowly upstairs.

Luella was there. Luella was only fourteen, but a big, courageous-looking girl, and prematurely wise from many maternal confidences. "Now you sit down and rest," she said. "I'll set the table and call Willie and everything. Baby's asleep all right."

Willie, shrilly summoned from the window, left his water wheel reluctantly and came in dripping and muddy.

"Never mind, mother," said Luella. "I'll fix him up in no time; supper's all ready."

"I can't eat a thing," said Mrs. Beazley, "I'm so worried!" She vibrated nervously in the wooden rocker by the small front window. Her thin hands gripped the arms; her mouth quivered—a soft little mouth that seemed to miss the smiles naturally belonging to it.

"It's another of them deeds!" she was saying over and over in her mind. "He'll do it. He's no right to do it, but he will; he always does. He don't care what I want—nor the children."

When the supper was over, Willie went to bed, and Luella minding the store and the baby, Mr. Beazley tipped back his chair and took to his toothpick. "I've got another deed for you to sign, Mrs. Beazley," said he. "Justice Fielden said he'd be along tonight some time, and we can fix it before him—save takin' it to town."

"What's it about?" she demanded. "I've signed away enough already. What you sellin' now?"

Mr. Beazley eyed her contemptuously. The protest that had no power of resistance won scant consideration from a man like him.

"It's a confounded foolish law," said he, meditatively. "What do women know about business, anyway! You just tell him you're perfectly willin' and under no compulsion and sign the paper—that's all you have to do!"

"You might as well tell me what you're doin'—I have to read the deed anyhow."

"Much you'll make out of readin' the deed," said he, with some dry amusement, "and Justice Fielden lookin' on and waitin' for you!"

"You're going to sell the Rockford lot—I know it!" said she. "How can you do it, William! The very last piece of what father left me!—and it's mine—you can't sell it—I won't sign!''

Mr. Beazley minded her outcry no more than he minded the squawking of a to-be beheaded hen.

"Seems to me you know a lot," he observed, eyeing her with shrewd scrutiny. Then without a word he rose to his lank height, went out to the woodshed and hunted about, returning with an old piece of tin. This he took upstairs with him, and a sound of hammering told Mrs. Beazley that one source of information was closed to her completely.

"You'd better not take that up, Mrs. Beazley," said he, returning. "It makes it drafty round your feet up there. I always wondered at them intuitions of yours—guess they wasn't so remarkable after all.

"Now before Mr. Fielden comes, seein' as you are so far on to this business, we may as well talk it out. I suppose you'll admit that you're a woman—and that you don't know anything about business, and that it's a man's place to take care of his family to the best of his ability.''

"You just go ahead and say what you want to—you needn't wait for any admits from me! What I know is my father left me a lot o' land—left it to me—to take care of me and the children, and you've sold it all—in spite of me—but this one lot.''

"We've sold it, Mrs. Beazley; you've signed the deeds.''

"Yes, I know I have—you made me.''

"Now, Mrs. Beazley! Haven't you always told Justice Fielden that you were under no compulsion?''

"O yes—I told him so—what's the use of fightin' over everything! But that house in Rockford is mine—where I was brought up—and I want to keep it for the children. If you'd only live there, William, I'd take boarders and be glad to—to keep the old home! and you could sell that water power—or lease it—''

Mr. Beazley's face darkened. "You're talking nonsense, Mrs. Beazley—and too much of it. 'Women are words and men are deeds' is a good sayin'. But what's more to the purpose is Bible sayin'—this fool law is a mere formality—you know the real law—'Wives submit yourselves to your husbands!' ''

He lit his pipe and rose to go outside, adding, "Oh, by the way, here 'tis Friday night, and I clean forgot to tell you—there's a boarder comin' tomorrow.''

"A boarder—for who?"

"For you, I guess—you'll see more of her than I shall, seein' as it's a woman."

"William Beazley! Have you gone and taken a boarder without even askin' me?" The little woman's hands shook with excitement. Her voice rose in a plaintive crescendo, with a helpless break at the end.

"Saves a lot of trouble, you see; now you'll have no time to worry over it; and yet you've got a day to put her room in order."

"Her room! What room? We've got no room for ourselves over this store. William—I won't have it! I can't—I haven't the strength!"

"Oh, nonsense, Mrs. Beazley! You've got nothin' to do but keep house for a small family—and tend the store now and then when I'm busy. As to room, give her Luella's, of course. She can sleep on the couch, and Willie can sleep in the attic. Why, Morris Whiting's wife has six boarders— down at Ordway's there's eight."

"Yes—and they are near dead, both of them women! It's little they get from their boarders! Just trouble and work and the insultin' manners of those city people—and their husbands pocketing all the money. And now you expect me—in four rooms—to turn my children out of doors to take one—and a woman at that; more trouble'n three men! I won't, I tell you!"

Luella came in at this point and put a sympathetic arm around her. "Bert Fielden was in just now," she told her father. "He says his father had to go to the city, and won't be back for some time—left word for you about it."

"Oh, well," said Mr. Beazley philosophically, "a few days more or less won't make much difference, I guess. That bein' the case you better help your mother wash up and then go to bed, both of you," and he took himself off to lounge on the steps of the store, smoking serenely.

Next day at supper time the boarder came. Mr. Beazley met her at the station and brought her and her modest trunk back with him. He took occasion on the journey to inform the lady that one reason for his making the arrangement was that he thought his wife needed company—intelligent company of her own sex.

"She's nervous and notional and kinder dreads it, now

it's all arranged," he said; "but I know she'll like you first rate."

He himself was most favorably impressed, for the woman was fairly young, undeniably good looking, and had a sensible, prompt friendliness that was most attractive.

The drive was quite a long one and slower than mere length accounted for, owing to the nature of rural roads in mountain districts; and Mr. Beazley found himself talking more freely than was his habit with strangers, and pointing out the attractive features of the place with fluency.

Miss Lawrence was observant, interested, appreciative.

"There ought to be good water power in that river," she suggested; "what a fine place for a mill. Why, there was a mill, wasn't there?"

"Yes," said he. "That place belonged to my wife's father. Her father had a mill there in the old times when we had tanneries and saw mills all along in this country. They've cut out most of the hemlock now."

"That's a pleasant looking house on it, too. Do you live there?"

"No—we live quite a piece beyond—up at Shade City. This is Rockwell we're going through. It's a growin' place—if the railroad ever gets in here as they talk about."

Mr. Beazley looked wise. He knew a good deal more about that railroad than was worth while mentioning to a woman. Meanwhile he speculated inwardly on his companion's probable standing and profession.

"She's Miss, all right, and no chicken," he said to himself, "but looks young enough, too. Can't have much money or she'd not be boardin' with us, up there. Schoolma'am, I guess."

"Find school teachin' pretty wearin'?" he hazarded.

"School teaching? Oh, there are harder professions than that," she replied lightly. "Do I look so tired?"

"I have a friend in the girls' high school who gets very much exhausted by summer time," she pursued. "When I am tired I prefer the sea; but this year I wanted a perfectly quiet place—and I believe I've found one. Oh, how pretty it is!" she cried as they rounded a steep hill shoulder and skirted the river to their destination. Shade City was well named, in part at least, for it stood in a crack of the mountains and saw neither sunrise nor sunset.

The southern sun warmed it at midday, and the north

wind cooled it well; there was hardly room for the river and the road; and the "City" consisted of five or six houses, a blacksmith shop and "the store," strung along the narrow banks.

But the little pass had its strategic value for a country trader, lying between wide mountain valleys and concentrating all their local traffic.

"Maria!" called Mr. Beazley. "Here's Miss Lawrence. I'll take her trunk up right now. Luella! Show Miss Lawrence where her room is! You can't miss it, Miss Lawrence— we haven't got so many."

Mrs. Beazley's welcome left much to be desired; Luella wore an air of subdued hostility, and Willie, caught by his father in unobserved derision, was cuffed and warned to behave or he'd be sorry.

But Miss Lawrence took no notice. She came down to supper simply dressed, fresh and cheerful. She talked gaily, approved the food, soon won Luella's interest, and captured Willie by a small mechanical puzzle she brought out of her pocket. Her hostess remained cold, however, and stood out for some days against the constant friendliness of her undesired guest.

"I'll take care of my own room," said Miss Lawrence. "I like to, and then I've so little to do here—and you have so much. What would I prefer to eat? Whatever you have— it's a change I'm after, you know—not just what I get at home."

After a little while Mrs. Beazley owned to a friend and customer that her boarder was "no more trouble than a man, and a sight more agreeable."

"What does she do all the time?" asked the visitor. "You've got no piazza."

"She ain't the piazza kind," answered Mrs. Beazley. "She's doing what they call nature study. She tramps off with an opera glass and a book—Willie likes to go with her, and she's tellin' him a lot about birds and plants and stones and things. She gets mushrooms, too—and cooks them herself—and eats them. Says they are better than meat and cheaper. I don't like to touch them myself, but it does save money."

In about a week Mrs. Beazley hauled down her flag and capitulated. In two she grew friendly—in three, confidential, and when she heard through Luella and Bert Fielden that his father would soon be back now—her burden of trouble overflowed—the over-hanging loss of her last bit of property.

"It's not only because it's our old place and I love it," she said; "and it's not only because it would be so much better for the children—though that's enough—but it would be better business to live there—and I can't make him see it!"

"He thinks he sees way beyond it, doesn't he?"

"Of course—but you know how men are! Oh, no, you don't; you're not married. He's all for buyin' and sellin' and makin' money, and I think half the time he loses and won't let me know."

"The store seems to be popular, doesn't it?"

"Not so much as it would be if he'd attend to it. But he won't stock up as he ought to—and he takes everything he can scrape and puts it into land—and then sells that and gets more. And he swaps horses, and buys up stuff at 'vandoos' and sells it again—he's always speculatin'. And he won't let me send Luella to school—nor Willie half the time—and now—but I've no business talkin' to you like this, Miss Lawrence!"

"If it's any relief to your mind, Mrs. Beazley, I wish you would. It is barely possible that I may be of some use. My father is in the real estate business and knows a good deal about these mountain lands."

"Well, it's no great story—I'm not complainin' of Mr. Beazley, understand—only about this property. It does seem as if it was mine—and I do hate to sign deeds—but he will sell it off!"

"Why do you let him, if you feel sure he is wrong!"

"Let him!—Oh, well you ain't married! Let him! Miss Lawrence, you don't know men!"

"But still, Mrs. Beazley, if you want to keep your property——"

"Oh, Miss Lawrence, you don't understand—here am I and here's the children, and none of us can get away, and if I don't do as he says I must, he takes it out of us—that's all. You can't do nothin' with a man like that—and him with the Bible on his side!"

Miss Lawrence meditated for some moments.

"Have you ever thought of leaving him?" she ventured.

"Oh, yes, I've thought of it; my sister's always wantin'

me to. But I don't believe in divorce—and if I did, this is New York state and I couldn't get it."

"It's pretty hard on the children, isn't it?"

"That's what I can't get reconciled to. I've had five children, Miss Lawrence. My oldest boy went off when he was only twelve, he couldn't stand his father—he used to punish him so—seems as if he did it to make me give in. So he never had proper schoolin' and can't earn much—he's fifteen now—I don't hear from him very often, and he never was very strong." Mrs. Beazley's eyes filled. "He hates the city, too, and he'd come back to me any day—if it wasn't for his father."

"You had five, you say?"

"Yes—there was a baby between Willie and this one—but it died. We're so far from a doctor, and he wouldn't hitch up—said it was all my nonsense till it was too late: And this baby's delicate—just the way he was!" The tears ran down now, but the faded little woman wiped them off resignedly and went on.

"It's worse now for Luella. Luella's at an age when she oughtn't to be tendin' store the whole time—she ought to be at a good school. There's too many young fellows hangin' around here already. Luella's large for her age, and pretty. I was good lookin' when I was Luella's age, Miss Lawrence, and I got married not much later—girls don't know nothin'!"

Miss Lawrence studied her unhappy little face with attention.

"How old should you think I was, Mrs. Beazley?"

Mrs. Beazley, struggling between politeness and keen observation, guessed twenty-seven.

"Ten years short," she answered cheerfully. "I was thirty-seven this very month."

"What!" cried the worn woman in calico. "You're older'n I am! I'm only thirty-two!"

"Yes, I'm a lot older, you see, and I'm going to presume on my age now, and on some business experience, and commit the unpardonable sin of interfering between man and wife—in the interest of the children. It seems to me, Mrs. Beazley, that you owe it them to make a stand.

"Think now—before it is too late. If you kept possession of this property in Rockwell, and had control of your share of what has been sold heretofore—could you live on it?"

"Why, I guess so. There's the house, my sister's in it now—she takes boarders and pays us rent—she thinks I get the money. We could make something that way."

"How much land is there?"

"There's six acres in all. There's the house lot right there in town, and the strip next to it down to the falls—we own the falls—both sides."

"Isn't that rather valuable? You could lease the water power, I should think."

"There was some talk of a 'lectric company takin' it—but it fell through. He wouldn't sell to them—said he'd sell nothin' to Sam Hunt—just because he was an old friend of mine. Sam keeps a good store down to Rockwell, and he was in that company—got it up, I think. Mr. Beazley was always jealous of Sam—and 'twan't me at all he wanted—'twas my sister."

"But, Mrs. Beazley, think. If you and your sister could keep house together you could make a home for the children, and your boy would come back to you. If you leased or sold the falls you could afford to send Luella away to school. Willie could go to school in town—the baby would do better down there where there is more sunlight, I'm sure—why do you not make a stand for the children's sake?"

Mrs. Beazley looked at her with a faint glimmer of hope. "If I only could," she said.

"Has Mr. Beazley any property of his own?" pursued Miss Lawrence.

"Property! He's got debts. Old ones and new ones. He was in debt when I married him—and he's made more."

"But the proceeds of these sales you tell me of?"

"Oh, he has some trick about that. He banks it in my name or something—so his creditors can't get it. He always gets ahead of everybody."

"M-m-m," said Miss Lawrence.

Mr. Beazley had a long ride before him the next day; he was to drive to Princeville for supplies.

An early breakfast was prepared and consumed, with much fault finding on his part—and he started off by six o'clock in a bad temper, unrestrained by the presence of Miss Lawrence, who had not come down.

"Whoa! Hold up!" he cried, stopping the horses with a spiteful yank as they had just settled into the collar.

"Maria!"

"Well—what you forgotten?"

"Forgot nothin'! I've remembered something; see that you're on hand tonight—don't go gallivantin' down to Rockwell or anywhere just because I'm off. Justice Fielden's comin' up and we've got to settle that business I told you about. Sce't you're here! Gid ap!"

The big wagon lumbered off across the bridge, around the corner, into the hidden wood road.

When Mr. Beazley returned the late dusk had fallen thickly in the narrow pass. He was angry at being late, for he had counted much on having this legal formality in his own house—where he could keep a sterner hand on his wife.

He was tired, too, and in a cruel temper, as the sweating horses showed.

"Willie!" he shouted. "Here you, Willie! Come and take the horses!" No hurrying, frightened child appeared.

"Maria!" he yelled. "Maria! Where's that young one! Luella! Maria!"

He clambered down, swearing under his breath; and rushed to the closed front door. It was locked.

"What in Halifax!" he muttered, shaking and banging vainly. Then he tried the side door—the back door—the woodshed—all were locked and the windows shut tight with sticks over them. His face darkened with anger.

"They've gone off—the whole of them—and I told her she'd got to be here tonight. Gone to Rockwell, of course, leavin' the store, too. We'll have a nice time when she comes back! That young one needs a lickin'."

He attended to the horses after a while, leaving the loaded wagon in the barn, and then broke a pane of glass in a kitchen window and let himself in.

A damp, clean, soapy smell greeted him. He struck matches and looked for a lamp. There was none. The room was absolutely empty. So were the closet, pantry and cellar. So were the four rooms upstairs and the attic. So was the store.

"Halifax!" said Mr. Beazley. He was thoroughly mystified now, and his rage died in bewilderment.

A knocking at the door called him.

It was not Justice Fielden, however, but Sam Hunt.

"I heard you brought up a load of goods today," said he

easily; ''and I thought you might like to sell 'em. I bought
out the rest of the stuff this morning, and the store, and the
good-will o' the business—and this lot isn't much by itself.''

Mr. Beazley looked at him with a blackening countenance.

''You bought out this store, did you? I'd like to know
who you bought it of!''

''Why, the owner, of course! Mrs. Beazley; paid cash on
the nail, too. I've bought it, lock, stock and barrel—cows,
horses, hens and cats. You don't own the wagon, even. As
to your clothes—they're in that trunk yonder. However, keep
your stuff—you'll need some capital,'' with this generous
parting shot Mr. Hunt drove off.

Mr. Beazley retired to the barn. He had no wish to consult his neighbors for further knowledge.

Mrs. Beazley had gone to her sister, no doubt.

And she had dared to take this advantage of him—of the
fact that the property stood in her name—Sam Hunt had put
her up to it. He'd have the law on them—it was a conspiracy.

Then he went to sleep on the hay, muttering vengeance
for the morrow.

The strange atmosphere awoke him early, and he breakfasted on some crackers from his wagon.

Then he grimly set forth on foot for the village, refusing
offered lifts from the loads of grinning men who passed
him. He presented himself at the door of his wife's house
in the village at an early hour. Her sister opened it.

''Well,'' she said, holding the doorknob in her hand,
''what do you want at this time in the morning?''

''I want my family,'' said he. ''I'll have you know a man
has some rights in his family at any rate.''

''There's no family of yours in this house, William Beazley,'' said she grimly. ''No, I'm not a liar—never had that
reputation. You can come in and search the house if you
please—after the boarders are up.''

''Where is my wife?'' he demanded.

''I don't know, thank goodness, and I don't think you'll
find her very soon either,'' she added to herself, as he turned
and marched off without further words.

In the course of the morning he presented himself at
Justice Fielden's office.

"Gone off, has she?" inquired the Judge genially. "Or just gone visiting, I guess. Forgot to leave word."

"It's not only that, I want to know my rights in this case, Judge. I've been to the bank—and she's drawn every cent. Every cent of my property."

"Wasn't it her property, Mr. Beazley?"

"Some of it was, and some of it wasn't. All I've made since we was married was in there, too. I've speculated quite a bit, you know, buying and selling—there was considerable money."

"How on earth could she get your money out of the bank?" asked Mr. Fielden.

"Why, it was in her name, of course; matter of business, you understand."

"Why, yes; I understand, I guess. Well, I don't see exactly what you can do about it, Mr. Beazley. You, technically gave her the property, you see, and she's taken it—that's all there is to it."

"She's sold out the store!" broke in Mr. Beazley, "all the stock, the fixtures—she couldn't do that, could she?"

"Appears as if she had, don't it? It was rather overbearin' I do think, and you can bring suit for compensation for your services—you tended the store, of course?"

"If I knew where she was—" said Mr. Beazley slowly, with a grinding motion of his fingers. "But she's clean gone—and the children, too."

"If she remains away that constitutes desertion, of course," said the Judge briskly, "and your remedy is clear. You can get a separation—in due time. If you cared to live in another state long enough you could get a divorce—not in New York though. Being in New York, and not knowing where your wife is, I don't just see what you can do about it. Do you care to employ detectives?"

"No," said Mr. Beazley, "not yet."

Suddenly he started up.

"There's Miss Lawrence," said he. "She'll know something," and he darted out after her.

She came into the little office, calm, smiling, daintily arrayed.

"Do you know where my wife is, Miss Lawrence?" he demanded.

"Yes," she replied pleasantly.

"Well—where is she?"

"That I am not at liberty to tell you, Mr. Beazley. But any communication you may wish to make to her you can make through me. And I can attend to any immediate business. She has given me power of attorney."

Justice Fielden's small eyes were twinkling.

"You never knew you had a counsel learned in the law at your place, did you? Miss Lawrence is the best woman lawyer in New York, Mr. Beazley—just going kinder incog, for a vacation."

"Are you at the bottom of all this deviltry?" said the angry man, turning upon her fiercely.

"If you mean that Mrs. Beazley is acting under my advice, yes. I found that she had larger business interests than she supposed, and that they were not being well managed. I happened to be informed as to real estate values in this locality, and was able to help her. We needed a good deal of ready money to take advantage of our opportunity, and Mr. Hunt was willing to help us out on the stock."

He set his teeth and looked at her with growing fury, to which she paid no attention whatever.

"I advised Mrs. Beazley to take the children and go away for a complete change and rest, and to leave me to settle this matter. I was of the opinion that you and I could make business arrangements more amicably perhaps."

"What do you mean by business arrangements?" he asked.

"We are prepared to make you this offer: If you will sign the deed of separation I have here, agreeing to waive all rights in the children and live out of the state, we will give you five thousand dollars. In case you reappear in the state you will be liable for debts, and for—you remember that little matter of the wood lot deal?"

"That's a fair offer, I think," said Justice Fielden. "I always told you that wood lot matter would get you into trouble if your wife got on to it—and cared to push it. I think you'd better take up with this proposition."

"What's she going to do—a woman alone? What are the children going to do? A man can't give up his family this way."

"You need not be at all concerned about that," she answered. "Mrs. Beazley's plans are open and aboveboard. She is going to enlarge her house and keep boarders. Her sister is to marry Mr. Hunt, as you doubtless know. The children are to be properly educated. There is nothing you need fear for your family.''

"And how about me? I—if I could just talk to her?''

"That is exactly what I advised my client to avoid. She has gone to a quiet, pleasant place for this summer. She needs a long rest, and you and I can settle this little matter without any feeling, you see.''

"What with summers in quiet places, and enlarging the house, you seem to have found a good deal more in that property than I did,'' said he with a sneer.

"That is not improbable,'' she replied sweetly. "Here is the agreement; take the offer or leave it.''

"And if I don't take it? Then what'll you do?''

"Nothing. You may continue to live here if you insist—and pay your debts by your own exertions. You can get employment, no doubt, of your friends and neighbors.''

Mr. Beazley looked out of the window. Quite a number of his friends and neighbors were gathered together around Hunt's store, and as each new arrival was told the story, they slapped their thighs and roared with laughter.

Judge Fielden, smiling dryly, threw up the sash.

"Clean as a whistle!'' he heard Sturgis Black's strident voice. "Not as much as a cat to kick! Nobody to holler at! No young ones to lick! Nothin' whatsomever to eat! You should a heard him bangin' on the door!''

"And him a luggin' in that boarder just to spite her,'' crowed old Sam Wiley—"that was the last straw, I guess.''

"Well, he was always an enterprisin' man,'' said Horace Johnson. "Better at specilatin' with his wife's property than workin' with his hands. Guess he'll have to hunt a job now, though.''

"He ain't likely to git one in a hurry—not in this county—unless Sam Hunt'll take him in.'' Wiley yelled again at this.

"Have you got that deed drawn up?'' said Mr. Beazley harshly—"I'll sign.''